The shining splendor of our Zebra Lovegram logo on the cover of this book reflects the glittering excellence of the story inside. Look for the Zebra Lovegram whenever you buy a historical romance. It's a trademark that guarantees the very best in quality and reading entertainment.

SARAH HAD BEEN WAITING FOR THIS TO HAPPEN HER ENTIRE LIFE

She could feel Travis's heart pounding against hers, and she saw her own wonder and uncertainty mirrored in the sky blue of his eyes. When he would have released her, she slid her arms up to his shoulders and around his neck.

With a groan, he kissed her, crushing her to him as if to take her into himself. Open-mouthed, he devoured her lips in a desperate claiming to which she submitted willingly, eagerly. Sarah hadn't known she could feel like this, ecstatic and desperate, fulfilled yet wanting, euphoric but terrified. Desire scorched through her, igniting sensations she'd never dreamed existed and needs for which she had no name. She thought she knew all the secret things between men and women, but Travis's touch had lifted her into a realm beyond her imaginings, a realm she could explore only with him. . . .

SURRENDER TO THE PASSION

LOVE'S SWEET BOUNTY (3313, $4.50)
by Colleen Faulkner

Jessica Landon swore revenge of the masked bandits who robbed the train and stole all the money she had in the world. She set out after the thieves without consulting the handsome railroad detective, Adam Stern. When he finally caught up with her, she admitted she needed his assistance. She never imagined that she would also begin to need his scorching kisses and tender caresses.

WILD WESTERN BRIDE (3140, $4.50)
by Rosalyn Alsobrook

Anna Thomas loved riding the Orphan Train and finding loving homes for her young charges. But when a judge tried to separate two brothers, the dedicated beauty went beyond the call of duty. She proposed to the handsome, blue-eyed Mark Gates, planning to adopt the boys herself! Of course the marriage would be in name only, but yet as time went on, Anna found herself dreaming of being a loving wife in every sense of the word . . .

QUICKSILVER PASSION (3117, $4.50)
by Georgina Gentry

Beautiful Silver Jones had been called every name in the book, and now that she owned her own tavern in Buckskin Joe, Colorado, the independent didn't care what the townsfolk thought of her. She never let a man touch her and she earned her money fair and square. Then one night handsome Cherokee Evans swaggered up to her bar and destroyed the peace she'd made with herself. For the irresistible miner made her yearn for the melting kisses and satin caresses she had sworn she could live without!

MISSISSIPPI MISTRESS (3118, $4.50)
by Gina Robins

Cori Pierce was outraged at her father's murder and the loss of her inheritance. She swore revenge and vowed to get her independence back, even if it meant singing as an entertainer on a Mississippi steamboat. But she hadn't reckoned on the swarthy giant in tight buckskins who turned out to be her boss. Jacob Wolf was, after all, the giant of the man Cori vowed to destroy. Though she swore not to forget her mission for even a moment, she was powerfully tempted to submit to Jake's fiery caresses and have one night of passion in his irresistible embrace.

Available wherever paperbacks are sold, or order direct from the Publisher. Send cover price plus 50¢ per copy for mailing and handling to Zebra Books, Dept. 3410, 475 Park Avenue South, New York, N.Y. 10016. Residents of New York, New Jersey and Pennsylvania must include sales tax. DO NOT SEND CASH.

SWEET TEXAS SURRENDER

Victoria Thompson

ZEBRA BOOKS
KENSINGTON PUBLISHING CORP.

With love to my two creative daughters,
Lisa the artist and Ellen the writer.

ZEBRA BOOKS

are published by

Kensington Publishing Corp.
475 Park Avenue South
New York, NY 10016

First printing: June, 1991

Printed in the United States of America

Chapter One

The first time she set eyes on him, Sarah knew he was the man she'd been looking for. How she could have known was anyone's guess, since at the time he was unconscious, soaked in his own blood, and being carried on a plank by two cowboys into Dr. Bigelow's house, but she knew nonetheless.

A third cowboy stood beside the spring wagon in which they had brought the injured stranger to town, waiting for his fellows to return. Sarah schooled her expression to mild concern and approached him.

"Good morning," she said, allowing her gaze to drift almost reluctantly toward the doctor's front door through which the cowboys were carrying their unfortunate burden.

" 'Morning, Miz Hadley," the young man replied, blushing scarlet. Sarah judged him to be no more than sixteen or seventeen, and although she couldn't recall ever having seen him before, she was not surprised that he knew her name. Everyone knew the Widow Hadley.

"Who is that poor man being taken into Dr. Bigelow's?"

"Don't know, Miz Hadley," he replied stiffly, looking

terribly ill at ease. Sarah supposed he rarely had an opportunity to converse with respectable ladies. Or maybe he just didn't want to be seen talking to Widow Hadley. "We found him like that out on the range."

"Has he been shot?"

"Yes, ma'am, more'n once, too." He seemed to warm to the subject. "He's a hard case, if you ask me."

"A hard case?" Sarah repeated, pretending she didn't know the meaning of the term and concealing her surging excitement.

"Yes, ma'am, a real tough character. See, we didn't find him right off. Found his horse first. Poor critter had been rode to death. We seen the vultures and figured it might be one of our cows, but of course it weren't."

"Of course," Sarah agreed encouragingly.

"Way we figured, after his horse dropped out from under him, that hombre started walking, even shot full of holes like he is. He was dripping blood the whole way, so we didn't have no trouble tracking him, even though he'd gone near a mile. We fetched a wagon and brung him in here."

"Didn't he tell you who he is or how he came to be shot?"

"No, ma'am, he didn't say nothing. Couldn't. He was out cold the whole time. I reckon we wasted our time bringing him in, though. He'll prob'ly die."

Sarah nodded soberly, but she didn't agree. A man so tenacious would not die easily, and if there was any chance of saving him, James Bigelow would find it.

"Perhaps I should see if Mrs. Bigelow needs any help," Sarah said, carefully concealing her eagerness. "Thank you, young man."

"No trouble, ma'am," he said, tipping his ridiculously

large Stetson as Sarah turned and hurried toward the Bigelows' gate.

She wasn't really intruding, she told herself. Amabel Bigelow was one of her dearest friends and had invited her for afternoon tea, in any case. The current emergency would preclude social intercourse, but Amabel would need help, and Sarah knew how to make herself useful.

Without bothering to ring—Amabel would have enough to do without answering the doorbell—Sarah stepped into the front hall. Her black dress blended into the shadows of the mahogany-paneled entranceway, so no one noticed her at first.

The two cowboys were coming out the door to the left that led to Dr. Bigelow's office, originally one of the two large front parlors of the huge house. They were both looking back over their shoulders at James.

"You think he'll make it, Doc?" one of them asked.

"He will if I have anything to say about it," James Bigelow replied from inside the room. Sarah imagined him already bent over the wounded man, stripping away his blood-stained clothing to assess the damage.

"We'll tell the sheriff what happened," the second cowboy said. "He'll probably want to talk to him."

"This fellow won't be talking to anyone for a while yet. Close the door, will you, boys?"

They did, cutting off what little light filtered into the hallway from that source, and when they turned, they both jumped at the sight of Sarah standing there.

In unison, they touched their hat brims, looking somewhat nonplused. Sarah smiled serenely.

"The doctor's got a patient right now," one of them said apologetically. Perhaps they imagined she'd come to consult James for a medical opinion.

"I know," she replied. "I was looking for Mrs. Bigelow." Feeling no need to explain further, she swept past them, down the long hallway to the door that led to the kitchen. Inside the large, brightly lit room she found Amabel.

"Oh, Sarah, I'm so sorry," Amabel exclaimed, looking up from her task. She was filling a pail with hot water from the boiler over the stove. "I'm afraid our afternoon visit will have to wait for another time. They've brought in an injured man, and I have to help James."

"I know; I was in the street when they carried him in," Sarah said, removing her black bonnet and hanging it carefully on a peg beside the back door. "I figured we wouldn't get much visiting done this afternoon, but I also thought you might need some help."

"Bless your heart," Amabel muttered distractedly. "I have to take this hot water to James and get him some bandages. Would you mind terribly starting some soup? If this man lives, he'll need something to help replace all the blood he's lost. I've got some soup bones somewhere. . . ." She gestured vaguely.

"I'll find them," Sarah assured her. "Just worry about that poor man."

Amabel's plump figure disappeared through the door with a swish of skirts and a slosh of hot water. Without hesitation, Sarah went to the pantry where she found the bones, carefully wrapped, and the few other ingredients she would need to make a thin gruel. Ordinarily, Sarah didn't care much for cooking, but the preparation of this meal held a special significance for her. If she could, in however small a way, contribute to the survival of the man who lay in James Bigelow's examining room, she would do so, because that man was going to help save Sarah Hadley.

8

She lifted her face heavenward and squinched her eyes shut. "You can't let him die!" she informed the Almighty.

Sheriff Monroe arrived a few minutes later. Amabel had not returned, so Sarah hurried to answer his ring. His stocky figure filled the doorway, and he frowned at the sight of her. Like most people in the county, he did not approve of Widow Hadley.

"I heard Doc Bigelow's got a wounded man here," he said gruffly.

"Yes, he's treating him now. I have no idea how long he'll be, but if you'd care to wait . . ." She stepped aside so he could enter, and he sidled past her with exaggerated care, as if afraid any contact might contaminate him. Sarah hid a contemptuous smile. "If you'd like to join me in the kitchen, I've made some coffee, and Mrs. Bigelow has a cake."

Plainly, Sheriff Monroe had no desire to join her anywhere. "I'll just wait here," he said, indicating the wooden bench by the office door on which Dr. Bigelow's patients sat when the doctor was otherwise engaged.

"Suit yourself," she said, smiling sweetly and returning to the kitchen. Sheriff Monroe's prejudices had cheated him out of a slice of Amabel's legendary lemon cake, but it served him right. Anyone so narrow-minded had no right to Amabel's cake.

Sarah made enough soup to save an army of wounded men, then took to scrubbing Amabel's immaculate stove just to keep busy during the interminable wait. How she envied Amabel, whose privileged status as James's wife allowed her to assist in the operation, while Sarah was left to wring her hands and worry.

9

Once, she thought to wonder how the welfare of a total stranger could matter so much, but she quickly dismissed the idea. It just did, that was all, and he wouldn't die. He couldn't, because she needed him too much.

After what seemed hours, Sarah heard Amabel's voice in the hall, and she hurried out to find her friend explaining the patient's condition to Sheriff Monroe.

"He's quite weak and hasn't regained consciousness yet, but my husband feels he has a good chance."

Sarah breathed a silent prayer of thanks as she approached Amabel and the sheriff.

"I'd like to question him," the sheriff was saying.

"But I told you, he isn't conscious," Amabel insisted. Her smooth, round face creased into a disapproving frown.

The office door opened, and James Bigelow's tall, lanky frame appeared. "My patient needs complete rest for the next few days, Sheriff. I'll notify you the moment he is able to answer questions."

Plainly, Sheriff Monroe felt Dr. Bigelow was being unreasonable. "The man was shot," he reminded them all sternly. "That means he was either attacked by bandits or he is a bandit himself. In either case, the law has been broken, and I need to know about it."

James Bigelow smiled tolerantly. "Not even the law can get answers from an unconscious man."

Although the light was poor, Sarah thought Sheriff Monroe's face reddened. "Then I'd like to at least see him. Maybe he's on a wanted poster, and if he is, I'll have to post a guard here at the house."

"Let me assure you, whether he is wanted or not, this man will not be in any condition to escape for several days," James said impatiently, but Sheriff Monroe was not going to be put off.

10

"It can't hurt if I just look at him, now can it?"

No one could argue. "All right," James sighed reluctantly, "but you can only stay a moment."

"I'd like to see him, too."

Only when three pairs of startled eyes turned on her did Sarah realize she had spoken her wish aloud.

"Why would you need to see him, dear?" Amabel asked.

Sarah glanced at Sheriff Monroe, and his disgruntled frown told her she'd better come up with a good excuse for such an odd request. The lie came with surprising ease. "Surely I must have told you, Amabel. I've been expecting my . . . my cousin from Tennessee. We haven't seen each other since we were children, and although I only caught a glimpse of the man before he was carried inside, I thought perhaps . . . Well, if it is him, I'd certainly want to know."

Sheriff Monroe's scowl called her a liar, and James Bigelow coughed to cover a grin, but sweet Amabel believed every word. "I had no idea. I thought all your family was dead."

"My *immediate* family," Sarah corrected her without a trace of remorse. She would explain it all later, and Amabel would cheerfully forgive her. "I still have quite a few cousins in various places. James, may I see the man?"

"He's in bed!" the sheriff objected in outrage before James could reply.

Sarah widened her eyes at him. "How gallant of you to be concerned for my sensibilities, Sheriff, but I've seen a man in bed before. I was married for over six years, or have you forgotten?"

This time there could be no doubt the sheriff's face had reddened, and his expression held more than disap-

11

proval. Perhaps he even blamed her in some way for Philip Hadley's untimely death. Others did, she knew.

"The man is decently covered," James said, not bothering to hide his amusement at the sheriff's outrage. "If Sarah wants to see if he might be her relation, I believe she can do so without embarrassment to either him or herself."

Sarah rewarded James with a smile and ignored the sheriff's disgruntled "Humph."

James opened the door after cautioning them to be quiet, and led the way into the office. Someone had drawn the drapes so the normally sunny room lay in shadow. To one side sat James's large rolltop desk with its comfortable clutter of papers. Beside it was an overstuffed chair on which his patients sat to tell him of their ailments. On the opposite wall stood the tall glass-fronted cabinet that held James's formidable collection of medical instruments.

At the far side of the room was the bed on which the patient now lay, his body motionless beneath the blanket that had been pulled up to the middle of his chest. Above the blanket she could see the stark whiteness of the bandages stretching to his armpits and looping over one shoulder. His arms lay outside the blanket, the corded muscles evident even in repose.

Sheriff Monroe strode directly to the bedside, but in spite of her previous boldness, Sarah held back a bit, responding to some innate reluctance to violate the man's privacy any further. For the first time, she got a good look at his face. His skin was unnaturally pale beneath his suntan, and if she hadn't seen the reassuring rhythmic rise and fall of his chest, she might have feared the worst.

Nothing about his countenance marked him as a

"hard case." He was rather ordinary-looking, not ugly but not particularly handsome, either. The corn-yellow hair that someone had carefully brushed off his forehead and the matching pale eyebrows made him seem amazingly young, much younger than the squint lines beside his eyes and the grooves running from his nose to the corners of his mouth proclaimed him to be. Sarah judged him to be between five and ten years older than her own twenty-three.

Because he was lying down, she found it difficult to guess his height, but he seemed short, perhaps no taller than her own five feet, five inches. Certainly he lacked the brawn of Sheriff Monroe or the lankiness of James Bigelow, yet Sarah again sensed something in him, the same aura of latent power that had struck her out in the street, the sort of strength that would have enabled him to walk a mile when other, lesser men would have given up and died. The thought raised gooseflesh on her arms and she shivered in reaction.

"Scrawny little runt, ain't he?" the sheriff remarked, turning away.

To Sarah's surprise, the man opened his eyes, eyes so blue she almost gasped aloud, and gave Sheriff Monroe a look that would have drawn blood on a rawhide boot. He hadn't been asleep or unconscious at all!

As if sensing her gaze, the man turned his amazing azure stare on her. His eyes widened in surprise, as if he, too, felt the sudden jolt of recognition that took her breath and shook her to her toes. *Recognition?* How could she recognize him when she'd never seen him before in her life?

"Well, Miz Hadley, is he your cousin or not?" Sheriff Monroe asked skeptically.

Sarah blinked, and when she looked again, the man's

13

eyes were closed once more, his face as blank as if she'd imagined the whole episode. "No, I'm afraid not," she murmured, still somewhat shaken by the impact of her strange reaction.

"I ain't surprised," he replied with some satisfaction.

"And do *you* recognize him, Sheriff?" James asked, echoing the sheriff's skepticism.

"Not right off," Monroe admitted, "but I'm going back to check my posters. I'll let you know if I find anybody fits his description."

The sheriff headed for the door, and James took Sarah's arm to escort her out, but she couldn't resist one last glance at the stranger. With his eyes closed, his face was still as unremarkable and expressionless as before, but she noticed his hands had closed into fists. He didn't like being considered a fugitive. He didn't like it one bit.

James nudged her arm, and she looked up to find him grinning down at her conspiratorially. He must have seen the stranger open his eyes, too. Had he known all along that the man was conscious? Sarah wouldn't embarrass him by asking, but she felt certain he had. From the expression on his face, he'd thoroughly enjoyed thwarting the sheriff's plans, too.

When they were out in the hall again, James closed the door softly behind them.

"Is he your cousin?" Amabel asked anxiously.

"No, I've never seen him before," Sarah replied, not daring to glance at the sheriff.

"You let me know as soon as he wakes up," Sheriff Monroe was saying to James. "I'll be real interested to find out how he got himself all shot up."

"I certainly will," James promised, seeing him to the door.

As soon as he was gone, Sarah asked, "Do you

14

really think he'll be all right?"

"His wounds weren't really very serious. Someone hit him with a load of buckshot, but not from close range. I dug a lot of lead out, but none of it was in very deep. Mostly he's suffering from loss of blood, exhaustion and shock. He'll probably be as good as new in a few weeks."

As good as new! Sarah felt an enormous sense of relief. "I'm glad to hear it. Perhaps I'll come by when I'm in town next week to see how he's doing."

"You'll most certainly come by for the visit we didn't get to have today," Amabel told her. "But before you leave, you must tell me about your cousin and why he's coming to see you."

"Yes, Sarah, tell us everything," James prompted, his sly grin entirely too smug for Sarah's taste.

"Why, Amabel, you know I don't have any living relatives," Sarah began, as they made their way back to the kitchen. She was already planning what she would say to the stranger when she finally got to speak with him next week.

The following Saturday, Sarah left her buckboard in front of the general store where she had placed her order for the supplies she needed at her ranch. Her only necessary errand completed, she made her way with unseemly haste to the Bigelow house.

The previous week had passed more slowly than any period of time Sarah could recall living through in her entire life, and she had spent most of it trying to imagine what she would do if the stranger refused the job she was going to offer. Of course, he would have no reason to refuse unless Amabel or James had told him about her. She really should have warned them off before she left that first day, but she hadn't thought of it until too late.

Well, if he knew, she'd prepared several arguments to convince him anyway. She wouldn't know which one to use until she'd had an opportunity to judge his character a little more thoroughly, though. Most men would respond to the "helpless female" argument, but she hoped she wouldn't have to use that one, since any fool could see Sarah Hadley had never been helpless in her entire life.

Still, she'd taken great pains with her appearance in the hope of fostering at least a hint of femininity, just in case he could be swayed by such things. Her widowhood severely limited her choice of apparel, but she'd selected her best black crepon. Elizabeth Williams had spent an inordinate amount of time getting it to fit and fall just right so it showed off Sarah's modest figure to the best possible advantage. It came closer than anything Sarah owned to making her look demure and respectable — just the image she wanted to project today.

She'd even spent a little time curling her dark hair this morning, instead of just brushing it straight back and pinning it into a bun. Amabel would probably remark on the corkscrew curls dancing around her face, but Sarah would simply say she'd finally decided to take Amabel's advice and do something with herself. She only hoped all this effort hadn't been a total waste of time.

By the time she rang the Bigelows' doorbell, she was fairly breathless with anticipation and anxiety over the coming meeting. She'd let Amabel ply her with tea and cake before asking to see their patient, so she would have a chance to compose herself.

"Sarah! I'm so glad to see you," Amabel exclaimed, motioning her inside.

"I trust you aren't as busy today as you were last week," Sarah said, her voice only slightly unsteady as her gaze darted automatically to James's closed office door.

"Oh, no, I'm not busy at all, not since Mr. Travis left."

"Who?" Sarah asked in alarm.

"Mr. Travis, the man who was shot. He told us to call him Travis, and of course we didn't ask any questions. You remember, don't you? They brought him in while you were here."

"He's *gone?*" Sarah couldn't believe it.

"Yes, he made a remarkable recovery. James urged him to stay for a few more days, at least until he was completely fit again. I certainly wouldn't have minded. He wasn't a bit of trouble — one of the most considerate patients James has ever had — but he wouldn't hear of it. He felt just awful because he had no money to pay James's fee, and he didn't want to take charity. Of course, when he found out they'd brought in his saddle, he sold it to pay for his care. He even wanted to pay for the clothes I gave him. I'd tried to wash the bloodstains out of his, but they were simply ruined, so I gave him some of James's old clothes. I told him they weren't worth a thing, but he insisted —"

"Amabel, has he left town?" Sarah asked impatiently.

"Oh, dear me, no. How could he, with no horse and no saddle? His horse died, did you know?"

Sarah felt close to panic. "Yes, yes, I knew. Where is he, then?"

"I believe James said he took a job at the livery stable. Anyone could see such a job was beneath him, but he's still much too weak for really hard labor, and who would

17

hire him for a riding job, with no horse and no saddle?"

"Who, indeed?" Sarah muttered, pulling open the front door.

"Where are you going? Sarah, I have tea already made!" Amabel called as Sarah hurried out and down the porch steps.

"I'll be back in a few minutes," Sarah assured her. "I just remembered something I have to do."

Why had she waited so long to come back? She should have known a man like that wouldn't linger abed unless he were dying. Thank heaven he was at least still in town, but she knew she'd better get to him before anyone else did.

Rolley Burns's Livery Stable was at the opposite end of town, a huge weathered barn with corrals adjacent. As she approached, Sarah consciously slowed her pace and began to take deep breaths, so she wouldn't give the impression of having run all the way across town even though she had. All the deep breaths in the world wouldn't still the pounding of her heart, however; that got increasingly worse the closer she got to the building.

She told herself she was silly to be apprehensive. He couldn't possibly know how important this was to her, and she would be an idiot to let him see. Besides, didn't she know in the depths of her pounding heart that he was destined to accept her offer? She'd known it the first time she'd seen him.

As usual, Rolley Burns was dozing outside the livery, seated in a ladder-back chair tipped against the wall, his battered hat pulled down over his eyes, his hands folded complacently over his huge belly. He must be thrilled to have someone to muck out the stalls, Sarah thought. Rolley had a terrible time keeping good help, and he certainly never did any of the work himself.

18

"Good afternoon, Rolley," she said loudly enough to rouse him.

He jumped, and the chair thumped down onto all four legs, jarring a moan from him. He lifted the brim of his disreputable hat and peered out cautiously at her. "Oh, 'afternoon, Miz Hadley. What can I do for you?"

She waited until he had pushed himself to his feet. "I understand you have a new man working for you, a Mr. Travis."

Rolley's face fell in almost comic dismay. "You don't want to hire this fellow, Miz Hadley. He's mighty poorly. Just come from Doc Bigelow's. Can't hardly work more'n a few minutes without resting."

"Thank you for your sterling recommendation," Sarah said with a ruthless smile. "May I speak to him myself?"

Rolley hesitated, obviously wondering whether he dared refuse her request. Sarah simply continued to smile, never batting an eye, silently warning him he'd be wasting his time. After about a minute, his shoulders sagged in defeat. But as he turned toward the barn door, he couldn't resist one last barb. "He prob'ly won't want to work for you when he finds out what he'll be doing, anyways."

Suddenly Sarah's smile felt stiff as she considered the very real possibility that he was right.

"Travis, somebody out here wants to see you," Rolley called grumpily into the cavernous interior of the barn. He flashed her a murderous look, then made his way back to the chair, slumped down into it, and sat there glaring at her for what seemed a long time until the man called Travis finally appeared in the doorway.

She'd been right; he wasn't big or tall, and wearing James Bigelow's castoff clothes made him look even

19

smaller, but the gun strapped to his hip reassured her. God had made some men big and some men small, but Mr. Colt had made them all equal.

He carried a pitchfork in one hand, and the pieces of straw clinging to his worn boots told her he'd been doing just what she'd imagined—mucking out the stalls. He wore no hat, and the corn-yellow hair had been carefully oiled and combed. The brilliant blue eyes squinted, trying to adjust from the dimness of the barn to the bright sunlit afternoon. She knew the instant he recognized her. His whole body went as rigid as the pitchfork handle he held.

"You're the woman at the doctor's office," he said. His voice was deeper than she'd expected, but it held exactly the note of arrogant authority she had known it would.

"Yes, I'm Sarah Hadley. I'm pleased to meet you at last, Mr. Travis."

She held out her gloved hand. He stared down at it for a second or two, then glanced at his own and, apparently judging it too dirty, let it fall to his side. Sarah quickly withdrew her own, folding it against the churning in her stomach.

"Well," Sarah said, feeling somewhat breathless and uncharacteristically flustered, "Mrs. Bigelow tells me you've made a complete recovery. I'm very glad to hear it."

"Are you?" Plainly he couldn't imagine why it should matter one way or the other to her.

"Yes," she continued doggedly. "You see, I'm somewhat shorthanded, and I was wondering if you'd like a job."

"What kind of job?"

Rolley Burns coughed, and Sarah resisted the almost overwhelming urge to glare at him. "A riding job. At my ranch," she explained with creditable nonchalance.

Travis's blue gaze slid past her, and he glanced around as if he were looking for someone. Or trying to determine whether she was indeed alone.

"Does your husband always let you do the hiring?" he asked when he met her eye again.

"My husband is dead," she said baldly, having learned long ago to say the words without emotion.

She half expected him to express his condolences. Most people did, but he didn't. Instead he seemed to find some mysterious significance in her words, a significance he had to consider carefully. She waited while he did so.

Travis Taylor looked the woman up and down. The curls and the fancy dress didn't fool him one bit. She was bossy and overbearing. He could see the iron will reflected in the green of her eyes. It was no wonder she was a widow. She'd probably driven her husband into an early grave.

"I never worked for a woman before," he said, looking straight into her eyes. What color were they, anyways? A second ago he'd thought green, but now he could see some brown in them, too. Cat's eyes, he thought derisively.

"A woman's money is as good as anyone else's," she pointed out with a logic he found irritating. "And a woman, or at least this woman, is going to understand that you're still recovering and won't be able to put in a full day's work right away."

"I put in a full day's work no matter what," he informed her, even more irritated to hear the defensiveness in his own voice. She was too tall, almost as tall as he and maybe even taller if he hadn't had on high-heeled boots. God, he hated tall

21

women, especially tall women who were bossy.

"Good, then I'll pay you forty a month and found."

Instantly, he was suspicious. Thirty a month was the usual wage for a rider. "Fighting wages?" he guessed.

"Not unless you're planning to start some fights," she replied, but he could see she was lying. For some reason she needed hired guns, and somehow she'd gotten the idea his was for sale.

"I've already got a job," he said.

He almost winced when he saw her knowing smile. "Oh," she said, pretending to be surprised. "I didn't realize you enjoyed cleaning out the stalls. And I suppose Rolley lets you sleep in the loft. It would be difficult to give all that up."

Travis felt the heat rising in his neck, and he wondered what it would take to shock some of that arrogance out of her. Damnit, that was the trouble with a woman: you couldn't knock her on her butt in the dirt even if she *was* just as big as you were. Or bigger.

"Forty a month, Mr. Travis," she repeated; then she looked him up and down, making him uncomfortably aware of what a poor figure he cut in hand-me-down clothes with horse shit on his boots. "You'll need a new outfit, too. Go to the store, get your saddle out of hock, and tell them to charge whatever you need to my account. I'll take it out of your first month's wages. Are the terms satisfactory?"

She knew damn well the terms were satisfactory, so satisfactory he couldn't possibly turn her down. He recalled an old saying about how beggars couldn't be choosers, but it galled him to know he was a beggar. Unable to let her have it all her own way, he said, "I don't have a horse."

"I know. We'll take care of that when we get to the

22

ranch. I drove my wagon to town today. It's parked in front of the store. If you'll give me about three hours to complete my visits, you can bring the wagon and fetch me at the dressmaker's shop. Do you know where it is?"

The gall was bitter in his throat, but God knew, nobody else would be crazy enough to hire on a stranger who'd come to town shot to doll rags. "No, but I'll find it," he assured her grimly.

For just a second her assurance seemed to slip, almost as if she was surprised he'd accepted, but he knew she couldn't be surprised. Women like her always got their way. If they didn't at first, they just kept pushing until they did, knowing damn well a man couldn't push back.

"Well, then," she said, complacent in her success, "I'll see you in a few hours. Good afternoon, Mr. Travis."

"Good afternoon, Mrs. Hadley," he muttered, watching the way her bustled behind switched as she strode away, back toward town. Damn her to hell, she would have to be a handsome woman. A little on the thin side, but round in all the right places. He always had liked black hair, too. He wondered how hers would look without those fussy curls, hanging down loose, brushing her white breasts . . .

"I don't reckon you're gonna finish up inside, are you?" Rolley asked crossly, startling him back to reality.

"Afraid I won't have time," Travis said apologetically.

"Folks do say that woman is trouble," Rolley remarked. " 'Course, she never caused *me* none before now. Reckon it was just my turn."

Or mine, thought Travis, leaning the pitchfork against the wall and arching his back against the persistent ache of his healing wounds. Well, it wouldn't be for long, in any case. As soon as he was well, he had a few scores to settle, so he supposed he wouldn't be working for the widow longer than it took to draw his first wages. Meanwhile, he had a lot to do in the next three hours, because he had no intention of appearing before Sarah Hadley again in cast-off clothes smelling of horse shit.

If Sarah had thought the previous week passed slowly, for the next few hours time seemed virtually to stand still. Amabel had served her tea and regaled her with anecdotes about Mr. Travis's convalescence that only confirmed Sarah's already high opinion of the man. A hard case he might be, but he wasn't mean.

"Changed his own bedclothes, carried his dishes back to the kitchen, and he never failed to thank me for the meal," Amabel reported. "Always as polite as he could be, too, and never a complaint, although I'm sure he suffered something awful from those wounds. Some of them are still pretty bad."

"Did . . . did the sheriff ever question him?" Sarah asked at one point.

Amabel laughed gaily. "Oh, yes, and it was the funniest thing! Sheriff Monroe couldn't find any hint that he might be wanted, and when he asked Mr. Travis how he'd come to be shot, Mr. Travis said he'd done it himself when he was cleaning his gun."

"Surely the sheriff didn't believe it!" Sarah exclaimed.

"Of course not, but what could he do?"

Afterward Sarah had gone to Elizabeth Williams's house. Elizabeth was making her a new bonnet, but Sarah had spent most of her visit playing with Elizabeth's three-year-old son Paul. Ordinarily, Paul provided more than enough diversion to take her mind off any other problems, but as the clock inched toward the appointed hour, Sarah found herself anxiously watching the road.

"You don't think he'd change his mind, do you?" Elizabeth asked, when Sarah's trips to the window became too frequent to ignore.

Sarah shrugged and turned to the woman she had once hated for being everything Sarah wished she could be. A frown marred Elizabeth's exquisitely beautiful face, and her emerald-green eyes were full of concern.

"I can't imagine that he would turn down my offer . . . Unless he found out my deep, dark secret."

"Who would tell him?" Elizabeth scoffed.

"Anyone. Rolley might, just to try to keep him on at the livery."

"Perhaps he already knows and doesn't care."

"Even if he cares, I can't see that he has any other choice, unless he really does enjoy cleaning out stalls."

"Unless . . . Well, you can be a bit intimidating," Elizabeth suggested gently.

Sarah knew better than to take offense. Elizabeth's nature simply didn't allow her to be deliberately cruel, but her words stung, nevertheless. They both knew only too well how intimidating Sarah could be, how she could drive a man right out of her life and into the arms of another woman.

Before Sarah could think of a suitable reply, she heard the rattle of a wagon stopping in front of Elizabeth's house, and her heart leaped.

"Is that the man you're waiting for, Aunt Sarah?" Paul asked, scrambling to his feet and running to throw open the door.

"Yes," she breathed on a relieved sigh when she had peeked out the curtain to make certain.

"My goodness, Sarah, you're blushing," Elizabeth exclaimed in amusement.

25

"I most certainly am not!" Sarah insisted, plucking her bonnet from the coatrack and positioning it on her head with suddenly clumsy fingers.

"He ain't coming in," Paul reported from the doorway.

" 'Isn't' coming in, darling," Elizabeth corrected absently, moving to the window with the studied grace Sarah had always envied. "I suppose we'll have to wait for our chance to meet him, then."

Sarah felt guilty for the sense of relief this brought her, although she didn't allow herself to wonder why she should care if Mr. Travis made unfavorable comparisons between her and Elizabeth Williams. Since Philip's death, such things had ceased to be important, hadn't they?

"I'll have the bonnet finished when you come to town next week," Elizabeth said.

"Thank you," Sarah replied, her attention already out in the street where Mr. Travis waited with her wagon.

"Paul, give Aunt Sarah a kiss."

Paul obediently lifted his cherubic face, but Sarah wasn't quite ready to part with him yet. "Walk me to the gate, will you, sweetheart?"

"Sure!" he agreed eagerly, clasping her gloved hand and fairly pulling her out onto the porch.

Sarah waved her farewell to Elizabeth, who stood in the doorway, smiling tolerantly at her son's antics. Then Sarah looked out toward the street where Mr. Travis waited. He'd climbed down from the wagon seat and stood leaning against the wheel, smoking the cigarette he had just rolled.

He'd taken her at her word and bought himself some clothes. The new shirt and Levi's fit much better than what he'd been wearing before, and his old boots showed the results of a spit shine, revealing that they had been custom-made. His Stetson wasn't new, either, but its quality indicated he usually took great pride in his appearance. How he must have hated wearing James's old things.

He watched her approach from beneath the shadow of his hat brim, so she couldn't quite read his expression. Still, she could feel the intensity of those azure eyes, and for the first time in years she felt self-conscious about her appearance. Were her curls drooping? Was her dress wrinkled?

She tried to tell herself she was being ridiculous. What did his opinion matter, anyway? He was just one of her hired men. This concern was probably only her silly pride rearing its head at a particularly inopportune moment. She would simply ignore it. Heaven knew, she'd swallowed her pride often enough in the past.

As she and Paul approached the gate, Mr. Travis pushed himself away from the wagon wheel, took one last drag on his cigarette, and tossed it away. Sarah half imagined he intended to step forward and open the gate for her, but Paul dropped her hand and raced ahead so he could perform the chore himself.

"Thank you, Paul," she said with mock formality.

"You're welcome, Aunt Sarah," he replied, with an impish grin that made her want to hug him. He looked so like his father when he smiled—the same curve of the lips, the same brown eyes. Her heart ached with regret.

"Now you may give me my kiss," she said, leaning over until her face was even with his.

He puckered again, threw his arms around her neck, and planted a wet smack on her cheek. She kissed him back, inhaling the agonizingly sweet scent of little boy and allowing her own arms to go around his precious body for one all-too-brief moment. Then she released him, ruffled his hair affectionately, and stepped resolutely through the gate he had opened for her.

"Be sure the gate is latched behind me," Sarah cautioned.

"Yes, ma'am," he replied brightly, jumping up to cling to it for a ride as it swung shut with a click.

She turned and finally allowed herself to look Mr. Travis full in the face. If he disapproved of anything about her, she couldn't tell from his carefully blank expression. She pretended to notice his clothing for the first time. "Quite an improvement."

If she had expected a reply or any hint of gratitude, she was disappointed. Instead, he merely offered his hand to help her up to the wagon seat. This time, apparently, he'd taken great pains to ensure it would be clean, and when she caught a whiff of lye soap above the scent of new clothes, she realized he must have gotten a bath at the barbershop. Perhaps she wasn't the only one concerned about appearances this afternoon.

Buoyed by the thought, she placed her black-gloved palm in his and allowed him to assist her onto the seat. He was much stronger than she had expected a man his size to be, especially a man still recovering from several gunshot wounds. If the effort caused him any discomfort, he gave no indication.

In another moment, he was on the seat beside her, untying the reins from the brake handle. Suddenly, she wondered if the strain of driving might be too much for him. Hadn't Amabel said some of his wounds were still unhealed?

"I can drive if it bothers your . . . your injuries," she said.

He turned the full intensity of his blue eyes on her, and she suddenly wished she hadn't thought to make the offer. "I can handle it," he said, plainly contemptuous.

She had a childish urge to inform him she'd been driving wagons like this for years, but bit it back. There was no use giving him a *reason* to be contemptuous. If he started bleeding, however, she'd graciously take over. He released the brake and slapped the team into motion.

"Good-bye, Aunt Sarah!" Paul called, waving furiously.

Sarah turned on her seat and waved back, including Elizabeth, who had stepped out onto the porch for a better look, in the farewell. She wondered what Elizabeth thought of her companion, but she would have to wait until next week to find out. She found herself amazingly reluctant to allow Elizabeth close enough to form an opinion, and wondered why it should possibly matter.

After he asked her which way to go, they rode for a while in silence. Sarah cast about for a topic of conversation, but couldn't think of a single thing that might not invite inquiries she didn't want to invite, so she was stymied into silence.

Travis glanced at her from time to time out of the corner of his eye. Stuck-up, he decided, on top of being bossy. Too good to talk to the help. He just wished she didn't smell so damn good, like flowers or something. Flowers and the tantalizing scent of woman. He caught himself wanting to lean over closer, maybe until his lips were almost touching the smooth white skin of her throat, so he could take a big, deep breath of her.

The thought of her probable reaction to such a liberty almost made him smile, although he had to admit even getting pushed off the wagon seat might be worth it. But he hadn't been this close to a woman in longer than he cared to remember, and he decided he'd better behave himself if he wanted it to last.

The curls around her face had relaxed into wisps the wind was teasing into her eyes, and she kept reaching up to brush them away. He remembered the feel of her hand in his, strong fingers gripping his through the thin barrier of her gloves. She probably could drive the wagon as well as he, and if he had any sense at all, he'd let her. Unless he was terribly lucky or she lived a lot closer to town than he thought she did, he'd be bleeding all over his new shirt before they reached her ranch. So much for pride.

When a mile had fallen behind them, Travis began to wonder at her continued silence. Being stuck-up was one thing, but surely she must be curious about him. She was his employer now, and a woman into the bargain. Any other woman would have asked him a dozen questions by now, demanding to know where he was from and how he'd come to be carried into town on a plank. He had expected the questions to start any second, but when several thousand seconds had ticked by without any, he lost patience.

"Aren't you going to ask me how I got shot up?" he snapped.

She stared at him in amazement. "I already heard the story of how you were cleaning your gun. Do you have any intention of telling me something different?"

"Well, no," he admitted in surprise.

"Mr. Travis, I've spent most of my life in Texas, so I know better than to question a man about his background. I will admit to a great deal of curiosity, however, and anytime you want to confide in me, I'll be happy to listen to your story."

Travis couldn't imagine ever wanting to confide in

her. Still, she'd earned his grudging respect. Not many women had such self-restraint. "I do have a lot of experience with cows," he told her by way of compromise. "You won't be sorry you hired me."

"Have you ever been a foreman?"

The question surprised him. Surely she wouldn't put a complete stranger in charge of her ranch. "Yes."

"You struck me as the kind of man others would respect," she said, surprising him again. "I recently lost my foreman, and none of the other men are willing to take on the responsibility. Of course, you don't have to, either, and you certainly don't have to make up your mind until you've had a chance to meet the other men. But the job is yours if you want it."

Now he *knew* something was wrong. If he had a lick of sense, he'd stop the wagon, thank her very much, walk back to town and ask Rolley Burns very humbly for the opportunity of working for him again. Unfortunately, he already owed her, for the clothes on his back, for the rest of his gear packed carefully in the wagon with her supplies, for the saddle he'd piled on top, and even for the bath he'd taken this afternoon. She must've planned all this, making him beholden so even when he did find out what her trouble was, he wouldn't be able to leave. Damn her, he already had enough trouble of his own. He sure as hell didn't need anybody else's.

Since he couldn't think of a suitable reply to her invitation to confide in her, they fell silent again. He wasn't a man given to casual conversation, so normally he wouldn't have minded, but something about Sarah Hadley's silence set his teeth on edge. It was almost like she could hear the things he wasn't telling her, or like she could see things he didn't want her to see. His unease drove him to speak.

31

"Your nephew is a fine-looking boy," he said, choosing the safest topic he could think of.

"My nephew?" she repeated sharply, and when he looked up, her hazel eyes were shadowed.

"Yeah, the little boy back there." Could she have forgotten him so quickly?

"Oh." She looked hastily away, almost as if she were embarrassed, and her hands began to twist in her lap. What on earth had he said now?

Sarah stared off into the distance, only vaguely aware of the rolling prairie and the vermilion glory of the setting sun. No one had ever called Paul her nephew before, but then, everyone else knew the whole sordid story already. It was really none of his business, of course, but sooner or later someone would tell him, and when they did, she didn't want him to get the wrong impression. She didn't want him to pity her.

"Paul isn't my nephew," she said resolutely.

"What?"

"I said, Paul, the little boy who called me 'Aunt Sarah,' isn't my nephew."

"Oh." Plainly she had only confused him.

She drew a deep breath and plunged in. "You'll hear the story sooner or later, so you might as well hear it from me. Paul is my husband's son."

The disturbingly blue eyes narrowed as he tried to figure it out. "I thought you said your husband is dead."

"He is. He died a little over a year ago in a riding accident." She wouldn't mention that Philip had been drunk, how he'd often been drunk those last months as he'd tried to drown the guilt of what he had done. "Before he died he fathered a child by another woman, a young widow in town."

"The dressmaker? That woman back there you were

32

visiting?" he asked in astonishment.

She clenched her hands more tightly in her lap. "Yes," she replied stiffly, acutely aware of his shock. "You must think it strange that I would be at her home."

"Strange doesn't even cover it, lady," he muttered. "Did this happen while he was married to you?"

"Yes," she admitted reluctantly, the shame of it still sharp enough to sting. "Philip and I married very young, or at least I was young, barely sixteen. We'd known each other almost all our lives." No use to tell him Philip had never loved her, that he had only married her because his parents had insisted. "At first we were only neighbors, but my parents and my brothers died when I was thirteen. It was some sort of fever. We all had it, but I was the only one who survived. Afterwards, the Hadleys took me in and raised me like their own daughter."

And took care of her ranch as if it were their own, too. In fact, so much like it was their own that eventually it became imperative for her to actually be their daughter so they would never have to explain to her where the money had gone or why all her cattle now bore their brand.

"When I was old enough, Philip and I married." A besotted sixteen-year-old girl marrying a twenty-year-old man who had no interest in or desire for marriage but who had always been a dutiful son and who was smart enough to have his eye on the main chance. "Mr. Hadley died shortly afterwards, and Philip inherited the responsibilities of the ranch. I suppose he was too young for a burden like that."

She glanced at Mr. Travis and was surprised to see anger glinting in his disturbing eyes.

"So he started whoring around with other women," he guessed.

Not exactly the word Sarah would have chosen, but fairly accurate, nevertheless. She nodded stiffly. "Elizabeth Williams and her husband came to town when Philip and I had been married about three years. Mr. Williams was consumptive, and he soon passed away. Elizabeth had no money and no place else to go, so she supported herself by making dresses for a time, until . . ."

"Until her little sin became too obvious."

"Yes." Sarah felt the heat rising in her face, but she ignored it and continued doggedly with her story. "For a long time no one knew who was responsible for her . . . her predicament, and even when people found out, no one told me." How odd, she thought, to be so ashamed when she had done nothing wrong. "You probably think I was incredibly stupid."

"Young and innocent, more likely," he said, his voice remarkably kind. Sarah studied him for any hint of condescension but found none. Satisfied, she continued.

"Anyway, I had no idea at all until after Philip's death. Reverend Gilbert, our minister, told me the whole story."

"Real nice of him," Mr. Travis remarked grimly.

"He didn't do it to hurt me, although I can't say I realized that at the time. You see, when people found out about . . . about Elizabeth's predicament, the ladies in town had stopped hiring her to make dresses for them. Since she couldn't work, Paul supported her. All those years, I'd never understood why we couldn't seem to make any money on the ranch, and suddenly it all made sense. Reverend Gilbert pointed out that with Philip dead and Elizabeth unable to earn a living because of her disgrace, she and the boy would starve to death."

"I can't believe you would've cared."

"I didn't!" Sarah assured him, feeling once again the pain and humiliation. "Reverend Gilbert told me it was my Christian duty to forgive her. He asked me to go see her and the child before I made up my mind."

"What difference would it make if you forgave her or not?"

"You mean besides easing my soul?" Sarah asked with irony. "Reverend Gilbert seemed to think I should be concerned for the survival of my husband's bastard son. If I would forgive Elizabeth and patronize her shop, the other ladies would, too. Elizabeth would be able to earn a living again."

"At least he didn't expect you to keep supporting them yourself," Mr. Travis said, shaking his head in wonder.

"I'm sure he knew better than to ask, and certainly not even God would expect me to be so generous."

"You wouldn't think so."

"In any case, I went to see her. I can't say my motives were good or kind. I wanted to humiliate her, but I was too late. Until I saw her that day, I don't think I'd ever realized what it meant to be truly an outcast in the community. Not one other woman had so much as spoken to her for years. We turned away when we saw her, of course, so no one would think we condoned her scandalous behavior."

His grim smile made her wonder if he, too, hadn't been the object of community scorn.

"When I met her that day, though, and saw what we had done to her, how we had shattered her pride and shut her off from human contact, I finally understood the difference between being humiliated and being ru-

35

ined. In the face of her tragedy, of what Philip had done to her, my own embarrassment seemed insignificant."

"So because of that, you forgave her?" he asked skeptically.

It wasn't a good enough reason. She'd never convince him it was, and for reasons she didn't care to examine too closely, she knew she had to tell him the truth, or at least part of it. "She . . . she told me some things about my husband, things I hadn't known. And when I knew them, I couldn't help but forgive her."

Mr. Travis frowned in disbelief. "Did she tell you he never stopped loving you or something?"

"I'd hardly be likely to believe something like that, especially from my husband's mistress."

She could see from his expression he couldn't imagine what else Elizabeth might have said to turn the hatred of a woman scorned into forgiveness and friendship. Although she had no intention of telling him, Sarah couldn't resist remembering the day she'd called on Elizabeth, how Elizabeth had stared at her in terror, her lovely green eyes red-rimmed and still streaming tears. All the invectives Sarah had planned to hurl had died on her lips in the face of such cringing fear, and instead she had listened to Elizabeth's broken and abject apologies.

No, Philip had never loved his wife, and Sarah would have scorned such a lie. But Elizabeth knew a secret Sarah would have killed to know. She knew that Philip admired Sarah, envied her strength and her indomitable will.

By the time Philip met Elizabeth Williams, Sarah had come to despise her husband's weakness and his failure. Sarah always knew the right decision to make, the right course to follow, while Philip wallowed in uncertainty and indecision. This mere slip of a girl could have run his ranch far better than he, if only he hadn't been too proud to take her advice. She could even have saved it after Philip's stubborn refusal to listen to her had driven them almost to bankruptcy, if only he hadn't been so afraid of her scorn.

In his shame, he'd sought refuge in Elizabeth's arms, gentle Elizabeth who would never criticize, never complain, not even when Philip's love took from her everything else she valued in the world. And poor Elizabeth, who'd known she could never have preeminence with a man whose one futile, driving passion was to earn the love and respect of his wife, a woman whom he would never love in return.

But of course Sarah couldn't share all this with Mr. Travis. Instead, she would placate him with something he might be able to understand. "And I fell in love with the boy. Not even I could hold an innocent child responsible for what his parents had done, and I couldn't help thinking that by rights he should have been my child." She'd shocked him again, but what did it matter? "Since I'll never have children of my own now, Paul will be a fine substitute."

Mr. Travis considered. "Isn't it a little early to decide that? You might marry again."

"Why should I marry again? I have a ranch to run, a successful ranch, so I don't need a man to support me, and I certainly don't need a man who might take over and ruin everything I've done."

His frown told her he didn't for one minute believe any man couldn't do far better than any woman in running a business. Sarah should have argued with him, but suddenly she felt too tired to make the effort. Besides, they were approaching the entrance to her property.

The sign above the barbed-wire gate proclaimed the entrance to the Golden Hoof Ranch.

"Here we are," she said, pointing to the gate.

He reined the team to a halt and jumped down to open the gate. She noticed a small red stain on the back of his shirt and had to bite her tongue to keep from crying out in distress. It was, after all, his back, and if he chose to drive until he dropped in exhaustion, he wouldn't appreciate her scolding him for it. Hadn't she learned her lesson with Philip?

Lifting the loop of rawhide that held the gate shut, he swung it wide and started back for the wagon. She noticed him checking the fence with a practiced eye for any signs of weakness, and when he stopped and veered off to examine a nearby section more closely, she assumed he'd found one.

She was wrong. He bent down and plucked a clump of fuzz from the lower strand of wire, then peered at it closely. Oh, dear, she thought with foreboding, as he strode angrily back to her.

His neck had reddened, and the intense blue eyes were practically sparking when he glared up at where she sat above him on the wagon seat. "Just what in the hell is this?" he demanded, thrusting the offending clump of fuzz under her nose.

She briefly considered reminding him he was addressing a lady, but thought better of it. "What do you think it is?" she countered.

His glare turned murderous. "I think it's the reason you needed a hired gun, Mrs. Hadley. I think it's fleece off a goddamned *sheep!*"

Chapter Two

"Mr. Travis, I'll thank you to watch your language," Sarah said primly, trying to match him glare for glare.

"You're a fine one to be worried about how other people act after you lied to me."

"I never lied to you!" She'd taken great care not to say anything that would require her to lie.

"You said I'd be working *cattle!*"

"And you will!" she informed him. "Although the sheep are proving more profitable, I'm still running cattle, too. You won't be asked to herd sheep, Mr. Travis."

He looked a little mollified, but only a little. Plainly, like most cattlemen, he hated the very thought of sheep. Before he could say anything else, she said, "I'll drive the wagon through the gate so you can shut it behind us."

Without waiting for his reply, she slid over, untied the reins, and slapped the team into motion. When the wagon was clear of the gate, she stopped it and waited, not daring to look back for fear he'd just be standing there, debating with himself the best way of getting back to town. Then she heard the gate slam shut and allowed herself a moment's relief while she waited for him to mount the wagon again.

As she handed him the reins, she hazarded a glance at his face. He refused to meet her eye, and she could see he was still furious. From his expression, she could imagine his plan for getting back to town was to simply murder her and take the wagon.

But he started the team without making any threatening moves, following the track that would eventually lead to her house and the other ranch buildings. They rode in silence, and when the silence became oppressive, she said, "I suppose you're wondering why I decided to raise sheep."

"And I suppose you have every intention of telling me," he replied, mocking her earlier reluctance to question him.

Her peek was wasted, since he didn't deign to glance at her. "If you've worked with cattle as much as you claim, you surely know how difficult it is to make a profit at it, Mr. Travis," she said determinedly.

"It ain't easy to make money no matter what you do nowadays."

"And what if you're wrong?" she challenged. "There's an old Spanish proverb that says, 'Wherever the foot of the sheep touches, the land turns to gold.'"

" 'The Golden Hoof,' " he muttered in disgust.

"My father-in-law named the ranch years ago, but when I found out how profitable sheep raising could be, I thought the name must be an omen."

"Aren't omens usually bad?"

Sarah sighed. "I can see you harbor the same prejudices as the other cattlemen around here."

"I ain't prejudiced. I just know the trouble sheep can cause."

40

"But that's just it; they don't cause any trouble at all!" Sarah exclaimed in exasperation. "I know cattlemen say they ruin the grass by eating it down to the roots and cutting up the sod with their hooves, but that only happens if they're herded improperly. In truth, they actually help the grass. Did you know sheep droppings are better fertilizer than cattle droppings? And you must know cattle only eat tall grass. Sheep eat the short grass and weeds the cows don't touch, so the two can graze on the same pastures."

"Cattle won't graze after the sheep have stinked the place up."

"You've just proved you don't know anything about it!" Sarah exclaimed in triumph. "The sheep smell only lingers on the ground for a few minutes, and I've grazed cattle after sheep many times. The system works beautifully. And of course sheep are a much more practical stock to raise. You can only sell a cow once, but you can sell a sheep's fleece many, many times while she's also producing lambs for you."

"You can only sell the fleece if the sheep stay alive, Mrs. Hadley, and don't tell me you ain't worried about keeping your sheep alive, because you wouldn't've been so all-fired anxious to hire me if you weren't."

Sarah pressed her lips together, fighting the urge to deny his charge. She certainly didn't want to give him a reason to accuse her of lying again. She settled for "No one has tried to harm my sheep."

"Yet," he replied ominously. "Can you say nobody's threatened to?"

"Most every cattleman would say he'd walk a mile out of his way to kick a sheep," Sarah hedged.

41

"I'd guess somebody's threatened to do more than kick them. The only thing I can't figure is what makes you think I'll be any help to you."

Sarah was beginning to wonder the same thing. For some reason, she hadn't counted on his being so obstinate. "You said you had a lot of experience working with cattle, and that's why I hired you."

"You hired me before I said that," he reminded her. His eyes were the color of the Texas sky just before a thunderstorm, and she felt a frisson of unease. "Mrs. Hadley, if you're going to hire a gunfighter, you'd do a lot better to pick somebody who'd won the last fight he'd been in."

She suspected the admission of defeat had cost him, and she respected him for it. "I appreciate your advice, Mr. Travis, but I have a feeling you aren't exactly used to losing. Don't forget, I saw the look you gave the sheriff that day in Dr. Bigelow's office. Besides, I've learned that winning isn't everything. Sometimes simply being able to outlast your opponent is the way to real victory. When I heard how hard you'd fought to survive, I knew you were exactly the kind of man I needed on my side."

"And you think because you're paying my wages, I'm on your side?" he scoffed, but his bravado didn't fool her.

"I think you're a man who honors his commitments, Mr. Travis. You ride for the brand, and when you took my offer of a job, I got your loyalty, too."

His eyes narrowed, and something twitched in his jaw, but as much as he might have liked to deny her claim, he couldn't, just as she'd prayed he wouldn't. He might despise sheep and even those who ran them,

42

but he was her man now, and he'd fight for what was hers.

Her man. The words caused an odd sensation in the pit of her stomach, almost like apprehension but not so unpleasant. She wondered why she should find the thought disturbing, and decided it was because possessing a man like this was a lot like having a tiger by the tail. She'd been lucky so far, but she'd be wise not to push him too far.

Still, she couldn't help noticing the red stain on his back had spread. "Mr. Travis, would you be willing to let me drive for a while if I told you you're bleeding again?"

He glanced over his shoulder in a vain attempt to see for himself.

"I really didn't intend to work you back into your sickbed on the very first day," she added, holding out her hands for the reins. With almost palpable reluctance, he passed them to her.

Sarah knew better than to gloat over this small victory. Men hated being bested by women, or even *suspecting* they'd been bested by women, and betraying a physical weakness before one must be galling to a man like Mr. Travis. Still, she allowed herself a tiny feeling of satisfaction. Mr. Travis had turned out to be even more interesting than she'd expected.

Travis shifted on the seat, trying to ease the ache in his back. Damn Sarah Hadley for being right. He'd add that to her list of sins, along with being bossy and good-looking. And he mustn't forget smelling good. Her scent teased at him against the wind, a constant reminder of her presence even when he was able to tear his gaze from her.

He decided he must be weaker than he'd thought, to be so affected by her nearness. Usually, he had more sense than to let a woman distract him. Of course, he couldn't exactly remember the last time he'd had the opportunity of being distracted by any woman, but he had the uncomfortable feeling Sarah Hadley would've bothered him even if he'd just finished up his turn at a bawdy house.

It was her black hair, he decided, as dark and shiny as a raven's wing. The heavy coil on her neck hinted at long, luxuriant waves reaching almost to her hips. The darkness would provide a delicious contrast to the milk-white skin he imagined under her widow's weeds.

He tried to imagine what her breasts would be like — small but full, with upturned nipples as pink as her lips and pursed just as tightly. A sweet handful if a man could get her to hold still long enough to savor it. Unfortunately, he couldn't imagine her ever doing so, at least not for him. No, Sarah Hadley wasn't for the likes of Travis Taylor. She deserved a man who'd stick, not a fiddle-footed drifter who'd left his best and only friend lying dead while he ran for his own life. And certainly not a man who probably wouldn't be here a month from now, who might not even be alive, because he had to avenge his friend's death no matter what it cost him.

"There it is," she said suddenly, startling him back to the present.

Up ahead he saw the cluster of buildings that composed the Golden Hoof Ranch. He told himself he shouldn't have been surprised. Naturally a woman would put more store in appearances than a man, but Sarah Hadley must be determined to let every other rancher in the county know how prosperous she'd become. Not only were the buildings in good repair, they sported a fresh coat of whitewash, making the whole place appear to be made of ice cream.

Her house looked as if it had grown from the usual two-room dogtrot, with rooms being added as family expansion demanded, until the place had become a sprawling monstrosity. Sarah Hadley had softened the effect with an equally sprawling veranda running the entire width of the house and furnished with wicker furniture. Travis wondered grimly what her men thought about living among all this pristine purity. Personally, he felt as comfortable as a whore in church.

She stopped the wagon in the yard in front of the house. Travis looked around, uneasily aware of what a poor impression he would make, having been driven to the ranch by Mrs. Hadley. A few men lounged on the porch of the bunkhouse, but they seemed more wary than interested. The instant the wagon stopped, one of them who had been sitting a little apart from the others got up and started across the yard toward them.

Travis needed only a glance to know the fellow wasn't a cowman, even though he wore the same type of Levi's and shirt Travis himself had just purchased. In place of the usual boots, this man wore regular shoes, and his hat bore absolutely no resemblance to a cowboy's Stetson. His sturdy build would tend toward fat in later years, Travis judged, and the fiery red hair visible beneath the ridiculous hat confirmed his worst fears about the fellow. A goddamned Scot.

With a sigh of resignation, Travis climbed down

from the wagon and prepared to meet him face-to-face. Mrs. Hadley was scooting over on the seat, so he had no choice but to help her down. Once again her hand gripped his as she descended from the high seat in a rustle of skirts and petticoats. Travis averted his eyes so he wouldn't catch any tantalizing glimpses of white lace or well-turned ankle. He'd have enough trouble not thinking about Sarah Hadley's feminine charms without knowing exactly what they were.

"Mr. Cameron," Sarah said to the redheaded man when he had reached them, "this is Mr. Travis. I've just hired him to help with the cattle."

Travis looked into blue eyes cold enough to freeze the gonads off a brass monkey. Cameron had the type of skin that would never tan. It just burned beet red, peeled and burned again. He was burning just now, or maybe he just got red in the face whenever Mrs. Hadley did something he didn't like. Travis noted with some satisfaction that Cameron's eyes were only an inch or two higher than his own. At least he wasn't tall.

"Mr. Travis, this is Owen Cameron," she continued, as if she hadn't noticed the way Cameron was scowling at him. If he'd been a snake, he'd've been rattling. "Mr. Cameron is my *mayordomo.*"

"Sheepman," Travis said tightly.

"Aye," Cameron replied, just as tightly.

Neither of them offered to shake hands, and Mrs. Hadley frowned in disapproval. Travis half expected her to scold them for being ill-mannered, but she must've thought better of it.

"Mr. Cameron manages everything to do with the sheep," she said with forced brightness.

46

"Only God and a Scotchman would see any good in a sheep," Travis said, quoting an old maxim.

Cameron smiled as if he'd been complimented. "Then I'll be in good company."

Travis knew he should resist the impulse, but since Cameron already hated him, he couldn't see the harm. He turned to Sarah. "Didn't anybody warn you not to hire a Scot to tend your sheep?"

"Because he'll end up owning the whole flock?" she replied. Her smug smile lit up her eyes, which now looked startlingly green. "I've heard that, but I'm not afraid of Mr. Cameron. He's made it clear he intends to build his own flock while he's working for me, but he's promised to leave me a few."

"A man who'd steal from a woman would be a poor man indeed," Cameron growled.

"You don't have to steal from her to get the sheep, and you know it," Travis growled back. "Just take your pay in lambs, and before long, you'll own more of them than she does."

"Ye seem to know a lot about sheep, Mr. Travis," Cameron said with sudden interest, and Travis stiffened in alarm. When would he learn not to yield to temptation and keep his big mouth shut?

"I've heard talk. Seems like everybody's cussing sheep nowadays."

"Cussing them or raising them, Mr. Travis," Sarah said briskly. "I happen to be raising them, and I'll thank you to remember the money they earn is paying your wages. Mr. Cameron, I've offered Mr. Travis the foreman's position."

Plainly, Cameron found the idea offensive. "Mrs. Hadley," he protested, but Travis noted his tone gen-

47

tled when he addressed Sarah, and the cold blue eyes softened noticeably. "What can ye be thinking? The man's a stranger. Ye don't know a thing about him."

"I know I need someone to take charge of the cowboys, and none of them are willing." Travis caught himself studying her for signs of the same gentling Cameron had shown. Were the two lovers? For some reason, Travis found the idea abhorrent, but when he looked at Sarah, he saw no hint of tenderness toward the man. Instead, he thought he detected a flicker of irritation in those hazel eyes. Apparently Sarah Hadley didn't like being patronized by her hired help. "I would appreciate it if you would show Mr. Travis where to put his things," she added sharply.

Cameron also showed a flicker of irritation, but he answered civilly enough. "I'll send someone to unload the wagon. Come, Travis."

He turned and stalked off without waiting for Travis, who decided to take his time getting the paper-wrapped parcel containing his new outfit from the bed of the wagon. When Cameron realized Travis wasn't following, he was forced to wait. By the time Travis caught up, the man was fuming.

He looked Travis up and down contemptuously, taking in the spanking new clothes and the package. "Got ye all togged out, did she?"

"Against my future wages," Travis said, wondering if the man's animosity could possibly be jealousy. Of course, that was absurd. If Cameron wanted Sarah Hadley, Travis Taylor wouldn't be an obstacle.

The icy eyes narrowed again. "Just so ye don't get the wrong idea, Mrs. Hadley treats all her hired hands the same way she treated ye. Ye needn't think you're something special."

He *was* jealous! Travis realized incredulously. He could have put the poor man's mind at ease, but he decided to let him stew for a while. The fellow looked like he could do with some humbling. "Maybe I *know* I'm something special," he replied smugly, and walked off toward the bunkhouse alone.

The sight of the three men on the porch quickly wiped all thoughts of Owen Cameron from his mind. Travis had rarely seen a sorrier bunch of men. They eyed him suspiciously as he approached, as if afraid he might do them some bodily harm. He climbed the steps cautiously, the way he would have approached a wild animal who might startle and run.

"Afternoon, boys," he said, although he judged all of the men to be older than his own twenty-nine years. When none of them returned the greeting, he added, "They call me Travis. Mrs. Hadley hired me to work with you."

"Cattleman?" the oldest of the three asked. Two beady eyes stared out of his weathered face like brown marbles. His clothes looked a little the worse for wear and hung loosely on his lanky frame. Although Travis would have judged him tall, he slouched almost apologetically.

"Yeah," Travis replied. "Cattleman."

The three visibly relaxed.

"The name's Quinn," the skinny fellow said, offering his hand. Although Travis made it a habit not to tie up his gun hand, he decided to make an exception in this instance. Besides, none of these fellows looked the least bit dangerous.

"They call me Shorty," the second one said when

49

Travis turned to him. Travis noted with irritation that the man wasn't any shorter than he, surely not small enough to have merited such a nickname. Shorty's grin revealed a gaping hole where his two front teeth should have been. He seemed younger than Quinn, but probably only because he was rather stout, so his face didn't look so wrinkled.

The third fellow, a bandy-legged man with a prodigious mustache, introduced himself as Ace.

"Maybe you boys can show me where to put my gear," Travis suggested.

The three of them glanced past him as if looking for Cameron's approval, but they saw the *mayordomo* had gone to unload the wagon himself. Travis wondered if he dared ask the man to take his saddle over to the barn, but decided not to push him too far just yet.

Quinn led the way into the bunkhouse, a long log building lined with single bunks. Most of them appeared to be taken.

"Sheepherders," Quinn said, gesturing to the far side of the room. "We're down here." They passed several empty bunks on the near side of the room until they came to three in a row which obviously belonged to the three cowboys. Although he figured the segregation probably wasn't too healthy, Travis dropped his package on the empty bed nearest theirs. There was no use in antagonizing the cowboys so early in the game.

"You're the fellow they brought into Doc Bigelow's, ain't you?" Shorty asked suddenly.

Travis resisted the instinctive defensiveness and forced himself to answer mildly. "Yeah. I had a little trouble, but it didn't follow me here."

50

Obviously, they wanted to know more, but they also knew how hazardous it could be to ask a man too many questions about his past. "I see you don't have a horse," Quinn said.

"No, they tell me I rode mine to death, poor bastard. I reckon I was too far gone to know what I was doing. He was a damn fine animal, too."

"We'll get you a string in the morning," Shorty said. "Mrs. Hadley keeps a first-class remuda."

Travis glanced around the comfortable bunkhouse. "She keeps a first-class everything, looks like." He eased himself down onto the bunk in a silent invitation to confidence.

The others responded, instinctively drawing closer. Quinn and Shorty sat down on the opposite bunk, and Ace moved to lean against the wall.

"I reckon you know about the sheep," Quinn ventured.

"I didn't find out until after I took the job," Travis informed them, letting his disapproval show.

"Mrs. Hadley couldn't help it," Shorty insisted. "The boss left her in a terrible fix when he died. She couldn't even pay our wages. She called all the men together and told us what she planned to do. There's some fellow down in Kerrville'll lend money if you promise to put half of it into sheep, so that's what she done. 'Course some of her men wouldn't stay once the sheep come."

"You mean most of them," Travis guessed.

"Not all of them left right at first," Quinn said. "A few did, but the others got scared off gradual."

"Then you've had some trouble?" Travis asked, mentally cursing Sarah for lying again. He'd asked

51

her right out, too.

"Not what you'd call real trouble. Some fences cut, a few sheep found dead, but nothing real serious," Quinn explained. "Mostly it's just threats, hints, you might say, about what might happen some dark night."

"And little things," Shorty added, aggrieved. "Like when we go into the saloon and nobody'll stand at the bar with us."

Travis nodded. He knew only too well how effective such subtle ostracism could be. "But you fellows stuck with her."

They exchanged a sheepish glance. "We didn't have a lot of choice. We ain't exactly top hands, mister," Quinn said. "Besides, we figured we owed the old man something."

"Mrs. Hadley's husband?" Travis asked.

"No, his pa. Old Man Hadley started this place. Him and Mr. Flynn, Mrs. Hadley's pa, was the first settlers here. They come right after the war, almost twenty years ago now. After his old man died, Phil Hadley about run things into the ground, but she was determined to keep the ranch, so we figured the least we could do was help her."

"Tell me about her husband. How'd he die?"

Again the men exchanged a glance, as if silently determining how much to reveal. Travis decided to make it easy on them. "I already know about the dressmaker and his kid. I want to know what kind of a boss he was."

Quinn frowned sourly. "It ain't right to speak ill of the dead, but Phil Hadley wasn't worth the powder to blow his brains out."

"Is that what somebody did?" Travis asked sharply.

52

"Hell, no. Didn't I say he wasn't worth it? He was a drunk, and one night when he was coming home from visiting his woman, he fell off his horse and busted his head open."

"They figured something spooked the horse," Shorty added, as if compelled to justify the accident.

"Some*thing* or some*body*?" Travis asked.

Quinn shrugged. "Ain't no reason to think anybody'd want him dead except maybe Mrs. Hadley, and she didn't even know about the kid then. We sure as hell didn't have sheep yet, so what could he've done to make somebody mad enough to kill him?"

"Maybe somebody didn't like your fences," Travis suggested.

"Didn't have fences then, either. Hadleys didn't care who used their water, and God knows, most folks needed to one time or another."

"Are you saying Mrs. Hadley controls the only reliable water around?"

"Most of it," Quinn confirmed. "When Phil Hadley married Sarah Flynn and put the two ranches together, he got hisself a gold mine, or so everybody thought. Didn't anybody guess he'd neglect it and spend all his money on some other woman."

Phil Hadley had been an even bigger fool than Travis had previously thought. If Travis Taylor had been gifted with just half of what Phil Hadley had, he never would've been forced to hire out his gun to earn his living. Travis marveled at the degree of animosity he felt for a man whom he had never met, and hoped he was only envious of Hadley's squandered opportunities.

He certainly had no right to envy Hadley his wife.

53

Disturbed by the thought, he pushed it aside and changed the subject by inquiring about the ranch and the condition of the cattle he would be tending. If he was going to be foreman of this godforsaken place — and he didn't see where he had much choice — he'd better learn as much as he could.

Sarah went straight to her room, removed her bonnet, and washed her hands and face. Hearing someone carrying in her purchases, she returned to the front room that she had furnished as a formal parlor. There she found Owen Cameron holding an armload of packages.

"Just take them into the kitchen and put them on the table," she said, following him across the hallway that had once been the open passageway or "dogtrot" between the original two rooms of the house, into the large kitchen. When the Hadleys had first built it, the kitchen had served as a combination kitchen, dining room and parlor while the second room, the current parlor, had served as sleeping quarters.

Owen laid the bags of flour and coffee on the pine table. When he turned, she saw the stubborn set of his jaw and the determined glint in his eyes, and she braced herself for the lecture she'd been expecting.

"He'd be the man they found half dead out on the range, won't he?"

"Yes," she said resignedly.

"What do ye know about him?"

"He knows cattle, and he's a man the others are likely to respect. You know Quinn can't handle the job, and neither can either of the others, and besides,

54

we're terribly shorthanded. I'd hire two or three more men if I could find anyone willing to work for me."

"Which is exactly the problem, missus," he replied in exasperation. "As long as we run sheep, you'll never find any men to work for ye, and if ye get rid of the sheep, ye won't have money to pay them. Get rid of the bloody cattle and be done with it!"

"Mr. Cameron," Sarah said, holding her temper with difficulty, "as I have explained to you before, I keep the cattle so I will have at least something in common with my neighbors. If I give the place over entirely to sheep, I wouldn't last a week!"

"I can't believe you're afraid of that lot of cowards!" he exclaimed.

"Killing defenseless sheep and hanging an unarmed sheepherder are acts only a coward would perform, Mr. Cameron," she informed him, losing the battle with her temper. "You haven't been in Texas long enough to be an expert in such matters, but I hope you will have sense enough to accept the benefit of my greater experience."

He frowned, and she could see he was trying to remember she was his employer. Unfortunately, he could never forget she was a woman. After a moment, the anger drained out of him and his eyes went all soft and pleading. "Experience or no, ye shouldna have to deal with this on your own. Ye need a man, Mrs. Hadley."

He took a small step toward her, and for one awful moment she thought he might actually reach for her. Fortunately, his control held, and he stood fast, waiting to see her reaction to his implied offer.

Sarah didn't know whether to laugh or to cry. Didn't

he know that marriage was the least attractive of her options? But of course he didn't. Men always assumed their mere presence was the answer to every maiden's prayer, even if the "maiden" in this case was a slightly harassed widow instead. Wishing to save his pride, she chose to deliberately misunderstand him. "I already have a man, Mr. Cameron. Several, in fact. I have you to look after my sheep, and now I have Mr. Travis to look after my cattle."

Cameron flushed crimson. "And would that be the only reason ye hired him?" he snapped.

"No, it wouldn't, as I think you know. I hired him because we need someone around here who knows how to fight."

"We need someone who knows how to win," Cameron corrected her. "What makes ye think this fellow does?"

"That's exactly what he asked me," Sarah recalled with amusement. "Regardless of Mr. Travis's most recent experience, however, I believe he's a man used to winning, and I think he'll go to any lengths to avoid another defeat."

"And what if you're wrong?"

Sarah's anger came back in a rush. "Then I will be the one to pay the price, Mr. Cameron, not you."

He stiffened under the rebuke, and Sarah instantly regretted her hasty words.

"I'm sorry, Mr. Cameron. A man who has been as loyal as you deserves better than that."

"It's more than loyalty."

She knew that, of course, but she dared not acknowledge it. "I know, your future is at stake here, too, and I have no intention of letting either of us fail.

56

However much you may disapprove, I'm afraid Mr. Travis's presence here will go a long way toward ensuring our success. As difficult as it may be for you, you will have to learn to tolerate him and what he stands for."

From his expression, she could see it would be difficult indeed, but she had no pity for him. A man who'd never even owned a gun before he came to Texas less than a year ago would need all the help he could get.

"I'll do it, missus," he said grimly. "But only because ye ask it."

Now Sarah simply wanted to cry. One thing she didn't need was Owen Cameron complicating her personal life when the rest of her life was in such a shambles. "Thank you, Mr. Cameron. I appreciate your *loyalty*," she said as formally as she could, and turned away, anxious for the privacy of her bedroom.

When she reached it, she closed the door behind her and sagged against it, savoring the comfort of her private refuge. When she looked around at the heavy mahogany furniture, a legacy from her parents' home, and the treasured keepsakes adorning her dressing table, she could almost believe she'd locked her problems outside the door.

Almost, but not quite, she realized, involuntarily remembering Owen Cameron's beseeching expression. What on earth had put the idea of marriage into the man's head? She wished she could believe he was really in love with her, but Philip Hadley had disabused her of any notions she might once have entertained about her ability to attract and hold a man's affections. No, Owen might admire her and even respect her, but, like most men, he had his eye on the main chance. In his native Scotland, he'd had no opportunity even to own land, but here in Texas, he could actually become a wealthy man. Who could blame him for wanting to take a shortcut toward that goal by marrying her? Sarah could almost admire his audacity. Still, she had no intention of sacrificing her own freedom to help him along his way.

She walked over to the wicker armchair sitting by the front window and sank down on it. From here she could see the bunkhouse, and quite naturally her thoughts strayed to Mr. Travis. She wondered if Cameron had seen him settled in, or if he'd left it to the other men. And what had Travis thought of the other men, that motley crew of misfits to whom Sarah owed so much? Once they'd been the backbone of the Golden Hoof's operation, and now that age had made them less than desirable to anyone else, they would continue to hold together the ranch their very sweat had built.

Unfortunately, she couldn't expect Mr. Travis to see all that in them. Somehow she would have to convey it to him. She only hoped it wasn't already too late. If he'd let them see his contempt . . . But somehow she knew he'd have more sense than to judge the men by appearances. Hadn't she known he was just the type of leader they needed?

Or had she been deluding herself, imagining virtues where she wanted and needed them to be? She certainly hoped not. Facing up to her own foolishness would be difficult enough, but facing up to Owen Cameron's I-told-you-so would be unbearable.

She thought affectionately of the burly Scot with his orange hair and his stubborn streak. He wanted so

58

badly to help her, and sometimes the burden of carrying this ranch and its crew became so great, she yearned for another pair of shoulders to share the yoke. Owen Cameron certainly had the shoulders for it. Too bad she could never bring herself to love him.

Movement outside caught her eye, and she saw Travis coming out of the bunkhouse with Quinn. The two men were talking, or rather Quinn was talking and Travis was nodding. She wished she could hear what they were saying, but she was gratified to see them apparently getting along so well. Quinn knew every detail about the Golden Hoof, and if he chose to, he could teach Travis whatever he needed to know. Apparently, he had chosen to.

The two men were heading for the wagon, which was still parked out in front of the house. Travis strode with confidence across the dusty ground, his lithe body as sleek and graceful as a panther's. He gave no indication of weakness, but Sarah suddenly recalled the red stain on his shirt. Would one of the other men notice and help him get the shirt off without tearing the wound open again? Would they think to check his back for signs of infection? Would Travis even allow them to?

They had reached the wagon, which Cameron had just finished emptying. What could they be after? she wondered; then remembered Travis's saddle. Good heavens, he wouldn't try to carry it himself, would he?

Sarah was out of her chair and through the bedroom door before she could even wonder why she should care. The reason, of course, was obvious: she had an investment in the man. She couldn't stand by

59

and let him hurt himself. When she reached the porch, Travis was just getting ready to hoist the saddle onto his shoulder.

"Mr. Travis!" she called without even knowing what she would say.

He looked up at her expectantly.

Oh, dear, she couldn't very well order him not to take the saddle. "Uh, Quinn, would you mind taking Mr. Travis's saddle over to the barn? I need to speak with him for a minute."

"Sure, Miz Hadley," Quinn said, willing as always to do her slightest bidding.

Travis frowned, obviously suspicious, but she wasn't worried. As his employer she had every right to be concerned about him, and certainly every right to speak to him. "Would you come inside, Mr. Travis?"

He started up the porch steps just as Cameron came out the front door behind her. Both men stopped and eyed each other warily, like two tomcats, Sarah thought uneasily.

"Will ye be needing anything else, Mrs. Hadley?" Cameron asked, planting his sturdy legs as if prepared to guard her door from this interloper.

"No, thank you, Mr. Cameron. You may go."

His expression showed his patent disapproval of her decision to have this man in her home, but he stepped grudgingly aside to let the two of them pass.

Just as Sarah entered the house, Cameron called reassuringly, "I'll be right outside if ye need me."

Sarah almost laughed out loud, but behind her Travis muttered something that sounded like "Bastard."

Oh, dear, she'd have to find some way to get these two to settle their differences, she thought grimly, then suddenly realized she had absolutely nothing to say to Mr. Travis now that she had him in the house.

But then she remembered what she had been concerned about in the first place, and led him into the kitchen. Without hesitation, she went directly to the cabinet where she kept her medical supplies. Pulling out the box, she turned to face him. He'd paused just inside the room, hat in hand, and was looking around as if he'd never been in a kitchen before.

Travis couldn't ever remember being in a kitchen like this one before. Everything was so clean, he was afraid to move for fear of contaminating something. Flowered curtains covered the shelves and the area beneath the sink and billowed at the windows. The air was redolent of yeasty bread and fragrant coffee and a dozen other mouth-watering aromas. The smells stirred something deep inside him, a long-forgotten memory that whispered *home*.

Startled by the thought, he glanced at Mrs. Hadley, who stood there staring at him expectantly, her mysterious eyes glowing green in the afternoon sunlight. She looked even more desirable than he'd remembered—all soft and rounded beneath the elegant black dress—and for one wicked moment he wondered how she would taste if she were to open her mouth beneath his.

"If you'll take off your shirt, Mr. Travis, we can get down to business."

"What?" he exclaimed, stunned.

"Your shirt. I think someone should tend to your back before it gets infected. Dr. Bigelow would never forgive me if I let you undo all his hard work."

Oh! he thought, feeling like an idiot. What did he

think, that she'd brought him into her kitchen to seduce him? But she couldn't seriously expect him to undress right here in front of her. "I'll get one of the men to look at it."

"Nonsense. I always tend to the men's injuries. If you're worried about my sensibilities, I assure you I have none, and if you're simply shy, I promise not to look at you."

The promise was ridiculous, of course. How could she tend his wounds if she didn't look at him?

She set the box she held on the table beside the supplies Cameron had piled there, and began unbuttoning her cuffs. He found the sight disturbing, almost as disturbing as if she'd actually started to undress.

"The water in the boiler is still warm, warm enough for our purposes, anyway," she said, as she rolled back first one sleeve and then the other, revealing slender wrists and softly rounded forearms. He hadn't moved a muscle, and she gazed at him quizzically, her eyes darker now. "Perhaps you should straddle this chair," she suggested, pulling out the one nearest her and turning it so the back faced away from her. Then she turned and went to the sink for a basin and proceeded to draw water from the boiler.

Travis watched her small, white hands in fascination. Already he could imagine how they would feel against his naked flesh, soft and gentle, soothing the persistent burning in his back. He really had no right to such ministrations, but hadn't she said she cared for all the men? What a treat it must be to get hurt around here. Travis told himself he'd be a fool to refuse her help, and without allowing himself to think of the reasons why he should, he laid his hat on the

62

table and began unbuttoning his shirt.

He'd just pulled out the tail when she turned, basin in hand. He resisted an instinctive impulse to jerk the shirt closed and cover himself from that clear green gaze, but he still couldn't quite bring himself to take it completely off. The sight of his bare chest was hardly likely to impress her, sensibilities or not.

As if sensing his reluctance, she said, "Sit down, Mr. Travis. I promise not to hurt you any more than is absolutely necessary."

Taking little comfort in the promise, Travis quickly straddled the chair, and with his back safely to her, he slipped the shirt over his shoulders and let it fall down to his waist, still keeping his arms in the sleeves so he could slip it back on just as quickly before she got too good a look at him.

"Good heavens!" she cried, and only then did he consider how much damage the shotgun blast must have done. He probably looked as if he'd been chewed up and spit out. What had possessed him to subject her to this?

"Never mind," he said, struggling to get his shirt up again, "I'll get one of the men—"

"Absolutely not!" She clamped a hand on his shoulder to hold him in the chair, and the feel of her velvety smooth skin against his drained all thoughts of resistance from him. "If I'd known how bad this was, I never would have permitted you to drive the wagon at all. How could you stand it?"

Travis closed his eyes, thinking the torment of his wounds was nothing compared to the torment of her touch. Could he really have forgotten so thoroughly how wonderful a woman's hand could feel, or was Sarah Hadley's caress so very different from every other he had known?

Her hand left his shoulder, and he heard a soft splash as she drew a rag from the basin of water and wrung it out. Gently, carefully, she bathed him, murmuring apologies when his breath hissed involuntarily. He didn't bother to explain that his reaction was to the acute pleasure of her delicate fingers on his naked skin.

When she had finished cleansing, she said, "I have an ointment. It smells terrible, but the men swear by it."

"All right," he muttered, gritting his teeth in anticipation of the continuation of the delicious torture.

He heard the snap of a can lid being popped, and smelled the rotten-egg stench of sulfur. She started on his shoulder where the damage was worst, stroking cautiously, her fingers dabbing and sliding sensuously across his sensitized flesh. Her warm breath stirred the hair on the back of his neck, and he could smell her tantalizing female scent even over the stench of the ointment. He felt the sweat breaking out on his face and under his arms, and tightened his grip on the back of the chair.

God, why had he ever agreed to this? he thought, while at the same time his blood roared in his ears as it raced like liquid fire through his body. Although he fought them, tantalizing images flickered behind his eyelids, images of Sarah Hadley with her long black hair hanging down and her naked breasts filling his hands while her fingers caressed him until he was hard and . . .

Oh, God, he *was* hard! he realized in horror. What

in the hell was he going to do now?

Sarah was trying to be as gentle as she could, but was not gentle enough, apparently. She couldn't help but notice how stiffly he held himself, braced against what must be the agony she was causing him. Tears of sympathy stung her eyes, and she scolded herself. She'd treated all her men at one time or another, and none of the myriad injuries had made her want to weep in sympathy.

Perhaps she was only reacting to Mr. Travis's courage. What other man could have endured what these wounds told her he had endured? His back bore more than a dozen open gashes where buckshot had gouged his flesh and James Bigelow's knife had cut it out. True, some had already closed, but others would be weeks in healing.

"You should really have these bandaged," she said. "I can't understand why Dr. Bigelow let you go with them exposed like this."

"He didn't," Travis explained, his voice tight and strained. "I couldn't move right, so I cut them off."

"Cut them off!" Sarah echoed, more outraged than she should have been. "What on earth were you thinking? You shouldn't have been moving around, anyway. Didn't Dr. Bigelow advise you to stay in bed a few more days?"

"Are you done yet?" he snapped, and Sarah realized she had overstepped her authority as his employer. Men hated to be nagged, as she knew perfectly well from bitter experience. Nagging rarely did any good anyway. Most men were pigheaded enough to do even what they knew was bad for them, just to spite a nagging woman.

Still, she couldn't surrender when his well-being was at stake. "I'll just put a bandage on the worst of them. Since tomorrow is Sunday, you don't have to work, so you won't have to worry about moving around. If you want to cut them off on Monday, it will be your business."

He drew a deep breath and released it in a long sigh, but he didn't object, so she pulled out a roll of old sheeting she had torn up for the purpose, and began to wrap it around him.

Good heavens, he was thin, she realized as she unwound the roll across his ribs. Here was a man who'd seldom if ever tasted a meal cooked especially for him by a woman who was concerned primarily for his comfort and happiness. The knowledge stirred some primitive female need to nurture, a need she'd thought Philip's betrayal had extinguished forever.

Startled by the sensation, she found herself staring at the too-long golden hair molding his finely shaped head. Something fluttered in her stomach, and she drew an unsteady breath, inhaling the musky male scent of the moisture she saw beading on his bare shoulders. Even the sulfur stench couldn't mask it, and she knew an urge to lean closer and press her mouth to the naked flesh so she could taste the warmth of the satiny skin she'd been caressing.

Caressing? she thought in alarm. She hadn't been *caressing* him at all! And why on earth would she want to kiss a man's shoulders? A *strange* man, and his *shoulder*, for heaven's sake? What had come over her?

Quickly, with hands that were suddenly unsteady, she cut the end of the bandage and tied it off.

"You done?" he asked again, this time openly impa-

66

tient.

"Yes," she said, amazed to find herself slightly breathless. She stepped back and busied herself with putting her medical supplies back in their box.

Mr. Travis jerked his shirt back up and began buttoning it without rising from the chair. She thought this must be quite awkward, since he had to lean away from the back of the chair to do it, but she certainly wasn't going to point this out.

When she had everything back in the box, she turned back to him, wondering why her cheeks felt so warm. He'd finished his buttoning, but he still hadn't moved, and she saw his shoulders rise and fall in another sigh. Perhaps her treatment had been harder on him than she'd supposed, she thought guiltily. Just because he hadn't complained didn't mean he hadn't felt pain.

"Would you like some . . . some tea?" she ventured. "Or coffee?"

"No," he said quickly. Too quickly? Well, she couldn't blame him for not wanting any more of her company after what she'd put him through.

At last he began to rise from the chair, slowly, carefully.

"Mr. Travis?" she said when he was standing again, his back still to her.

"Yeah?" he replied, only half turning, as if afraid that facing her completely would cause him even more discomfort.

"You should put that shirt into cold water to soak so the bloodstain doesn't set."

"Sure," he said, not quite meeting her eye.

He had the smoothest cheeks, almost like a boy's.

Not at all like Philip with his dark, bristly whiskers. She imagined his beard would be soft and golden, like his hair, and wondered why she should care.

"Did Quinn tell you what you need to know about the ranch?"

"Yeah," he said, finally turning completely toward her, although he still looked wary, as if she might yet do something untoward.

"Quinn and the others have been extremely loyal. Quinn used to work for my father years ago, and when Papa died, he went to work for Mr. Hadley. It's difficult for me to hire cowboys since I got the sheep."

"I guess so," Travis said acerbically, and Sarah almost winced.

"What I'm trying to say is that my crew may not look like much, but you'll never find better men," Sarah explained in some irritation.

"I can see that," he told her, and she blinked in surprise.

She shouldn't have been surprised, of course. Hadn't she known he'd have good judgment? "Well," she said, casting about for something else to say, "I don't suppose you've had time to decide about the foreman's job yet, but —"

"Yes, I have."

"What?" she asked, startled.

"I've thought about it, and I'll take it."

"Well," she said again, inordinately pleased and knowing she shouldn't let it show. "I . . . Thank you. . . . I mean, I'm relieved, knowing you'll be in charge."

"Maybe you'd better be the one to tell the others."

"Oh, yes, certainly. I'm sure they'll be relieved, too."

68

She stared at him for a long moment, lost in the intensity of his blue eyes, until she remembered something else. "I'm sorry, but Mr. Cameron has already taken the foreman's room, so you'll have to sleep out with the rest of the men."

"I don't mind." He frowned, making her think he really did, until he said, "Do you know the sheepherders sleep on one side of the bunkhouse and the cowboys on the other?"

"No, I didn't, but I'm not surprised. My sheepherders are Mexicans, so naturally . . ." She gestured vaguely, conveying the futility of trying to overcome the decades of hostility between Texans and Mexicans.

"It's hard enough fighting your neighbors without having your hands fighting among themselves, Mrs. Hadley."

"Do you have any ideas for making peace in the bunkhouse, Mr. Travis?" she replied in kind.

"Not yet," he said, picking up his hat, "but I'll be working on it."

Without another word, he turned and left the kitchen. Sarah stared at the empty doorway until she heard him leave the house, then she sank down onto the chair in which he had sat. She felt suddenly weak, as if she'd been released from a great strain. Her heart was beating quickly and she couldn't seem to get her breath. What on earth was wrong with her?

For some inexplicable reason she had an urge to ask Mother Hadley about it. During the time Sarah had lived in this house, Philip's mother had comforted her many times, often without even realizing it, but Sarah had never really appreciated the older woman until after she died.

Sarah wasn't sure she would ever forgive Mother Hadley for dying, either, for turning her face to the wall after Philip's accident and willing herself to join him. Hadn't she known Sarah would need her? Hadn't she known she was leaving her daughter-in-law alone and helpless?

Sarah almost smiled at the thought. Of course she hadn't, because Sarah Hadley would never be helpless, not so long as she had the use of her tongue. In chagrin she recalled how she had chided Mr. Travis about his bandages. She couldn't blame him for being annoyed, and wondered what had inspired her outburst. In all the months she'd worked with Mr. Cameron, she'd never become irritated with him, either, until this afternoon when they'd argued over Mr. Travis. Mr. Travis had raised her ire the very first day she met him.

How long had it been since she'd reacted so strongly about anything? she wondered idly, and the truth came to her in a blinding flash: *not since Philip's death.*

When Philip died, he took with him every source of irritation in her life, her feeling of being at the mercy of a man who seemed determined to ruin them all. Certainly she'd chided her husband, nagged him relentlessly in fact, but only because she'd cared so very much. *Someone* had to warn him, and his mother could never see any wrong in him, so Sarah was the only one left.

But why should she react that way over Travis? He was only a hired hand, and she couldn't possibly care about him the way she'd cared about Philip.

Could she?

Chapter Three

"He's somebody, Miz Hadley," Quinn told her later that evening when she'd informed him Travis would be their new foreman. She and Quinn were standing on her front porch. "He's a known man."

"I suspected as much," Sarah admitted. When Sheriff Monroe hadn't been able to find Travis on any wanted posters, she'd been left with the only logical explanation: he was a hired gun. "Do you have any idea who he might be?"

Quinn shook his head. "He ain't gonna tell us, neither, but it's plain as the wart on a billy goat's nose. You seen his gun, I reckon."

Sarah nodded, recalling the pistol with its worn ivory grip, and the carefully oiled gunbelt. Travis wore it with the ease of long familiarity, not like Quinn and the others, who carried their guns like unwanted baggage. "Mr. Cameron thinks I was foolish to hire him in light of what recently happened to him."

"Aw, shoot, Miz Hadley, anybody can get hisself in a pickle every now and then. If a man's shot up too bad to fight, his best bet's to pull his freight like Travis done."

71

"But won't he want to go back and get revenge on the men who shot him?" she asked, voicing her secret fear that he would leave.

Quinn shrugged. "Maybe, but he ain't gonna be fit for manhunting for a while yet, and by the time he's ready to go, he might not want to leave."

"What do you mean?"

Quinn grinned with the insolence of a man who'd known her since girlhood. "Well, you already got one of your foremen in love with you."

"Quinn!" Sarah cried, mortified. How could he have guessed her problem with Cameron, and couldn't he see Cameron was only interested in her sheep?

"Not that I blame him, o' course. You're a fine-looking woman when you remember to smile."

"Thank you," Sarah said, smiling in spite of herself, even though she knew Quinn's opinion was prejudiced.

"Now, I ain't suggesting you oughta lead Travis on or anything," Quinn continued, ignoring Sarah's outraged cry. "All I'm saying is he might not be able to help hisself."

"I appreciate your insight," Sarah said acerbically, "but I have absolutely no reason to expect to earn Mr. Travis's loyalty so dramatically. What I would like, however, is for you to keep your eyes and ears open for any clue as to his identity."

"Sure thing," Quinn replied smugly. "I'd've done that anyways."

They looked up at the sound of an approaching wagon and saw the herders were returning from their afternoon off.

"They're mighty quiet," Quinn noticed ominously.

"Prob'ly dead drunk."

Shading her eyes with her hand, Sarah peered out across the vast yard. No heads were visible above the sides of the wagon, and the driver swayed dangerously on the seat, so she had to agree with Quinn's assessment. "As long as they're sober when they work for me, I don't care what they do on their days off. Where were they, anyway?"

"Some kind of fandango down in Spanishtown, Cameron told me. Maybe a wedding."

Sarah sighed. "I wish you boys would go to town on Saturday nights like you used to."

Quinn grunted contemptuously. "Ain't nothing to do in that flea-bitten burg anyhow."

But Sarah knew why they stayed here week after week, and she knew it was her fault, hers and her sheep's. She wouldn't have hurt the men for anything, but she also knew she couldn't have kept them on without the sheep, either.

They watched in silence from the front porch as the wagon rolled in and lurched to a halt in front of the bunkhouse. The men inside were not actually herders, of course. The true herders lived with the sheep twenty-four hours a day, seven days a week. The men in the wagon were the link between those herders and the ranch. The *vaqueros* supervised two herders each, making sure all was well with each flock. The *caporal* supervised the *vaqueros*, apportioning pasturage, helping locate lost sheep, inspecting animals for disease, and otherwise attending to the welfare of the sheep. The *caporal* reported directly to Cameron, who oversaw the entire operation. Without outside interference, the system would work beautifully.

Travis, Ace and Shorty were lounging in ladder-back chairs on the bunkhouse porch when the wagon arrived, and they watched as the three *vaqueros* half climbed, half fell out of the wagon bed. One of them stumbled, grabbed his companion to keep from falling, and pulled both of them down in a heap. The third man stared at them through bleary eyes, then burst out laughing as the two on the ground struggled unsuccessfully to rise.

Someone should help them, Sarah thought in dismay, knowing none of the cowboys would dirty their hands on a Mexican, particularly a Mexican sheepherder. Then, to her surprise, Travis pushed himself out of his chair and strode over to the men on the ground. He spoke to them, and although she couldn't hear the words from this distance, she knew from their expressions that he was addressing them in Spanish.

She saw the flash of Pedro's gold tooth when he grinned in reply; then he took Travis's offered hand and allowed the cowboy to pull him to his feet.

"I'll be damned," Quinn muttered, and Sarah knew he must be thoroughly overwhelmed, because she couldn't remember him ever swearing in her presence before.

"It looks like Mr. Travis could use some help with the crew," Sarah observed wryly.

Quinn gave her a quelling look. "I'll fetch Cameron, then," he replied, sauntering off.

Sarah covered a smile. Mr. Travis was obviously a man of his word. Already he'd begun to make peace with the sheepmen, but he'd have a way to go before he got the rest of the cowboys to go along with him.

* * *

Sarah told herself she was only inspecting her property the way she usually did every week or so. Just because she'd inquired this morning to learn exactly where each of the men would be working today didn't mean she'd actually planned to find Mr. Travis on the range. She'd simply never seen him in action and wanted to observe him for herself.

Certainly, the other men had nothing but praise for his first week on the job, and even Cameron had remarked on how he'd managed to keep the cattle from interfering with the sheep. Faint praise, but any praise at all from Cameron was significant.

When Sarah saw the rider in the distance, she felt a strange fluttering in her stomach, and she automatically reached up to pat her hair back into place beneath the broad-brimmed hat she wore. By now her riding habit was hopelessly dusty, but she brushed at the skirt a few times anyway, and made sure it was spread smoothly across the horse's side.

Riding sidesaddle did have its advantages if a woman wished to look picturesque, she noted with a self-mocking grin, then slapped the horse gently with the quirt and made for the lone rider.

She had recognized Travis at once from the way he sat his horse. Although she told herself she hadn't been paying any particular attention, she couldn't help noticing he rode with the same cocky assurance with which he did everything else.

At the moment, Travis sat his horse, his back to her, on top of a rise. Obviously, he had found something of interest below, and she thought she might sneak up on him while he was thus distracted. To her dismay, he not only heard her approach, but when he turned, he had his hand on his gun before she could call a greeting.

Quinn was right, she thought. Travis was a known man, someone whose name she would most likely recognize if only she knew it. He removed his hand from his gun and touched his hat brim respectfully as she approached, but he didn't return her greeting.

"Good morning," she said, wishing he looked a little more pleased to see her. His startlingly blue eyes were narrowed, and his finely shaped mouth turned down in a frown. Then she glanced away to see what he had been observing and realized the reason for his displeasure. Below them a herd of sheep grazed.

From here they looked like a thousand gray rocks some giant hand had scattered across the emerald grass, but Sarah felt a perverse pride in what they stood for. And a profound irritation in Mr. Travis's refusal to recognize it.

"You probably can't tell from here, but under those sheep, the land is pure gold," she said.

" 'Wherever the sheep's foot touches, the land turns to gold,' " he quoted sourly.

"Scoff if you want to, Mr. Travis, but those sheep saved my ranch."

"Quinn told me about the loan you got, about how you had to use half of it for sheep."

"Don't get the wrong idea," Sarah cautioned him stiffly. "Mr. Schreiner will only loan money if the borrower promises to invest half of it in sheep, but I had decided to buy sheep long before I went to him."

"How long?" he asked sharply.

"How long what?" she asked, startled by his sudden interest.

"How long ago did you decide to buy sheep? Was it before your husband died?"

Now it was Sarah's turn to frown. "Well, yes, but my husband had nothing to do with it. I was studying the possibility on my own, but when I suggested it to him, he wouldn't hear of it, not even if it meant the difference between losing the ranch and keeping it."

"So nobody would've killed him for bringing in sheep."

Where on earth had he gotten an idea like that? "No one killed him at all. His death was an accident. I thought I told you that already."

Travis shifted in his saddle and folded his gauntleted hands across the pommel. "Most things that happen in this life happen on purpose, Mrs. Hadley. You struck me as a woman who might know that."

"You may be right, Mr. Travis, at least about *most* things, but my husband's death was truly an accident. He didn't have an enemy in the world." No, she recalled bitterly; everyone loved the charming, dashing man she'd married, or at least those did who hadn't suffered from his weaknesses. "I'm going down to look at the sheep," she said, to change the subject. "Would you like to ride with me?"

"Are you ordering me?" he asked, with just a hint of challenge. Somehow Sarah had the impression he was just waiting for her to say yes so he could refuse to go.

"No, I'm not ordering you," she informed him in annoyance, "but if you're going to work on this ranch, you should learn as much about sheep as possible, if only so you'll know best how to stay out of their way, Mr. Travis."

"It's just 'Travis,' " he said, looking as irritated as she felt.

Sarah frowned in confusion. "What?"

"Just call me 'Travis.' No 'mister.' "

So, just as she'd suspected, "Travis" wasn't his last name. His first? Or perhaps just a name he'd pulled out of the air. Sarah stared at him, trying to read some emotion in those azure eyes, but he showed her nothing. "All right, *Travis,* are you coming or not?"

Without waiting to see, she switched her horse with the quirt and started down the hill. Although she would have died before admitting it, she was holding her breath in anticipation until she heard his horse fall in behind hers. The victory was surely minor, but Sarah savored its sweetness nevertheless. Somehow she knew this man didn't give in very often.

Seeing their approach, the sheepherder rose from where he'd been sitting in the shade of a scraggly tree and waved a greeting. Carefully skirting the grazing sheep, Sarah rode up to him.

"Good morning, Mr. Sanchez. How is everything going?"

"Buenos días, señora," Sanches replied. He looked as disreputable as ever, his long black hair and beard tangled by the wind, his baggy coat and pants threadbare and worn, his serape filthy. She noticed he'd been knitting a sock, a common pastime among the herders. "The sheep, they are fine. Many lambs this year, señora."

"I hope you're right," Sarah said, sliding down from her horse. She dropped the reins to the ground, knowing her well-trained mount wouldn't wander off if he were ground hitched, and started toward the sheep.

Behind her she thought she heard Travis make a sound of disgust, but then she heard the creak of his saddle as he dismounted, too, and she purposely slowed her pace so he could easily overtake her.

When he was beside her, she glanced over at him. His smooth cheeks looked a little ruddy, but she chose not to notice his pique. "You never came back to have your bandages changed," she recalled with a slight twinge of regret. "Can I assume your wounds have healed satisfactorily?"

"Watch out," he said sharply, grabbing her arm to prevent her from stepping in a pile of sheep droppings. "Better look where you're going," he advised in disgust as he drew her around it.

Sarah felt her face burning, absurdly grateful for being saved the humiliation, and she looked up to thank him. Her gaze locked with his blue one, and the words of thanks died on her lips. Suddenly, she couldn't quite breathe, as if an iron band had closed around her chest and started to squeeze. He still held her arm, and his fingers tightened, biting into the tender flesh until the grip was almost painful.

Almost, but not quite, although his touch seemed to burn right through his heavy leather gloves and the fabric of her sleeve to scorch the skin beneath. Something flickered in his eyes, something hot like the blue center of a flame, and the heat of it swept over her like wildfire.

Then, just as suddenly, his eyes went blank again, and he released her arm as if he, too, had felt the searing heat. He took a quick step backward, putting some distance between them, and Sarah almost imagined he was embarrassed by the momentary contact.

"Thank you," she managed at last, relieved to note she could breathe again.

He gave her what might have been a half grin. "Now you know one thing cowboys have against sheep: you never have to watch where you step when you're working cattle."

"Because you never get off your horse," Sarah said, shaking her head. How well she knew the contempt cowboys had for anyone who went afoot. They often bragged they wouldn't do any job that couldn't be done from the back of a horse. Sheep, on the other hand, were worked by a lone man who walked among them.

A nearby ewe looked up from her grazing, eyed them morosely, and let out a plaintive "baaa."

Sarah smiled fondly at the matted bundle of fleece and drew a deep, satisfied breath. "Can you smell it, Travis? The smell of success."

"The stink of sheep," he contradicted her.

"Cows don't exactly smell good, either," she reminded him, although even she had to admit she preferred the comfortable bovine scent to the acrid odor of sheep.

"You trying to make me think you really like these infernal woolybacks?" he asked in disbelief, gesturing toward the animals grazing before them.

"But I do like them," she assured him. "Not only are they going to make me wealthy, but they . . ." Her voice trailed off as she realized what she had been about to reveal.

"They what?" he prompted, and when she looked

80

into his blue eyes again, she saw not the cold blankness he usually showed, but a trace of the warmth she'd seen a moment ago. Unlike most men, who only humored her, Travis seemed genuinely interested in what she'd been about to say.

But could he understand? She decided to test him. "Do you think they look sad?"

"The sheep?"

She nodded.

He studied the one that had bleated at them. "You mean because they all look like they're crying?" Mature sheep had glands beside their eyes which secreted a fatty substance that looked like constantly falling tears.

"Yes," she replied in delight at his observation. "Some people would think us fanciful for saying so."

"Nothing fanciful about it," he scoffed. "From the minute it's born, ain't no critter on earth more set on dying than a sheep."

Mr. Cameron had made the same observation to her during their very first interview when explaining to her the hazards of raising the animals, but how would Travis know a thing like that? She stared at him in amazement. "You seem to know a lot about sheep for a man who professes to hate them," she observed.

No doubt about it, this time his face did turn red, although she thought he was more angry than embarrassed. "I told you before, everybody's talking about them. I just know what I've heard. Do you intend to go traipsing through this bunch or not? 'Cause if you do, I'll stay right where I am, if you don't mind." He glanced meaningfully down at the pile of sheep dung into which she had almost stepped a moment ago.

81

She might have smiled at his disgust if she hadn't been so intent on figuring out why he seemed more knowledgeable about sheep than he should have been, and why he wouldn't admit to where he'd gained the knowledge.

Travis held her gaze, silently cursing her for being so smart. He'd add that to her list of faults, which had grown amazingly long for so brief an acquaintance. He just wished she'd get back up on her horse. Standing here eye-to-eye with her made him uncomfortably aware of how tall she was. For sure he'd have to be careful not to ever let her catch him without his boots.

Everything would've been fine if she hadn't tried to step in that pile of shit. So long as he didn't touch her, he could almost convince himself he'd forgotten she was even a female. She sure as hell didn't act like any female he'd ever known.

"I think the reason I like the sheep so much is because they look so sad," she said. Damn if he didn't think she was purposely trying to confuse him.

"Do you like misery, Mrs. Hadley?" he asked, wondering if that was why she'd taken him in. God knew, he'd been in a world of hurt the first time he'd ever set eyes on her.

"No one *likes* misery, Mr. Travis," she said, then caught herself. "I mean, *Travis*." He just wished she wouldn't say his name as if it felt good in her mouth or something. He couldn't remember ever hearing anybody say it quite that way. "But as you know, my life hasn't been exactly happy up until now. I've lost everyone—my entire family and my husband's family, too, and I've been faced with financial ruin."

Not to mention shame and disgrace, he thought, remembering what the no-good bastard she'd married had done to her. He noticed she hadn't mentioned him as one of her losses, though. At least she wasn't mooning over him. Travis didn't think he could stand it if she was. Still . . .

"Excuse me for saying so, but you don't look like you're losing any sleep over the past," he pointed out.

"I try not to," she replied, smiling in that way she had that made him want to reach for her. The sun had turned her nose pink, and he wanted to feel the warmth of it with his lips. "But I'm a woman, and even when a woman can forget all the reasons why she should be sad, there's always a few men around to give her some new ones."

Travis felt a surge of outrage, hot and bitter. What men was she talking about? If he ever got his hands on them, he'd . . . "What kind of reasons?" he asked.

"Oh, the usual things," she replied, more lightly than he would have thought possible "A gentle reminder every now and then that I'm only a female and therefore not quite bright, not quite up to running a ranch by myself, not quite to be trusted. I should sell out to someone more fit, some *man* more fit, so I can go someplace safe and quiet and do my knitting in peace."

"Did somebody really tell you to go off and knit?" he asked in amazement.

"Not specifically." Her eyes were as green as the Texas grass and filled with laughter. He caught himself wondering what her laugh would sound like and figured he'd never find out. "They do drop hints, though. You see, many men consider women to be no better than sheep, Travis. They think we're stupid and worthless and a nuisance. Good in our place perhaps, so long as our place doesn't interfere with where the men want to be."

Travis frowned, wondering if he hadn't been guilty of the same sort of prejudice. Oh, he'd never for one minute thought Sarah Hadley was stupid or worthless, although the way she was haunting his dreams *was* getting to be a damn nuisance. Still, hadn't he suggested she get her husband to do the hiring the day she'd come by the livery for him? "They can't criticize you anymore, not after the way you've made this place go."

She shook her head in mock dismay. "But don't you see? My success only makes things worse. If a man had done what I did, turned this place around by bringing in sheep, he would have earned a grudging respect. No one respects me, Travis. Most of them hold me in contempt, and a few actively despise me. I'm like these sheep. I've turned a profit when the cattlemen couldn't, so they make up stories about me so they can justify their hatred."

"Jealousy, you mean." He looked away, no longer able to hold her green gaze without letting her see the fury boiling inside him. By God, he wanted to strangle every man who'd ever made Sarah Hadley suffer. Jamming his hands in his back pockets, he stared out blindly at the flock and willed himself to calmness.

"Jealousy," she mused as if she'd never considered the possibility before. "I suppose I never credited them with enough sense to realize they *should* be jealous. Maybe I underestimated them."

"I don't reckon it matters much *why* they want to put you out of business," he said when he could trust

84

his voice. "Just so long as we're ready when they do."

"Are we ready, Travis?"

He turned back to her in surprise. "I thought that's why you hired me."

She smiled her lazy smile again, the one he always pictured when he imagined her lying beneath him, and he felt the same bleak longing he always felt when he remembered that would never happen. "I knew I could count on you, Travis."

Travis wanted to swear. He wanted to warn her not to count on him. He wanted to tell her the last person who'd counted on him had got his brains blown out. But when he looked into those emerald eyes, he couldn't. Instead he said, "If you're counting on me, then I reckon I'd better get back to work."

He turned on his heel, ready to leave her here to admire her sheep, but she followed, matching him stride for stride until he wondered if maybe she intended to follow him around for the rest of the day.

"The lambs will start coming soon," she said. "With sheep we plan the breeding much more carefully than we do with cattle. We keep the bucks separate from the ewes until we're ready to breed them. We started breeding late last October, so the first lambs will arrive in late March. I expect at least two hundred a day for about a month. But then, maybe you already know all that."

He looked at her sharply, determined not to reveal anything else to her. "Do you expect me to play midwife?"

"Certainly not, but I thought you should know, because during lambing time we'll be most vulnerable to attack."

Travis wanted to groan.

"Perhaps you'd like me to make you up a powder, Mr. Cameron," Sarah remarked, as she counted out the coins for the men's monthly pay.

"A powder? For what?" he asked, shifting uneasily in his chair. He sat beside her desk as she dropped the coins into a leather sack.

She smiled sweetly. "From the way you've been scowling at me lately, I can only assume you're suffering from dyspepsia."

His scowl deepened, and Sarah had a fierce urge to shake him. Since the man outweighed her by a good fifty pounds, the urge presented an interesting challenge.

"If I've got stomach problems, there's only one way ye can cure them," he informed her.

Sarah knew a moment of alarm as she considered the possibility that he was referring to his offer of marriage, but she quickly regained her composure. "Yes, I know," she said, amazing even herself with her nonchalance. "You want me to fire Mr. Travis."

"He doesna like being called 'mister,'" Cameron reminded her grimly. "Missus, the others do not think 'Travis' is his real name."

Sarah widened her eyes at him. "Is that why you've been walking around here like you've been sucking on a lemon for the past ten days? I know you're new to the West, Mr. Cameron, but one thing you should have learned by now is how few men out here give their true name when asked."

"No honest man would be afraid to tell his

true name," Cameron insisted.

"I can think of many reasons why a man wouldn't want his identity known," Sarah said. "He may be in danger."

Cameron snorted in disgust. "He's got no right laying his danger on your doorstep then, missus. Ye've troubles enough without adding his."

Sarah leaned back in the armchair from which her husband and her father-in-law had run the Golden Hoof, and considered her *mayordomo*. "How are you coming with your marksmanship, Mr. Cameron?"

The question struck a nerve, and his face reddened. "An honest man has no need to fire a gun."

"In Scotland, perhaps, but things are different here," she reminded him, knowing exactly how she was humiliating him but having no choice. Owen Cameron had never fired a gun until entering her employ, and although the cowboys had tried to teach him, his natural distaste for violence and the weapon itself had hampered any progress.

"I havena seen any difference between here and Scotland," he insisted. "The cattlemen complain, but they do no more than curse the sheep and threaten. I canna believe any of them would attack a woman."

"Oh, my person is probably safe enough, but my womanhood won't protect the men who work for me, and it certainly won't protect my sheep. And you know perfectly well they wouldn't have to even use violence to destroy me. One scab-infested sheep turned loose in a flock would do it."

Cameron frowned. Although Sarah had only read about the damage the tiny mite that caused the disease called scab could do to a flock, Sarah knew he had

87

seen it firsthand. "I willna let that happen to your sheep, missus."

Sarah knew she was supposed to feel comforted by this masculine assurance, but she didn't. "And if it does, I know we can dip the sheep and probably save most of them, but don't you understand? If they're afraid of us, they'll never dare do anything in the first place."

"She's right."

They both looked up to where Travis stood in the doorway. As always, Sarah felt surprised by him, by how slight he was and yet how imposing. His blue eyes seemed to burn in his otherwise expressionless face.

As if Cameron couldn't stand letting Travis have the advantage of height, he jumped to his feet. Sarah noticed his hammy hands closed into fists, and she wondered wryly what Travis would do if Cameron chose to use those fists on him. If the man outweighed her by fifty pounds, he had a good twenty on Travis, too, but somehow she wasn't worried. She instinctively knew Travis would never come to blows with any man, because his size would be too much of a disadvantage. Travis was the sort of man who would long ago have learned never to put himself at a disadvantage.

"What do ye know about sheep, *Mr.* Travis?" Cameron challenged, goading him with the title.

Travis didn't even blink. "Not as much as you, but I know a sight more about cattlemen. They're biding their time now, but the closer Mrs. Hadley gets to success, the madder they'll be."

"And if I ship as many lambs as I plan to and the shearing goes well, I'll pay off my debt this fall," Sarah informed them both. Neither of them had a reply.

"Here, Mr. Cameron," Sarah said, feeling suddenly weary of the old arguments. She handed him the sack of coins for the herders.

He hefted it as if he could tell by the weight whether she had counted correctly, then he frowned at Travis, who waited expectantly, hat in hand. Plainly, he was loath to leave her alone with him, and Sarah had to bite back a smile. "Thank you, Mr. Cameron," she said by way of dismissal. "Would you sit down, Travis?"

Grudgingly, Cameron moved away so Travis could take the chair he had occupied, but still he made no move to leave. This time Sarah wanted to box his ears, since he was acting like a little boy. Or a dog in a manger. "You may go, Mr. Cameron," she said sternly, leaving him no choice.

Although he shot Travis an evil look, he obeyed, walking as slowly as he could. When he reached the door, he hesitated and turned back, but before he could speak, Travis said, "You'll be outside if she needs you."

Sarah clapped a hand over her mouth to keep from laughing aloud, and Cameron's expression grew positively thunderous. "Aye, that I will, and don't be forgetting," he warned, stomping out. He left the door open behind him.

Sarah coughed discreetly, and when she could trust her voice, she said, "I'm sorry. Mr. Cameron feels protecting me is part of his duty."

"It's part of mine, too, or don't he know that?"

She smiled wryly. "Perhaps you should explain it to him."

Travis crossed his arms over his chest and frowned, while she began counting out the coins for the cowboys' pay, which Travis would give them. "Anything I should know about the cattle?" she asked to fill the silence.

He gave her a report on the condition of the grass and the prospects for the calf crop. As she listened, Sarah tried to decide what it was about his voice she liked so well. The gruffness, perhaps. The way he took such pains to keep his tone impersonal even though she could hear the faint echo of gentleness, something she never heard when he spoke to one of the men. He couldn't forget she was a woman any more than Cameron could, but for some reason this didn't annoy her the way Cameron's condescension did.

"You won't lose money on your cattle, either," he informed her when he had finished his report. "In fact, if you'd turn a little more of the range back over to cows, I could probably do even better for you."

"I'm satisfied with things just as they are, thank you, Travis." She had counted out enough to pay Quinn, Shorty and Ace, and was just about to put the money into a sack similar to the one she'd given Cameron when she had another idea. Figuring quickly in her head, she added ten days' wages for Travis, too.

"Here you are," she said, holding out the sack to him.

He took it from her with a gloved hand.

"Do you always wear gloves?" she asked, thinking it odd he hadn't removed them when he came in.

He glanced at his hands as if he'd been unaware that he was. "I guess so."

"Even in the summer?"

Instantly his eyes went blank, and his wariness was like an aura she could almost see. How stupid of her to have forgotten the unwritten law of the West that forbade asking personal questions!

He probably should have told her to mind her own business or simply gotten up and left without replying. Instead he said, "They protect my hands."

Something about the way he said it sent a chill over her. If he were a gunfighter, his hands would be important. A rope burn or even heavy calluses would slow his draw or maybe even ruin it altogether. "Oh," she said, unable to think of anything more profound.

He jiggled the bag as Cameron had done and rose to his feet.

"I didn't mean to pry," she told him apologetically.

He just nodded once, and she thought the expression in his eyes was very close to sadness. As he walked to the door, she had an impulse to call him back, but since she had absolutely nothing else to say to him, she didn't.

He closed the door behind him, and the instant he did, Sarah was on her feet. Her desk was in the hallway between the kitchen and the parlor, the former breezeway of the house, and she hurried into the parlor. She went straight to the front window and peered cautiously through the curtain.

From here she could see the men gathered in front of the bunkhouse to receive their wages. Cameron was already busy paying the *vaqueros* and the *caporal*, although Sarah noticed he was trying to watch Travis out of the corner of his eye at the same time.

Travis made quick work of distributing the money among the cowboys, and Sarah held her breath as she

91

saw him puzzling over the extra coins in the bottom of the bag. Although she couldn't read his expression from here, she had no trouble at all guessing his mood as he strode stiffly back toward the house. Why on earth would he be angry?

Before she could decide, he was on the porch, and just as she hurried back toward the hall, her front door burst open.

"Mrs. Hadley," he said, apparently expecting to find her still seated at the desk. When he didn't, he hesitated and glanced around until he saw her in the doorway.

His eyes blazed, and his neck burned crimson, but he spoke slowly and deliberately, as if trying to hold his temper in check. "You gave me too much."

For some reason, his anger unnerved her. "I know," she said, a little breathless. "I gave you ten days' wages for yourself, too."

She'd surprised him, and she saw some of the anger drain away. "Why?"

"Because you've worked for ten days."

He considered this. "Did you forget I owe you for my outfit and for getting my saddle back?"

Why did he make her feel so defensive, as if she'd done something wrong? "No, of course I haven't forgotten," she told him testily. "I'll take that out of your first full month's wages. I just thought you might need some money for . . . for tobacco or whatever. I know you didn't have anything when you left Dr. Bigelow's."

Fury flared in his eyes again and colored his cheeks, but still he held himself in check. With slow, deliberate strides, he went to her desk and dropped the bag onto it. The few silver dollars tinkled forlornly. "I don't want your charity."

"Charity!" she cried, stung. "How dare you insult me like that?"

She'd surprised him again. He crossed his arms in silent challenge. "If it's not charity, what is it?"

Sarah lifted her chin defiantly and thought fast. "Look around, Travis. I'm a woman alone. I'm raising sheep, which makes me the enemy of every cattleman in the county. I've got three cowboys nobody else would hire, a handful of Mexicans who'd probably hide at the first sign of trouble, and a Scotsman who couldn't hit the ground with his hat. Didn't it ever occur to you that I might want . . . no, *need* to have a man like you in my debt?"

Characteristically, he thought this over. Meanwhile, her heart pounded so loudly, she thought surely he could hear it across the room. Dear Lord, what had she done? But then, who would ever have imagined her impulsive act would have so thoroughly offended him?

After what seemed an inordinately long time, his lips twitched. "He couldn't hit the ground with his hat?"

Oh, no! Had she really said that about Cameron? "Mr. Cameron is one of the best sheepmen around," she explained hastily. "He simply isn't used to defending them with a gun, and even if he were, the cowboys aren't likely to follow him, now are they?"

"I reckon not."

"But they are likely to follow you, so I very desperately need your loyalty."

He glanced at the bag on her desk, and his expression hardened. "I just thought maybe . . ."

93

"Maybe what?" she prompted when he didn't continue.

"I thought maybe you were testing me, to see was I honest enough to tell you about the extra money."

She gaped at him, horrified. No wonder he'd been so furious! "Certainly not! If I'd had any doubts about your character, I would never have hired you in the first place!"

His lips flattened skeptically. "Excuse me, Mrs. Hadley, but you didn't know a damn thing about my character when you hired me, and you don't know much more now."

Normally, she would have been outraged at being addressed in such a manner, but not this time. She crossed her arms in mocking imitation of his own defiant stance. "On the contrary, Travis. Your reaction just now tells me everything I need to know about you."

His blue eyes widened in amazement, but only for a moment before narrowing again. "Not exactly everything, Mrs. Hadley, but I'll tell you the rest of it right out, so you won't misunderstand again. You can't buy my loyalty. A man doesn't put himself on the line because he's grateful or because you've paid him more wages than he's earned."

"Then why does a man put himself on the line?"

She could see he'd never had to answer the question before, perhaps had never even considered the answer, but she knew the moment he'd settled on it. His blue eyes clouded and his mouth set in a grim line. "Sometimes he does it because he believes in something, but other times he does it because he just doesn't give a damn anymore."

94

He was gone before she could ask him which was his reason for helping her.

Early March brought spring in earnest. Calves began to drop, and Cameron started preparation for the lambing. After the discussion over his pay, Travis had avoided Sarah except when forced to speak to her about some aspect of the ranch work. Even then, he would often send her word through Quinn, who wasn't a bit shy about expressing his curiosity over the situation.

"Could be he's one of them fellows who's scared of females, but I didn't think that hombre was afraid of nothing," Quinn theorized, the third time Travis had sent him with a message.

"I can make no judgments about Travis's courage," Sarah replied, "but I can assure you, he isn't afraid of me." Briefly, she explained the misunderstanding over his pay.

Quinn grinned, showing tobacco-stained teeth. "You don't need to worry none about Travis having spending money. He pretty near cleaned us out playing poker the other night."

"You mean you boys have been gambling in the bunkhouse!" Sarah exclaimed, thoroughly shocked.

"We do it all the time," Quinn informed her, unconcerned. "Mostly we play for matches, but since we don't have nothing much to spend our wages on, we played for money when we got paid."

Sarah should have reprimanded Quinn, but she doubted it would do any good. Had Philip known the men gambled? Probably, she thought with dismay, and realized her husband wouldn't have minded in the least. "Well, I'm glad to know I needn't be concerned about Travis being able to buy tobacco. And tell Travis he shouldn't be such a stranger," she added wryly.

"I surely will, ma'am," Quinn said, with another grin.

But of course, Travis had continued to avoid her, and to her annoyance, Sarah found herself standing at the window each evening when the men came in, so she could watch him surreptitiously as he unsaddled his horse and made his way to the cookhouse for the evening meal.

On Sundays she took her dinner with the men in the cookhouse, but the rest of the time she ate alone in her kitchen, knowing her presence put a damper on their conversation. Usually, she didn't mind eating alone. She didn't need the company of others, and when she'd become a widow, she had resigned herself to spending the rest of her life without a man. Why, then, had she begun to feel lonely, to long for the sight of another face across the table from her? And why did the bed she had once been relieved at no longer having to share suddenly seem so empty?

By mid-March, Sarah began having trouble sleeping. Awakened by troubling dreams, she would toss and turn for hours, unable to keep her eyes closed for more than a few minutes at a time. She told herself she was only anxious about the lambs that would soon be born, worried that a norther might swoop down to freeze the newborns before they even had a chance at life, worried that a pack of wolves might come, attracted by the scent of birthing, and snatch away her hopes and dreams.

But as often as she would try to "count sheep," she knew the woolybacks weren't the only thing keeping her awake, because the troubling dreams concerned not only freezing winds and howling wolves. The dreams also concerned a blue-eyed gunfighter who called himself only Travis.

She was, she told herself time and again, acting like a schoolgirl. Travis was nothing to her but a hired hand, a man whose real name she didn't even know, a man who might be gone before the next full moon. Still, he appeared to her at night, his strange eyes glowing with blue fire while he warned her time and again to get rid of her sheep before it was too late.

"The lambs will start in a day or two," he told her this time. "Then I won't be able to protect you anymore."

Sarah opened her mouth to protest, and the sound woke her with a start. She stared up at the black ceiling of her bedroom, shaking with fury, her heart pounding in her chest. How dare he tell her what to do with her sheep? she demanded of no one in particular, then threw off the covers and bolted from the bed, unwilling to lie there another moment and be frightened by phantoms.

Her robe lay at the foot of the bed, and she snatched it up, jamming her arms into the sleeves even as her feet found the slippers she'd discarded a few hours earlier. Muttering a curse at the now-departed phantom, she paced restlessly around the darkened room, loath to light a lamp lest any of the men see the light and wonder if something was amiss.

Who did Travis think he was, anyway? she asked herself. She was starting to be sorry she'd ever hired him. The man wouldn't even speak to her unless she spoke to him first, and what good was a foreman who avoided her like the plague?

Restless, she strode to the window and pulled back the curtain to stare at the night sky. The stars twinkled down like a thousand eyes, and Sarah could almost imagine they were watching over the sheep for which Travis felt such contempt. The thought gave her a moment's satisfaction, until she noticed the strange glow in the distance.

Dawn? Surely, it was far too early. Then she realized the glow came from the wrong direction. Only one thing could light the night sky in such a way, and the knowledge stabbed her heart like a shard of ice.

Without a conscious thought, Sarah turned and ran, out into the parlor and onto the porch where the old dinnerbell hung. Snatching up the rusting clanger, she thrust it into the iron triangle and struck the three sides with all her might, around and around until the noise filled the silent night, echoing off the outbuildings and reverberating in her head.

After what seemed hours, but that must have been only minutes, the men began to stumble from the bunkhouse, tucking in shirts and stamping into boots as they came. When Sarah heard their shouts above the ring of the bell, she at last let the clanger drop and hurried out into the yard to meet them.

Cameron was there first. His orange hair stood up in spikes around his head, and his shirttail hung loose. "What is it, missus?"

"Fire," she gasped, surprised to find herself breathless.

"The house?" Travis demanded, rushing up beside

98

Cameron. He'd forgotten his hat, and his fair hair looked silver in the moonlight.

"No, out on the prairie." She pointed to the orange glow on the horizon.

The other men came running up, and they all stared in the direction in which she pointed.

"Somebody's house, maybe," one of the men guessed.

"Who lives out that way?" Travis asked.

"Nobody," Quinn said.

The two men exchanged a glance. "Grass fire?" Travis said, but even Sarah could hear the doubt in his voice.

"This time of year?" Quinn scoffed. "Grass ain't hardly up yet, and it sure as hell ain't dry enough to burn."

Then what could be burning? Sarah wanted to ask, terror clawing at her stomach, but she didn't dare voice the question for fear of what the answer might be.

Travis turned to her, his eyes glittering obsidian in the darkness. "Break out the rifles. Give every man a rifle and a pistol. Sheepmen, too," he added, raising his voice and making it a command. "We'll all go. Quinn, see to the horses."

"Right," Quinn called over his shoulder as he jogged toward the corrals.

Travis took her arm, and before she could think, they were heading back to the house.

"Wait a bloody minute," Cameron snarled, trotting at their heels. "What do we need guns for?"

"To scare off whoever is burning something out there," Travis explained impatiently, propelling Sarah up the porch steps.

99

"Why should we want do a thing like that?" Cameron demanded, following them inside.

Sarah went to her desk and lit the lamp with trembling fingers. If Travis wanted rifles, the danger was even greater than she had feared.

Wasting no time, Travis had already gone to the gun cabinet that stood in the hallway opposite her desk. He threw open the door. "Because I've got a feeling whatever's burning out there is Mrs. Hadley's property, and it ain't burning by accident."

Cameron watched as he pulled a Winchester out and cracked it open to check the load. Satisfied, he snapped it shut and tossed it to Cameron, who caught it instinctively, although Sarah noted he looked at it with as much revulsion as if it had been a live snake.

"But my men aren't trained to fight," Cameron protested.

"Don't aim to fight," Travis informed him, mechanically checking each rifle in turn before laying it on the floor. "If we can catch them by surprise, we can scare them off. If they had any courage to start with, they wouldn't need to attack by night with their faces covered. Now get your men in here so I can show them how to use these guns."

Forgotten, Sarah leaned against the wall, hugging herself against the night chill and her own terrors, and watched in admiration as Cameron bent to Travis's will and summoned his Mexicans. Contrary to Cameron's protests, they seemed more than eager to do battle. Their dark eyes gleamed with a feral light as they listened closely to Travis's instructions, delivered in rapid-fire Spanish. Even Pepe, the fat cook, seemed eager for the challenge. Each took a rifle and headed

100

out the door.

Quinn pushed past them on his way in. "Horses are all ready, boss," he reported, taking the rifle Travis handed him, and Sarah felt a pang. Since Philip's death, no one had been called 'boss' at the Golden Hoof. The title rightly belonged to her, but no one would think of addressing a woman like that.

But she had no time to dwell on the thought. Travis said, "Quinn, I'll need you to stay here with Mrs. Hadley."

Quinn's homely face fell, as if Travis had denied him a special treat, but she noticed he did not object.

"Ye can't think there's danger to Mrs. Hadley," Cameron said, his florid face beet-red with indignation.

"I can and I do. Whoever's out there might be planning to hit the house next."

"Then what good would one man be?" Cameron challenged.

"None," Travis replied hotly, "but he can help her get away safe. Now get out of here and get on your damned horse."

"I don't take orders from any nameless little—"

"Gentlemen!" Sarah cried in despair.

Both men turned in surprise, as if they'd forgotten she was there, and for a moment she couldn't think of a thing to say. Then she pulled herself up to her full height and attempted to look imperious, although she was painfully aware she stood there in her nightdress and robe. "I'll thank you to remember you both take orders from me. In view of Travis's superior experience in these matters, Mr. Cameron, I'm putting him in charge tonight. You will kindly follow his instruc-

101

tions."

Cameron's scowl made her wince, but she refused to look away, and at last his heavy shoulders sagged in resignation.

"Aye, for this night," he said, turning his glare on Travis. "But tomorrow we'll have this settled once and for all."

"Fine. Now get moving," Travis said. "Quinn, grab a rifle for Ace. I've got one for Shorty."

The men filed out, Cameron first and reluctant, Quinn quick and eager. As Travis turned to follow, Sarah called his name. He looked at her slowly, almost cautiously.

"Do you know . . . ?" she began, but the words caught in her throat and she had to try again. "Do you know what's burning?"

"No," he said, but she knew he lied. Part of her wanted to berate him for trying to protect her, but another part very much needed such protection.

"Be careful," she heard herself say.

Something flickered in his azure eyes, something very like surprise, and just as quickly was gone. "Sure," he said gruffly, and hurried out.

Chapter Four

Travis stopped Quinn on the front porch. "Make sure she gets dressed to ride and have two horses saddled and ready. Do you know someplace safe to take her?"

"I know a couple hidey holes, but I'd try to get her to town if I can. She'd be safe with Doc Bigelow."

"Good," Travis said, satisfied he'd left Sarah in good hands. He only hoped she'd have sense enough to run if she needed to. Unfortunately, he didn't have time just now to discuss the matter with her, and even if he did, he didn't dare go back in the house. The thought of being alone with Sarah Hadley when she was wearing nothing but a nightdress and a flimsy little robe made him break out in a cold sweat. "When we come back, I'll fire off three shots so you'll know it's us."

Quinn nodded, and Travis started down the porch steps.

"I'm thinking even ye can't expect us to win a fight like this," Cameron said when he reached the bottom.

"Lucky for us, winning won't depend on how good we are," Travis replied, not even breaking stride as he hurried toward where Quinn had left the horses ground hitched in the yard.

"On what will it depend, then?" Cameron insisted,

keeping pace with difficulty.

"I told you—surprise," he explained impatiently. They'd reached the horses. The other men had mounted, and he handed the second Winchester up to Shorty. Travis winced when he noticed how awkwardly the Mexicans handled their rifles. If one of them didn't shoot himself, it would be a miracle. He raised his voice so everyone could hear. "I figure we're dealing with gunnysackers, and a man who'll cut holes in a sack and put it over his head so nobody'll see his face isn't going to stand and fight. All we have to do is ride up shouting and shooting, and they'll run for cover."

"Do you want us to shoot at the men, señor?" José asked doubtfully. Travis figured none of them had ever shot at another man. The prospect was bound to disturb them, so he'd make it as easy on them as he could.

"I know most of you couldn't hit the side of a barn, but nobody can shoot accurately from a running horse anyway. Just fire at the sky if you don't trust your aim, and try not to hit any of your own men, but don't do anything at all until I give the signal." He slipped his rifle into the scabbard hanging from his saddle, stuck his foot into the stirrup and swung up. "Let's ride."

They started out at a ground-eating lope, and the pounding of the horses' hooves filled the dark silence. Before them, the orange glow increased, like a tiny false dawn, and Travis cursed. At least they wouldn't have to worry about the flames racing across the prairie as they would have later in the year, when the summer sun had turned the grass to tinder. But when he thought of what *was* burning, he cursed again and spurred his horse into a run, heedless of the danger of riding blindly into the night. The ground blurred beneath him as the miles fell away, and the orange glow swelled on the horizon.

They smelled it first, the sickening stench of burning wool and roasting meat. Then they heard the frantic bleating above the pounding of their horses' hooves, the blood-curdling screams of dying sheep. At last they saw it, the scene illuminated by the flaming fleeces of hundreds of sheep driven mad by pain and terror.

Six masked men chased the sheep on foot, flapping flour sacks in their faces to frighten them into a milling throng so the flames could jump more easily from animal to animal. And the flames did jump, catching the wool of each sheep as if it had been a torch and sending another animal into an agonized frenzy.

Knowing he could never hope to hit anything, Travis pulled his pistol from its holster and fired at random into the melee. This was the signal, and suddenly the night exploded with gunfire as his men followed his lead.

As one, the gunnysackers looked toward the sound. Instantly recognizing their danger, they turned and ran for their horses with almost comic haste. Travis emptied his pistol, then jammed it back into the holster. By then, the gunnysackers were riding away, but Travis reined up when he reached the camp.

Cameron brought his horse to a sliding halt beside him. The Scot's face was scarlet in the brightness of the burning sheep. "Aren't ye going after the bastards?" he shouted above the din of agonized bleats and dwindling gunfire.

"Find the herder first!" Travis shouted back, scanning the camp as he spoke. He found the man almost at once and vaulted from his saddle.

Travis recognized the herder instantly as the one Sarah had called Mr. Sanchez. He slumped, apparently unconscious, his arms wrapped around the trunk of a lone cottonwood and tied at the wrists, his naked back a bloody mass. Travis raced to him, reached into his boot, pulled out a knife and sliced through the rope with one swift thrust. Cameron, who had followed at his heels, caught Sanchez and lowered him gently to the ground.

"What in God's name have they done to him?" Cameron demanded.

"Whipped him," Travis replied, tasting the bitterness of fury. "Is he alive?"

Sanchez groaned, and his eyes flickered open. "The sheep . . ." he muttered.

"I'll take care of him," Cameron said, as angry as Travis had ever seen another living soul. "Ye can go after them."

"We've got work here first," Travis said, waving both arms to signal the other men, who had ridden on a little way after the fleeing raiders but who had now slowed, having realized Travis and Cameron were no longer with them.

"Ye can't let them go!" Cameron protested in outrage.

"As you pointed out, we ain't got much chance of beating them in a fight, so I figure our best bet is to save as much of Mrs. Hadley's property as we can. Ace! Shorty!" he shouted, running out to meet the returning riders. "Ride into that mess and cut out the burning sheep."

106

The horses were already shying from the flames. *"How,* boss?" Shorty asked, fighting for control of his mount. "They won't go near the fire."

"Take off your shirts and tie them over the horses' heads so they can't see it." He turned to the Mexicans and addressed them in Spanish. "Ace and Shorty are going to try to separate the burning sheep from the rest. You boys herd up the good ones and get them as far away from the burning ones as possible."

"Sí, señor," José said, sliding down from his horse. As Ace and Shorty rode off, the Mexicans followed on foot.

"What will *ye* do?" Cameron asked, as Travis jogged past him on his way to his horse. But Travis didn't have time for conversation.

He didn't stop until he reached his mount and had pulled the Winchester from its scabbard. Turning, he came face to face with the *mayordomo.* The Scot's bulk was blocking his way, and he knew Cameron wouldn't move until he'd had an answer. "I'm going to put the ones that aren't already dead out of their misery."

Cameron's broad face twisted in despair, but he stepped instantly out of Travis's way. "I'll see to the herder," he called, as the gunfighter strode toward the flaming flock.

Travis barely heard. The roar of bleating agony filled his head, a sound so close to a woman's scream he could hardly stand it. Although every nerve and every muscle in his body resisted, he raised the Winchester to his shoulder. Ace drove a bunch of sheep toward him. They ran in maddened panic in a futile attempt to escape their own blazing backs, their eyes rolling wildly, their mouths gaping with terrorized

107

shrieks. Travis took aim at the closest black face, gritted his teeth, and fired.

Hour after hour, her riding skirt slapping against her boots, Sarah paced across the ranchyard and back, watching the orange glow slowly fade and die. Did that mean her men had found the fire and put it out? Or did it mean the fire had simply gone out by itself? And where were her men and what had happened to them? *And where was Travis?*

Although Quinn had fully intended to guard Sarah, he sat in a chair on the front porch, rifle across his lap, head tipped back against the wall of the house, snoring sonorously. She didn't begrudge him his rest, and she was perfectly capable of recognizing danger herself, but she desperately needed someone to talk to. She marched over to the porch steps.

"Quinn!"

His whole body jerked, and in the next second he was on his feet, rifle raised, ready to fight.

"Don't shoot!" Sarah cried, fighting an absurd urge to laugh. "I just want to ask you a question."

He blinked in the lanternlight and scanned the horizon. "Fire's out, looks like."

"Do you know what was burning?"

Quinn stiffened in silent resistance. "Didn't Travis say?"

"No," she said, not wanting to admit she hadn't wanted to ask. "Do you know?"

She could almost smell his reluctance to reply. "Can't you guess?"

Unfortunately, she could. She laid a hand over her

churning stomach. "What would they have done to the herder?"

Quinn looked away, and the rifle drooped in his hands. "Don't rightly know."

Sarah opened her mouth to demand a straight answer, but at that moment they both heard the sound of approaching horses. Sarah held her breath until the three pistol shots pierced the night silence, then released it in an agonized sigh.

"Quinn, get some more lanterns." She wanted to see, *needed* to see who rode up. If anyone had been hurt . . . But she wouldn't let herself think of that. Instead she waited, hardly daring to breathe, while Quinn fetched two more lanterns from the bunkhouse and carried them out to illuminate the yard.

Apprehension tightened in her chest as the riders drew closer, and then she saw Travis leading the group. He rode upright, his golden hair gleaming in the moonlight, visibly weary but obviously unhurt, and relief coursed through her on a bittersweet wave.

Only then did she notice Cameron and the blanket-wrapped burden he carried on his horse. What on earth was wrong with her? Travis wasn't her only concern! She hurried toward the Scot's horse.

"Who is it? What happened?" she asked as soon as she was within shouting distance. Then she realized none of the Mexicans had returned. "Where are the others?" she added in growing alarm, picking up her skirts and breaking into a run.

Just as she reached Cameron's horse, strong arms caught her and pulled her away. Outraged, she looked up into Travis's face and struggled against his hold.

"It's Sanchez," he told her, tightening his grip and

109

refusing to let her go. "They whipped him. He's alive, but he's not very pretty."

"Take him into the bunkhouse. I'll get my medicine box," she told Cameron, who had already ridden by on his way to the bunkhouse. "Where are the others?" she demanded again.

"We left them with the sheep." Travis's grip gentled, but he didn't let her go. Oddly, Sarah no longer wanted to be released. His touch felt almost comforting, and she needed comforting very badly.

"They . . . they burned the sheep, didn't they?" she forced herself to ask.

"Just one flock, and only about half of them. José and the others are taking the rest off to a safer place."

"Burned alive!" Sarah cried, the horror chilling her. "And poor Mr. Sanchez. How could anyone . . . ?" Travis's hands tightened again, and she saw her own rage reflected in his azure eyes.

"I tried to tell you," he said, giving her a little shake. "This is just the beginning. Next time they might come after *you*."

Sarah gaped at him, but before she could respond, Quinn came loping up, her medicine box under his arm. "You want me to take care of him?"

"No," she said, jerking free of Travis's grip. She took the box from Quinn. "Get me some hot water and some clean rags from under the sink in my kitchen. As soon as you're done, ride into town and fetch Dr. Bigelow."

Without so much as a glance at Travis, she started for the bunkhouse, but he wasn't finished with her. "You ever seen a man who's been whipped?" he asked coldly, matching her stride

110

for stride as she hurried across the yard.

"I've seen men gored by bulls and caught in stampedes," she replied just as coldly. "If you're worried about my sensibilities, I've already told you, I don't have any."

And even if she had, she would never reveal them to Mr. Travis Whatever-his-real-name-was. She didn't hesitate when she reached the bunkhouse door, but walked straight in. Only then did her step falter, and only for a second. Cameron had laid Sanchez facedown on a bunk near the door and unwrapped the blanket. The poor man's back looked like a chunk of raw meat, and the sickly sweet scent of fresh blood assaulted her. For an instant Sarah felt a wave of nausea rising in her chest.

She fought it down, however, and walked right up to the bed, pushing Ace and Shorty out of the way to make room for herself. She set her box on the next bunk and began rummaging in it for the supplies she would need. First she found the small brown bottle of laudanum.

"Shorty, get me a glass of water, will you?" She leaned over to Sanchez, trying to ignore the sight and stench of the blood. "Mr. Sanchez, can you hear me?"

His eyelids fluttered and finally lifted, and she saw that his dark eyes were clouded with pain. He tried to speak, but she wouldn't let him.

"Don't try to talk. I'll give you some laudanum for the pain; then I'm going to take care of you. You're going to be just fine."

"That's an order, Sanchez," Travis said, startling her. She hadn't realized he stood so close, but when she looked up at him, she saw his gaze was firmly on

111

Sanchez's face. "You ain't going to disobey Mrs. Hadley, now, are you?"

To Sarah's amazement, the injured man made a noise that sounded almost like a laugh. "Oh, no, señor," he croaked, and the other men chuckled. The sound was forced and unnatural, but she could see that even Sanchez relaxed afterward.

Shorty came in with the water, and Travis and Cameron helped Sanchez swallow the potion she prepared. When the injured man was resting more comfortably, Sarah started rolling up the sleeves of her shirtwaist, but Travis was already dipping a rag into the water Quinn had brought.

Before she could protest, he began to cleanse away the dried blood with amazing gentleness. As if unwilling to let Travis care for one of his men, Cameron snatched up another rag and began to help. In a matter of minutes, the wounds were clean, and Sarah saw they weren't quite as bad as she had imagined. Still, it would be weeks before Sanchez was fit to work again, and for him to have suffered the pain and humiliation of such an attack was monstrous.

And it was all her fault.

Her hands trembled as she spread the healing salve over the lacerated skin. A man had almost been killed, others had ridden in danger of their lives, and a thousand defenseless animals had been burned alive, all because Sarah Hadley refused to give in. What gave her the right to cause others such misery?

Her vision blurred, and someone took the roll of bandages from her nerveless fingers.

"Cameron, take care of this. I'll get Mrs. Hadley back to the house," she heard Travis say. He slipped

112

his arm around her waist. "Come on."

How dare he order her around? How dare he put his hands on her? Sarah tried to work up some outrage, but found she hadn't the strength for it. To her humiliation, she meekly allowed him to lead her from the bunkhouse and out into the blessedly clean night air.

"Are you all right?" he asked when they were outside.

She found she had to take a few deep breaths before she could answer him, and even then her "yes" sounded more like a denial. He muttered something profane, and his arm tightened around her.

Her eyes stung, and she recognized the unfamiliar urge to weep. She wouldn't, of course—certainly not in front of Travis—but the urge was almost overwhelming. Suddenly, she felt incredibly weary, too tired even to take another step, and her knees obligingly buckled.

A small cry escaped her, but Travis caught her before she could fall, and the next thing she knew, he'd scooped her up into his arms and was carrying her toward the house.

"I . . . This . . . You . . ." she sputtered, stiffening indignantly.

"Shut up," he said. "And that's an order. Damn female, I ought to let you fall on your face. Don't have sense enough to know when you've bit off more'n you can chew."

He continued muttering as he strode across the darkened yard, until he grew too short of breath from his burden. Sarah tried not to think about the myriad sensations coursing through the body that had been so

113

very close to fainting just seconds ago, but that now tingled as if she'd sustained an electric shock.

He might not be a big man, but he was certainly strong, strong enough to carry her and curse her at the same time, at least most of the way. She'd been forced to wrap her arms around his neck to keep from falling, and she didn't know which was the most disconcerting—feeling the tensile strength of his shoulder beneath her hands, or having her face so close to his.

Even in the darkness she could see the hint of golden stubble on his lean cheeks, and the dangerous glitter of his steel blue eyes. His corn-yellow hair was mussed, and she clenched her hands together more tightly as she resisted the impulse to smooth it. Still, she knew exactly how it would feel beneath her fingers: soft as silk and warm with life.

For some reason, she couldn't seem to get her breath—which was just as well, because every time she inhaled, she couldn't help smelling his musky, masculine scent, in spite of the lingering odors of burning wool and sweating horse that clung to him. She wondered how his skin would feel if she were to press her lips against his cheek, and knew a compelling desire to lay her head on his shoulder and do just that.

Oh, dear! She must be getting delirious!

With relief, she realized they were mounting the porch steps. In another instant they would be inside, he would put her down, and all these ridiculous thoughts would vanish from her head.

The door stood open, and Travis turned sideways so they could pass through it into the inner darkness. The lantern on the porch cast a feeble glow into the

114

hallway that served as her office. With an audible sigh, Travis set her on her feet just inside the door, although he kept his arm around her.

"If I leave you here and go light a lamp, will you keel over on me?" he asked, with far less respect than he should have shown his employer.

"Certainly not!" she informed him, suddenly remembering why kissing his cheek would have been most ill-advised.

In spite of her assurance, he still did not release her at once. Instead he slipped his arm away gradually, as if testing her stability before abandoning her completely. Although she would have died before admitting it, the loss of his touch left her feeling strangely bereft.

Hugging herself against a sudden chill, she leaned against the wall beside the door and waited while he found the matches and lit the lamp on her desk. The glow sent the night shadows fleeing to the far corners of the room and illuminated Travis's face. He looked furious.

"Good God, you're white as a ghost," he said. "Do you have any whiskey in the house?"

She did, but at the moment she couldn't exactly recall where it was. She shook her head.

"I shouldn't've let you go in there," he muttered, looking around as if he expected to find the whiskey sitting on her desk. "I should've known—"

"It wasn't the blood," she insisted, horrified at how faint her voice sounded. "I've seen blood before. I've just never . . ."

She shuddered, and he took a step toward her, but caught himself. "You never what?" he prompted.

115

How could she explain? "I've never seen anyone hurt because of me," she tried.

"You didn't hurt him. Your friends and neighbors did it for you," he said grimly.

"Maybe I didn't hold the whip, but this never would've happened if I hadn't brought in the sheep. Don't you see?" She reached out, beseeching. "It's all my fault."

To her horror, her voice broke and tears flooded her eyes. Travis muttered something savage, and in the next second his arms were around her. She should have been shocked, should have pushed him away, but she was so tired and cold and alone, and he was too strong and warm and consoling.

Instinctively, she clung to him, wrapping her arms around his narrow waist. His hands caressed her back, molding her to him; then he reached up and forced her head onto his shoulder. His long fingers delved into her hair, loosening the pins that held it.

He whispered her name, a sound so full of longing her own heart ached in response. His warm breath tickled her ear, sending delicious shivers racing over her, and the hot, sharp sting of her tears subsided. "It's not your fault," he said fiercely. "You've got every right to do what you want on your own land. Don't ever let them beat you, Sarah. Don't give in."

Stunned, Sarah jerked her head from his shoulder. "But you said—"

"I just wanted to protect you from all this, but it was already too late."

He'd wanted to protect her? How long since anyone had even cared whether she was safe or not? "Why would you want to protect me?" she whispered.

116

How could he tell her? Travis wondered, especially when he didn't even know himself. He only knew the compulsion he felt, the undeniable need to cherish her and shield her from the wickedness. He must be losing his mind. "Because . . . because you're a woman," he tried, although he knew that wasn't the reason. Regardless of her sex, Sarah Hadley didn't need protection—not his or any other man's.

But she *was* a woman, a fact of which he was acutely aware as he held her in his arms. Her slender body felt so good, so right, so wonderful, pressed against his. Her richly female scent filled his senses, drugging him until his will was no longer his own. He thought he'd never seen a woman so beautiful, with skin so perfect, with eyes so mysterious, with lips so sweet and inviting.

"Sarah, I . . ." he began, but there was nothing left to say, nothing left to do except kiss her; so he did, lowering his mouth to hers slowly in case she wanted to pull away.

But wonder of wonders, she didn't pull away, didn't move, didn't even breathe until his lips touched hers. Then she sighed, and he captured her sweet essence in his mouth as he drew her closer until he could feel the soft roundness of her breasts and belly pressing against his own desperate yearning.

Desire roared in him, desire for her body and for all the things she could bring him: happiness and peace, an end to wandering and, above all, love. Need tore through him like a dull knife, ripping away all his carefully constructed defenses and leaving only the agony of knowing she could never be more to him than she was at this moment.

117

With the last of his strength, he lifted his mouth from hers and looked down into her emerald eyes. She stared back at him with a mixture of confusion and vulnerability, but he steeled himself against it.

"I . . . This shouldn't have happened," he said hoarsely.

Sarah blinked in surprise. Her head still spun, and she could hardly think, but she knew he was wrong. She'd been waiting her entire life for this to happen. "Is this why you've been avoiding me?" she asked, still breathless.

He nodded, as breathless as she. She could feel his heart pounding against hers, and she saw her own wonder and uncertainty mirrored in the sky blue of his eyes. When he would have released her, she slid her arms up to his shoulders and around his neck. "Travis, I . . ."

But she didn't have to finish. With a groan, he kissed her again, crushing her to him as if he would take her into himself. Open-mouthed, he devoured her lips in a desperate claiming to which she submitted willingly, eagerly. At his urging, she opened to him, and his tongue plunged into her mouth in imitation of the ultimate claiming.

Sarah hadn't known she could feel like this, ecstatic and desperate, fulfilled yet wanting, euphoric but terrified. Desire scorched through her, igniting sensations she'd never dreamed existed and needs for which she had no name. She'd thought she knew all the secret things between men and women, but Travis's touch had lifted her into a realm beyond her imaginings, a realm she could explore only with him.

His hands moved over her urgently, as if he would

118

touch every part of her, and she offered herself freely, burying her fingers in the softness of his golden hair and holding his mouth to hers. At last he found a breast, cupping it tentatively, almost reverently, at first. His hand seemed to sear right through the fabric of her clothing straight to the naked flesh beneath, and her nipple hardened in startled reaction. Desire pulsed in her, a wanting so intense her body wept with it, dewing her most secret place.

His name thundered in her head, a name she wasn't even sure was his, but a name she knew was her destiny. When he tore his mouth from her and forced her away from him, she suddenly realized the name wasn't in her head at all.

"Travis! Where are ye?" Cameron called from outside.

Travis stepped back, and for one brief instant she saw a wild expression in his wonderful eyes, a combination of astonishment and despair. In the next instant it was gone, and he had turned away.

"In here," he called back to Cameron in a voice that sounded amazingly normal.

Sarah shook her head to clear it, and knew a momentary dismay that their very private moment might have been observed. But no, Cameron's call had sounded far too calm for him to have seen Travis kissing her, and she realized they'd been standing to one side of the open door, out of view of anyone in the yard.

She enjoyed only a second of relief, however, before she noticed that Travis had erased all trace of passion from his expression. He stood by her desk, half turned away, adjusting the lamp wick as if nothing untoward had happened. How could he . . . ?

Then she suddenly realized he had to conceal his physical reaction to their encounter from Cameron. So, he wasn't as unaffected as he appeared. The knowledge soothed her wounded pride and restored her confidence.

Cameron appeared in the doorway, his bulk seeming to shrink the small hallway even as it blocked the dim light from the lantern on the porch. He looked at Travis, then at Sarah. At the sight of what must have been her bemused expression, his own softened at once.

"Are ye all right, lass?" he asked, and Sarah was somewhat gratified to see Travis's head jerk up at the familiar form of address. Of course he had no way of knowing Cameron had never dared be so familiar before.

Before she could reply, Travis said, "*Mrs. Hadley* seems to think she's responsible for what happened to Sanchez."

"But 'twas no' your fault, missus," Cameron insisted. "How could ye think so?"

"Quite easily, Mr. Cameron," she said, glad to hear that her own voice sounded almost normal, too. "If I'd never brought in sheep, Mr. Sanchez would never have been whipped."

"He wouldn't've had a job, either," Travis pointed out grimly. "He knew the risks when he came to work for you."

Sarah wasn't so certain, but she wanted to believe him. She only wished he weren't looking at her so coldly, as if they hadn't kissed just moments ago, as if her body didn't still burn for his touch.

120

"That's true," Cameron said, obviously surprised to find himself in agreement with Travis. "We all knew what we faced when we came here."

Sarah sighed, knowing they were right but knowing she was right, too. Unfortunately, being right wouldn't change a thing or make Mr. Sanchez whole again.

"Gentlemen, I appreciate your concern, but as owner of the ranch, I must hold myself responsible for whatever happens here. I must also be the one to decide whether or not to continue putting my men at risk."

Cameron stiffened instantly. "Ye can't be thinking of selling out!"

At last Travis turned to face her, arms akimbo, frowning his disapproval. "You aren't going to back down! You can't let those stinking cowards win!"

Cameron's astonishment was comic, but Sarah didn't feel much like laughing. "I would like a little time to think things over before I decide," she said.

"Take all the time you need," Travis said, still frowning, "just so long as you make the right choice. Come on, Cameron. The lady's had a rough night. She needs some rest."

Cameron blinked as if recovering himself. "Aye," he said absently, then recalled his manners. "Will ye be needing anything before we go?"

"No, thank you," Sarah said, wishing she could think of some reason to ask Travis to remain behind so she could experience at least one more of his kisses to last her through the long, lonely night ahead. She was beginning to think she might have dreamed the whole encounter.

Looking at his face now, no one would ever guess

how tenderly he'd held her just moments ago. No one had held her in so very long, and she'd forgotten how wonderful it could feel. But of course she couldn't ask him to stay, certainly not without arousing Cameron's suspicion, so she watched in silence as he left.

Cameron lingered, obviously reluctant to leave her and even more obviously willing to give her the comfort she craved. "If ye need anything—" he began, but she cut him off.

"I'm fine, really, Mr. Cameron. Thank you for everything." She moved purposefully behind him and took hold of the door, preparing to close it behind him.

Taking the hint, he followed Travis out, still unwilling but resigned. Travis waited on the porch, hands on his hips again, and Sarah could imagine jealousy in his fixed expression as he watched to see if she would ask Cameron to stay. Somewhat gratified, she almost smiled.

"Good night, gentlemen, and thank you for everything. Tell the men they have the day off tomorrow. They've earned it."

They murmured their own good nights, and Sarah started to close the door, but she stopped just short of it, leaving just enough space for her to observe the two men as they strode across the yard.

All but oblivious to the stocky figure by his side, she watched Travis, admiring, as always, the fluid way he moved. He put her in mind of a panther, sleek and powerful, beautiful but dangerous. But Sarah didn't fear him. Hadn't he said he wanted to protect her?

When the two men disappeared into the bunkhouse, Sarah closed the door completely and sagged against it, unutterably weary. If only Travis really could protect her from the decisions she would have to make tomorrow. Luckily she was too tired tonight to think about anything, not her sheep or the attack or even her very disturbing encounter with Travis. All of it would have to wait for morning.

The next morning Sarah awoke with a start, unable to remember her dreams but knowing they had disturbed her. Then she recalled the events of the night before, the attack on the sheep, poor Mr. Sanchez, and her shocking behavior with Travis!

What on earth had she been thinking? she wondered, horrified to realized she had kissed a man she hardly knew, a man who worked for her, for heaven's sake! And if she'd only kissed him, things would have been bad enough, but when she remembered what else he had done, humiliation washed over her in a crimson tide.

Instinctively, she crossed her arms over her breasts as if she could undo the damage, as if she could by an act of will erase her wanton response to him. But it was far too late to be thinking of remedies. The damage was done, and so was she. Even now Travis was probably spreading the sensational story to the other men, telling them how the virtuous Sarah Hadley had offered herself to the first man who'd dared to put his hands on her.

How could he help but gloat to Cameron, who so obviously wanted her for himself? And to the men who had served her out of loyalty to the Hadleys, never suspecting their mistress was little better than a whore?

Tears of humiliation scalded her eyes, but she refused to let them fall. Facing the men would be ordeal enough, without letting them see the depths of her degradation. With a groan, she lurched from her bed and staggered over to the washstand, where she splashed icy water onto her face to douse the hot sting of her grief.

With trembling hands, she found the towel and patted herself dry, then stared wide-eyed at her reflection in the cloudy mirror. She looked remarkably unchanged, hardly like a woman who had thrown away her good name for a few moments of illicit passion. She only hoped she could maintain the facade when faced with the derision her behavior would bring down upon her.

Determined to appear unbowed, she bathed and dressed, perversely putting on her most modest black bombazine gown and brushing her hair until it shone before pinning it up into a severe knot on the back of her head. When she had finished, she checked her appearance again in the mirror. The face she saw reflected back seemed unnaturally pale but otherwise quite normal. She would show them nothing.

On leaden feet, she moved through the silent house to the kitchen, where she built a fire in the stove and mechanically made herself a pot of coffee. When she allowed herself to look out the window, she saw the sun was high in the sky and the men had just begun to stir.

They had all been as weary as she. Perhaps they didn't even know yet. Surely a man would wait until he had their undivided attention before revealing such a scandal. Last night they would have been too concerned with Sanchez to bother with gossip.

Or so she told herself.

When the coffee had boiled, Sarah poured herself a cup and slumped down at the kitchen table, hoping its warmth would calm the churning in her stomach. She'd managed only one sip when she heard the thump of boots on the front porch.

Her start of surprise sent hot coffee sloshing over the side of the cup. She set it down with a clunk and rose instinctively to her feet. Who was it, and what would she say to him? How could she explain? How could she justify her behavior?

But she knew she'd be a fool even to try. Once a woman sipped, nothing she did for the rest of her life could make up for it. Hadn't she seen the hard evidence in what had happened to Elizabeth? The poor woman didn't even dare speak to a man now, for fear of the gossip that was sure to result.

Whoever was on the porch knocked but didn't wait for her response. The door opened at once.

"Mrs. Hadley?"

Sarah's heart leaped into her throat at the sound of Travis's voice. What did he want? To gloat? Or worse, did he expect her to fall into his arms again? Did he expect even more this time?

"Mrs. Hadley?" he tried again when she did not reply. "Are you up?"

Swallowing the thickness in her throat, she managed to say, "Yes, I'm in the kitchen."

Steeling herself, she still wasn't quite prepared for the sight of him. He looked remarkably attractive in the light of day, his hat in his hand, his golden hair

125

oiled and combed, his chin scraped clean of stubble, his clothes immaculate.

He paused in the doorway, expression carefully blank, and she thought she sensed a wariness about him. They stared at each other in silence for what seemed an age before he said, "Thought you were up when I saw the smoke. Sanchez is doing real good. The laudanum helped a lot, and he slept until morning. The doc was here early, and he said we did as much as he could've done. He changed the bandages and put more of your salve on him. He thinks he'll be all right."

"Has Dr. Bigelow gone?" she asked, feeling strangely helpless.

"Yeah. He said not to wake you, since there was nothing you could do."

Sarah didn't know what to say. "I . . . thank you."

He studied her face for a long moment. "Are *you* all right?"

Sarah knew she would never be "all right" again. "Should I be?" she asked perversely.

He frowned and took a step forward. Sarah panicked. "No!" she cried in alarm, throwing up her hands in a protective gesture, as if she could ward him off.

He stopped instantly, and his frown faded into something very close to despair. "Look, about last night . . ." he began with something like uncertainty.

Sarah stiffened her spine and folded her arms defensively across her middle. "What about it?" she snapped.

He drew in a deep breath and let it out on a long sigh while Sarah wondered frantically what on earth he would say to her. "I know you were tired and scared and . . . and . . ." He gestured helplessly.

Apparently, he expected her to say something, but Sarah held her breath, unable to think of a single appropriate reply.

After a long minute, he made an exasperated sound. "Do you want me to leave?"

"Leave?" she repeated as if she had never heard the word before. Indeed, it was the last one she had expected to hear.

"Yeah, leave the ranch," he clarified grimly. "If you're afraid because of what happened . . . I mean, I can understand why you wouldn't want me around anymore, but it'll never happen again, I swear."

Sarah stared at him, speechless. She'd expected him to swagger, even to gloat, but never this. He was practically apologizing! "I'm afraid you may have gotten the wrong impression of my character, Mr. . . . uh, Travis," she tried, searching for some delicate way of confronting this most sensitive of issues.

"I don't have the wrong impression of anything," he informed her gruffly. "I know the kind of woman you are. Men talk, Mrs. Hadley, and if there was anything bad to know about you, I'd've heard it the first day I was here. I know you'd never . . . I know you wouldn't . . ."

He gestured again, and Sarah couldn't help remembering how that hand had felt caressing her so gently. Her face flamed in humiliation, but she resolutely refused to look away.

"I was upset last night," she said, sounding as if she were upset right now, too.

"Yeah, that's it," he agreed too quickly. "You were

127

upset, and I was mad. That's all. We made a mistake."

A mistake. Somehow she didn't like the idea that he regretted the incident as much as she did, and wondered why. A very unsettling possibility occurred to her. "Of course, if you *want* to leave, I'll understand perfectly."

He frowned again. "Look, Mrs. Hadley, if you want me to go, I will, but I'll tell you right out, you need me more now than you did when you hired me."

"But you were the one who didn't want to get involved in a fight over sheep," she reminded him in surprise.

"I didn't before, but now it's personal for me."

"Personal?" Sarah asked in alarm, wondering how many rights he thought one kiss had won him.

"When somebody attacks my men, I take it personal. I want to find the bastards who whipped Sanchez and make them sorry they was ever born."

Sarah knew she should have been relieved to learn his personal interest didn't include her person, but instead she felt slightly annoyed. "It seems you and I have the same goal, then, and I'm afraid you're absolutely right when you say I need your help more than ever now."

His disturbing eyes narrowed suspiciously. "Are you saying I can stay?"

She didn't want to seem too eager. "On the condition that . . . that . . . " She didn't know how to say it.

"Strictly business between us from now on," he assured her hastily. Too hastily, Sarah thought, irritated all over again. He could at least show a little regret at her rejection of his physical advances, instead of acting relieved. But then, what had she expected? She

128

knew men weren't attracted to her.

After a moment's thought, he added, "I think maybe we shouldn't be alone again."

Stung, Sarah nodded stiffly. Did he think that if they were alone, she might throw herself into his arms again? "Certainly not," she replied.

Before either of them could think of something else to say, Cameron came in the front door. "Mrs. Hadley?" he called, then saw Travis. "What is it?"

"I was just telling Mrs. Hadley how Sanchez is getting along," Travis said, turning away without so much as a backward glance. He put on his hat with elaborate care and started for the front door.

Sarah knew a pang at his departure, and chided herself for being a fool. She should be thanking her lucky stars that he hadn't told every living soul in the state about her indiscretion, and instead she was disappointed because he wanted to pretend it hadn't happened. She really must be losing her mind.

" 'Tis good news I've got for ye, missus. We only lost three hundred and thirty-eight sheep last night. I was thinking it was a lot more."

"I'm glad," Sarah said, managing a polite smile. "I was afraid it was a thousand or more."

"Aye, in the confusion, we couldna tell for sure. We left Pedro to mind the flock until we can hire another herder."

"Good," she murmured absently, thinking they wouldn't be able to hire anyone at all, not now. People would be afraid to work for her, and she couldn't blame them. Suddenly she felt the exhaustion of last night overtake her again. "Thank you, Mr. Cameron. Now, if you'll excuse me,

I haven't had my breakfast yet."

"Aye, missus, and you'd best try to rest today. Ye had a troublesome night."

Hers had been far less troublesome than anyone else's, she wanted to say, but she didn't. Instead she watched him leave, then sank down into her chair again. Well, at least she didn't have to worry about Travis spreading stories about her and destroying her reputation. She should have felt relieved and grateful and even happy. Instead she felt cross and irritable. Probably a result of the awful experiences she'd been through during the past twenty-four hours, she told herself.

Certainly her mood had nothing whatsoever to do with Travis Whatever-his-name-was or his eagerness to forget the kiss they had shared during one of the darkest times of her life. Unfortunately, she knew that if he were to come back at this very moment, she would be hard pressed to resist the comfort and excitement of his embrace.

Travis couldn't believe what he'd done. By rights, Sarah Hadley should have thrown him out on his ear, but only if she'd decided not to have him shot instead. All night long he'd tossed and turned, trying to figure out how he could have allowed his body to slip beyond his control like that. Something about Sarah Hadley had him a little crazy, he supposed. He hadn't been acting like himself at all since the first time he'd laid eyes on her.

And why he'd talked her into letting him stay, he'd never know. Didn't she realize she was in far more danger from him than she'd ever be in from her sheep-hating neighbors? Travis certainly realized it, and he knew he should hightail it before he did something they'd be a whole lot sorrier for. Instead, he'd practically begged her to let him stay on. He was so busy calling himself a fool, he almost didn't hear what Cameron was saying.

"Ye did a good job last night, man. I'm thinking you're a man who knows his way around a fight."

Travis winced at the compliment. "When you've been in as many as I have, you learn," he replied sourly.

But Cameron wasn't going to be put off. "I'm no' too proud to admit when I'm wrong, and I was wrong about ye. I couldna have done what ye did last night."

"For your sake, I hope you never have to." Travis would have walked on, but Cameron grabbed his arm and held him fast.

Ordinarily, Travis didn't allow other men to touch him, but Cameron's grip was entreating, not threatening. "Travis, I'm afraid for the lass. She doesna know the trouble she is in."

"Don't underestimate her, partner. Sarah Hadley knows exactly how much trouble she's caused. Why do you think she's having second thoughts?"

"Do ye think she knows she's in danger, too?"

"I told her, but I don't think she believed me."

Travis studied Cameron's broad face and saw his own concern for Sarah reflected in the Scot's blue eyes. "Ye ken we canna let her lose this fight."

"Why?" Travis challenged. "Afraid you'll lose out on the sheep you were going to steal from her?"

Cameron frowned, not the least offended. "I won't

lie to ye. When I came here, I wanted the sheep and nothing else, but now . . . now it's the lass herself. She . . ."

He pressed his lips together, dropped Travis's arm, and looked away, as if unwilling to let Travis see his pain. Which was just as well, Travis thought, since he didn't want the Scot seeing his pain, either. It was the lass that held them both, and Cameron had the worst of it, since he was obviously in love with her. Luckily, Travis wasn't that far gone, or at least he hoped to God he wasn't.

"I won't let anything happen to her," Travis said, aware of the irony of his promise. If Cameron knew what Travis had done to her last night, he'd kill him with his bare hands.

The Scot shifted his considerable weight and looked back at Travis. "I know ye'll look after her. Hell, ye'll look after all of us."

Travis couldn't help smiling at the dismay in the Scot's voice. "That's what I'm paid to do, but truth to tell, you didn't make too bad a showing yourself last night. You're a man to ride the river with, Cameron."

The Scot's wide mouth quirked. "I'm thinking that's a compliment. We'd best be careful, or we'll get to liking each other, Yank. That might make things difficult, since we're both in love with the same woman."

Travis's smile faded, but before he could dispute the Scot's claim, he heard riders approaching. They both turned to see a group of three men whom Travis didn't recognize.

Cameron drew in his breath on a hiss. "Mrs. Hadley's neighbors," he explained as they watched the men ride into the yard and up to the house.

132

The three were well dressed, sporting expensive hats and hand-tooled boots and riding first-class saddles. Ranchers, most likely, and Travis knew a twinge of envy. If he'd worked as hard at ranching as he had at fighting, he'd have made a success of his life, too.

One of them halloed the house, and Sarah came out onto the porch to greet them. She looked small and vulnerable in her black dress with her ebony hair drawn back from her pale face, and Travis had an urge to race across the yard and protect her.

He really was getting irrational where Sarah Hadley was concerned, he noted wryly. She wasn't likely to need protection from what were obviously respectable men on her own front porch, and she probably wouldn't welcome his interference either. They had a deal, and appointing himself her personal knight in shining armor didn't fit in with the deal at all. But still . . .

The men dismounted, and Travis noticed with dismay that one of them was quite tall, perhaps over six feet. He bounded up the steps and took Sarah's outstretched hand in both of his and held it as if he had the right.

Something burned in his chest, something as bitter as gall. "Who in the hell is that bastard?" he asked Cameron through gritted teeth.

"The *tall* one?" Cameron asked, with a knowing look. "Garth Richardson. He was Philip Hadley's best friend, and I'm thinking he'd like to be *Mrs*. Hadley's friend, too."

Before he knew it, Travis was on his way over to join the happy little group.

133

Chapter Five

Sarah winced when she heard the call from the riders in the yard. The last thing she needed right now was company, particularly company from the very men who had been trying for months to get her to give up her sheep.

Ignoring the throbbing ache behind her eyes, she rose and went outside, onto the porch. Two of her visitors were Abel Frank and Ed Smith, the two men she least wanted to see, but at least they'd brought Garth Richardson along with them. He'd make the visit bearable if nothing else.

She smiled as he swung down from his horse and climbed the porch steps two at a time. He took her hand in both of his. His grip was warm and strong, and he didn't let go right away. Sarah looked up into his dark brown eyes half a foot above her own and saw genuine concern.

"We heard about your trouble, Sarah. Was anyone hurt?"

"Someone horsewhipped one of my herders and set fire to a flock of sheep," she reported grimly.

"Good God," Garth exclaimed. His handsome face

creased into a frown of dismay. "Is the herder . . . ?"

"He's doing well, I'm told. Luckily, I woke up last night and saw the glow of the fire. Heaven only knows what might have happened if my men hadn't gotten there when they did."

"Do you know who done it?" Abel Frank inquired. He and Smith were coming up the porch steps behind Garth.

Garth released her hand and stepped aside to make room for them, and Sarah saw Travis striding angrily across the yard toward them with Cameron at his heels. What on earth?

"I said, do you know who done it?" Frank prompted.

Sarah forced her attention back to the wiry rancher. Frank stood only an inch or two taller than she, and his weathered face was squinched into a perpetual scowl, as if he so seldom saw anything in this world worthy of his approval that he had no reason to affect any other expression.

"I'm afraid the raiders wore masks," Sarah informed him, wondering if he were asking in order to find out if she might have identified some of his men. "Perhaps they were afraid of being recognized."

"Excuse me for saying so, Miz Hadley," Ed Smith offered, "but it prob'ly *was* somebody you'd know. Who else'd care that you brought in sheep?"

Who else, indeed? Sarah thought sourly, frowning at the portly rancher. Ed Smith was a man who apologized for everything, even if it wasn't his fault, but Sarah couldn't help wondering if he, too, had been involved in the raid last night. He hardly seemed resolute enough to be completely responsible, but if

135

someone else had planned it, he might have been willing to go along, particularly if the person who planned it was someone like Abel Frank.

Before she could carry her reasoning any further, Travis came up the porch steps, his step unmistakably purposeful. She glanced at him, surprised to see his face was ruddy, although the short sprint across the yard couldn't possibly have winded him. Then he glanced up at her, and she saw the cold glitter of his eyes. He was furious again, although what he had to be furious about she had no idea.

Her three visitors turned toward the newcomer, and Travis stopped at the top of the steps, his stance somehow casual and threatening all at once.

"This must be the new man you hired," Garth said, breaking the momentary silence. He smiled as if he had long been anticipating the pleasure of this meeting. "Garth Richardson," he said, offering his hand.

But Travis ignored the hand and merely nodded curtly. "They call me Travis."

Sarah bit back a smile at Garth's disgruntled expression. He apparently wasn't used to having his charm fail him quite so miserably. "Gentlemen, Travis is my new foreman. Travis, this is Mr. Abel Frank and Mr. Ed Smith. They're our neighbors. And," she added as Cameron reached the porch, "you all know Owen Cameron."

The other two ranchers mumbled an unenthusiastic greeting, Travis nodded again, and Cameron did nothing at all. The lines had been drawn and everyone knew on which side he stood. Although she would not have chosen to do so, Sarah had no choice but to observe the rules of hospitality. "Won't you gentlemen

136

come in? I have some fresh coffee made."

She left the men to find their own seats in the parlor and hurried into the kitchen, where she quickly filled six cups with the coffee she had made earlier. Knowing her guests would eschew anything so dandified as milk or sugar in their coffee, she placed the cups on an enameled tray that was a legacy from her mother, and carried it into the parlor.

The men had settled in rather awkwardly. Frank and Smith were sitting on her leather sofa, glaring at Travis and Cameron, who stood like sentinels on either side of the fireplace. Only Garth looked comfortable, his long frame relaxed in one of the two wing chairs. He jumped to his feet the instant Sarah entered the room, although the other two ranchers made no move to rise.

"I've missed your coffee, Sarah," he said, taking a cup from the tray when she stopped in front of him.

"If you want some, all you have to do is stop by now and again," Sarah replied, unable to resist returning his smile. He really was a dear man. She'd forgotten how agreeable he could be.

Her smile faded when she turned to offer Travis some refreshment. His eyes were like blue ice, and when she looked into them, she felt chilled. Suddenly, she realized at least some of his anger was directed at her, although she couldn't imagine what she had done to irritate him. He took a cup from the tray with his left hand and set it on the mantel, plainly having no intention of drinking it.

Puzzled, she moved to Cameron, who, oddly enough, seemed almost amused. He, too, set his cup on the mantel, but Sarah took no time to decide what the two of them were up to. Instead she served her other two guests, set the tray down on the sideboard and took the last cup for herself. Only when she had seated herself in the matching wing chair did Garth resume his own seat.

Her visitors made a great show of sipping the scalding beverage, and when Sarah could stand the suspense no longer, she said, "I think I'm safe in assuming you gentlemen didn't leave your own ranches in the middle of a workday and ride all the way over here just to drink my coffee."

The three exchanged a glance, as if silently deciding which of them should be the spokesperson. Garth received the nod. "Sarah," he said earnestly, leaning forward slightly in his chair, "what happened last night was a terrible thing."

"I agree," Sarah said, "and if you've come to offer your help in finding the culprits, I accept."

Garth might have winced slightly, but he wasn't going to be sidetracked. "I thought you said the men wore masks."

"They did, but someone knows who they were— probably a lot of someones," she said, deciding boldness was the wisest course. "If men as influential as the three of you were to investigate, I'm sure you could discover their identities in no time."

This time Garth frowned in mild disapproval, as if she'd committed some breach of etiquette for which he felt obligated to reprimand her. "Sarah," he said gently, patiently, "while none of us can condone violence or the destruction of private property, we all agree that you brought this trouble on yourself and that the only way to end it is to get rid of your sheep."

Sarah gasped, but before she could reply to this outrageous statement, Travis said, "I thought this was a free country."

Everyone looked up, as surprised as if a piece of furniture had spoken.

"I beg your pardon," Garth said, disconcerted.

"I said, this is a free country. Far as I know, there ain't no laws against running sheep, so what Mrs. Hadley does on her own property is her own business."

"You're right, of course," Garth said with a tolerant smile, then turned pointedly back to Sarah. "Certainly no one can force you to give up running sheep, but each of us has a certain responsibility to the rest of the community, a responsibility not to offend our neighbors, and many of your neighbors find sheep extremely offensive, Sarah."

Sarah feigned astonishment. "Is that true?" she asked Frank and Smith, who so far had listened quietly, content merely to nod in agreement with each of Garth's points. "Are you gentlemen offended by my sheep? And if so, you need only tell me what they have done to offend you, and I'll make them apologize at once!"

"Now, Mrs. Hadley, there's no need . . ." Smith blustered, flushing furiously, but Frank cut him off.

"You know what Garth is saying, Miz Hadley, and let's call a spade a spade. Maybe you've run your sheep without bothering anybody. You keep 'em on your own land, and even though some of us wish you hadn't fenced off your water so's we can't use it when we need it, we got no legal right to complain."

"You certainly don't," Sarah said stiffly, "and you also know that when and if you need water, you only

139

have to say so and I'll open my gates to you and your stock at once."

"Excuse me, Mrs. Hadley, but it shames a man to have to ask," Smith pointed out. "In the old days—"

"But the old days are gone," Garth reminded him, smoothly changing the subject. "As much as we might all long for open ranges, we'll never have them again, so we must adjust to what we do have."

"And you gentlemen must adjust to the fact that *I* have sheep," Sarah said. She could feel the heat in her face, and realized she probably looked as furious as Travis had a few moments ago. But she didn't want to lose her temper and, with it, control of the situation.

Garth smiled his conciliatory smile. "I believe what Abel was trying to say is that although you run your sheep in an orderly manner and never bother anyone else, the mere fact that you have sheep at all invites an invasion of people who might not be so considerate of others."

"You know who we mean," Frank assured her, scowling even more fiercely than usual. "We're worried about drifters moving in, men with no land of their own who'll run their sheep on ours until it's ruined, then move on to somebody else's."

"And you think that by driving me out of business, you'll protect yourself from the drifters?" Sarah demanded.

"Now, Sarah, there's no need to get upset," Garth insisted. "We're thinking about your welfare, too. After all, sheep aren't branded. Right now you don't have to worry about rustlers because yours are the only sheep in the area, but if drifters move in . . ." He smiled apologetically, as if he were too kind to

140

even mention the consequences to a lady.

Sarah wanted to box his ears. "For your information, sheep are earmarked, the same as cattle, and you will forgive me if I refuse to believe you're all here to convince me to get rid of my sheep just so they won't someday be stolen."

"Well, it is something to think about," Smith offered meekly, earning a scowl from Frank. He winced and shifted his bulky frame uncomfortably on the sofa.

"Miz Hadley, this is cow country," Frank said, turning his attention back to Sarah. "There's places in Texas where they do run sheep, but this ain't one of them, and never will be."

"On the contrary, Mr. Frank, it already is, and my sheep are the proof of it. I've also proved you can run sheep and cattle together and both will flourish. The only trouble my sheep have caused has been from those who want them gone. If you could convince whoever it is to leave me alone, we could all live together in perfect harmony."

Frank turned his scowl on Garth. "See? I told you there'd be no reasoning with a female."

Smith nodded morosely. "Phil would've listened."

"And *Phil* never would've brought in sheep in the first place," Sarah snapped, at the end of her patience. "He preferred to see the place go bankrupt."

"Better to go bankrupt than shame his pappy's good name by bringing in sheep," Frank said dourly.

Sarah gaped at him, unable to believe such stupidity even from Abel Frank, but before she could think of a suitable reply, Garth once again tried to smooth things over. "Sarah, no one faults you for trying to make a success of your ranch, but do you really think

141

Phil would want you to make yourself a pariah just so you can make money?"

Since Philip hadn't particularly cared what Sarah wanted when he was alive, Sarah didn't feel obligated to consider what he might have wanted now that he was dead. Unfortunately, she couldn't exactly say so without scandalizing her visitors even more than she already had. Instead, she gave Garth a condescending look. "Would you have me starve in genteel poverty, then?"

"Of course not!" Garth exclaimed, genuinely distressed.

"Nobody expects you to starve," Frank insisted, although Sarah had her doubts. "We're ready to buy you out so's you can take your sheep someplace where they'll be welcome."

"What!" Sarah exclaimed, stunned by his audacity. She looked at Garth, hoping he would assure her Frank spoke only for himself, but she was disappointed.

"I would have broken the news a little more tactfully," Garth said, frowning his disapproval at Frank, who ignored him. "But Abel is right. We're prepared to offer you a fair price for your land and your cattle. If you decide you'd like to go someplace a little more civilized, I'm sure you could sell the sheep, too. You'd be able to settle in a city, Sarah, someplace with libraries and theaters, the kind of place where a woman like you belongs."

Sarah could hardly believe her ears. Garth Richardson had known her for years, yet he didn't really know her at all. How could he imagine she would be happy in a city, away from her home and her land? Hemmed

142

in by houses and people, robbed of her purpose for being, she'd wither and die. No one would ever suggest to a man that he'd be happier giving up the only life he'd ever known and moving to a strange place among stranger people. Only because she was a woman did they dare try to uproot her.

Fairly trembling with rage, Sarah rose imperiously from her chair. "Garth, it may come as a shock to you, but a woman like me belongs right here, and I have no intention of selling out, to you or to anyone else. Now, if you have no further business, I'll thank you all to leave."

She was vaguely aware of Travis moving closer, his presence a palpable force of which the others instantly became aware. They eyed him warily before rising from their seats.

Still, Abel Frank wasn't intimidated. "Don't be too hasty, Miz Hadley," Frank warned as he moved toward the door. "You've still got time to change your mind."

Sarah bit her lip to keep from telling him exactly where he could take his offer to buy her out. Good manners required her to see her guests to the door, but when she moved to do so, Garth stood his ground.

"Sarah, I'm sorry," he said, laying a hand on her arm. "This wasn't my idea, but I felt you should at least hear the offer so you'd know you had a choice." His dark eyes convinced her of his sincerity, and some of her anger drained away, although she wasn't quite ready to forgive him completely. "I handled this badly. I never intended to upset you."

"I don't see how you could have handled it any other way," Sarah said, somewhat mollified. "Any offer to buy me out would have made me mad."

Garth glanced over his shoulder to make sure the other two ranchers had gone, then glanced at Travis and Cameron, who had moved even closer to her. "Maybe if we could have a few minutes alone, you'd feel differently."

Sarah couldn't help smiling at his confidence. "Are you going to charm me into selling out?"

"Could I?" he countered, his finely molded lips parting in a mischievous grin.

"Look, Richardson," Travis broke in, "Mrs. Hadley asked you to leave."

Garth's jaw flexed, the only sign of his irritation, but his gaze never left Sarah's. "Just five minutes. Please?"

As annoyed as she was with him, she also couldn't forget he had been Philip's friend, and since Philip's death, he'd always been her friend, too. "All right, five minutes."

Travis made an odd sound, but when she looked at him, he'd wiped all expression from his face. Only his eyes betrayed the fury still burning within, but they both knew he had no right to care about whom she spoke with. Not unless she'd given him the right, which of course she hadn't.

"Will you please excuse us?" she asked Travis and Cameron.

Cameron started immediately for the door, his expression still slightly amused, but Travis lingered just long enough to register his reluctance before following him. Sarah watched him go, trying to decide why he was making such a scene, when he paused in the doorway and turned back.

"If you need me, I'll be right outside," he said, echoing almost verbatim the warning Cameron had given several weeks ago when he had left Sarah alone with Travis.

Cameron made a choking sound, and Sarah had to cover her mouth to keep from laughing aloud. Only Garth failed to see the humor in the situation. His aristocratic features stiffened, and he pulled himself up to his full six feet in silent challenge.

Travis merely looked him over from head to foot with total contempt and strode out.

When Garth turned back to Sarah, his cheeks were crimson. "He's awfully protective of you, Sarah."

Did his tone hold a hint of accusation? If so, Sarah chose to ignore it. "I pay him to protect me," she reminded him. "Now what did you want to say to me?"

With a visible effort, Garth got his temper back under control, and he managed a version of his winning smile. "Perhaps we should sit down."

Intrigued, Sarah allowed him to escort her to the sofa where they sat, side by side. Garth gazed at her for a long moment as if he'd never actually seen her before, and she gazed back, curious as to what on earth he had to say that would provoke such a soulful look.

"Sarah," he said at last, "you must know how much I've always admired you."

Admired? she thought. What an odd choice of words. "And I've appreciated your friendship, Garth. Until today, I've always felt I could count on your support."

He gave her a self-mocking grin. "I can understand why you think I betrayed you today, but I must confess, I had an ulterior motive."

"Oh?"

145

"I thought perhaps if you were a little frightened, you'd . . . But I'm getting ahead of myself. You must forgive me. I'm not very experienced at this."

"At what?" Sarah asked, totally confused.

"At courting," he told her with another smile. "And don't look so surprised. Surely you must know how I feel about you."

She'd thought she did, but now she wasn't sure. "Garth, what are you talking about?"

He sighed. "I can see I've bungled this whole thing. Sarah, what I'm trying to say is I want to marry you. I've wanted to for a long time, but I've been waiting for some sign from you that you were ready to think about marriage again. Unfortunately, with things as they are, I can't wait anymore. You must know you need a man to take care of you, to deal with the problems your sheep have caused, and to keep you safe. I want to be that man."

Sarah couldn't believe her ears. Was Garth saying he loved her? No, of course not. How could he? A man as handsome as Garth Richardson wouldn't ordinarily even *notice* a woman like Sarah Hadley, much less fall madly in love with her. Sarah looked into his eyes and saw not passion — she'd seen passion recently enough to recognize it — but kindness. For some reason, dear, sweet Garth wanted to protect her, and he was willing to marry her in order to do it.

Touched, she had to swallow the lump in her throat before she could reply. "I can't tell you how grateful I am for your offer, Garth, and I'll never forget you made it, but I can't let you make this sacrifice for me."

"Sacrifice?" he echoed in apparent confusion. "What are you talking about?"

146

"Your being willing to marry a woman you don't love out of kindness."

He blinked in surprise, then smiled slowly. "Sarah, I'm not being kind. You'd bring quite a dowry with you even if you weren't a very desirable woman, which you are."

Desirable? Was he serious? But he didn't give her an opportunity to decide.

"And as for love, you must know I'm extremely fond of you, and have been for a long time. I'm conceited enough to think you're fond of me, too. I don't believe in the fairy-tale kind of romance, Sarah, and I don't think you do either, but I believe we could have a good life together."

Sarah certainly didn't believe in the fairy-tale kind of romance, and she well knew there was no such thing as happily-ever-after, but something in her rebelled at surrendering her hard-won freedom to a man of whom she was merely fond, even if she did believe she needed a man's protection, which she didn't. She'd thought she had loved Philip, and look how disastrously her first marriage had turned out. She couldn't subject herself or Garth to such unhappiness.

She reached out and took his hand. "Garth, I'm sorry, but I can't let you do this."

"Do what?" he asked in some exasperation, his fingers closing tightly around hers. "Sarah, you act like marrying you would be some tragic mistake. Can't you see it would be the best thing for both of us? I need a wife, and you need a husband. If we put our two ranches together, we'd have one of the biggest spreads in the state. We like each other, and we get along. Thousands of marriages do well without half as many things in their favor."

"I'm sure you're right, but you must remember I have more experience at marriage than you do, and you'll understand if I'm a little cautious about taking another husband."

"I'm not Philip," he told her solemnly. "He treated you badly, Sarah, but not all men are cut from the same cloth. I'd never leave you for some trollop."

Sarah waited for the flicker of pain she always felt at the mention of Philip's betrayal, and was surprised to find how little it hurt this time. She must truly have recovered from her humiliation. But how could she explain to Garth that she wasn't so much afraid of losing her husband as she was of losing control of her life again? Garth would never believe she didn't need a man to take care of her, so she was probably foolish to try to convince him. "If I *were* interested in getting married, your offer would be irresistible. Unfortunately, I'm not, Garth. In fact, I don't plan to ever marry again."

Something flickered in his dark eyes, something very like anger, but was gone before she could be sure. He sighed dramatically. "You certainly are hard on a man's pride."

She didn't believe him for one moment. "Your pride is in perfect working order, Garth Richardson, and don't try to pretend I've broken your heart, either. If the truth were told, you're probably relieved I turned you down."

"No, not relieved," he assured her. "I really do need a wife, and I can't think of any other woman I'd rather have."

Which was a shame, Sarah thought. She knew of a

woman who really did need a husband and a father for her son, but Garth Richardson would never even consider Elizabeth Williams. Hadn't he just called her a trollop, and not for the first time? Philip Hadley had a lot to answer for.

"If you can't think of any other possible candidates, you just haven't been thinking hard enough," she told him gently, withdrawing her hand from his. "And besides, I wouldn't want to spoil our friendship by marrying you."

His fine mouth twitched into a reluctant grin. "And you wonder why I admire you. Sarah, you are a piece of work."

"And you, Garth Richardson, probably have work to do." She stood, signaling the interview was at an end, and he slowly rose from his seat to tower over her.

For one second she enjoyed feeling small and feminine against his masculinity, but only for a moment. Philip had been tall, dark, and handsome, too. She started for the door, and he followed behind.

Out on the porch, Sarah saw Travis and Cameron lurking near the door, as if they really expected she might have to call for help. Smiling at the thought, she turned to Garth and offered him her hand.

He took it, and to her surprise, raised it to his lips. The gallant gesture startled a laugh from her, and when he lifted his teasing gaze to hers again, he said, "At least promise you'll save me the first dance."

"Dance?" she echoed stupidly.

"Next week. Don't tell me you've forgotten."

"Oh, of course!" The community dance had been the furthest thing from her mind. "I just didn't realize it was so soon. I'll be glad to save you the first dance unless my sheep have started lambing by then, in which case I'll be too busy for dancing or anything else."

He grimaced in distaste. "Surely you don't involve yourself in such things."

"Everyone on a sheep ranch is involved in lambing. Sheep require a bit more care than cows, I'm afraid."

He shook his head, silently remonstrating, but he refrained from voicing his criticism. "Sarah, what shall we do with you?" he asked of no one in particular, putting on his hat and setting it at a jaunty angle.

"You could start by convincing my neighbors to be a little more tolerant," she suggested, but he only shook his head in mock despair.

"Next week, then," he said, lifting his hand in salute as he bounded down the steps and untied his horse from the hitching rail in front of the house.

"Next week," she replied, waving as he mounted and rode slowly out of the yard.

He hadn't even cleared the ranch buildings when she felt Travis's presence at her elbow. Startled, she glanced over and met his steely blue gaze. The intensity of his silent fury fairly took her breath, and once again she knew at least part of his anger was directed at her.

"What is it?" she asked, more sharply than she had intended.

Travis's face reddened beneath his tan. "Did he talk you into quitting?" he asked tightly.

Was that what he was worried about? "No, of course not."

"Are you still thinking about it?"

Was she? "Not after this little visit," she decided. "Maybe it's my Irish blood, but nothing makes me more determined to succeed than a bunch of men determined to see me fail."

Some of the tension went out of him, but he still held himself stiffly, and when he looked out where Garth Richardson's masculine figure was disappearing into a cloud of dust, his lips tightened. When his gaze came back to hers, his eyes had gone cold. "Does he make a habit of kissing your hand?"

Of all the impertinence! How dare he ask her a question like that? But then, why would he ask unless the gesture had disturbed him? She couldn't believe he was jealous, but the possibility was too delicious to ignore.

"No," she replied with creditable nonchalance, "but then, he doesn't make a habit of proposing to me, either."

"*Proposing?*"

The question came from Cameron, not from Travis, who looked entirely too shocked to reply.

"Do ye mean to say he asked ye to marry him?"

Oh, dear, she'd forgotten Cameron had some aspirations in that area himself. "Well, yes," she admitted, sorry she had mentioned the subject. When would she learn not to surrender to these female impulses?

"And did you accept?" Travis asked as if the question had been dragged from his throat.

"Of course not! He was only being kind." She turned on her heel, intending to go back into the house and put an end to this uncomfortable conversation, but Travis followed her as if he had every right to walk into her home anytime the mood took him. She

151

stopped in the hallway and turned to face him, arms crossed belligerently, determined not to let this go any further. "Was there something else?"

"Kind?" he repeated as if she hadn't spoken. "Where I come from, men don't ask women to marry them out of kindness."

"Oh?" she asked in feigned surprise. "And why *do* they ask?"

His blue gaze drifted over her, touching her breasts, her belly and down, to her toes and back again. To her chagrin, she felt the look as if it had been a caress, as if his smooth, gunfighter's palms were stroking over her naked flesh, and her body stirred in reaction, remembering how his caress had felt and tingling in response. When his eyes met hers again, her face burned with a combination of humiliation and something else entirely, although she didn't allow herself to decide what that something else might be.

"They ask," he said, reminding her of the half-forgotten question, "because they want the woman."

Some distant part of her brain understood that if Garth had looked at her as Travis was looking at her now, she would have had no choice but to accept him. But Travis wasn't asking anything, she reminded herself sternly. "Garth is an old friend," she said, amazed to hear how steady her voice sounded when her heart was trying to beat its way out of her chest. "He thinks I need someone to take care of me."

Travis nodded sagely. "I took him for a fool the minute I saw him."

Sarah didn't know whether to be angry or flattered. From the doorway, Cameron made a choking sound, the same sound he'd made earlier when Travis had

152

quoted him, and both Travis and Sarah looked at him in surprise.

His sunburned face was crimson, although Sarah couldn't tell what emotion had inspired his flush, but his eyes were mild as he looked first at Travis, then at Sarah, then at Travis again. "I'm thinking one of those three sent the raiders last night."

"Maybe all of them did," Travis confirmed.

"Nonsense!" Sarah contradicted. "Ed Smith doesn't have the nerve, and Garth would never—"

"Never say never," Travis cautioned.

"He'd hardly send raiders to kill my sheep at night, then show up on my doorstep proposing marriage the next morning," she pointed out.

"He would if he wanted to convince you that you needed a man to take care of you," Travis pointed out right back.

Sarah stared at him in horror. Hadn't Garth hinted at that very thing? But surely he wouldn't have said it if it had been true! "Not Garth!" she insisted. "He was Philip's best friend!"

"So good a friend, he wants to marry his widow."

How could he twist things so? Sarah wondered in outrage. He made Garth sound so . . . so . . .

"Easy, man," Cameron cautioned, and to her surprise, Sarah saw amusement in his eyes. "Mrs. Hadley'll think you're jealous of the tall Mr. Richardson."

Jealous? What an absurd idea! Travis instantly confirmed her theory.

"I'm just wondering if a man could be greedy enough to kill his best friend, knowing his friend's ranch was about to go under, so he could get it from the widow for next to nothing. Then, when the widow

153

turns it around, he sets his sights on her. Easy pickings."

"I'm not 'easy pickings,'" Sarah protested in outrage, then flushed when she saw the skepticism in Travis's steely eyes. He did, of course, have reason to believe she was vulnerable to male attention, and she had no idea how to convince him the kiss they had shared was an aberration. "Besides," she tried, wishing she didn't sound quite so defensive, "Philip wasn't murdered. How many times do I have to tell you?"

"His death was pretty convenient, though," Travis pointed out. "From what I heard today, there's some folks want your water pretty bad, maybe bad enough to kill for. I reckon everybody knew the shape you was in, and nobody figured a woman alone could make a go of the place, not if her husband couldn't do it."

"But there was no reason for anyone to kill him. Philip hadn't fenced the water. Anyone could use it then," she argued.

"He would've fenced sooner or later, though. You did, first chance you got."

She supposed he was right. Indeed, even those who couldn't afford it had now taken out mortgages to cover the cost of barbed wire so they could secure their property.

"Ye think someone killed him to get the ranch?" Cameron asked.

"I think we shouldn't rule it out. The people who attacked the sheep camp weren't playing games. Whoever wants your ranch is running out of patience."

"*If* someone wants my ranch!" she protested. "You haven't yet convinced me there's a conspiracy."

"Three men just sat in your parlor and offered to

154

buy you out," Travis reminded her grimly. "What more proof do you need?"

"Why would they offer to buy me out if they thought they could scare me off?" she countered.

"They scared you so you'd be more willing to sell," he replied, exasperated. "Look, you don't have to believe it; you just have to admit it's possible and be ready."

Much as she hated to, she had to agree. "Actually, I'd already decided Abel Frank was perfectly capable of attacking my sheep camp, and Ed Smith might have sent some men along to help," she admitted.

"What about Richardson?" Travis prompted.

"Absolutely not," she insisted. "Garth Richardson would never condone such a thing, much less participate in it. He's just one of those men who truly believes a woman isn't suited for running a business. He thinks he's helping by offering to buy me out."

"Oh, yeah, I forgot, he's *kind*, " Travis said sarcastically.

Sarah ignored the remark. "So what do we do?"

Travis and Cameron exchanged a glance. Neither of them looked pleased. "Nothing we *can* do yet," Travis said. "We just wait for whoever it is to show his hand."

Between tending Mr. Sanchez and catching up on her rest, Sarah had time for little else the remainder of the day. She slept fitfully that night, disturbed by the new fears Travis's theories had raised and by her equally unsettling encounters with Travis and Garth. She wondered if perhaps the phase of the moon could account for this sudden explosion of romance—if indeed a furtive kiss and an unwelcome proposal of marriage truly counted as romance.

The next morning was Saturday. Sanchez had recovered sufficiently to sit up and, having lost her patient, Sarah found herself too restless and full of questions to remain at home. Only in town could she find someone with whom she felt comfortable discussing these mysterious developments in her life. When her Mexican workers got ready to go to town, Sarah asked Quinn to hitch up the wagon for her.

Waiting on the porch, she watched Travis striding across the yard toward her. How strange that she could now tell his mood simply from the way he walked. Or perhaps she had no trouble because lately he seemed *always* to be in high dudgeon about something.

Even when he was angry, he moved gracefully, his finely made hands swinging past the gunbelt strapped around his narrow hips. Sarah couldn't help remembering how those hands had held her and caressed her, and how safe she had felt for those few precious moments in his arms.

She knew she was crazy to torture herself with such memories. She should, in fact, have been ashamed of her own behavior, and most of the time she was. By the time he reached the bottom of the porch steps and glared up at her, she had managed to recall that shame.

"Just where to you think you're going?" he demanded.

"Wherever I please," she replied in irritation. "And I'll thank you to remember you are the one who works for me, not the other way around."

156

Her reasoning did not impress him. "Are you taking anybody with you?"

"I didn't think anyone here would want to go visiting with me," she informed him haughtily.

"I mean, are you taking anyone along as a *guard*," he explained with exaggerated patience.

"Why would I need a guard?"

"To *guard* you!" he snapped, his patience ended. "Honest to God, I didn't take you for a fool!"

"You can't think I'd need a guard just to drive to town and back in broad daylight," she said, irritated at being called a fool, especially when she had a sneaking suspicion his caution might be justified.

"I think you need to be careful. Are you taking anybody with you?"

"I was going to ride along with José and the others. The cowboys don't feel welcome in town, so I don't like to ask them." And, she thought, I don't dare ask you, not after what happened between us.

He nodded, giving grudging approval to her plan. "You'll be back before dark."

It wasn't a question. "*Well* before dark," she confirmed, wishing she felt less like a child being cautioned by an overprotective parent. Still, his concern touched her in a perverse way. If he didn't care about her on some level, he wouldn't be so angry at the prospect of her setting out unprotected. But perhaps he was only concerned because she paid his wages.

Sobered by the thought, she wished him good day, stalked down the steps past him, and set out across the yard toward where Quinn had the wagon waiting. She didn't even look back.

The wagonload of Mexicans followed behind as

157

Sarah drove her own wagon and tried not to think about Travis or anything else, but visions of his startling blue eyes haunted her. She found it increasingly difficult to believe she had once fallen into his arms, wept on his shoulder, and surrendered to a passion so strong its mere memory could shorten her breath and set her nerve ends to tingling again. How could a man as hard as he appeared to be have revealed such compassion and such passion? Had it been an aberration for him, too? She reached town without coming to any conclusions.

Leaving her wagon in front of the store, she placed her weekly order for supplies and strolled down the street to the Bigelows' house. Amabel greeted her enthusiastically and took her straight into the parlor, where she served a lavish tea.

When they were sipping at the dark brew and nibbling the cakes Amabel had set out, Amabel said, "You must tell me everything about the attack on your herder. James pretended he didn't know any of the details. He's so worried about protecting me from unpleasantness just now."

Marveling at this predilection some men had for such things, Sarah briefly filled her friend in on all the gory details of poor Mr. Sanchez's ordeal.

"It seems you did well in hiring Mr. Travis," Amabel remarked when Sarah had finished.

"He . . . he has proved valuable," Sarah admitted.

"Do you have any idea who was responsible for the attack?"

"Not really, but I had a visit yesterday from Abel Frank, Ed Smith and Garth Richardson. The three of them offered to buy me out so I could take my sheep someplace else. Travis suspects a connection."

"You can't think . . . I mean, Garth couldn't be involved, could he?" Amabel asked, visibly shocked.

"Certainly not," Sarah confirmed, glad to finally find someone else who shared her views on the matter, "although Abel Frank is just the sort of skunk to send masked men to do his dirty work."

Amabel shuddered delicately. "I admit I've never liked him, but still . . ."

"I know, it's difficult to imagine someone you know doing something so wicked, but I'm afraid it just *has* to be someone we know. Only people I know are interested in getting rid of my sheep."

Amabel's round face puckered in concern. "Have you thought about selling?"

"For a few minutes after they brought Mr. Sanchez in and told me what happened to the sheep, but I quickly came to my senses. I'm not going to let a bunch of sneaking cowards drive me from my home."

"Good girl!" Amabel exclaimed, her good humor restored. "A great many women in this county are looking to you. We don't want you to fail."

Sarah sighed. "If only I could hire them on as riders, then I wouldn't have to worry about my sheep."

Amabel laughed at the notion of female riders. "Sometimes I do think women could run things just as well as men if we didn't have our own responsibilities of home and family," she remarked, reminding Sarah of the topic she had really wanted to discuss with her friend.

"Did I mention that Garth Richardson asked me to marry him?" she asked with creditable nonchalance.

"No!" Amabel exclaimed, her eyes going wide. "Do

159

tell? When? How? What did he say? What did *you* say?"

"He asked me yesterday after the others had left. I turned him down, of course."

"Why 'of course'?" Amabel asked in disapproval.

"Oh, Amabel, he only asked me because he thinks I need a man to look after me, and I expect he feels some sense of loyalty because he was Philip's friend."

Amabel shook her head. "If he felt an obligation to take care of Philip's messes, he'd be courting Elizabeth Williams, but we both know his opinion of poor Lizzie. I can't believe you think he'd propose to you out of *loyalty*, for heaven's sake!"

"Well, he didn't confess his undying love, if that's what you're thinking," Sarah explained, glad to note the admission cost her nothing more than a small prick to her pride. "He said he admires me and is fond of me, and he thinks we would do well together."

"He's probably right, too. Sarah, it's been almost two years. You're still young, and you deserve a little happiness."

Sarah smiled tolerantly. "If I thought we'd be as happy as you and James, I'd marry Garth in a minute, but I don't think I'd be happy with anyone. I'm just not cut out for marriage, Amabel."

"Nonsense! Every woman is cut out for marriage to the right man," Amabel insisted.

"Then I guess I just haven't found the right man yet," Sarah said, trying to dismiss the subject, but to her dismay, she found herself thinking of another man entirely, and a whole new set of questions occurred to her. "How . . . how would I know when I have? Found the right man, I mean?"

160

Amabel smiled slyly. "I suppose if you have to ask, then you definitely haven't found him yet."

Knowing she was entering dangerous territory, still Sarah couldn't resist asking, "Is it . . . does it have something to do with the way he makes you feel?"

"Oh, yes," Amabel assured her, setting down her cup and leaning forward eagerly. "It's sort of a breathless, fluttery feeling here," she explained, laying a dimpled hand on her stomach, but she didn't really need to show Sarah, who knew only too well the feeling she described. "And when he kisses you . . ."

"When he kisses you, what?" Sarah prompted when Amabel hesitated.

Amabel gave an embarrassed laugh. "I just remembered you've been married. You must know all about this."

Sarah felt the heat in her face, but she wasn't going to let a little humiliation leave her in ignorance. "I'm afraid I never felt any of this with Philip, or if I did, I've forgotten."

"Oh, dear," Amabel murmured sympathetically. "I hadn't realized . . ."

"So when he kisses you, what?" Sarah insisted. "Is it exciting and frightening all at once? Like you want him to keep doing it but you want it to stop, too?"

"Well, yes," Amabel admitted with a surprised smile. "Did Garth kiss you?"

"Who?" Sarah asked absently, then recovered herself. "Oh, no, I mean, of course not. I was just . . . just trying to imagine."

"You're doing amazingly well," Amabel said, her lovely eyes speculative, but Sarah was too lost in her own thoughts to care.

She was remembering how she had felt when Travis kissed her, as if her body was on fire and only he could quench the flames, as though she'd been alone her entire life and had finally found the solace for which she'd been searching. But all that was ridiculous, fanciful. She'd been exhausted, mentally and emotionally, that night. Probably if he kissed her today, she'd feel nothing at all, just as she'd always felt nothing on the rare occasions when Philip kissed her.

"And of course," Amabel went on, her eyes bright with conspiracy, "you'll welcome other liberties, too."

"Other liberties?" Sarah echoed warily, recalling the feel of Travis's hand on her breast and how she'd wanted him to go on touching her.

As if Amabel, too, were remembering that scandalous moment of surrender, she pinkened prettily. "Oh, yes. I know some women claim they merely endure their marital duties, but, well, I've always found . . ."

"Found what?" Sarah prompted again. Her cup clattered in its saucer, and she quickly set it down.

Amabel couldn't quite meet her eye, but she said, "I've always found the marriage relationship quite . . . quite pleasant. In fact . . ."

Amabel was too modest to go on, but Sarah needed no further explanation. She knew exactly what her friend would say, that the physical relationship between a man and a woman could be desperately thrilling and overwhelming and even glorious—all the things she'd experienced in those brief moments in Travis's arms.

Why couldn't she have felt that way with Garth, a man who actually wanted to marry her, instead of with a drifter, a man whose name she didn't even know, a man who might be gone from her life tomorrow?

"Oh, dear, I've shocked you," Amabel said; misreading her dismay. "I'm so sorry! I didn't mean—"

"You didn't shock me at all," Sarah assured her. "I was just thinking how sad that I'll never know that kind of happiness with a man."

Amabel smiled knowingly, shaking her head. "Never say never, my dear," she said, echoing Travis's earlier warning with alarming accuracy. "The man you're looking for may be just over the next rise."

Or even at her very own ranch, Sarah thought gloomily.

"And you mustn't stop looking for him, Sarah," Amabel went on. "I know you're doing a wonderful job managing the ranch, but I also know that's not all you want out of your life. A woman's destiny is a home and a family, children of her own . . ."

Amabel's voice trailed off meaningfully, and for an instant Sarah thought of Paul Williams, the son who should have been hers. Her heart ached with longing for the child she had never borne; then she noticed Amabel's beatific smile. Her friend had laid a hand over her own abdomen, and suddenly all Amabel's subtle hints made sense.

"Amabel, are you . . . ? You're going to have a baby?" she asked, her own longing coalescing into the bitterness of envy.

"Yes!" Amabel confirmed, oblivious to her friend's dismay.

Somehow Sarah conjured a smile and forced all the properly congratulatory phrases past her constricted throat. She really was happy for her friend. Amabel

163

and James had been married almost three years, and Sarah knew they had begun to despair of ever having a child. If only she could share Amabel's joy without also feeling her own sense of loss. Even if Sarah did find a man to share her life, she couldn't allow herself to hope for children of her own. Six years of marriage to Philip hadn't given her one, and she well knew Philip hadn't had any trouble at all getting another woman with child.

"So you see," Amabel told her, "I'm especially sensitive to these things right now, and I can't help thinking how much happier you'd be if you'd marry again. Promise me you'll at least consider it."

Since she'd already been doing that very thing, Sarah promised.

As soon as she could politely do so, Sarah took her leave of Amabel. She'd planned a visit to Elizabeth Williams, and now more than ever she felt compelled to go there. Elizabeth was sensitive to different things and wouldn't dream of encouraging Sarah into another relationship with a man.

"Sarah, what a nice surprise," Elizabeth said when she opened the door. As usual, she looked like a picture, every hair in place, her perfect figure elegantly clad in a dress of her own design. "Come right in. Paul! Aunt Sarah is here!"

The boy came charging out of the back room and straight into Sarah's arms. She scooped him into her arms and hugged his sturdy little body fiercely. "My goodness, you're getting so big, I can hardly lift you anymore!"

"I am!" he assured her, wrapping his small arms around her neck to return her hug. Sarah buried her face in the soft curve of his neck. He smelled so sweet, she wanted to weep. "Mama even said I could wear trousers now. See, she made me some," he announced, pushing away from her.

"Very handsome they are, too," Sarah said, reluctantly releasing him and setting him back on his feet to admire them when he started to squirm. "I guess you're not a baby anymore."

"No, ma'am," he assured her solemnly, and she resisted an almost overwhelming urge to take him back into her arms. Aching from the need to hold his little body again, she allowed him to take her hand instead. "Come see what I'm building, Aunt Sarah. If I had some more blocks, I bet I could build us a whole new house!"

He drew her into the back room where he had constructed a lopsided tower over which she oohed and aahed with appropriate enthusiasm. She even knelt down and helped him add to his tower until the unstable structure teetered and fell with a crash.

She cried out in dismay, but Paul laughed uproariously, clapping his hands in delight at the disaster he had caused, and quickly began to construct a new edifice. Sarah watched, fascinated at the way his chubby hands clasped the blocks with such confidence and stacked them one upon another. He was such a beautiful child, and she loved him so very much . . .

"Aunt Sarah, are you crying?" Paul asked with a frown, shocking Sarah back to the present.

"Of course not, silly," she said, with a forced laugh. "The wind was blowing, and I must have gotten some dust in my eye." Hastily, she brushed away the moisture and scrambled to her feet again, knowing she couldn't stay here with Paul another moment and maintain her dignity.

When she turned, she saw Elizabeth standing in the doorway, her lovely face a mask of concern.

"Sarah?"

Sarah managed a smile. "Amabel is expecting," she said, moving past Elizabeth into the other room.

"Oh, my," Elizabeth said, taking Sarah's hand as she passed and squeezing it. "Are you all right?"

Of course Elizabeth understood. Hadn't Sarah known she would? Wasn't that why she'd come here? "I'll be fine in a minute," Sarah assured her, returning her squeeze.

Elizabeth led her to the sofa and seated her. "Stay right there. I'll make us some tea."

Sarah had already had as much tea as she wanted this day, but she waited obediently. By the time Elizabeth came back with her tray, Sarah had her emotions under control again, and she'd decided she didn't want to discuss the subject of babies anymore.

"We had some excitement out at my place the other night," she said.

"I heard about it," Elizabeth said with a delicate shudder. "Oh, Sarah, I'm so sorry. How is that poor man?"

"He'll be fine, thank heaven, although I suppose I should thank my men instead. If they hadn't gotten to him when they did, God only knows what might have happened."

"I heard that new man led them, the one who came here all shot up."

"Yes," Sarah said, trying to remember Travis as he had been then, helpless and unconscious, but failing

166

in the attempt. "He's . . . he's very good with a gun. I was lucky to find him."

"Do you know anything about him? About where he came from or who he is?"

Or how long he plans to stay or where he'll go when he leaves? Sarah thought, but didn't say it. "No, I . . . he doesn't say much about himself, but I can't complain." Well, she could, but what good would it do, and she certainly didn't want Elizabeth to know what a fool she'd made of herself over him.

"You never complain about anything," Elizabeth said, flashing her charming smile, the one Sarah had always envied. If she were as beautiful as Elizabeth, would Philip still have betrayed her? If she were as beautiful as Elizabeth, would Travis Whatever-his-name-was have turned away? "I wish I could be like you, Sarah."

"Like me?" Sarah asked in surprise. "Whatever do you mean?"

"You're so strong and brave and smart." Elizabeth's perfect features twisted in despair, and she turned away. "You'd never let a man ruin your life."

If only Elizabeth knew how close she'd come to doing just that! For the first time Sarah realized she could finally understand what had prompted Elizabeth to go against everything she knew as right just for the luxury of having a man's love. "Nobody's that strong," she said, with more truth than she liked to admit. "Did you ever think I'm virtuous because no man was ever interested in seducing me?" Not even the one who had practically done so.

Now Elizabeth was surprised. "Is that what you really think?"

"It's what I *know*," Sarah insisted grimly.

"Then you're wrong. Oh, Sarah, every man in the county would dearly love to seduce you if only they weren't afraid of you."

Sarah gaped at her. "Where on earth did you get an idea like that?"

Elizabeth shrugged gracefully. "Everyone knows. Ask Amabel. She'll say the same thing. Sarah, you're an attractive woman, and now you're wealthy, too. If you'd give them the slightest encouragement, gentlemen callers would be beating down your door."

Sarah considered this. "Well, I did get a marriage proposal yesterday."

"You did? From whom?" Elizabeth asked, delighted.

"Garth Richardson."

Elizabeth's smile vanished. "Did you . . . did you accept?"

Oh, dear! Sarah thought, recognizing her disappointment. Was poor Elizabeth infatuated with Garth? Sarah couldn't have imagined a more tragic turn of events, knowing, as she did, Garth's contempt for her friend. "No, I didn't accept. I'm not in love with Garth, and he's not in love with me either," she added, thinking she could at least offer Elizabeth a small bit of comfort. "He's just concerned about me, and I think he feels a certain amount of responsibility for . . . for the ranch." She had almost said, "for Philip's widow," and caught herself just in time. There was no use in adding insult to injury.

"Sarah, men don't propose out of a sense of responsibility, not even when they have every reason to feel one," Elizabeth said with authority, and Sarah ac-

168

knowledged her greater experience in the matter. "If you'd take off those widow's weeds and start going out in company again, you'd find out I'm right."

Sarah glanced down at her modest black gown and sighed. She *was* getting awfully tired of wearing black. "Maybe I should at least go into gray. Not to please any men," she quickly added, "but just because I want to."

"For whatever reason," Elizabeth confirmed.

"I don't have anything gray, though," Sarah remembered.

Elizabeth smiled and shook her head. "Now you'll think I'm trying to get you to hire me to make you a new wardrobe."

"Well, you should be," Sarah said, glad for the opportunity to make Elizabeth the subject of the conversation. "You aren't nearly forceful enough about getting yourself extra business. Every woman in this town could do with a new dress or two. You should talk them into it instead of just meekly turning their collars and cuffs for them so they can make do with what they've got."

"As I said, not all of us are as strong and brave as you, Sarah," Elizabeth said wistfully.

"Nonsense," Sarah scolded. "It has nothing to do with courage. You'll be doing them a favor. Now, what would you suggest in the way of a half-mourning gown for me? And," she added, remembering, "can you have it ready in time for the dance next Saturday?"

An hour later, having selected a style and a fabric and having garnered a bittersweet farewell hug from Paul, Sarah left Elizabeth's house and walked back to Main Street, where she found her

169

wagon had been loaded with her supplies.

Checking the position of the sun, she realized the hour was later than she had realized, and knew she should be starting for home soon. Suddenly she realized she had no idea where her Mexican herders were or how to find them. They had probably gone to Spanishtown, the section of town south of the creek where the Mexican population lived.

She could, of course, have gone over there and rousted them out, but she found the prospect daunting. Respectable white women never went to Spanishtown, and even if she were able to find them, she had no guarantee they would be sober. She tried to remember Travis's reasons for insisting that she have a guard, and decided he was being entirely too cautious. What could possibly happen to her between town and home on a public road in broad daylight?

Since she could think of no answer, she climbed up into the wagon seat, released the brake, and slapped the horses into motion.

Chapter Six

"Ye're going to wear out the boards, man," Cameron chided from his seat on the bunkhouse porch.

Indeed, Travis had been pacing for the better part of the afternoon while he waited for Sarah and the other men to return. She'd promised to be home well before dark, but the sun was edging toward the horizon and there was still no trace of her.

"Where in the hell could she be?" he demanded of no one in particular.

"Ye know how women are," Cameron said, not even bothering to hide his amusement. What was wrong with the man? He was the one who claimed to be in love with her. Didn't he even care?

"No, I don't know how women are. I don't know a goddamned thing about them," Travis growled, turning when he reached the edge of the porch so he could stride back down the length of it.

"If ye don't care about the boards, ye ought to at least consider your boots," Cameron advised. "Ye've probably walked farther today then ye have in the last year."

Travis thought he was probably right, but who could

sit still with Sarah out God-knew-where? Who except a damn Scotchman, he amended sourly. "Where in the hell could she be?" he asked again.

"Probably got to visiting with her lady friends and forgot the time, but if ye're so concerned, ye could ride out to meet her. I'm thinking she'll be glad to see your smiling face."

Travis scowled at Cameron's feeble joke, but he didn't seem to notice. The Scot just kept grinning. "Why're you so anxious to send *me* after her? I thought you were in love with the woman."

His grin faded, and Travis recognized the pain he saw clouding the Scot's eyes. "Aye, laddie, that I was, but I know failure when I see it, and I've seen it in the way Mistress Sarah looks at ye."

"Looks at me? What does that have to do with anything?" Travis demanded in disgust.

"Everything, laddie, and if ye don't know of what I speak, ye'd best get on your horse and find Mistress Sarah so ye can see it for yourself. As I said, she'll be mighty glad to see your smiling face."

No, it wasn't true, he told himself. Cameron was just riding him. Sarah didn't have any feelings for him, certainly not *those* kinds of feelings. Sure, she'd let him kiss her once, but only because she hadn't realized what she was doing. Women like Sarah Hadley didn't fall in love with no-account drifters, not when they had men like Garth Richardson slavering after them, damn him to hell.

"She'll be glad to see me, all right," Travis allowed, "but only so she can tear a strip off me for something. Come on, let's go."

Travis hopped off the porch and started for the corral. He'd gone several steps before he realized Cameron hadn't followed. Turning back, he saw the Scot's stocky figure still planted firmly in the chair. "I wouldn't think of intruding," he said cheerfully. "Give the missus my regards, will ye?"

"You're a coward, Cameron," he tried, "afraid she'll be mad because we went to meet her."

"Aye, that I am," he agreed, without the slightest indication he had taken offense. "In fact, I'm hoping she'll be thoroughly disgusted with ye, but I'm prepared to be disappointed. Much as Mistress Sarah pretends otherwise, I'm thinking she likes being fussed over."

"I'll fuss over her," Travis grumbled, setting out for the corral again. Damn her, if she said one word about him going out to meet her, he'd . . . he'd . . . Well, he'd think of something, and if she'd gotten herself into any kind of trouble, so help him, he'd murder her with his own hands.

The ride did him good. In fact, Travis realized he should've set out earlier and saved himself the aggravation of waiting. Feeling calmer with each mile that fell behind him, he kept scanning the road ahead for the telltale dust of approaching wagons. At least he'd insisted she have some company for this trip, he told himself. Not that he had much confidence in José and his bunch if it came to a fight, but nobody'd approach her as long as they were with her.

Instinctively, he watched the road for tracks, although trying to pick out Sarah's wagon from among the myriad marks of other travelers was impossible.

173

Besides, he told himself, if he hadn't encountered her, he'd hardly see her tracks, because she wouldn't have passed yet.

But if he hadn't been watching, he might have missed the wagon altogether.

The first thing he noticed were the wagon tracks leaving the road. How strange, he thought, fighting a sense of foreboding. Probably somebody wanting to take advantage of the shade from a small stand of cottonwoods nearby for a little nap, he told himself, squinting to make out the wagon concealed among the drooping branches. Odd, he couldn't see a horse.

The hairs on the back of his neck prickled. He drew his gun and kicked his horse into a slow walk. "Hello, the wagon," he called, watching for any sign of movement, but nothing stirred except the relentless Texas breeze.

Even before he reached it, he knew what he would find: Sarah's wagon, all her supplies neatly packed in the back, untouched, and Sarah's purse lying on the floor in front of the seat.

But Sarah was gone.

Terror twisted his stomach. "Sarah!" he shouted, willing her to appear, to emerge from some hiding spot where she'd been lurking to torment him. But only silence greeted his call.

His heart turned to stone, and the sweat chilled on his body. *Sarah!* his mind cried, but he fought the desperate urge to panic, to race off madly, blindly. No, if he were to find her, he'd have to be careful. He'd have to take his time, no matter how the rage boiled inside of him, no matter how the visions of her captivity tormented him.

Who had her and why, and what would they do to her?

But he couldn't let himself think of that, not now, not yet. Closing his eyes, he drew a calming breath and forced himself to swing down from his saddle. Walking carefully so he wouldn't disturb the sign, he studied the ground for a clue as to what had become of her.

Sarah awoke slowly, aware of the pounding in her head, the roiling nausea in her stomach, and her aching body jouncing painfully. Something was wrong, so very wrong. This must be a nightmare, except that when she opened her eyes things only got worse.

Oh, God, she groaned, or would have if she hadn't been gagged. The ground sped by just a few feet below her face, and she slammed her eyes shut against the sight. What on earth was wrong? She seemed to be upside down, slung over a horse, over some man's lap, her head throbbing . . . And then she remembered.

She'd been riding home in her wagon when she'd come across a lone rider, a stranger. He'd been walking his horse as if the animal had gone lame, so naturally she'd stopped to see if she could help.

Instantly, she'd regretted stopping. The man looked totally unsavory, but he'd been polite enough, smiling and calling her "ma'am." He'd even taken off his hat when he approached the wagon to inquire whether she knew of any jobs for which he might apply.

She'd opened her mouth to reply when he suddenly reached up, grabbed her arms and yanked her from the seat. In that split second she'd known abject terror and the certainty that she would be raped; then his fist had

175

connected with her jaw and everything went black.

She tried to remember. What had happened then? But she knew nothing from that instant until now. Of one thing she was certain: she hadn't been raped, because that was practically the only part of her anatomy that didn't ache. Apparently he'd simply slung her over his horse, and they were going somewhere, but where and why? If he'd wanted to attack her, he could have done so by now. Why would he carry her off?

Her head hurt too much to figure it all out, and she swallowed around the gag, trying to keep from vomiting as another wave of nausea washed over her. Instinctively, she tried to pry the gag from her mouth and found her hands were tied. Still, she fumbled with the gag until something slammed into her back, driving the air from her lungs and sending excruciating pain reverberating through her.

"Hold still," her captor warned, "or I'll hit you again, and this time I won't be so gentle."

Gentle? She knew a hysterical urge to laugh in spite of her pain, but she swallowed it along with a brand-new wave of nausea. Dear God, how long could she bear this?

But bear it she did, long after she thought her head would burst, long after she prayed for death to end her agony, until at last he stopped his horse, swung down from the saddle and dragged her to the ground.

Now, she thought, now it will come; but when she opened her eyes, her captor was leading the horse away. She glanced around and was astonished to see they were at one of her deserted line shacks. In the days before fencing, cowboys would be stationed at these outposts and would spend their days riding the boundary

176

lines of the ranch, driving back stray cattle from both sides and doing their best to keep everyone's cattle on their own property. Fences now did the job much more efficiently, so "riding the line" was no longer a necessary occupation.

Her captor was putting his horse into the lean-to shed attached to the cabin. The instant he disappeared from sight, Sarah rolled over on her side and pushed herself up on one elbow so she could better evaluate her situation. When she tried to move her legs, she discovered he'd tied her feet, too, so running was out of the question even if she could have convinced her numb limbs to function.

Her whole body seemed reluctant to respond to her commands, and she wondered if this were some lingering result of the blow she had taken or simply a consequence of having been slung over a horse for heaven only knew how long. As near as she could tell, she and her captor were alone, but since she was unarmed and presently helpless, she could do nothing except think. And plan. And pray.

Travis had been right, she recalled with a pang; she really had needed a guard. She only hoped she would have the opportunity of telling him so quite soon. Sarah checked the position of the sun. There were at least two hours until darkness set in. Would Travis begin to worry before then? Would Cameron? Would the Mexican herders notice her abandoned wagon on their way home? Would *somebody* be coming after her?

The answer, she thought with despair, was no. No one would miss her for hours. If she were to escape, she would have to depend on herself. She tensed, hearing her captor approaching again.

"Well, now, honey, let's get you inside," he said, squatting down beside her. She could smell the now-familiar odor of his unwashed body, and almost gagged again.

Sarah glared at him, furious at his presumption at calling her "honey," but he ignored her. She studied his face, trying to remember whether she'd ever seen him before. His pockmarked skin and beady brown eyes rang no bells, however, nor did his crooked nose or the leering smile that revealed yellowed, scraggly teeth. His wiry body was stronger than it looked, she realized as he hauled her to her feet. Fighting him would be a waste of time and energy. Better to conserve her strength for a time when she might really need it.

"Come on," he said, prodding her forward and cursing when she stumbled and almost fell. Apparently, he'd forgotten her feet were tied, and of course she couldn't remind him because of her gag. He let her slump to the ground, heedless of the jarring she received, but she bit back her groan and waited in stoic silence while he untied the ropes binding her legs.

The instant he released them, the life flowed back into her feet like a thousand shards of glass. This time she could not repress her moan, but he ignored her and hauled her up again. Her full weight on her feet jarred an agonized cry from her throat, but he only grinned and shoved her toward the cabin.

When she would have lurched forward on her face, he grabbed her arm, nearly wrenching it from the socket, and half-dragged, half-carried her the rest of the way. By then she could feel her feet as more than two lumps of agony, but when she stumbled into the dimness of the cabin, she gratefully collapsed into one of the two rickety chairs sitting by the makeshift table in the center of the room.

Sarah glanced around, getting her bearings. She hadn't been inside one of these shacks in years, but they were all the same. A single, sparsely furnished room with a bunk built into one end, a table and chairs in the middle, a crude hearth on the wall opposite the door, and a few boxes nailed to the fourth wall to serve as cabinets.

In days past, the cabinets would have held a supply of canned goods. Now they stood empty. To her surprise, however, someone had left a sack on the table. From the looks of it, it hadn't been there long, either. Supplies prepared ahead of time for her abduction? Suddenly she realized something else about the cabin: it should have been dusty from long disuse. Instead, it was clean and freshly swept, with not a cobweb in sight. Even the bunk had been made up. This abduction had been very carefully planned.

Her captor took the other chair and grinned at her. Frustrated beyond endurance, she reached up and jerked the gag out of her mouth. Fully expecting her companion to protest, she steeled herself for a blow. To her surprise, he made no move to stop her, and just continued to stare at her benignly as she massaged her jaw back into working order.

"Who . . . who are you?" she asked when she could speak again.

"You can call me Zeke."

She debated her next question, since she wasn't really certain she wanted to hear his answer to "What are you going to do with me?" She settled for, "If you're after a ransom, I'm a wealthy woman. I'll pay whatever

179

you want if you'll let me go unharmed."

"A real tempting offer, honey, but I already been paid to take you, and my boss wouldn't like it if I took money to let you go."

"Your boss?" she echoed in surprise. "You mean someone hired you to kidnap me? Why?"

"That's the trouble with women, they always want to know things that ain't none of their business," he remarked cheerfully. "You hungry? I sure am. Let's see what the boss left for us."

He looked into the bag and frowned. "Wouldn't you know? Jerky and cold biscuits. Not even any coffee, but then, he did say not to make a fire, now didn't he? You want a biscuit?"

He held out a gray lump, and Sarah's stomach lurched in protest. She shook her head and looked quickly away, praying she wouldn't humiliate herself by throwing up.

"Suit yourself," he remarked, still maddeningly cheerful, and proceeded to stuff the biscuit into his own mouth. He fished two tin cups out of the sack and headed toward the door.

"If you're going for water, I'd like some," she called after him.

He flashed his evil grin over his shoulder. "Sure. Just be sure you don't go away now."

Sarah glared at his disappearing back and fumed at her own helplessness. She might use this opportunity to make a run for the horse, but he'd most certainly unsaddled it, and how could she hope to climb onto a reluctant, unsaddled animal with her hands tied and her arms and legs still rubbery from her ordeal? He'd be on her in a trice, and remembering the "gentle" thump

180

he'd given her earlier simply for trying to get her gag loose, Sarah didn't relish the prospect of getting caught.

No, if she intended to get away, she would have to wait for a better opportunity. In the meantime, she would try to find out as much from her captor as she could.

Zeke returned in a few minutes with two cups of water which he'd filled from the pump outside. He set one on the table in front of Sarah, who grasped it awkwardly with her bound hands and lifted it to her lips. She drank thirstily in an attempt to wash away the taste of the gag and of her own fear. When the cup was empty, she set it down again.

In the quiet stillness of the cabin, her headache was beginning to ease and her stomach had begun to settle. In a few minutes she would be fine except for her bound hands. Maybe if she could get on her captor's good side, he would untie her.

"Where are you from, Zeke?" she asked.

"Around," he replied, gnawing on a piece of jerky. His beady eyes glittered knowingly, as if she didn't fool him for a moment.

"I don't think I've ever seen you before. You must be new around these parts."

"I've been here long enough to know all about you, little lady. You're the one brought in them damn woolybacks to stink up the countryside." He grinned again, showing his ugly teeth, and he straddled the other chair. "Know what I like? I like to take a wagon spoke and bust their brains out. Makes a popping noise, you know? Then them brains come pouring out and the little bastards scream something fierce."

181

Sarah stared at him in mute horror. So much for getting on his good side. "Is that . . . is that what you plan to do with me?" she heard herself asking.

"Hell, no," he chuckled as if she'd made a joke. "That'd be a waste of good woman, now wouldn't it? And God knows, there ain't near enough women in this world as it is."

He grinned again, taking her in from head to toe with his beady gaze. Sarah felt an urge to cover herself and a definite urge to shudder in disgust. If he put his hands on her, what on earth would she do?

"My boss feels the same way," he added. "In fact, he's planning to put you to good use when he gets here."

Travis glanced up to check the position of the sun. Less than an hour of daylight left. What drove him crazy was not knowing how long Sarah had been a captive and imagining all the things that could have happened to her. Was she still alive? And if she were, would she ever be the same woman again? He'd seen what happened to women who were raped in Indian attacks. Sometimes their minds just gave out. Would Sarah be strong enough to survive?

In his more rational moments, he told himself she hadn't been abducted for anything so ordinary as rape. No, whoever had Sarah had something far more important in mind than her delectable body. Ransom? He could hardly credit it, but then, why not? Rumor said she was a wealthy woman. If he'd thought God would listen, he would've prayed that it was ransom they wanted.

Travis got down and studied the prints in the fading

light. The bastard hadn't even bothered to hide his trail. Travis had easily read the sign of what had happened. Whatever else he did, this bastard had put his hands on Sarah and knocked her to the ground. If he'd done nothing else, that was reason enough for Travis to want to kill him.

He just hoped to God he had the opportunity before it was too late for Sarah.

Through the open door Sarah could see the sun had turned to a red ball and was about to disappear behind the horizon. After revealing his boss's plans for her, Zeke had fallen silent, ignoring her questions as if afraid he'd already revealed too much. Indeed, Sarah wasn't sure she even wanted to know what was going to happen, particularly when she saw the way Zeke kept leering at her.

"When is this boss of yours going to show up?" she asked, when she could stand the silence no longer.

Zeke stared at her thoughtfully for a long moment, his feral eyes narrowed. "I don't expect him 'til about midnight. He's got some fun planned for you."

"Fun?" Sarah echoed, her blood cold in her veins.

Zeke grinned again. "Yeah, fun. You know, man-woman stuff. You're a widow. You know what I mean."

"Why?" Sarah demanded, horrified.

The question surprised Zeke. "I reckon because he likes it." His grin turned to a leer, and he rubbed his crotch suggestively. "Most men do, you know."

Repulsed, Sarah looked away, feeling the heat of humiliation in her face. Still, she tried to make sense of it. Why would a man pay to have her kidnapped just so he could rape her himself? He could have paid a whore and accomplished the same thing more cheaply and far less dangerously. But even if she couldn't figure it out, she had to try to stop it.

"Aren't you worried, Zeke?" Sarah tried, swallowing the fear clogging her throat. "I mean, if anyone finds out you're the one who kidnapped me, they'll string you up."

"How'll they find out?" Zeke asked confidently.

Sarah certainly didn't want to remind him that she could identify him. Zeke didn't seem like the kind of man to hesitate about murdering her if he thought it was in his best interest to do so. "The men who work for me won't rest until they find the man who did it," she said, knowing instinctively that it was true.

Zeke clicked his tongue and shook his head in mock dismay. "You got the wrong idea here, lady. You think folks'll be mad about this, but you're wrong. Fact is, they'll be mighty pleased to find out the Widow Hadley's getting herself hitched again."

"Hitched?" Sarah couldn't have heard him right.

"That's right," Zeke confirmed, obviously pleased with himself. "See, my boss is going to pay you a little visit tonight. Now he didn't tell me 'xactly what he's got in mind, but I figure he'll start by stripping you down and tying you to the bed so's you can't object to nothing. Then he'll . . ."

Sarah tried not to listen as he poured out his filth, but the horror of it chilled her, terrified her. How could anyone even *think* of such things? How could any woman endure them? She wanted to scream and cry and run and hide, but she couldn't even cover her ears. She settled for pressing her bound hands to her face.

184

"Now don't take on so," Zeke advised when he had savored her revulsion for a minute or two. "See, that's only half the plan. Once he's done with you, he figures you'll be too ashamed to tell anybody what happened and you'll be grateful to marry him."

"Marry?" Sarah echoed, stunned.

"Oh, yeah," Zeke assured her. "You told me yourself you're a wealthy woman. He wants your land and your money and even those stinking woolybacks, I reckon, 'cause he can sell 'em and put the money back into cattle." Zeke grinned again, and the sight filled Sarah with horror. "Marrying a woman is the easiest way to get what she's got, or at least that's what the boss says. Legalized stealing was what he called it. 'Course you also get a free whore who can't say no." Zeke's cackle made her shudder.

Who could have planned this? Who did she know who was even capable of thinking of such evil? Before she could decide, she noticed Zeke had wandered over to the bunk and was eying it speculatively.

"All that talk's got me to thinking. We got a long wait until the boss gets here. Hours," he muttered, absently rubbing his crotch again.

Panic welled in her, hot and sour. "Your boss won't want damaged goods," she informed him, hoping he couldn't hear the high note of hysteria in her voice.

"Aw, it ain't like you're a virgin or nothing," he reminded her. "What's one more slice off a loaf already's been cut, I always say. He won't know the difference."

"I'll know! I'll tell him," she tried, glancing toward the door and wondering at her chances for escape now that she was rested.

But she had no time to plan. As if reading her

185

thoughts, Zeke strode back to her and hauled her out of the chair. "I been wondering what you look like under all them clothes, missy. I'll bet you ain't half so stuck-up when you're buck-naked with your legs spread."

"No!" she screamed, struggling frantically, pushing against his chest, but he pulled her closer until the bulge in his crotch pressed against her. He gyrated obscenely, his fetid breath hot in her face, gagging her.

"You'll like it, honey. They all like it," he said hoarsely, one hand cupping her buttocks through the thickness of her skirts.

With a burst of superhuman strength, she simultaneously shoved against his chest and brought her knee up between his legs. His howl of agony told her she had hit her mark, and the next instant she was free, racing for the door.

In another second she was outside. She wasted a precious moment deciding whether or not to go for the horse, then knew she must if she were to have any hope of escaping. The animal was tied in the lean-to. Fortunately, Zeke had left his bridle on. She grabbed the reins and clumsily unlooped them with her bound hands and drew the now-frightened animal out of the lean-to. He balked, but Sarah fought him.

"You bitch!" Zeke shouted from the doorway of the cabin. He stood hunched over, holding his injured crotch, but the expression of pure hatred on his face gave Sarah a new burst of strength. She grasped the horse's mane and jumped, throwing her leg up, but the animal snorted and shied, sidestepping. The mane jerked from her hands, and she fell in a heap.

Too frightened to feel pain, she scrambled to her feet

186

again, not daring to look back, but just as she lunged toward the horse again, something caught her hair and jerked her backward.

She screamed in terror, but Zeke's arm clamped around her throat, cutting off her wind and her scream.

"You sneaking little hellcat. Now you're going to be sorry. I'm gonna wallow you right here on the ground like the bitch you are, and then I'm gonna stake you out naked so when the boss comes, he'll find you ready, your ass in the dirt and your—"

"Let her go!"

Sarah heard the command faintly, as if it came from the end of a long, dark tunnel, a tunnel that was closing in on her, but she recognized the voice, or thought she did.

Zeke jerked in surprise, relaxing his grip long enough for Sarah to draw one desperate breath before he dragged her around until she was between him and the voice. He fumbled for his gun and held it out in front of them.

Through the tunnel Sarah could see Travis calmly sitting his horse, his own gun drawn and pointed steadily at them. *Shoot him!* she wanted to cry, but she couldn't speak, couldn't even breathe, and the tunnel was getting darker by the second.

Something exploded in her face, and powder smoke billowed around them. Zeke's gun! He'd shot Travis! Blinking through the smoke, she could no longer see him anywhere. Dear heaven, was he dead? Then they were moving, she and Zeke, his arm still around her throat, his gun still out in front of them. "Come on, bitch," he grunted into her ear as she stumbled back-

187

ward, clawing at his arm, trying frantically to pull it away.

"Fall down, Sarah!" Travis called.

He's alive! she thought even before his command registered. Fall down? How could she when Zeke's arm was around her throat? Then she realized he couldn't hold her if she simply collapsed, but before she could consciously do so, her legs buckled of their own accord.

"God damn it!" Zeke shouted, struggling to hold her up one-handed, but she slipped out of his grasp and fell to the ground, where she instinctively curled into a ball. He'd kill her, she knew it, and when the second explosion roared, she jerked, holding her breath against the burning pain.

But it never came. Instead, Zeke screamed in anguish and began to run. Sarah covered her head, gasping for the precious air and praying Travis wouldn't be hurt. Zeke's horse whinnied in protest and he cursed again; then she heard the sound of running hooves.

Booted feet pounded up to her, and she instinctively braced herself again.

"Sarah, are you all right?"

Travis!

"Yes," she croaked as he pulled her hands away from her head, cursing when he found them tied.

"Thank God. Was he alone?" He pulled a knife from his boot and swiftly slit her bonds.

She gasped with pain and relief as the blood surged back into her fingers. "Yes, but . . . someone else . . . He'd been hired by someone else to kidnap me."

"Who?" With surprising gentleness, he massaged the life back into her hands.

"I don't know," Sarah said, wondering how he could

188

look so angry and touch her so tenderly.

"I'm going after him, then, so we can find out. Will you be all right?"

"Yes . . . yes, get him," she gasped.

For one second his massage stopped and the fire in his eyes flickered out. She saw something else there, something as soft and gentle as his touch, but only for a second, not long enough for her to identify the emotion. Then the anger returned and he released her hands.

"I don't think I'll be gone long. He won't get far with a slug in him."

She nodded, remembering Zeke's scream after the second explosion. "Don't worry . . . about me. I'm fine," she lied, hoping he wouldn't notice how she quaked from head to foot.

"Stay put," he said, giving her arm an awkward pat, and then he was gone.

Sarah hugged herself when she heard his horse galloping away. He'd come for her, she thought. He hadn't waited until dark. He must have gone out looking even before anyone suspected she was missing, the presumptuous, arrogant, stubborn . . .

In spite of everything, Sarah smiled, and she felt a pervading warmth steal through her, touching places that had been cold for such a long time. *Travis had come after her.* No matter what he tried to pretend, no matter how he tried to dismiss the kiss they had shared, he cared about her. Not even Cameron, who fancied himself in love with her, had come, but Travis had. He'd been unable to stay away.

Sarah couldn't remember how she'd felt when she'd imagined herself in love with Philip Hadley, but she knew it couldn't have been anything like what she felt now for Travis. The trembling of terror gradually gave way to a completely different kind of trembling as Sarah began to understand the magnitude of her emotions. Travis Whatever-his-name-was might not be anyone's idea of the ideal man, but Sarah had somehow managed to fall in love with him.

The knowledge should have terrified her, but for some inexplicable reason, it brought her a peace and a confidence she'd never known before. She knew it was foolish. The man was a virtual stranger, and heaven only knew what he'd done before she met him. She had no guarantee he wouldn't walk out of her life tomorrow, and part of her insisted she should hope he would. And what would poor Amabel say? Sarah couldn't imagine a man less suited to the quiet domesticity of home and hearth that Amabel had prescribed for her. Sarah would do better to try to housebreak a mountain lion.

Still, in spite of all this—or perhaps because of it—Sarah knew she loved him. The danger of heartbreak only added to the thrill of it, and Sarah hugged herself tighter, as if she could somehow keep him closer by doing so.

How long she lay there, she never knew, but gradually she became aware of her cramped position and the folly of lying in the dirt. Slowly, stiffly, she unfolded her body and rose to her feet. Her black dress was dusty, her hair hanging down her back. She didn't want Travis to see her like this, as if she had been a helpless victim. Zeke might have threatened her with unspeakable things, but he hadn't done more than smack her a time or two. She wasn't cowed and she wasn't humiliated and she certainly didn't want anyone to think so.

Forcing her hands to steadiness, she brushed away as much of the dirt as she could, then moved carefully back into the shack. The sun had set, and evening cast eerie shadows into the corners of the cabin. Sarah would have liked a fire, but the sack of supplies held no matches. She rubbed her hands together, feeling much colder than she should have on such a warm night. What she really wanted, she thought wryly, was to feel Travis's arms around her and to know the heat of his kiss.

The thought brought a smile to her lips. She must be in shock after her fright, to be imagining such fanciful things.

Sarah sank wearily into the chair she'd been sitting in for the past few hours, and absently began to pull the remaining pins from her hair and finger-comb the tangles from it. She'd probably look like a witch with her hair hanging loose, but there was no remedy for it. When she'd done what she could with her hair, she let her hands fall idly into her lap and stared blankly out the door for a long time, straining to hear the sounds of Travis's return.

At first she tried to imagine how he would greet her. Would he sweep her into his arms and seal their love with a kiss? Unlikely, she judged, since he had no idea she loved him. No, he would probably return just as angry as he'd been when he left, ready to berate her for going off alone after he'd warned her not to.

In fact, he'd probably return with a wounded Zeke, who might or might not be ready to confess who had hired him, she thought with a start. The thought of facing Zeke again, even a captive Zeke, unnerved her.

But what if Travis didn't catch up with him? What if

Zeke circled back, possibly in search of the bag of supplies to aid him in his escape? The prospect of encountering a wounded, vengeful Zeke brought her to her feet. And what if Zeke had been mistaken about when his boss would come for her? What on earth was she doing sitting here like a lovesick fool when her murderer might even now be stalking the cabin?

Travis had told her to stay put, but he'd never intended for her to put herself in danger. Imbued with new energy, Sarah hurried out of the cabin. Once outside, she studied the treeless terrain in dismay. She couldn't go far, not if she expected Travis to find her again, but where on earth could she hide so Zeke or her other mysterious enemy couldn't find her?

In the distance she could hear the sound of a rider approaching.

Travis raced back to the cabin, cursing the man who lay dead somewhere behind him. Why in the hell couldn't he have surrendered like any reasonable human being, instead of pulling his gun and forcing Travis to kill him?

Of course, any man who'd kidnap a woman didn't deserve to live, so Travis couldn't feel too much regret over the act, especially when he remembered the threats he'd overheard the bastard making to Sarah. Travis and Cameron would have seen him hanging from the nearest tree before too long anyways. Maybe the son of a bitch had guessed as much, and had decided to go out like a man instead. Whatever his reasoning, he now lay dead without having revealed the name of the man who'd hired him, may he rot in hell.

The line shack was a darker shadow in the darkening night. It looked deserted and empty and somehow forbidding. Sarah was nowhere in sight. Shaking off his feeling of foreboding, Travis reined in and leaped from his saddle, leaving his horse ground hitched. The cabin door stood open, and he strode inside, expecting to find her waiting. Instead, the empty silence mocked him. He glanced around again, thinking his eyes must be playing tricks on him. Where could she have gone? Surely she wouldn't have set out for home on foot, and he'd told her to stay put, that he'd be right back. Unless . . .

Dear God, she'd said the bastard he'd killed was only a hireling. What if his boss had come for her? The thought filled Travis with a nameless terror, a despair so deep he could almost feel himself falling. *No!* his mind cried, and his voice shouted, "Sarah!"

In her hiding place in the lean-to, Sarah went weak with relief. *Travis had come for her!* She wanted to laugh and cry at the same time. How could she ever have doubted him? Wasn't he the most stubborn man alive? If he made her a promise, he'd keep it or die trying. What she hadn't let herself admit was the possibility that he might have died trying. She shivered.

"Sarah!" came the cry again, this time almost frantic, and Sarah realized he must think she'd been taken again. Pushing up out of her hiding place, she allowed herself a small smile at the desperation in his voice, almost as if the prospect of losing her was as wrenching to him as the prospect of losing him was to her.

"Here; I'm here!" she called back, joy sluicing through her as she groped her way out of the lean-to into the cool night air. Then he was there, strong and solid, his arms around her, crushing her to him as if he would never let her go.

She clung to him, reveling in the solid strength of his back and shoulders, inhaling his blessedly familiar scent.

"Did he . . . did he hurt you?" His voice was hoarse, his breath warm against her ear.

"No," she breathed. "No, I'm fine, really."

His arms tightened for a second, as if in gratitude, and she felt the hot sting of tears.

"Where . . . where is he?" she asked.

"Dead." His voice held no inflection, and Sarah found she had no desire to hear the details so long as she knew Travis was safe.

Travis sighed unsteadily. "God, you're shaking like a leaf," he said, and to her surprise, she realized it was true. "Come on; I'll get you inside and get a fire going."

She nodded against his shoulder, but still he held her for another second, as if as loath to release her as she was to be released. At last his arms relaxed, but to her relief he didn't let her go completely. With his arm around her waist, he led her back to the cabin and seated her in the chair she was beginning to think of as hers.

When his hands left her completely, she felt suddenly alone, and shivered in the chill. He was no more than a shadow in the darkness. "I'll make a fire," he said, although he made no move to do so, but stood hovering over her as if afraid to leave her side.

"I'm all right," she assured him again, glad to hear her voice sounded steadier.

"God, you scared me to death," he said sharply. "Where in the hell were you?"

"Hiding. I . . . I couldn't be sure it was you." She shivered again at the memory, and the motion seemed to galvanize him into action.

He strode to the hearth and quickly struck a match. The cabin's last occupant had followed Western custom and laid a fire for those who came after him. The ancient tinder caught instantly, and within seconds a cheerful flame sent the shadows scurrying to the far corners of the room.

Sarah watched Travis as he took a small log from the pile beside the hearth and laid it carefully across the flickering flame. The firelight's glow softened his features until Sarah could almost believe he had a gentle side, but when he turned back to face her, she saw she was mistaken.

"What happened to José and the rest of them?" he asked, but the accusing tone of his voice told her he already suspected.

"I . . . They . . . I couldn't find them when I was ready to come home, so . . ." She shrugged, hating the way he always managed to put her in the wrong.

"Didn't I tell you not to travel alone?" he demanded, rising to his feet. The firelight sent his shadow looming out over her, but she refused to be intimidated.

"How was I supposed to know someone would be waiting on the roadside to kidnap me?" she asked indignantly.

"You were supposed to show good sense," he snapped, then stiffened, as if he had just realized he shouldn't berate a female who had just gone through an ordeal. "All right," he said more calmly, moving to the other chair and straddling it. "Tell me exactly what happened."

195

Sarah drew a deep breath and folded her still-unsteady hands in her lap. "I was about halfway home when . . . when I encountered a man. He was walking his horse. I assumed the animal had gone lame, so naturally, I stopped."

"Naturally," Travis said without the slightest trace of sympathy.

She ignored him. "He said his horse had picked up a stone and had a sore foot. I didn't offer him a ride," she informed him. "I told him I'd send one of my men back for him; then he started asking me if I knew where he could get work. He wasn't the least bit threatening," she added defensively.

Travis's eyes looked indigo in the dimness, but were no less intense. "Not until he dragged you out of the wagon and threw you on the ground," Travis remarked through gritted teeth.

"How did you know?" she asked in surprise.

"I read the sign. Then what did he do?"

"He . . . he hit me," she admitted, unconsciously touching her jaw where his fist had landed, and Travis's entire body went rigid. "He knocked me out, and when I woke up, I was slung across his horse, bound and gagged. He brought me here."

"He was alone all this time?" Travis asked tightly.

"Yes, but he kept referring to his 'boss,' the man who'd hired him to kidnap me."

"What did he say about him?"

Sarah winced, wondering how she could explain without totally humiliating herself. "Nothing that would help us identify him, if that's what you're thinking. Zeke—that was the man who kidnapped me—he said 'the boss' would be coming here around midnight

196

tonight to . . . to . . ." She looked away, unable to meet his eye.

"To what, Sarah?" Travis insisted.

She had to force the words past her constricted throat. "He . . . he thought if he dishonored me, I'd have to marry him. Then he would have possession of my ranch."

Travis swore and slammed his hands down on the back of the chair, startling her. "Now do you see what I meant when I said you're easy pickings?"

"I still wouldn't have married him!" she informed him, indignant again.

"You don't know what you would've done when he got through with you," Travis snarled, his blue eyes terrible. "You might've been *glad* for him to put you in a *brothel!*"

"How dare you?" she demanded, jumping to her feet, arms akimbo.

"*Somebody* better dare to tell you the truth, lady," he exclaimed, flinging his own chair out of the way as he rose to face her. "You're a woman, for God's sake. You've got no protection at all!"

"Oh, you're wrong there!" she cried triumphantly. "I've got a foreman who follows me around like a hound on the scent!"

He flinched as if she'd struck him, but he recovered instantly. "Somebody has to follow you around, since you don't have any more sense than a one-eyed mule!"

"But why does it have to be *you?*" she demanded, poking him in the chest with her forefinger.

He grabbed her hand and glared at her. They stood so close she could see the tiny golden hairs of his beard and the way his nostrils flared, as if he really were

197

catching her scent. His eyes were fierce, and danger radiated from him like an aura, but Sarah wasn't afraid.

Travis wanted to shake her. Didn't she know how close she'd come to disaster tonight? Didn't she know what a man could do once he had her in his power? But the clear green eyes staring back at him held no trace of knowledge, no hint of the terror she must have felt.

She looked like a wicked angel, with the firelight gilding her alabaster skin and dancing off her lush, ebony hair. God, it was even more beautiful than he had imagined, streaming down her back like a black silk cape. He could still remember how it had felt against his hands when he'd held her just moments ago, how *she* had felt, all soft and vulnerable pressed up against him. His body quickened at the thought, and he silently cursed his own weakness.

He suddenly realized he still held her hand in a bone-crushing grip. He tried to let her go, but she wouldn't let him. Her fingers tangled with his, holding his palm against the softness of hers.

"Why did you come after me?" she asked, her voice no more than a whisper of sound in the silence of the cabin. Her gaze locked with his, her eyes asking other questions, questions he didn't dare to answer.

"You were late," he answered thickly, willing himself to breathe against the tightness in his chest.

"No, I wasn't," she insisted, her fingers squeezing his, "not late enough for you to be worried. Why, Travis? Couldn't you wait to see me again?"

She knew, he realized with alarm. She knew how he felt about her, and she was mocking him. Rage swelled in his chest, choking him. *"Couldn't wait to see you again?"*

he mocked in return. "Lady, you *pay* me to watch over you. I was just doing my job."

She reared back, stung, and he instantly regretted his harshness. He'd only meant to protect himself, not hurt *her*, but to his horror he saw tears in her eyes.

"Sarah, I . . ." he tried, but she wrenched her hand from his grasp and backed away, her beautiful face twisted in anguish. "Look, I didn't mean . . ." As usual, he couldn't find the proper words.

She encountered the bunk and sat down abruptly, her eyes wide and glittering with unshed tears and silent accusations.

Sarah stared up at him through the red haze of pain, aware his image had blurred but unwilling to blink lest she dislodge a tear and send it rolling down her face. What a fool she was! How could she have imagined a man like this capable of tender feelings, of *love?* She must be destined always to give her heart to the wrong man.

Despair washed over her, and she thought of the emptiness of her life, and the loneliness, the years past and the years ahead with no one to share her happiness or her pain, no one to care whether she lived or died except the men she paid to care.

The tears scalded her eyes, flooding them until Travis disappeared before the burning wave. Humiliated, she covered her face with both hands. She wanted to fight, to resist, but she had no strength left, no choice but to let despair claim her. She choked on a sob.

"Oh, God, Sarah, don't cry!" Vaguely, she heard the pleading in his voice, but it only made her cry harder.

Mortified, she hunched her shoulders, wishing she could hide herself from him. She would gladly have died rather than let him witness her disintegration, but no one had offered her the choice. Instead, she could only cover her face and surrender to the sobs that wracked her body.

At some point he pressed a bandana on her. She took it gratefully, burying her face in the soft cloth that carried Travis's distinctive male scent. Fairly aching with the need to be held and comforted, she hugged herself and let her tears fall into this poor substitute until at long last she managed to regain a somewhat tenuous control over her emotions.

It was the shock, she told herself as she scrubbed at the remnants of her tears. Anyone who'd been kidnapped and threatened with a fate worse than death would have been upset. The weeping had actually done her good. She felt cleansed. Cautiously, she lifted her moist gaze to Travis, who still hovered over her. To her astonishment, his blue eyes glinted with renewed fury.

"Did he hurt you?" he demanded. "I know you said he didn't, but—"

"He punched me in the jaw," Sarah said, gathering the tattered remains of her pride around her. "He said unspeakable things, and he threatened me, but other than that, he didn't hurt me, although he probably would have if you hadn't come along when you did. I'm grateful to you," she added stiffly, glad to hear her voice sounded only a little hoarse.

"If you're not hurt, then why were you crying?" he asked skeptically.

Why, indeed? Thinking of her foolish assumptions about him, and how cruelly he'd dashed them, she felt the heat come to her face, but surely the dim light would conceal her humiliation. "It was . . .

just a reaction to being kidnapped, I guess."

"He's dead," Travis reminded her. "You're safe now. I won't let anything else happen to you."

Sarah could have laughed out loud at the irony of his promise, but how could she explain to Travis that *he* was the one from whom she most needed protection?

"I suppose I'm a lucky woman to have a man like you working for me," she remarked bitterly. "I'd just like to know one thing. If you were afraid something had happened to me, why didn't you bring the rest of the men with you?"

He frowned, disgruntled, and she knew she'd at least succeeded in making him a little uncomfortable. "Cameron wouldn't come. I . . . I didn't ask the others."

"Why not?" she asked in genuine surprise.

He put his hands on his hips and looked away, his lips pressed tightly together as if holding back his reply.

"Travis?" she prompted.

When his gaze swung back to her, it was accusing. "You got any idea who might've hired this fellow to kidnap you?"

The question caught her off guard. "I . . . I haven't really had much chance to think about it. Someone who wants my ranch, of course."

"And someone who wants you," he added grimly.

Outrage stiffened her spine. How dare he make fun of her? "Don't be ridiculous. As you pointed out, I'm just 'easy pickings,' a means to an end, nothing more."

"Is that what you think?" he demanded, anger darkening his cheeks. "Well, you're wrong. Whoever planned this wants you every bit as much as he wants your land. Why do you think he went to all this trou-

201

ble?" He gestured to the newly cleaned cabin and the neatly made bunk on which she sat. "He could've just kept sending night riders to kill your sheep, if he's even the one who did it in the first place, which I doubt. He could've infected your sheep with scab or poisoned your water or done any one of a hundred things to put you out of business, but he didn't just want to run you off, *Mrs. Hadley;* he wanted *you.*"

Sarah's face burned with outrage. She knew only too well no man wanted *her,* not Garth Richardson, who'd only proposed out of a sense of duty, not Owen Cameron, who had his eye on her sheep, and certainly not Travis Whatever-his-name-was, who didn't want anything at all.

Ignoring the lingering weakness in her knees, she rose from the bunk and met Travis's gaze eye-to-eye, haughty and unflinching. "And what, pray tell, makes you think my mysterious kidnapper wants *me?*"

Travis's jaw tightened, and his gaze swept over her, taking her in from head to toe in one swift, heated glance. For the second time that day, Sarah experienced the urge to cover herself, but this time she felt much more vulnerable. "Because," he said, his voice ragged, "any man in his right mind would want you."

Chapter Seven

Stunned, Sarah could hardly find her voice. "And are you . . . in your right mind?" she managed.

A tremor went through him, and his eyes blazed as if a fire raged inside him. "God, yes," he whispered brokenly.

His hands closed into fists, and Sarah saw her own anguish and her own need reflected in his face. Dear heaven, he *did* want her! He really did care! Wonderingly, she lifted her hand and touched his cheek, but he flinched as if her touch had burned him.

"Don't," he commanded through gritted teeth, grasping her wrist to pull it away.

"Why not?" she challenged, lifting her other hand, but he grabbed it, too.

"Because." He spoke as if the words were being torn from his chest. "It's all I can do to keep my hands off you as it is!"

"Then don't!" Sarah cried in frustration. "I *want* you to touch me. I *need* you to hold me! *Please!*"

His fingers tightened on her wrists for a second, and then his arms were around her, crushing her to him. His heart thundered against hers, and his breath rasped in his throat. He groaned her name as his hands moved over her back, molding and caressing, as if he would take her into himself and never let her go. Sarah clung to him, reveling in his power and his need. Wrapped in the haven of his arms, for the first time in so very long she felt truly safe.

She rubbed her cheek against his, savoring the delicious sensation of his bristly beard on her tender skin; then his mouth found hers unerringly. His kiss was urgent, demanding everything, and she gladly surrendered to his claiming.

His tongue swept her mouth, devouring her essence until her own tongue met his for a sensual duel that left them both gasping. Desire surged through her, driven by every pounding heartbeat, hot and heady and compelling. The heat melted her bones and, weakened, she sank backward onto the bed.

He came with her, catching himself on one elbow as he fell on top of her. He groaned again, half-need, half-protest. "Sarah, don't . . . I can't . . ."

She silenced him with a kiss. His lips burned against hers, igniting flames in her heart and in her belly, flames that burned out an aching emptiness only he could fill. He found her breast, and her nipple tightened against his palm, straining for release. His kneading fingers sent shafts of longing racing through her, and she thought she might die of wanting him.

Pushing off his hat, she buried her fingers in the softness of his hair, holding his mouth to hers for a kiss she never wanted to end. The fire inside her raged out of control, searing away caution and reason and even will. Nothing mattered except being as close to him as she could be.

When his fingers fumbled with the buttons of her bodice, Sarah found the buttons of his shirt and swiftly opened it to her exploring hands. He gasped when she touched the lightly furred wall of his chest and ran her hands around to stroke the corded muscles of his back.

In a frenzy now, he fairly tore her bodice open. The cool night air teased at her overheated skin, but his mouth quickly warmed her as he lavished kisses over every inch of flesh exposed to him. When he reached the lacy edge of her chemise, he jerked the fragile fabric away, freeing her aching, swollen breasts to his sensual assault.

He captured one throbbing nipple in his mouth and suckled. Sarah cried out at the startling burst of pleasure, and arched her back, offering herself, offering him everything. He feasted on her while she gloried in the feel of his heated flesh against hers. Instinctively, she pressed her hips to his, seeking the union for which she'd never before felt a desire, never until now.

And now desire was compulsion. He already owned her heart, so she must give him her body, also. Then she would be his, and they would be one, inseparable.

She ran her hands down his sides, caressing the bare flesh until he shuddered in response. Emboldened by her own passion, she stroked lower, clutching his flanks; then she slipped one hand between them and found the hard evidence of his desire. He started in surprise and groaned her name in protest, but she knew what she wanted.

"Love me, Travis," she begged. "Please, love me."

His breath caught, and when he released it, the words came out in a ragged sigh. "I do, Sarah. I do."

His confession shattered the last of her restraint. She threw her arms around him and forced his mouth back to hers for a kiss so wild she felt as if she were soaring through the night sky, streaking past a million stars into a realm of which she had only dreamed.

Her breasts chafed eagerly against his hair-roughened chest, and her hips rocked against his in timeless rhythm. When his gunbelt bumped against her, he reached down and released it, letting it fall to the floor. Sarah's hand followed his, fumbling with the buttons on his pants, teasing over his hardness until he moaned in surrender and helped her with the buttons. In the next second, she held the hard, silken length of him in her palm.

Shocked by her own boldness, she nevertheless reveled in her power. He drew his breath in a hiss as her fingers explored him, stroking, testing, teasing. But he bore it for only a moment before he yanked her hand away.

"Witch," he gasped. "Let's see how you like it." Before Sarah's befuddled brain could register the threat, he'd shoved her skirt and petticoats up to her waist and found the place where her drawers opened between her legs.

She cried out when he touched her, a touch so gentle she couldn't believe the pleasure streaking through her. No one had ever touched her like that, but he had only begun. Murmuring his approval at her reaction, he began to stroke, lightly at first, teasing. The burning she had felt everywhere began to center beneath his fingers as they taught her the mysteries of her own body.

Her hips shifted restlessly as the heat grew unbearable. She wanted him to stop, wanted him to finish, wanted him . . . wanted him . . . She arched, pressing herself into his palm, pleading silently for what she could not ask aloud. She opened, offering herself, and whispered his name.

"Oh, God, Sarah," he said hoarsely, and Sarah heard the undercurrent of doubt. He knew he shouldn't take her, and she was desperately afraid he might be strong enough to resist.

"Yes, my darling," she murmured, and found his still-rigid shaft.

"Sarah, don't . . ." he tried, but the protest died in a gasp of pleasure when her fingers closed around him. She knew her power now and used it, caressing him as he had caressed her, until his breath came in ragged gasps and she knew he could no longer resist.

"Love me, Travis," she entreated again, drawing him to her.

He came, looming over her in the flickering light, his eyes glowing like coals in the fire. She lifted to him in blatant surrender, and he slid into her in one swift thrust that wrenched a cry of surprise from her throat. He swallowed it with a kiss that went on and on while he held himself completely still, filling her, holding her, claiming her, while her body seemed to dissolve into one molten mass of need.

When neither of them could breathe, he lifted his mouth from hers. For a long moment they simply stared at each other, and in that breathless space of time, with their bodies joined, Sarah could see inside his soul. She saw the pain and anger and loneliness, the need and want and despair, but also the wonder at having found, after so very long a time of searching,

207

someone who could make everything right again.

He said her name as if it were a question, as if he couldn't quite believe it, and because she couldn't quite believe it either, she slipped her arms around him and pulled him back to her again.

This time his kiss was demanding and his body began to demand. Moving within her, he stirred the flames to life again. They licked against her nerve endings, sending the scorching heat racing over her body.

At first she lay still, afraid to move, terrified by the unfamiliar sensations. What was happening to her body? What *would* happen? Travis moved slowly, sliding out with torturous care, then filling her again with even more tormenting gentleness. Each time he brought her more pleasure, more pressure, more desperate need, until she could no longer resist.

Instinctively, she met his thrust, and the world spun away in a dizzying whirl. He grasped her hips and taught her the rhythm, guiding her in this mysterious dance with patience and an urgency she inhaled with every gasping breath.

She saw the stars again, racing past as she soared out of control, out of the world, out of her mind. Nothing existed now but the two of them, their bodies joined, their hearts thundering and the flames searing, scorching, melding them into one desperate, frantic entity.

Sarah wrapped her legs and arms around him, compelled to hold him, to hold herself, against the roiling, swirling maelstrom that carried her up and up and up until she couldn't see or hear or breathe, and when she thought she must surely die, her body con-

208

vulsed with pure, unadulterated joy. She cried out at the wonder of it, clinging to him while he pulsed within her, filling her with the gift of life.

Slowly, gradually, the fire within burned down to embers, leaving them panting and gasping. Travis rolled off her, as far away as the narrow cot would allow, and threw one arm over his eyes as he fought for breath. Somewhat stunned, Sarah hugged herself against the sudden chill and tried to gather what was left of her wits. The instant she did, she only wanted to be back in Travis's arms again. Responding to the need, she turned to him, wrapping one arm around his waist and snuggling against him.

He lowered his arm and slipped it around her, settling her head more comfortably on his shoulder. Knowing this was where she'd longed to be, she sighed in blissful contentment.

The silence stretched for a long moment, until Sarah responded to the need to verify the wondrous thing that had happened between them. "I . . . I never knew it could be like that," she said, her voice strangely hoarse.

He released his breath in a shuddering sigh. "Neither did I."

Sarah didn't like the note of despair in his voice. "Travis, I—"

"Shhh," he cautioned, laying a finger across her lips. "Don't say anything you might regret later."

Regret? What on earth did he mean? She would never regret anything about this night, not even the kidnapping, because it had finally driven Travis to admit he loved her.

And he did love her. She knew it now. Nothing else

could explain what they had shared. She touched his cheek and pressed her lips to the bristly skin. "Travis, I love you."

Her words cut him like a knife. Of course she thought she loved him, he told himself bitterly. A woman like Sarah Hadley would have to find some justification for what had just happened between them. She might even convince herself she had to marry the man, and Travis, if he had a brain in his head, would let her do just that. Wasn't this the chance he'd been waiting for all his life? He'd have a place of his own, a *home,* and the kind of woman he'd never even known existed until he'd met Sarah Hadley.

But what would *she* have? A drifter, a man who'd killed more times than he ever wanted to think about, a man who'd kill again if he had to, a man who wasn't good enough to touch Sarah Hadley's hand, but who'd bed her when she was scared and alone and vulnerable. Somebody ought to blow his brains out for what he'd just done, and here she was telling him she loved him.

He wanted nothing more than to hold her just like this for the rest of the night, for the rest of his *life,* to hear her whispering sweet things and feel her luscious mouth against his, and her luscious body beneath him, and believe she really could belong to him. He also knew he couldn't do that to her, not to a woman he loved. The only thing he could do now was wait until she came to her senses and let her run him off. Until then . . .

"I'd better get you home," he said gruffly, easing out of her embrace with what he hoped was seemly haste.

"Didn't you say Zeke's boss was coming here tonight?"

He sat up and began to button his shirt, forcing himself not to look at her.

"Not until midnight," she replied, pushing herself up, too. He winced when she slipped an arm around his back and laid her head on his shoulder so trustingly while he finished with his shirt buttons. "That's hours from now. Can't we stay just a little longer?"

Her scent engulfed him, as enervating as an opiate, but he fought it. "Cameron'll be half-crazy wondering where we are, and the rest of the men, too."

Somehow he found the strength to shrug out of her embrace and push himself up off the bed. Swiftly, he tucked in his shirttail and buttoned his pants. "I just hope my horse hasn't wandered off too far," he remarked, as he picked up his gunbelt and strapped it on.

"Travis?" she said, and his heart ached at the uncertainty in her voice. Every instinct told him to turn around and take her in his arms, but that would just be adding insult to injury. Instead, bracing himself for the sight of her, he turned to face her.

This time she looked like a wanton angel with her dark hair tumbling around her shoulders, her lips swollen from his kisses, and her creamy white flesh visible beneath her open bodice. Somehow he managed to control the overwhelming urge to drag her into his arms again. With a hand that was far from steady, he reached out and touched her cheek with just the tips of his fingers. "I want you home where you'll be safe. Do you understand?"

She covered his hand with hers and pressed it

211

against her face. "I feel safe anywhere, as long as I'm with you."

Her eyes were black in the shadows, but he could see the trust and adoration in them. What had he ever done to deserve such a tribute? "I can't protect you from everything, Sarah," he said, thinking he hadn't even been able to protect her from himself. "Now quit arguing and get yourself together." He forced a smile. "Cameron'll be having apoplexy as it is."

She smiled back, but when she made a move toward him, he bent to retrieve his hat and hurried out to find his horse. He couldn't risk letting her touch him again, because he knew what would happen, and he didn't want her to have anything else to regret about this night.

The trailing reins had kept his horse from going too far, and in a matter of minutes, Travis had led him back to the cabin. Sarah stood in the doorway waiting for him, fully clothed and looking almost respectable again, except for that glorious hair.

"You ready?" he asked around the tightness in his throat.

Instead of answering, she came to him, slipped her arms around his waist and pressed her precious body to his. For one awful second he felt the compulsion again, the same irresistible hunger he'd felt when he'd been inside her, possessing her and knowing she could never truly be his. Using every ounce of strength, he made himself pull away from her embrace.

"Don't get me started again," he cautioned in a poor attempt to sound playful. God, he didn't even know how to talk to a woman like Sarah, a *lady*. He saw the confusion in her eyes, but he didn't know how to deal

212

with that, either. "We'll have to ride double. Can you sit up behind me?"

"Of course," she said, sounding more like herself, a little annoyed that he would even ask.

He swung up into the saddle, then kicked his foot free of the stirrup and reached down to give her a hand up.

To his surprise, she brought her leg over the horse's rump to sit astride, and to his dismay, she wrapped her arms around his middle and snuggled up as closely as she could against his back.

He could feel every soft curve of her, and the wind blew a strand of dark, silken hair across his face. He caught it, remembering fantasies in which she'd bent over him, her ebony hair falling down around them to make a private world for just the two of them, in which she would love him and nothing else would matter.

But other things did matter. He brushed the hair away and said, "We'll have to ride quiet, so I'll hear in case anyone follows."

"All right," she said, resting her chin on his shoulder and pressing her soft cheek against his. He could feel her warm breath and smell the sweet woman scent of her body. Gritting his teeth against the surge of renewed desire, he kicked his horse into motion. It would be a long ride home.

Only when she finally allowed herself to relax against Travis did Sarah begin to feel the effects of her trying day. Her jaw ached and so did her head, probably because she hadn't had anything to eat in a while. Her scalp was sore where Zeke had pulled her hair, her whole body fairly throbbed with weariness and the

213

pounding she had taken on the back of Zeke's horse, and she would probably find numerous bruises in the morning. Still, in spite of her discomfort, Sarah had one brand new ache she didn't mind at all.

Smiling at the thought, she nuzzled Travis, pressing her lips to the soft spot below his ear and inhaling his unique scent. She never wanted to be any farther away from him than this again. Travis belonged to her now. They were as close as two people could be without being married, and they'd take care of that as soon as possible.

Of course, Travis hadn't said anything about getting married, but he hadn't exactly had an opportunity, either. When two people loved each other the way she and Travis did, and when they had made love the way she and Travis had, marriage was the only logical step. Never again would she awaken in the night aching with loneliness. Never again would she envy the happy couples she knew. And never again would she have to worry about when Travis might leave her.

She laid her head on his shoulder and flattened her palm against his chest so she could feel the reassuring beat of his heart. She truly must be besotted, she supposed, since she didn't even know what her name would be when she married Travis. There were many mysteries about him to which she would soon discover the answers. A man wouldn't keep secrets from his wife, now, would he?

And wouldn't everyone be surprised? Well, perhaps not Amabel or even Elizabeth, who must have suspected Sarah's feelings even though she'd try to deny them to herself. Certainly, her kidnapper would be surprised to learn she was no longer vulnerable to his schemes as she had been as a widow.

Widow! Good heavens, what was she thinking! If she were to marry Travis now, she'd make *him* the target of whoever was trying to get her land, and while her enemies wouldn't dream of actually killing a woman, what was to stop them from killing her husband? Hadn't Travis even suggested that Philip's death had been intentional? If so, then Travis was in double danger, or would be if she married him.

"Oh, dear!" she said aloud.

His body stiffened to attention. "Did you hear something?" he asked, his hand on his gun as he scanned the darkness.

"No, I . . . I just realized something. We can't . . ." She'd almost said they couldn't marry right away, but since he hadn't suggested it yet, she thought perhaps she should, for once, be discreet. "I mean, if whoever was behind this kidnapping finds out we . . . finds out about *us,* you'll be in danger. They might try to kill you the way you think they killed Philip."

She sensed something in him, a silent resistance, and she knew she'd made a mistake. Men, particularly men like Travis, wouldn't feel they needed a woman fussing over them, trying to protect them. "I mean, I just think it would be a good idea to keep our . . . our feelings for each other a secret for now," she tried lamely. "Just until all this trouble blows over, and things settle down."

"Yeah, sure," he said, but something was wrong. He sounded resigned, almost defeated, as if she'd said something he'd been dreading to hear.

"Travis?" she tried, not even knowing how to ask the question.

215

"I thought I told you to ride quiet," he said, feigning irritation, and Sarah smiled. He wasn't upset about her; he was upset about the situation, and rightly so. If she had the sense she'd been born with, she'd shut her mouth.

"Yes, sir," she replied, with equally feigned meekness, and laid her head back on his shoulder. At least she could savor this closeness for as long as it lasted. Heaven only knew when they'd have a chance to be alone again.

By the time they reached the ranch, Sarah had almost dozed off. Cameron's shout roused her, and she looked up to find the ranch yard ablaze with light and all her men gathered on the bunkhouse porch. What on earth?

They all came running to meet them. Cameron was the first to reach their side, and he looked up at Sarah with terror in his eyes. "Good God, man, where've ye been? Are ye hurt, missus?"

Sarah opened her mouth to reply, but Travis beat her to it. "She was kidnapped," he told them all, swinging his leg over the pommel and sliding to the ground.

"We know," Cameron said, as Travis reached up and lifted Sarah off the horse. "José and the others saw her wagon, but they didn't know what to do, so they came here to get ye."

"We wanted to go after you," Quinn said, "but it was almost dark, and Cameron said we should stay put 'cause you'd prob'ly do better on your own anyways."

"He was right," Travis said, giving Cameron an approving glance. "You never would've found us." Travis held one of Sarah's arms to steady her until she was

216

firmly on her feet, then instantly let her go, as if they were still no more than employer and employee. Sarah felt the loss of his touch, but told herself they would have to learn to conduct themselves discreetly sooner or later, so it might as well start now. "You were right to stay here," Travis added. "They might've attacked the ranch, with everyone gone."

"Who took her?" Cameron asked.

Sarah was beginning to get annoyed at being spoken of as if she weren't present. "A man named Zeke," she informed Cameron. "He was alone, but he said he'd been hired by someone to kidnap me. We don't know who it was."

"Where's this Zeke now?" Quinn asked Travis, oblivious of Sarah's disgruntled frown at being ignored again.

"Dead," Travis said curtly. "Look, we can hash all this out in the morning. Mrs. Hadley, don't you think you'd better get on inside?"

Her heart leapt. He wanted a few minutes alone with her. "Yes, I . . . I am feeling the effects of the day, I'm afraid," she said, glad to escape the scrutiny of her men.

"I'll see to your horse," Quinn offered, taking the reins and leading the animal away. Shorty, Ace and the herders followed him after murmuring their awkward assurances that they were glad she'd gotten home in one piece. Cameron, however, stayed by her side.

As she turned toward the house, he took one of her arms but, to her disappointment, Travis didn't take the other. Instead he said, "If you'll see Mrs. Hadley inside, Cameron, I've got some business to attend to."

Before Sarah could protest, he was walking away,

leaving her alone with the Scot. When she'd told him they would have to be careful, she hadn't expected him to take her quite so literally! But, she consoled herself, maybe he would come later.

"Are ye hurt?" Cameron asked solicitously, guiding her toward the house. "Should I summon the doctor?"

"No, I'm fine," Sarah assured him. "A little the worse for wear, but nothing a good night's sleep in my own bed won't cure."

"How did Travis find ye?" Cameron asked as he helped her up the porch steps.

"He tracked me, I suppose. That Zeke person knocked me unconscious and carried me off on horseback to one of our old line shacks. He was going to hold me there until his boss showed up to claim me." Sarah shuddered at the memory of the terror she had felt.

"There, now, it's over. Are ye sure ye don't want me to fetch someone for ye? One of the ladies from town?"

"No," Sarah said, thinking she wouldn't dream of disturbing any of her friends at this time of night. The passion she and Travis had shared had blotted out most of the ugly memories of the kidnapping, and she was fairly sure she could comfort herself with dreams of Travis and hold the nightmares at bay.

Cameron insisted on taking her inside and lighting all the lamps for her while she slumped in a chair. When he had finished with the lights, he turned back to her and, seeing her clearly for the first time, frowned ominously. "Are ye sure ye're not needing the doctor, missus?"

Sarah shook her head wearily. "I know I must look a fright, but most of it will probably wash off."

"Would ye be wanting a bath, then?"

A bath! How glorious! Her reaction must have shown on her face, because he nodded knowingly. "I'll fill the tub for ye. Where do ye want it?"

The prospect of Cameron performing such an intimate task for her brought the heat to Sarah's face, but she did very desperately need a bath and she also didn't feel physically capable of seeing to it herself. "In . . . in the bedroom, I suppose. The tub is . . ."

But he'd already gone to fetch it. She laid her head back against the chair and closed her eyes, willing herself to stay awake until she'd had a chance to take advantage of the luxury Cameron was preparing for her. She dozed lightly while she listened to him moving back and forth between the kitchen and her bedroom, carrying the tub and the buckets of water.

At last he stopped before her. "Missus?"

She forced her eyes open and managed a grateful smile. "Thank you, Mr. Cameron. I'm forever in your debt."

He returned her smile, only his was a little rueful. "I'm thinking ye owe Travis a bigger debt."

A debt she would be willing to spend the rest of her life repaying, she thought, but she said, "Yes, he's quite a hero, isn't he?"

"Did he tell ye how he happened to come after ye?"

"Well," she admitted archly, "he did mention you wouldn't come with him."

Cameron flushed scarlet. "He did ask, and I would gladly have gone if I'd known ye were in real trouble, but I didna know. I thought ye might like to see Travis alone."

She saw the speculation in his eyes, and this time *she*

219

blushed. "How very perceptive you are, Mr. Cameron."

"Ye should have seen him, missus, pacing the floor like a wild man when ye didna come home."

Suddenly, Sarah felt warm again, as if Travis's arms were around her once more. "Thank you for telling me, Mr. Cameron."

Cameron nodded. "I'm thinking he might not want ye to know. He's a proud man."

"That he is, but . . ." She silently debated just how much to tell him. "Travis and I . . . we understand each other now."

"Do ye, now?" Cameron replied with some amusement. "I'm thinking that must be a near miracle." Before she could respond to this outrageous statement, he added, "Best enjoy your bath before the water turns cold."

With that he turned on his heel and left, with Sarah glaring impotently at his back. If he weren't the best sheepman in Texas, she might be tempted to tell him exactly what she thought of his unsolicited analysis of her relationship with Travis. But, she thought, as she rose stiffly from the chair and made her way into the bedroom, he might be too right. In spite of the way she and Travis had made love and the intimacies they had shared, Sarah still knew precious little about the man.

The bath steamed invitingly, and Sarah began to strip out of her soiled clothing, remembering, as she undid the buttons, how Travis had wrenched them open in the heat of passion just a few hours earlier. Humming at the golden memories, she had worked her way down to her chemise when she heard Ca-

220

meron calling her.

"Missus! Mrs. Hadley!" he fairly shouted, the sound of his booted feet running across the porch echoing through the house.

Alarmed, Sarah grabbed her robe and shrugged it on, hurrying to the bedroom door. When she threw it open, Cameron stood on the other side, poised to knock, his broad face beet-red.

"What is it?"

"It's Travis. He's gone."

"Gone? What on earth do you mean?"

"I mean, he's taken his bedroll, saddled a horse and gone."

Sarah stared at him incredulously. This couldn't be happening. She must have misunderstood. Cameron must be mistaken.

Cameron studied her face for a long moment. "Then ye didn't know. Ye didn't send him away."

Too shocked to speak, she shook her head in vehement denial. Dear God, how could he have left her *now*, after what they'd shared? But then, what *had* they shared except a few moments of lust? He hadn't spoken of love, not really, and certainly not afterward, when she'd confessed her own feelings to him, and he hadn't spoken of marriage at all. When she'd told him they would have to keep their relationship a secret, he hadn't even argued! The pain of betrayal ripped through her like a dull knife.

Something flickered in Cameron's eyes, something very like pity, before his expression hardened to steel. "I can see ye don't want him to leave. His work isna finished here, is it?"

Sarah barely heard him as a thousand "why's"

221

echoed through her head, but he didn't wait for her response. For the second time in as many minutes, Cameron left her. His shouted commands registered with some distant part of her brain. He was mustering the men to ride.

Mechanically, she closed the bedroom door and moved toward the bed. Sleep, that's what she needed. In the morning this would all make sense, she told herself, as she sank down into the inviting depths of the feather mattress. In the morning she would understand everything.

If only the pain didn't kill her first.

Travis checked the stars and tried to judge the time. If he were lucky, very lucky, he could settle this thing once and for all tonight. Sarah might already have decided she didn't want anything to do with a worn-out gunslinger, but her safety would always be important to him. He would guarantee it before he left.

At first he didn't believe his ears when he heard the riders. Zeke had told Sarah his boss was coming to the line shack for the purpose of rape, not a task a man would need outriders for. He slowed his horse, thinking they couldn't possibly know he was heading for the shack, too. If he could manage to elude them and let them pass, he could follow behind undetected.

He was scouting for a likely hiding place along the road when he realized with alarm that the riders weren't behind him at all. They were beside him, on both sides, and closing fast.

Quickly, he considered his options. He could run for it or stand fast and fight. In view of the odds — he estimated at least half a dozen horses—he chose to run. He pulled his pistol and jammed his spurs home. His horse bolted, charging into the darkness, but instantly Travis knew he'd made a mistake. Riders were *ahead* of him, too, and he was riding right into their arms.

God Almighty, it was like they were after *him!* They materialized out of the darkness, mere shadowy figures racing toward him. Too late to turn and run, he pointed his pistol at the nearest one and fired. The explosion covered the whistling of the lariat, so he never knew the rope was coming until it locked around his chest and jerked him from the saddle.

The ground slammed into his back, stunning him, and the night turned even blacker and the stars disappeared for a moment.

"Got him!" he heard one of them yell, and was vaguely aware of being dragged a way while the roper got his horse under control.

When the stars reappeared, Travis realized some instinct had prevailed and he still held his gun. The riders with the ropes—there seemed to be two of them now—loomed over him, silhouetted against the night sky. He couldn't decide which one to shoot, and they wavered, so he aimed somewhere between them and squeezed the trigger.

The explosion sent the men flying from their saddles. Travis blinked, and the images merged into one shouting individual who seemed totally unscathed but almighty furious, judging from the stream of curses.

Travis took aim again, but someone on his other side shouted a warning, and just as he squeezed the trigger a boot appeared from nowhere and stomped on his arm. The shot went wild and the booted foot pinned his arm to the ground while the foot's owner wrested the pistol from his hand.

Travis felt his strength returning, and he braced himself, ready to leap to his feet the instant his assailant released his arm. But instead of releasing him, the burly figure bent down to him and yelled, "Jesus, Mary and Joseph, man, don't make us kill ye!"

Travis blinked again, trying to focus on the shadowed face. "Cameron?" he asked incredulously.

"Aye, you son of a bitch," he replied in disgust, releasing Travis's arm and grabbing it with his hammy hands to haul him to his feet.

Still woozy from the fall, Travis staggered a bit and shook his head in an attempt to clear it. "What in the hell is going on?" he demanded, furiously struggling free of the rope.

"We came for ye, man." Inexplicably, Cameron sounded as angry as Travis felt.

"What in God's name for?"

"Because no man walks out on Sarah Hadley," another familiar voice informed him. Quinn marched up, coiling his rope with furious jerks. Even in the darkness, Travis could see his rage.

"Walks out? What in the hell are you talking about?"

"We're talking about how you turned tail and run when things got a little rough, you yellow-bellied snake in the grass," Quinn informed him. "Maybe *we* don't have no use for you now, but Miz Hadley seems to want to keep you around, so—"

"You mean you came after me on purpose? To bring me back?" Travis exclaimed, his own rage swell-

224

4 FREE BOOKS

ing.

"Aye," Cameron snarled. He would have said more, but Travis cut him off.

"You roped me like a steer and almost broke my damn neck," Travis snarled right back.

"If it was my choice, your neck *would* be broke," Cameron assured him. "But we did it for *her.*"

"Sarah?" Travis raged. "Sarah put you up to this?"

"Aye, she—"

"And you just did her bidding like a bunch of trained apes," Travis shouted. "God damn it to hell, I ought to kill the lot of you and put you out of your misery!"

"Get his gun," someone cried, and there was a scuffle as some of the men tried to find it on the ground.

"We thought ye were one of us," Cameron declared ominously. "But just when she needs ye most, ye run out like a—"

"Shut your damned mouth before I shut it for you, Scot," Travis warned him.

"Ye and what army, little man?"

The "little" was the last straw. Travis launched himself at the Scot, fists flailing. He landed a punch on Cameron's face, but the burly Scot only grunted, and when Travis drove his fist into Cameron's stomach, it was like hitting a brick wall. He howled as his arm went numb to the elbow. Then the brick wall slammed into his face and once again he found himself on his back in the dirt, but this time the stars were inside his head.

Shaking himself, he managed to clear his vision, and he was halfway to his feet again when two men grabbed his arms. He roared in outrage and somehow

225

managed to wrench one arm free. He swung, connecting with solid flesh. Someone howled; then his other arm was free. Cameron shouted something, but Travis was too busy to hear it.

Afterward, no one could really say what happened or who actually hit whom or at what point in the melee. When the dust finally settled, four men held Travis pinned to the ground, and he might still have gotten up again if Cameron hadn't also been sitting on his chest.

"We should've let ye leave," Cameron bellowed into his face. "Sarah Hadley's too good for the likes of ye."

"Not that it's any of your damn business," Travis bellowed back, fighting for breath against the Scot's weight, "but I wasn't leaving! The man who ordered Sarah's kidnapping was supposed to come to the line shack at midnight to get her. I was *planning* to give him a little surprise when he arrived."

"Ye expect us to believe that?" Cameron scoffed. "Why were ye needing your bedroll then?"

"In case the bastard got away from me, and I had to trail him."

"Why didna ye tell us then? Why didna ye take some men with ye?"

"Because I travel best alone, and damn it, I did tell Pedro when I took the horse. He was the only one around, and I was in a hurry."

"Pedro?" Cameron challenged, looking around for the herder.

The man holding Travis's left leg said, "*Sí, señor,* he does say this to me, but when you say he has run away, I think he was lying and—"

Cameron roared a curse, scrambling off Travis as

226

quickly as his bulk would allow. "Let him go, you fools," he added when the others didn't quite comprehend.

The next instant Travis was free, and when he bounded to his feet again, the others backed away.

"Travis, we made a mistake," Quinn said in a soothing voice.

"Damn right you did," Travis growled, fury still boiling in him. "And I hope to hell you didn't make another one. You didn't go off and leave Sarah alone at the ranch, did you?"

"No!" Cameron replied, outraged. "I left Shorty and José with her."

"Thank God," Travis growled. "Where's my gun?"

"Now, Travis, there's no need—"

"Where's my goddamned gun? That bastard is probably at the cabin right now!"

Someone shoved his pistol into his hand.

"Take my horse," Ace offered. "Yours'll be halfway home by now."

Travis grasped the offered reins, thrust his foot into the stirrup, and swung up.

"Do ye want some company?" Cameron asked, rather sheepishly, Travis thought.

"Suit yourself, Scotsman," Travis replied, spurring the horse into a run.

The others were right behind him, and Travis didn't have to look around to know Ace would be riding double with somebody. None of them would be left out of this game.

Travis stopped them when they got close enough to be heard. The blood still roared in his ears, so he had to strain to listen for sounds of any other approaching

227

riders. He checked the stars again, and judged the time to be close to midnight.

"Quinn, Cameron, you come with me," he whispered. "We'll sneak up on foot in case he's already there. If he's not, we'll wait for him. The rest of you stay put and try not to make any more noise than you already have."

Cameron and Quinn followed as Travis darted through the brush. The cabin was a black rectangle in the darkness. When they paused to listen, they heard nothing except the normal sounds of night.

"We've beat him here," Cameron whispered.

"Unless all that shooting scared him off," Travis replied grimly. "I'll go up to the cabin and see if he's inside. You cover me."

Crouching to make a smaller target, Travis jogged across the open space up to the cabin door. Flattening himself to the wall beside it, he listened, pistol poised, holding his breath and trying to hear above the pounding of his heart. Hearing nothing, he ducked inside, flattening himself against the wall inside the door this time, but no one challenged him. He waited, listening for the sound of breathing, and heard nothing.

After a dozen heartbeats, he carefully drew a match from his pocket and, holding it at arm's length in case his adversary was waiting for a target, struck it on his thumbnail.

The blaze of light illuminated the wreckage of the cabin. Travis stared in disbelief at the overturned table, the smashed chairs, the scattered supplies, and the bedclothes lying in a heap on the floor. He jumped when the flame seared his fingers and instantly dropped the match. Swearing, he holstered his pistol

228

and shouted, "It's all clear. Come on."

Lighting another match, he moved to the hearth and managed to throw together a small pile of kindling. By the time Cameron and Quinn burst in, he had a tiny fire going, enough to illuminate the mess.

The two men looked around. "You and Zeke must've had quite a time of it," Quinn remarked.

Travis shook his head. "I got Zeke about a quarter mile from here. When we left, the cabin was neat." Except, he thought, for the mussed bedclothes, but of course he wouldn't mention that.

"Then who . . . ?" Quinn began before the truth dawned on him, too.

"I'm thinking our kidnapper was a mite irritated to find his prize was gone," Cameron said.

"Seeing how mean his temper is, I'm just glad he never got his hands on Sarah," Travis remarked grimly, rising from where he'd knelt to make the fire. "We'd better take a look around in case he left any clues, but I guess my best bet'll be to track him in the morning."

The other two men did not respond, and Travis noticed they seemed to be waiting for something. He also noticed they hadn't holstered their pistols.

"You still got something in your craw, Cameron?"

The Scot's eyes narrowed. "Ye've got every right to be angry with us."

"Damn right I do."

Cameron and Quinn exchanged a glance. Quinn cleared his throat. "Look, Travis, we're mighty sorry for what happened. We was wrong, but if you think about it careful, you'll see we only wanted to keep you with us."

229

Travis couldn't remember ever receiving a more left-handed compliment. Still, he had to admire their loyalty to Sarah and the guts it had taken for them to come after him. He supposed he couldn't blame them for being so besotted with Sarah Hadley that they'd make asses of themselves to follow her every whim. "I reckon you're all just lucky Mrs. Hadley needs you boys so bad," Travis said with the ghost of a smile. "If there was a chance in hell of replacing you, I'd be sore tempted to send every one of you to your just reward."

The two men visibly relaxed, but neither of them put up his gun.

"Was there something else?" he asked mildly.

"Ye'll be going back to the ranch with us tonight, won't ye?"

Common sense dictated that Travis stay right where he was so he could get started on the trail at first light, and ordinarily nothing and no one would be able to change his mind. On the other hand, Cameron and Quinn looked mighty determined. Travis figured he could probably take them both if he had to, but he certainly didn't want to.

And now that he thought about it, going back to the ranch was an excellent idea, because Sarah was at the ranch and he had a few choice words to say to her about tonight's little adventure. "Of course I'm going back to the ranch," Travis said. "I've got some important business with Mrs. Hadley."

The lamp had long since sputtered out, and still Sarah lay wide-eyed, staring up into the darkness. If only she could cry, she thought for the thousandth

230

time, but her burning eyes refused to produce the cleansing tears. Perhaps it was her pride, forbidding her to succumb to this most damning sign of feminine weakness. Would Travis Whatever-his-name-was have wept if *she* had turned away from their love?

The very idea was preposterous. Men didn't cry. For all Sarah knew, men didn't even love. Perhaps that was the whole problem.

She heard the horses outside, but she didn't recognize the significance of the sound for a few moments. Then she remembered: Cameron and the others had gone after Travis. For all the good it would do them, she thought bitterly. All the king's horses and all the king's men wouldn't be able to catch him. What chance did a few has-been cowboys and some sorry sheepherders have?

"Mrs. Hadley?" Cameron's voice called.

Sarah briefly considered ignoring him, since she certainly had no desire to hear how he had failed, but she knew he wouldn't let her rest until he'd given his report.

Wearily, laboriously, she pushed her reluctant body off the bed and shuffled to the bedroom door, pulling her robe more snugly around her as she went. She opened the door a crack, prepared to send Cameron on his way as swiftly as possible, but to her surprise, he wasn't outside her door. Instead she caught a glimpse of several men standing in the parlor, and when she opened the door farther, she gasped in surprise.

"Wh . . . what . . . ?" was all she could manage.

Cameron and Quinn stood, hats in hand, looking awkward and ill at ease, and Travis simply stood, glaring at her as if he would gladly break every bone in her body.

"We found him," Cameron explained. "He hadn't really left. He'd just—"

"Save it, Cameron," Travis snapped, and only then did Sarah notice his blackening eye. Good heavens, he'd been in a fight!

"You didn't have to hurt him!" she cried, appalled, but when she turned her accusing stare on Cameron she noticed he sported a glowering bruise, too. She turned to Quinn and saw a trace of blood on the corner of his mouth. Her stomach dropped to her toes. "Oh, dear," she said faintly.

"You gents can go now," Travis said. "I don't think Mrs. Hadley wants you to hear what I've got to say to her."

Sarah didn't think she wanted to hear it either, but when Cameron said, "If ye want us to stay . . ." she shook her head.

"No, I . . . Travis is right. I have a few things to say to him, too."

Cameron frowned doubtfully, but Quinn beat a hasty retreat, obviously only too glad to escape what was rapidly becoming a very uncomfortable situation. Cameron lingered another moment until Sarah gave him a nod of encouragement. He backed into the hallway as if afraid to take his eyes off Travis. "If ye need me—" he began, but Travis cut him off.

"Get out!"

The Scot scowled, but obediently pulled the door shut behind him.

For a long moment, Travis just continued to glare, and Sarah found it hard to breathe, as if all the air in

232

the room had suddenly evaporated. At last she found her voice and said, "I never meant for them to hurt you."

"Exactly what did you mean for them to do, then? Truss me up like a Christmas turkey and dump me on your doorstep?"

"No!" she cried, appalled. "I . . . I didn't even want them to go after you!"

"Then where'd they get the idea?" he asked skeptically.

"I have no idea," she replied haughtily. What conceit to think she'd sent them after him! Her indignation increased her confidence. "Cameron came and told me you'd . . . you'd *run away*," she informed him, pleased with her choice of words and the way his eyes narrowed in fury. "Naturally, I was . . . upset," she continued, her face heating when she recalled just why she'd been upset. Ignoring her own humiliation, she jerked the lapels of her robe more tightly around her throat and lifted her chin defiantly. "After what happened between us, I thought . . ." But she couldn't say what she'd thought, so she let her voice trail off.

"What did you think, Sarah?" he taunted. "Did you think you'd bought my loyalty with one roll in the hay?"

She gasped in outrage, but he wasn't concerned about her sensibilities.

"Did you think I'd come to heel and be content just to sniff around your skirts from now on?" he continued mercilessly.

"No!" she cried, but he ignored her.

"Just so you understand, I left here tonight to find the man who had you kidnapped. I might've even

233

done it if you hadn't sent your trained apes after me."

"I didn't — !" she tried, but he wasn't finished.

"I was on my way back to the line shack when your boys jumped me. There was some shooting, which he probably heard, and he hightailed it, because when we finally got there, he was gone."

"How do you know he just hadn't arrived yet?" she challenged, her face burning now.

"Because he'd torn the place up when he didn't find you there. Whoever he is, he's a mean bastard, but I might've got him if your boys hadn't stopped me."

All her fury suddenly evaporated, and Sarah tried to swallow. Her throat felt raw, but she somehow held her voice steady. "Just so *you* understand, I *didn't* send my men after you."

"But you didn't stop them, either," he reminded her ruthlessly. "You thought I'd left you, and you let them go."

Sarah opened her mouth to deny it, but the words caught in her throat because she knew he was right. Somewhere down deep, in defiance of all reason, she'd wanted them to bring him back to her.

He must have read the truth on her face, because he said, "I won't be your lapdog, Sarah."

"I don't want a lapdog!"

"Don't you?" he challenged. "You're probably thinking if I'd asked your permission to go out tonight, none of this would've happened."

"Well, it wouldn't have," she insisted righteously.

"I'm not a man who asks permission, not to do the job you hired me to do in the first place, which is to find out who's behind all this business and stop him. The trouble is, you're a woman who likes to run

234

things, and you can't just let a man do what he has to do."

"I *have* to run things around here. I own this place, remember?"

"Oh, I remember, all right, but something tells me you'd be like this whether you did or not. Or maybe I'm wrong. How about it, Sarah, were you a meek little wife to Philip Hadley, or did you try to run him, too?"

Sarah wanted to slap the knowing look right off his face, but she suspected he'd simply slap her back. She settled for "You son of a bitch!"

"Guessed right, didn't I?" he said triumphantly. "You ran him, all right, ran him out of your bed and out of your house and into the arms of another woman."

"*No!*" she cried, wanting to cover her ears, but he was there, holding her so she couldn't, his fingers digging into her upper arms, forcing her to listen, forcing her to look into his blazing eyes.

"Listen to me, Sarah, because I'm only going to say this once. Don't think because of what happened between us you can bend me to your will. I'm not Philip Hadley. I'm not weak, and nobody is going to run me. You can't make me stay if I want to go, and you can't run me off if I want to stay, either. I do what I want, when I want. Do you understand?"

Rage boiled in her chest, choking her, but she forced the words out anyway. "Yes," she hissed. "I understand perfectly."

He held her for a long moment, as if waiting for some hint of insincerity. Then, satisfied, he released her. She staggered back a step, rubbing her arms

235

where his fingers had bruised her flesh, and he turned on his heel and strode to the door. He'd opened it before she found her tongue again.

"Which will it be then?"

He froze and turned slowly back to face her. "What?"

"Which will it be?" she asked again, hugging herself against the trembling that shook her. "Are you going or staying?"

He hesitated, and for a moment Sarah suspected he might not even have decided himself, but then he sighed and looked away, and she knew he was only trying to decide whether to admit it or not.

"I'm staying, God help us both."

Chapter Eight

Travis and Cameron were just coming out of the cookhouse after breakfast when they saw Sarah striding carefully across the muddy ranch yard. Travis didn't know what annoyed him more, the determined set of Sarah's jaw or the mud that was a painful reminder of the five days of rain they'd just had. The rain had begun just before dawn the morning after Sarah's kidnapping, and had effectively erased any trail her kidnapper might have left. The black clouds had matched Travis's mood since.

"What do ye suppose she's up to?" Cameron remarked.

"From the look in her eye, nothing good," Travis replied grimly. He braced himself as he watched her approach.

She wore what he had come to think of as her town dress, a black thing decorated with a bunch of fancy trimming, but even its furbelows couldn't disguise the real Sarah, at least not from him. He knew the soft feminine curves that lay beneath all those petticoats, and he knew the passion she usually revealed only as anger. He supposed he should count himself lucky for having seen even a glimpse of her other self, since she sure as hell wasn't ever going to let him see another, not if the way she'd been treating him this past week was any indication. He must be crazy to stay around here and endure the torment of seeing her every day and knowing he could never have her.

" 'Morning, missus," Cameron said as she reached them. He seemed entirely too cheerful, in Travis's opinion.

"Good morning, gentlemen," she replied, hardly sparing Travis a glance, which was just as well, because if she got too snippy with him, he'd be forced to take her in his arms and give her a gentle little reminder of just how much he knew about her.

As if she'd read his thoughts, she glanced back at him, her eyes startlingly green in the morning sunlight. Then she frowned. "I need to go to town," she announced.

Something in her tone set his teeth on edge, but he held his temper in check. "Tomorrow's Saturday," he reminded her.

"I know, and there's a dance at the schoolhouse tomorrow night. I asked Mrs. Williams to make me a new dress for the occasion, and I must go in today to fetch it."

"You're going to the dance?" he asked, feeling the first warning prickles.

"Certainly," she said imperiously. "Why shouldn't I?"

Travis could think of a dozen reasons, not the least of which was that he didn't much like the idea of her

238

dancing with a lot of other men, but of course he couldn't say such a thing. If she didn't laugh out loud at him, she'd give him one of her looks, and God only knew what he'd do then. "Your kidnapper'll probably be there," he said instead.

She stiffened, but if he'd frightened her, she gave no other indication. "Then perhaps this is a chance to catch him. He'll be the only one there who knows about the kidnapping besides us, so he might accidentally give himself away by mentioning it."

She had a point, but Travis wasn't about to admit it. "Do you think that's worth putting yourself in danger again?"

"I can't imagine how I'll be in danger with all my men there to guard me. You *will* be accompanying me, won't you?"

Travis had long since ceased to find community dances a source of enjoyment, and the prospect of watching Sarah in the arms of other men made this one particularly onerous. Still, he couldn't see where he had any other choice. "I've been counting the days 'til I get to kick up my heels," he informed her sarcastically. "How about you, Owen?"

Cameron blinked his surprise, but he jumped right in. "Aye, that I have. Perhaps ye'll save me a reel, missus."

"Certainly." She turned her bright green gaze on Travis as if she expected him to make a similar request, but he had no intention of giving her an opportunity to turn him down in front of Cameron. Travis knew an almost overwhelming urge to kiss that expectant smirk right off her pretty little mouth.

"So if you're going to town tomorrow anyway, why

239

can't you just pick up your dress then?" Travis said to change the subject.

"Because it might not fit, and then Elizabeth would have no time to alter it. I must go in today, but," she added with feigned meekness, "I've learned my lesson, and you will be happy to know I have no intention of going alone."

An irrational surge of jealousy almost choked him. "Who's going with you?"

She seemed surprised at the question. "Why, you, of course." She smiled triumphantly because she'd given him an order he wouldn't dare refuse to obey. They both knew he wouldn't trust anyone else with the job of guarding her. "It looks as if the rain has finally stopped, but let's take the buggy just in case we get another shower." She turned to Cameron as if she were completely unaware of Travis's seething rage.

"How soon do you think the lambs will start?" she asked him.

"Any day, missus," Cameron replied. "This rain has made the grass tender and sweet, so we donna have to worry. The early lambs willna starve on winter hay."

She smiled at Cameron as if he'd just told her the best news she'd ever heard. She never smiled at Travis like that. He had to grit his teeth to hold back the bitter bile of envy.

She glanced at Travis again as if surprised to find him still here. "I'd like to leave immediately, if you don't mind." It was another order, no matter how politely phrased, a none-too-subtle reminder of who was the boss and who was the hired hand.

240

"Yes, ma'am," he replied, in a parody of civility. As he strode toward the barn, he cursed the mud that forced him to go carefully lest he slip and make a complete fool of himself. Just how in the hell was he supposed to ride into town and back with her, alone, and not make an even bigger fool of himself?

Sarah frowned at his departing back and knew she'd probably made a terrible mistake in planning this trip. Travis had been right in suggesting she could pick up her dress tomorrow. Elizabeth had never yet failed to fit her perfectly the first time, and any minor alterations could be performed on the spot.

No, Sarah's trip to town had a completely different purpose. She wondered if she wasn't a fool, and indeed, she'd called herself one at least hourly since she'd first thought of this plan yesterday afternoon. Wasn't she satisfied with knowing Travis could barely tolerate her? They'd hardly exchanged a complete sentence in the five days since he'd turned her life upside down, so why was she torturing herself by forcing him to escort her into town?

Maybe Travis was right about her. Maybe she simply wouldn't be content until she'd driven him completely away, just as she'd done Philip.

Or until she'd discovered he couldn't be driven.

The trip to town seemed endless. Travis hardly spoke a word, and Sarah couldn't think of a single topic of conversation that wouldn't somehow bring up subjects she didn't want to discuss with him. To make matters worse, the rain had rutted the road, and more than once Sarah found herself thrown up against Travis in the close confines of the covered buggy. If their proximity disturbed him, he gave no sign except an occasional grunt of displeasure whenever the jostling of the buggy sent her practically into his lap.

For her part, Sarah found it intolerable to be so close to him. Her body didn't seem particularly concerned with whether or not he still wanted her. She still wanted him, and every nerve hummed with awareness until Sarah thought she might scream. She heaved a heartfelt sigh of relief when the weather-beaten buildings of town finally came into view.

"The fitting won't take long," Sarah said, forcing herself to remember her plan. Apprehension formed a hard lump in her stomach. Why was she doing this? Even though she couldn't quite recall the reason, she couldn't seem to stop herself, either. "Take your time doing whatever errands you need to do; then come and get me at Mrs. Williams's house."

"I'm not the one with errands," he reminded her sourly.

Sarah bit back a sharp retort. "Well, I'm sure you can find something to occupy your time for an hour or so, can't you?"

He didn't bother to reply, and she sighed again. Maybe she should just murder him right now and put them both out of their misery.

When they reached Elizabeth's house, he stopped the buggy as near to her gate as he could, then set the brake and jumped down to help Sarah out. The road here was practically a quagmire, and she looked askance at the mess.

He muttered something Sarah didn't catch, then reached up for her. Before she realized what he in-

242

tended, he had scooped her out of the buggy and into his arms.

"Travis, really!" she sputtered as he swung her legs up. Having no other choice, she locked her arms around his neck to keep from falling. Just exactly what did he think he was doing? How dare he take advantage of her like this?

For the short trip from the buggy to Elizabeth's porch, Sarah gritted her teeth and tried not to notice the hundred little things about Travis that she'd had no opportunity to notice for so many days. The way his golden hair curled out from beneath his hat, the way the sun-bleached lashes curved almost invisibly around his amazingly blue eyes, the tiny squint lines around those eyes, the greenish remnants of his shiner, and the inviting curve of his mouth, even when he frowned.

The worst part of being so close was that she couldn't help but smell his tantalizing masculine scent. She'd never noticed any other man having a particular scent before, and she found the discovery unnerving, practically as unnerving as the feel of his arms around her and the way her body responded almost automatically to his touch by going weak in the strangest places.

Fortunately for her emotional state, he set her down the moment he reached the lowest step and released her instantly, as if he'd found the encounter unpleasant. He seemed as breathless as she felt, and she wondered if he'd found carrying her a strain.

"I . . . Thank you," she managed, although she didn't think her voice sounded at all normal. But then, how could it, when her heart was trying to

243

pound its way out of her chest and her bones quivered like jelly?

"I'll be back later," he said, not quite meeting her eye, and for an instant she imagined he flushed. Then he turned away and she could no longer be sure. She laid a hand over her clamoring heart and tried to get her breath.

"Sarah!" Elizabeth exclaimed from the front door. Apparently, she'd been drawn by the commotion. "I didn't expect to see you today."

Reluctantly, Sarah turned from watching Travis's retreating figure and forced a smile for her friend. "I came for my dress."

"Aunt Sarah!" Paul cried, charging past his mother's skirts. He would have launched himself down the steps, but Elizabeth grabbed an arm as he flew by, and jerked him to a precipitous halt.

"Not so fast, young man," Elizabeth scolded, holding his squirming body as Sarah came up the steps. "I've had a time of it keeping him inside during the rain, and now it's too muddy for him to play outside. He's about to go wild!"

Paul gave Sarah an angelic grin that belied his mother's prediction, but Sarah wasn't fooled. "Maybe he just needs a new playmate. Would you like to build something with me?"

Paul gave a shout of approval that left Sarah's ears ringing, and she allowed him to pull her inside.

"First, Aunt Sarah has to try on her dress," Elizabeth warned. "It's right here." Elizabeth reached into the enormous wardrobe that dominated her front room, pulled out the gown, held it up, and smiled mischievously. "What do you think?"

Sarah could hardly believe her eyes. The color was the one she had selected, dove gray, but she recognized nothing else. From the simple bodice and draped skirt pattern Sarah always used, Elizabeth had created something entirely new. The bodice collar and cuffs were maroon, as was the piping Elizabeth had added to the seams, and the intricate drape of the skirt revealed an underskirt of the same color. A few tasteful bows adorned the edge of the drape and danced down the back below the bustle.

"Elizabeth," Sarah protested. "It's *red!*"

"Not red, magenta," Elizabeth corrected cheerfully. "Didn't you agree it was time you went out of mourning?"

"I didn't agree to wear red!" Sarah insisted. "Or even magenta."

"Try it on," Elizabeth suggested. "If you don't like it —"

"Oh, I'm sure I'll like it," Sarah groaned, taking the dress from Elizabeth and holding it against her. "I'm just not sure I'll be bold enough to wear it!"

Once she had it on, she changed her mind. Looking at her reflection in Elizabeth's cheval glass, she knew she not only could but that she *must* wear it. Elizabeth had cut the bodice slightly smaller than Sarah usually wore her clothes, so it fit more snugly and showed her modest curves to greater advantage. The skirt flared perfectly, making her waist seem tiny, and when Sarah swayed experimentally, she saw how delightful the gown would look when she danced.

But what she liked best was the color. "Did you say it was magenta?" she asked, fingering the collar lovingly.

"The perfect color for your skin. Oh, you look good in black, but a woman in black tends to fade into the background too much, don't you think?"

Since Elizabeth also wore black almost exclusively, Sarah knew she spoke from experience. Of course, until recently, they had both preferred being in the background. Elizabeth probably still did, but how had she known Sarah was ready to come out again?

Sarah turned around and looked over her shoulder in an attempt to see how she looked from behind. From the corner of her eye, she saw Paul staring at her from the doorway, his eyes enormous in his small face. "What do you think, sweetheart?" she asked.

"You look awful pretty, Aunt Sarah," he said in awe. "You're almost as pretty as Mama."

Sarah couldn't stop the heat that rose in her face at the comparison she most dreaded. She only hoped Elizabeth wouldn't notice. "That's high praise indeed," she managed, forcing a smile.

"Children always think their mothers are the most beautiful women in the world," Elizabeth explained hastily, so Sarah knew she'd noticed her distress. "But Paul is right. You do look lovely, lovely enough to catch the eye of a certain gentleman."

Sarah looked at her in surprise. "What makes you think I want to catch someone's eye?"

Elizabeth smiled beatifically, her perfect face fairly glowing with studied innocence. "Why, nothing at all, but when a woman gets herself a new dress when she doesn't really need one, she's usually trying to impress someone in particular, and usually that someone is a man."

"I most certainly am *not* trying to impress him,"

Sarah insisted. "He's nothing to me but a hired gun."

"Who?" Elizabeth asked curiously, and Sarah's cheeks burned when she realized she'd confirmed Elizabeth's suspicions.

"No one," she tried, but Elizabeth only shook her head.

"I saw him carrying you up to the house."

"The ground is muddy and . . . You can't think . . . I mean . . ." Sarah wasn't sure what she meant. "I don't even know his real name," she tried lamely.

"You must know a lot of other things about him," Elizabeth suggested.

Sarah thought her face might burst into flames. She only hoped Elizabeth hadn't guessed just how much she did know. "The only thing I'm sure about is that he's good with a gun, and that's the kind of man I need working for me right now," she said dismissively.

Elizabeth took the hint and began to inspect the dress again. "I think I could take another tuck here," she said, fussing with the skirt. "I'll do that while you play with Paul."

Gratefully, Sarah slipped back into Elizabeth's bedroom and stripped off the new dress. Well, the new dress might not impress Travis — and he didn't seem like the type of man to be impressed by such things — but at least it would boost Sarah's confidence. After today, it might well need a lot of boosting.

When she had given the dress back to Elizabeth for the alterations and put her own black gown back on, Sarah helped Paul set up an army fort with his blocks and his tin soldiers. She tried to lose herself in the experience, to concentrate on watching Paul's cherubic face and listening to his tinkling laughter, but she caught herself more than once straining to hear the sound of an approaching buggy.

The apprehension she'd felt earlier grew with each passing minute, until she noticed her hands were shaking. Closing them into fists to still their trembling, she called herself a fool. What did she think she was trying to prove? She must be crazy even to have thought of such a plan.

But, she realized, she had to go through with it. She simply had to know.

Travis stopped the buggy outside Elizabeth Williams's house, pulled the brake and tied off the reins. If he had a lick of sense, he'd sit right here and wait until she came out. The ride back was going to be hard enough without making things worse, and if he went to the door, he'd be sorely tempted to take her in his arms again. He'd needed most of the hour he'd spent waiting, to get over the first time. God, he'd never realized the hold a woman could have over a man. He supposed it could explain why so many men were willing to get married and settle down. And he had to admit the prospect of having Sarah Hadley in his bed every night for the rest of his life was enough to make domestic life actually seem attractive.

He must be losing his mind.

Before he realized it, he was out of the buggy and halfway up the muddy walk. Since it was too late to turn back, he went the rest of the way, pausing to scrape the worst of the mud off his boots before climbing the porch steps and knocking on the door.

He heard a child's voice yell, "I'll get it!" and the sound of running feet. In the next second, the door flew open, and the child Sarah had told him was Philip Hadley's son smiled up at him.

Travis could see at once how the boy had won Sarah's heart and why she would even be willing to befriend her husband's mistress in order to know him better. Travis couldn't help smiling back. "I'm here for Mrs. Hadley," he said.

"Please come in," he said, quoting a phrase he had obviously been trained to say, but his training hadn't extended far. *"Aunt Sarah!"* he shouted, dashing back inside.

Travis experienced a moment of uncertainty. He'd been invited in, but would the boy's mother really want him inside? His boots were still pretty muddy, and . . .

"Oh, hell," he muttered to himself and stepped into the parlor.

He saw Sarah at once, or thought he did. His eyes weren't yet adjusted to the dim interior light, and when she materialized into focus, he realized the woman wasn't Sarah at all.

Although she by God could've been her sister.

He stared in astonishment at the woman Philip Hadley had preferred over his wife. She was, without doubt, beautiful, her features fine, her figure lush and inviting. Her resemblance to Sarah was amazing, too—the same raven hair and alabaster skin, the same green eyes, the same height and build.

But she wasn't *exactly* the same as Sarah. Something was missing, and Travis could guess it was this difference that had drawn Philip Hadley: she was a serene, almost placid creature, the kind of woman who would never give a man a moment's trouble. She was Sarah without the fire.

"Elizabeth, this is Travis, the man I told you about."

Travis looked up to see Sarah in the doorway to what must be a back bedroom. Her hands were clasped tightly in front of her, and she had a strange expression on her face, half-expectant, half-apprehensive. He could almost feel the tension emanating from her. What on earth?

"Travis, this is Mrs. Williams," she continued, her voice strangely flat.

He looked back at Elizabeth, touched his hat brim politely and nodded.

"I'm very pleased to meet you, Mr. Travis," Elizabeth Williams said. God, even her voice was like Sarah's, only softer, lacking the edge of confidence and command. A proper lady's voice.

"Pleased to meet you, too, ma'am," he said perfunctorily while his mind raced. What was going on here?

"Won't you come in and sit down?" Elizabeth asked. The sweetness of her voice made the invitation sound like a plea, and not many men could resist such a plea. A woman like Elizabeth, a woman so gentle and vulnerable, made a man feel strong simply by existing. She needed help, needed someone to take care of her. Philip Hadley must have needed to be needed. Travis could understand the appeal, even though he didn't feel it himself.

"I'm kind of dirty for a social call," he said, gesturing to his boots.

"We don't mind, do we, Elizabeth?" Sarah asked,

250

although the tightness of her voice made it sound more like a command than a request.

"Certainly not," Elizabeth assured him, either oblivious of Sarah's tension or too ladylike to take notice of it. "I'm finished with Sarah's dress, and I was about to make tea. Won't you join us?"

He glanced at Sarah and saw her expression had changed. Her eyes had turned completely brown, and she looked almost afraid. *Sarah, afraid?* Afraid of what?

"If you're worried about your boots, you can take them off," Elizabeth suggested. "Can't he, Sarah?"

Sarah didn't reply, didn't do anything except squeeze her hands together until the knuckles were white, and then he knew: in spite of her assurances, she didn't really want him to sit down and drink tea with Elizabeth Williams. She didn't want him to be with Elizabeth Williams at all.

Then why was she trying to throw the two of them together?

The answer came to him with blinding clarity, and even though he tried to tell himself otherwise, he knew he was right. The knowledge infuriated him, almost enough to make him pull off his boots and plunk himself down in Elizabeth's parlor for the rest of the afternoon, Sarah Hadley be damned. Unfortunately, he couldn't take his boots off. With them on, he stood no better than eye-to-eye with Sarah. Without them . . .

"Thanks just the same, Mrs. Williams, but we should probably head on back. From the looks of those clouds, we're in for another storm, and I'd like to have Mrs. Hadley home before it hits."

Before either woman could reply, the boy stepped forward. Travis had almost forgotten he was there. He looked gravely up at Travis and said, "Are you the one Aunt Sarah was talking about? The hired gun?"

Both women gasped, and Travis felt the accusation like a thrust to his heart, but he managed not to show it. "I reckon I am," he told the boy solemnly, hunkering down to the child's level.

Paul eyed his pistol curiously. "I'm gonna have a gun when I grow up."

"Why do you think you'll need a gun?" Travis asked.

"To shoot bad people."

"Paul!" both women cried in unison, but Paul wouldn't deign to look at either of them, sensing the man's opinion was the most important.

Travis shook his head. "How'll you know who's bad and who's not?"

Paul frowned, considering his answer for a moment; then he brightened. "The same way *you* know!"

"But I don't always know. Sometimes it's hard to tell. What if you shoot the wrong person?"

Paul grew grave again. "I'd say I was sorry."

Travis shook his head again. "Not good enough, partner. Shooting somebody's a pretty serious thing. Once it's done, you can't undo it. And somebody might shoot you right back."

Paul's eyes grew wide. Plainly, this possibility had never occurred to him. Travis laid a comforting hand on his shoulder.

"I wouldn't lose too much sleep over it, partner. I figure by the time you're big enough to carry a gun,

252

you won't need to, unless it's to shoot a rattler or some other varmint."

Paul brightened again. "I'd shoot all them critters if I knew how. Can you teach me?"

Travis smiled in spite of himself. "You're a mite small right now."

"Will you teach me when I get big?" he asked hopefully.

Travis's smile faded. The future was one thing he never liked to think about, and instinctively, he glanced at Sarah. Her eyes were huge, her mouth a thin, colorless line.

"If I'm still around then, partner," he said, never moving his gaze from Sarah.

She started as if she'd received a jolt, and suddenly the color surged back into her face. "I suppose Travis is right," she said quickly, too quickly. "We should be on our way."

"Can't I show the man my soldiers?" Paul asked, affronted.

"Maybe he doesn't want to be bothered," Elizabeth suggested, drawing Travis's gaze. Her lovely eyes glittered with gratitude for the way he had handled the boy — gratitude and admiration. He would have killed to see that expression in Sarah's eyes.

"I don't mind seeing your soldiers," Travis said, rising, and he gave Sarah a look of silent challenge. "That is, if your Aunt Sarah doesn't mind."

"I still have to wrap Sarah's dress," Elizabeth said before Sarah could object. "That will take a few minutes."

"Come on!" Paul said, grasping Travis's hand and

pulling him forward with amazing strength for one so small.

"You heard your mother, Paul; he can only stay a few minutes," Sarah warned sharply, so sharply Travis suspected she was actually warning him.

Enjoying the novelty of being fought over, Travis gave Elizabeth a grin as Paul dragged him past her, but he let it fade when Sarah reluctantly stepped out of the way to allow them to pass into the other room.

She was fit to be tied, but that was all right, because Travis Taylor was just the man to tie her. All he had to do now was decide where and when.

"He's a nice man, isn't he, Mama?" Paul asked Elizabeth when their company had gone.

"Nice" was not exactly the word Elizabeth would have chosen to describe Sarah's gunfighter, but he had certainly been kind to her son. "Yes, dear, but you must remember not to pester grown-ups, particularly grown-ups you do not know."

"I know him," Paul insisted. "He's Aunt Sarah's friend."

Elizabeth smiled, wondering how Sarah would react to that statement. "But you don't know him very well. Only when someone has been your friend for a long time should you ask him for a favor, like teaching you to shoot a gun."

Paul squirmed a little under the reprimand, but as usual, he was ready to defend himself. "He said he would, so he must not've been mad."

"No, I don't think he was mad," Elizabeth allowed, sinking down onto the sofa.

254

"Aunt Sarah was, though," Paul observed, scrambling up into her lap. "Was she mad at me?"

"No, dear," Elizabeth replied, hugging him reassuringly while she recalled Sarah's white face when Travis had entered the parlor. If Elizabeth had noticed his surprise when he'd recognized the resemblance between the two women, then Sarah must have, too. That would explain her reaction, or at least part of it.

"Are you sure, Mama?" Paul insisted. "I don't want Aunt Sarah to be mad at me."

"She's not mad at you," Elizabeth soothed him. "She's mad at . . . at something else entirely, something that doesn't involve you at all."

Or perhaps it did, Elizabeth thought, as her son slipped out of her embrace and scampered away, back to his soldiers. Because if Paul hadn't been born, Sarah might never have known of her husband's betrayal. And she would never have wondered what he had found in another woman's arms that he hadn't found in hers.

Elizabeth wished she could talk to Sarah about it, could at least admit that she knew Sarah wondered, and reassure her, perhaps even tell her the truth about Philip, but she and Sarah simply did not discuss Philip. To do so would be to admit they were not really friends, only rivals who had established a mutually beneficial truce. Since Elizabeth benefited from it far more than Sarah did, she didn't dare breach it.

Elizabeth had been considering the problem for several minutes when someone knocked on the door. Paul was already on his feet and in the bedroom doorway, but Elizabeth called, "I'll get it!" before he could make his usual mad dash.

255

He frowned and stuck his lower lip out in a pout, but Elizabeth ignored his dramatics and opened the front door.

"Mr. Richardson," she cried in alarm. Automatically, she glanced past him in case he'd simply accompanied one of her regular customers, but he was alone. "Is there something I can—"

"I want to come in," Garth Richardson said, forcing her to step aside or be run over as he entered her house. He took several steps into the room before he turned back and gave her a questioning look.

Elizabeth still stood by the door, clinging to the knob as if for support.

"Aren't you going to ask me to sit down?" he inquired sarcastically.

"Do you have some business here?" Elizabeth asked, trying to maintain her composure.

"Maybe I want to order a dress," he said. "A dress for someone, oh, about your size," he added, looking her over from head to toe. "Something red. Red *is* what scarlet women wear, isn't it?"

"Mama?" Paul was frightened, probably because he sensed her fear, and Elizabeth desperately wished she could reassure him. Still clinging to the doorknob with one hand, she reached out the other, and Paul came running to her side.

Instinctively, he stood in front of her, as if he could protect her from this intruder. Richardson smiled contemptuously. "You could find a better protector than that if you put your mind to it, Lizzie."

Fury welled in her, fury at his insult and at her own impotence. "What do you want?" she demanded.

"Not what you think, so you can stop hiding behind your little bastard," he assured her mildly. Elizabeth winced at the epithet, but she refused to drop her gaze in shame. "I heard Sarah Hadley came to see you today."

"She left. If you hurry you might be able to catch up with her."

"Maybe I will, but first I wanted to ask you, did she tell you about her trouble?"

"What trouble?" Elizabeth asked, feeling a whole different kind of alarm.

"The kidnapping. Didn't she tell you all about her adventure and her daring rescue?"

Elizabeth wondered if he were trying to trick her somehow by telling her lies to make her feel stupid. "She didn't say a thing about it."

Richardson raised his eyebrows as if he thought she must be lying, but he said, "I wonder why she didn't. I heard it from one of my men, who heard it from one of her men. It must be all over the county by now."

"If you want to know about it, why don't you just ask her yourself?" Elizabeth asked, wondering if she dared order him out, and whether he would go if she did.

"Because I'm asking you." He eyed Elizabeth again, and she pulled Paul closer to her in a defensive gesture. "You'll see her tomorrow, won't you?"

Elizabeth nodded stiffly.

"Then you tell her people are talking. They're saying a woman has no business trying to go against the whole community. She was lucky this time, but she might not be so lucky next time."

"Why don't you tell her yourself?" Elizabeth snapped.

"I have, Lizzie," he informed her with a feral smile. "I have, but she doesn't listen to me. She thinks I'm just being protective of her. She doesn't know the kind of danger she's in, but you'll tell her, won't you?"

Elizabeth lifted her chin, too frightened to refuse but too proud to agree.

"Yes," he decided with infuriating confidence, "you'll tell her, but only because you're even more worried about her than I am."

He started for her, and she stiffened, prepared for she knew not what, but he was simply heading for the door. He paused beside her and glanced back at the parlor, eying the shabby furniture and the accouterments of her trade with disapproval. "Really, Lizzie, I can't understand why you put up with it. A woman with your . . ." He looked her over again with insulting thoroughness. ". . . with your *talents* shouldn't be wasting herself serving *women*."

Elizabeth held her breath, waiting for the next insult, praying Paul wouldn't understand any of this, but apparently Richardson had decided he'd done enough damage for one day.

"You won't forget to tell Sarah you think she should give up her sheep, will you?"

"I won't forget," Elizabeth said through gritted teeth, thinking that if she did, she'd do so for Sarah's sake, and certainly not because he'd ordered her to.

Sarah thought she might be ill. Travis hadn't spoken a word to her since he'd carried the parcel containing her dress out to the buggy and left her to mince her way through the mud by herself.

Of course, he might just still be mad from this morning. He'd hardly spoken to her on the way into town, either, but the silence of the return trip was different somehow, more ominous, almost as if he suspected . . . But of course he couldn't suspect what she'd tried to do.

Sarah supposed she should get used to his silence. Travis had made it perfectly clear he didn't want a relationship with her, not even a civil employer/employee type of relationship. It hurt, but she should be used to such things by now. As a sheep rancher in cattle country, she'd learned to ignore disdain. Surely she could learn to ignore Travis's, or at least not to feel it so much.

Her mistake had been in scheming to introduce him to Elizabeth. She must be crazy. Any other woman would have been more than satisfied with knowing a man simply didn't want her, without throwing him together with a woman he couldn't help but admire.

And he did admire Elizabeth. What man wouldn't? Sarah had seen his reaction to her beauty and the gracious smiles he bestowed upon her. He never smiled at Sarah that way. He never smiled at Sarah at all.

By the time the buggy rattled into the ranch yard, Sarah's head was pounding and her stomach felt as if it were filled with rocks. He stopped in front of the house and waited, making no move to get out and help her down. She considered thanking him for taking her to town but decided she didn't want to antag-

259

onize him further. She also didn't want to risk the inevitable sarcastic reply.

He slapped the horse into motion the moment she was clear of the vehicle, and headed for the barn. Sarah climbed the porch steps wearily and entered the empty house. The place was almost eerily silent, especially so after she had visited Elizabeth's place, which was always filled with Paul's childish laughter.

Even the ranch itself was silent. Sarah's men were all out working. Only the cook would be here at this time of day, and he seldom left his kitchen, particularly when he was busy preparing a meal.

Remembering her muddy shoes, she slipped them off and left them just inside the door. She went into the parlor, sank into one of the armchairs, leaned her head back, and closed her eyes. With a stab of remembrance, she realized she'd sat just like this the night of her kidnapping. The night when Travis had made love to her and made her believe in happy endings again.

She sat there for a long time, until the burning behind her eyes told her she'd better get moving or risk a humiliating fit of weeping. She was just about to get up when she heard the front door crash open.

"Sarah? Where are you?"

Sarah was out of her chair in an instant, but before she could respond, Travis appeared in the parlor doorway. He held the package containing her dress, and for one moment she thought he had simply brought it to her. Then she saw his eyes and knew she wouldn't get off so easily.

"Thank you for bringing my dress," she forced herself to say.

260

He strode into the room, tossed the parcel on the sofa, jerked his hat off, dropped it on top of the parcel, and turned to face her, hands planted on his hips. "Just what in the hell did you think you were doing?"

He didn't know, she told herself. There was no way he could have known. She lifted her chin and looked down her nose at him. "I don't know what you're talking about, and I'll thank you to remember you're addressing a lady—"

"A lady?" he scoffed. "Then how come you act like a pea-brained jackass so much of the time?"

She gasped her outrage, but he didn't give her time to reply.

"What did you think, Sarah? Did you think that once I saw *her,* I wouldn't want *you* anymore?"

Rage boiled up in her, drowning every other emotion. "As I recall, you didn't want me even *before* you saw her!"

"Don't make fun of me, Sarah," he warned.

"Don't make fun of *me,* Travis, or whatever your name is! Maybe you think because we . . . we . . ." she gestured helplessly, unable to think of an appropriate word to describe what had happened between them.

"Because we what?" he mocked. "I can't help you because I don't know exactly how you remember it. What was it for you, Sarah, screwing or making love?"

The burning behind her eyes increased until she could hardly blink for fear of dislodging a tear, and she clasped her hands over her churning stomach. "You said you loved me," she managed, past the thickness in her throat.

261

"And you said you loved me," he reminded her ruthlessly. "I can understand you changed your mind when you had a chance to think about it, but don't feel like you have to find me another woman to help me forget my troubles."

Sarah gaped, not quite certain she'd heard him correctly. "Changed my mind?" she echoed in confusion.

"Or came to your senses, whatever you want to call it," he said impatiently.

"Came to my senses about *what?*" she demanded in exasperation.

"About me," he snapped. "Look, I know it was a mistake, and you'd probably just like to forget it ever happened. You don't have to worry about me because I won't—"

"Wait a minute!" Sarah cried, planting her own hands on her hips. "Do you think I'm sorry for what happened?"

The question seemed to startle him. "You said you were."

"When?"

He frowned, and his hands dropped to his sides. "That night. You said we should pretend it never happened."

"I most certainly did not!" she exclaimed. "I said we shouldn't tell anyone because if people knew I was in love with you, you'd be in danger!"

"How could that put me in danger?" he scoffed.

"You're the one who thinks Philip was murdered!" she reminded him hotly. "If people thought I was going to have a new husband, a man who was far more dangerous than Philip, then somebody might decide to get you out of the way. Even if Philip wasn't mur-

262

dered, whoever kidnapped me isn't above resorting to violence to get what he wants. And," she added, "I didn't think what happened between us was a mistake, at least not until you said all those horrible things to me when you thought I sent the men after you. Which reminds me, if you really did think I sent the men after you, you should have been flattered instead of furious."

"*Flattered?*" he shouted incredulously. "You think I should be *flattered* because even though you didn't want me as a man, you still wanted to keep me around to kill for you?"

"I never said I didn't want you as a man, but you said you didn't want a woman who tried to run you!"

"I never said I didn't want *you!* I just said I wouldn't let you run me, and I won't!"

They glared at each other across the space separating them. Somehow that space had shrunk during the course of the argument, until now they stood almost toe to toe. Sarah could see the little flecks of gold in his eyes that looked almost like sparks, and as she stared, the fury faded and the sparks flickered out.

"Sarah?" The word held a wealth of questions.

Her mouth felt dry, and she swallowed. "I . . . I think we may have had a misunderstanding," she tried. Her heart was pounding, but whether from excitement or apprehension, she wasn't sure.

"Maybe," he allowed. "But what about this afternoon? If you weren't trying to play matchmaker between me and Elizabeth Williams, what *were* you doing?"

Sarah winced at the reminder of her foolishness. "I . . . I wanted to see if . . ."

263

"If what?" he prodded, crossing his arms. He looked prepared to wait all day if necessary.

Sarah looked down and studied her clasped hands, no longer able to meet his knowing gaze. "I wanted to find out if you would . . . find her attractive."

"Did you now?" he asked sarcastically, and she looked up to find the fury had returned to his eyes. "Maybe you wanted to know if I thought she was pretty, and maybe you wanted to know if I thought she was prettier than you."

"She is prettier than I am!" Sarah exclaimed before he could point it out. "Elizabeth is beautiful."

"And you figure that any man who likes you will like her a whole lot better. That's it, isn't it?"

Sarah felt the heat in her face, and she thought the wave of mortification might choke her, but she refused to look away again. "I don't know," she said, her voice little more than a whisper. "That's what I was trying to find out."

Travis shouted an expletive. Sarah jumped and automatically stepped back a pace, but he didn't stop. He kept going, cussing a blue streak, saying words Sarah had never even heard before, but she didn't have to know the meanings to catch the drift. He was furious, furious at her, and he thought she was an idiot!

"Were you born this stupid or did you have to practice up?" he demanded when he'd apparently run out of profanity.

"I am not stupid!" she informed him with as much hauteur as she could manage.

"Oh, yeah?" he challenged. "Only a complete jackass would imagine a man could prefer her to you."

264

"My husband did!" she reminded him through gritted teeth, her face blazing with humiliation.

"I said a 'man,' not some spineless, lily-livered lapdog without the gumption to blow his own nose! Oh, I know what your late husband saw in the 'attractive' Mrs. Williams. She's exactly the kind of woman a man like that needs. She probably patted his hand and told him nobody appreciated what a wonderful fellow he was and how big and strong he was, and she never yelled at him or expected him to stand up and be a man. Hell, they probably met in the first place because you sent him over to her shop to pick up something for you. He was feeling henpecked, and she gave him some sympathy."

Sarah stared at him, aghast. "I couldn't be running to town all the time," she said defensively. "I had to do the accounts and make sure the men knew what they were supposed to do and . . ." Her voice trailed off as she realized what she was saying. She hadn't ever even consciously tried to determine how Philip and Elizabeth had actually met, yet she'd known. She'd known because Philip had always been more than willing to run her errands, willing to grasp any excuse to get away from her, and she'd been happy to get him out of the way so she could do what needed to be done.

She felt the blood rushing from her head, and Travis grabbed her arms just as her knees went weak.

"Sarah?"

"You were right," she said hoarsely. "I did drive him away."

"And you were trying to drive me away, too."

"No!" she cried, clasping the fabric of his shirt in

265

both hands. "I don't want you to leave me! But I thought you already had, you see, so I wanted to know if . . ."

"If I'd go to her, too."

Sarah squeezed her eyes shut so she wouldn't have to see his contempt, and nodded. In the next instant, his arms were around her, holding her, cherishing her. He buried his face in the curve of her neck and gave a shuddering sigh.

"I told you before, I'm not Philip," he whispered against her skin. "I'm not afraid of you. I'm not afraid of your tongue or your schemes or your stubbornness, and I'm not afraid you're smarter than me. You can't scare me off or run me off, no matter how hard you try, and you sure as hell can't tempt me with another woman."

Sarah drew a breath and realized she was crying. "Travis?" she said on a watery gurgle.

"What now?" he asked, sounding impatient.

"I love you."

He groaned, and his arms tightened until she could barely breathe. Then he found her mouth, his lips slanting over hers as naturally as if they'd kissed like this every day of their lives. The kiss went on and on until neither of them could breathe, and at last, he lifted his mouth from hers.

He studied her face for a long moment, then reached up and touched her cheek with one finger. "Your friends would tell you not to waste your time with a man like me."

Sarah smiled serenely. "A sheepherder doesn't have any friends, remember? And besides, what's wrong with a man like you?"

"I've got nothing, Sarah," he informed her solemnly. "No woman in her right mind would look at me twice, and you've got your pick of men, *respectable* men. Even rich ones."

"I don't like respectable men," she countered playfully, slipping her arms around his neck and pressing herself more tightly against him. The feel of his solid body stirred all sorts of delicious memories, and she wished she could get closer still.

He settled her hips more firmly in the cradle of his thighs. "What kind of men *do* you like?"

Desire flowed through her like warm honey. "Men who stand up to me and who won't tell me their right names and who carry me off and ravish me whenever the mood strikes them."

He groaned again, then he kissed her again, his mouth hot and demanding, his tongue urgent against hers. She felt the world spinning, and when he cupped her breast, the warm honey turned to liquid fire.

"Oh, Travis, ravish me!" she begged against his mouth.

"The men . . . Cameron . . ." he argued, although his mouth never left her heated flesh, and she could feel the evidence of his own need even through the layers of her petticoats.

"They won't be back for hours. No one will know. Travis . . ." She ran her hand down his hip and across his belly until she encountered his hardness.

He gasped and jerked her hand away, but before she could protest, he'd scooped her up into his arms and was carrying her to the bedroom. He kicked the bedroom door shut with a resounding crash, but

267

Sarah hardly noticed. Gracious in her victory, she wrapped her arms around his neck and proceeded to nibble on his ear until he fell with her onto the bed.

His mouth found hers again for a resounding kiss. His hands moved over her, searching but finding little satisfaction through the restraints of her clothing. With a moan of frustration, he pulled his mouth from hers and pushed himself up.

"Can you get rid of some of these clothes?"

"If you can," she countered, running her stockinged foot up his leg. "Start with your boots."

In an instant he was sitting up and pulling them off. Sarah watched the play of muscles beneath the thin fabric of his shirt, then realized she should be removing something, too.

She started on the buttons of her bodice. She was almost finished when Travis turned back to her. His eyes were wonderful, as dark as a stormy sky, and lightning flashed in them, warming her to her toes.

While she finished on her bodice buttons, he started to undo her skirt, and when she sat up to pull the bodice from her arms, he helped, peeling the garment away and tossing it aside. Her skirt was already open, so she quickly untied her petticoats and lifted her hips so he could slide them off. They fell in a heap off the end of the bed, and she lay in just her undergarments. Travis would have taken her in his arms again, but she held him off.

"I didn't say *just* your boots," she scolded, reaching for the buttons of his shirt. As she worked them, he unbuckled his gunbelt and let it slide to the floor. When the buttons were open, he pulled the shirttail loose and stripped the garment from him, tossing it after her bodice.

Sarah had thought their first time together had probably been intensified by the threat of danger, but already her body thrummed with a need even more urgent than she had felt that night.

Shirtless, he looked as if he were carved from marble, his sinewy strength blatant in the bright sunlight streaming in the windows. She touched him, admiring him with her hands, testing the satiny breadth of his shoulders and trailing her fingers through the golden hair on his chest. "You're so . . . beautiful," she murmured, unable to find a more appropriate word.

He smiled and shook his head. "No, *you're* beautiful, more beautiful than you'll ever know," he replied, tracing the lacy neckline of her chemise with the tip of one finger until he found the sensitive valley between her breasts.

She drew in her breath and held it, waiting, until he lowered his head and kissed her, just there. Her heart thundered against her ribs, and her nipples puckered, begging to be touched. If he didn't soon tear away her chemise, she might just do it for him, but when he lifted his head, he simply reached for the tie and pulled the ribbon loose, drawing it out with agonizing slowness until Sarah thought she would scream with frustration.

Even when it was loose, he didn't hurry. Instead he gently parted the fragile fabric with both hands and slipped his fingers aside, splaying them to cover both of her breasts at once. Sarah released the breath she had been holding in a quavering sigh as she arched her back and pressed herself into

269

the delicious heat of his palms.

Then he began to knead, teasing her pliant flesh with his fingers while his thumbs tormented her straining nipples until they were throbbing, aching nubs and the flames of desire rose high enough to scorch her heart. When Sarah thought she would go mad with wanting, he lowered his head and soothed her with his lips. Gently, at first, he took each pebbled peak into the warm haven of his mouth and laved it with his tongue. Then he suckled, less gently, sending shockwaves pulsing through her, until she squirmed with need and wrapped her arms around his neck and tried to force his body onto hers.

He wouldn't budge, but while he continued to lavish attention on her breasts, his hand slipped under the hem of her chemise and found her hip. He began to caress, sliding along the thin silk, warming it, heating it, until the need became hunger and the hunger became passion. Instinctively, she parted her legs, and he quickly found the opening in the fabric.

"Oh, God, Sarah, you're so hot."

And she was, she was burning up, and she felt wild, out of control. His fingers worked their magic, finding the place that wept with wanting, and turning that wanting into obsession.

"Travis!"

This time he did not resist her importuning hands. He came to her, pausing only to release the buttons of his pants. Sarah helped him slide the Levi's down his hips; then she took his silken hardness and guided him to her, drawing her knees up and offering herself.

He eased into her slowly, torturously, filling her until she gasped with pleasure. He caught the gasp with his mouth and gave it back to her in a kiss that sent the world spinning away. She wrapped her legs around him and buried her fingers in the gold of his hair, holding her to him because she never wanted to let him go.

His hips began to move, and she moved with him, rocking in the ancient rhythms, striving with him in the ancient quest. Colors swirled behind her eyelids: blues and golds, like his eyes when they were angry or full of passion. Her heart thundered, and the color heated to purple, rich and voluptuous, enveloping her until she could hardly breathe, hardly think. Flames of desire licked through her, searing away doubts and fears, consuming the last remnants of her sanity, and finally destroying the very bonds that held her to the earth. The colors exploded into scarlet and crimson, and she soared with him into the realm of ecstasy where nothing could ever part them again.

For a long time afterward, she merely floated, aware only of the peace and joy she felt, and of him so close their hearts beat in time. All too soon, however, reality intruded, and when she tried to draw a breath, she found Travis's weight a burden. As if sensing her distress, he eased himself off her, although he didn't quite let her go. His arm still lay across her stomach and his leg still pinned one of hers to the bed.

His eyes, so close to hers on the pillow, were as clear as a rain-washed sky, as if their love had cleansed away all the hurt and anger between them. Sarah raised her hand to his cheek and caressed it. He closed his eyes, as if he were savoring her touch.

"Travis," she said.

271

"Hmmm?" he replied sleepily.

"Nothing. Just Travis. I love your name."

His eyes flickered open, and to her dismay, she saw wariness in them. "It is my real name, just not all of it."

She smiled, fighting to hold onto the closeness, not wanting too much reality to intrude. "If you don't want to tell me . . ."

His eyes went bleak, and the warm afterglow evaporated. He pushed away so they were no longer touching, and propped himself up on one elbow. "My name is Taylor, Travis Taylor."

Sarah was almost disappointed. The name meant nothing to her. She tried another smile. "Somehow I expected you'd be someone I'd heard of."

"I've got a nickname, too," he said in a voice so flat as to be emotionless. "Men like me usually do. Makes us seem more dangerous or something. They call me 'Colt' Taylor."

Sarah's disappointment disappeared under a wave of horror.

Chapter Nine

"*You're* Colt Taylor?" Sarah asked, fighting shock and hoping he couldn't hear her reaction in her voice.

"Most of what you've heard probably isn't true," he said grimly, rolling onto his back so he could fasten his pants.

Sarah pulled the edges of her chemise together with trembling hands and pushed the hem back over her thighs. "I haven't heard so very much," she lied, trying to sound nonchalant.

"How many men do you think I've killed? Twenty? Thirty?"

She winced at the bitterness in his voice. "I only know about the one you killed because of me."

"I never killed a man unless he didn't give me any other choice." He lay still, staring up at the ceiling, as if loath to meet her eye, his hands straight down at his side, his fists clenched.

"I know you didn't," she assured him. "You wouldn't."

"How do you know?"

"Because I know you. Because I love you."

He turned to her, his eyes as hard and cold as glass. "Just because you love a man, or think you do, doesn't make him good, Sarah."

"I don't 'think' I love you, Travis Taylor. I *do* love you, and knowing who you are doesn't change a thing. If I've heard things about you that aren't very nice, then I have to figure they're lies. Everybody knows about reputations and how they're like gossip; they change with every telling."

"I'm a hired gun, Sarah. There's no lie in that, and I've killed men for pay, men who would've killed me if they'd had the chance."

"I know," she said, laying a hand on his bare chest, just above his heart. She could feel it beating, and it quickened at her touch, but he held himself perfectly still, as if afraid to respond. "I knew the kind of man you were the first time I saw you, when they were carrying you into Dr. Bigelow's office, and I chose you then, even before I heard what Amabel Bigelow had to say about what a nice man you were and how you'd been a model patient and how you'd sold your saddle so you could pay them for your care. I may not have known I'd fall in love with you, but I was sure you were the man I needed to help me, the man I could finally depend on, the man I'd been looking for all my life."

He drew a deep breath and let it out in a long sigh. "I'm not like that, Sarah. Nobody's ever been able to depend on me. As soon as the job's over, I'm gone."

Apprehension thickened her throat. "Are you saying you'll leave me, too?"

He didn't reply at once, and with each second,

274

Sarah's apprehension grew. Had she been a fool? Had she once again chosen the wrong man?

"I've got some . . . some unfinished business," he said at last.

She opened her mouth to protest, then remembered just why he'd been carried into Dr. Bigelow's house that first day. "With the men who shot you before you came here," she guessed.

"They killed someone, a friend of mine."

"But they probably think they killed you, too. No one will expect you to—"

"*I* expect me to avenge my friend, Sarah," he told her harshly. "A man like me doesn't have much except his pride. If I lose that . . ."

"Is your pride more important than me and the life we could have together?" she argued.

His eyes narrowed dangerously. "I can't have any life with you at all unless I can look myself in the mirror every morning and not be ashamed. But then, maybe you want a man like that, a man you can bully and who won't talk back."

Sarah wanted to punch him. "You know perfectly well that's not true."

"Then don't be telling me my pride's not important," he warned her, levering himself up to a sitting position and throwing his legs over the side of the bed.

"Where are you going?" she demanded, sitting up herself.

"I've got work to do, and you've put me half a day behind," he informed her, leaning over to retrieve his boots.

"Travis, we haven't settled anything!" she cried,

the apprehension still clogging her throat.

"It's settled as far as I'm concerned. If you've got something else to say, I'm listening." He stood up and stomped his feet into the boots, then leaned over again to get his shirt.

"You can't just carry me in here and . . . and . . ."

"Ravish you?" he supplied helpfully, looking entirely too smug as he shrugged into his shirt.

"And then just go on about your business!" she finished, praying her face wasn't as red as it felt. Perhaps he would just think she was angry.

"What am I supposed to do? Hang around here so I can fetch and carry for you?"

Sarah scowled murderously, but Travis only shook his head, thinking she looked too deliciously wanton to leave, but knowing he'd better go while he still could. His pride wasn't the only thing he was intent on sparing. Now he had to protect the woman he loved, as well.

"Sarah," he said, trying for reason, "you said yourself it would be dangerous if people knew about us."

"Don't tell me I've finally convinced you to be careful," she scoffed.

"I don't mean dangerous for me," he informed her, fighting exasperation. "I mean dangerous. For one thing, how do you think the men would react if they knew what we just did there on your bed?"

Her cheeks grew rosy again, and her emerald eyes widened with understanding.

"Yeah," he confirmed brutally. "They'd call you a whore, and they'd horsewhip me *if* I was lucky and they didn't just string me up to the nearest cottonwood. Even if they were too afraid to actually do

276

anything, they'd never take another order from me again, and you'd be a laughingstock. Even the people who don't mind about the sheep would despise you. They'd treat you like Elizabeth Williams, only worse, because at least she had the good taste to take up with a respectable man. You lay down with a no-good saddle bum, a man you pay wages to, for God's sake."

She hugged herself, and her green eyes clouded with hurt. "You make it sound so dirty. Maybe you despise me, too."

He wanted to take her in his arms and kiss away every one of her doubts, and swear to God he loved her more than life itself and that he'd die before causing her pain. Unfortunately, his loving her was bound to cause her pain no matter how he might wish things otherwise. Even if she still wanted him when all this was over, he couldn't be sure he'd be around to make things right. If Sarah's enemies didn't get him, there were other folks more than willing. But if something did happen to him, he would at least leave Sarah's good name intact.

"All I'm saying is, nobody needs to know your private business," he tried. "You were the one wanted to keep things secret. All I'm doing is agreeing. You oughta be pleased as punch that for once I'm not arguing with you."

She looked anything but pleased. Unable to meet her eye, he jammed his shirttail into his pants, scooped up his gunbelt and began to strap it on.

"I don't trust you when you're not arguing with me," she informed him at last. "It makes me think you're pretending."

277

"What would I be pretending?" he asked impatiently.

"You might just be pretending you love me so you can have your way with me and . . . *Oh!*"

Travis descended on her in a flash, grabbing her arms and hauling her half off the bed until her lips were under his and his arms were around her, holding her to him so he could feel the softness of her breasts and taste the sweetness of her mouth. He held her to him, cherishing her, memorizing every curve of her beloved body, and he kissed her until she went limp and yielding in his arms.

Satisfied he'd made his point, he released her reluctantly and set her back down on the bed. "Now get some clothes on, woman, before somebody comes along and wonders what you've been up to."

He turned on his heel and hurried from the room, afraid to look back lest he be tempted to take her all over again. God knew, his sins were grave enough without adding any more to them. She called his name, but he didn't stop, snatching up his hat as he passed through the parlor, and loping for the door.

Sarah was off the bed before she realized she couldn't make a bigger fool of herself by chasing after him. She must, she decided as she sank back down on the mattress, be losing her mind. How could she have allowed—no, she had to admit it, she had actually *invited*—a man to seduce her, not once but twice? Although she could no longer claim she didn't know his true identity, knowing it made things even worse. No woman in her right mind would trust a man like Colt Taylor, much less give him her heart and take him to her bed.

278

If she had a lick of sense, she'd pay him off and get him out of her life before he could do any more damage to her poor heart or what was left of her pride. Then she remembered how he'd insisted they keep their relationship a secret, as if he really cared about protecting her good name. As if he really cared about *her*. And when she remembered how tenderly he had made love to her just moments ago, she shivered, wondering whether a man could be so loving if he didn't really love. And that parting kiss . . .

Nothing about Travis Taylor made any sense at all, but at least Sarah was sure of one thing: he'd be around until the job she'd hired him for was finished. Maybe by then she'd have him figured out. Maybe she'd even know how to keep him with her, assuming she still wanted to.

The next evening, Sarah stood before her mirror and studied her reflection with a critical eye. Thank heaven she'd asked Elizabeth to make this dress for her. At least she would have the assurance that she looked her best when she appeared at the dance tonight. Between knowing that someone in the crowd had probably arranged to have her abducted, and worrying over her relationship with Travis, Sarah anticipated a less than pleasant evening.

Giving her hair one last pat to make sure all her pins were secure, she carefully tied on a bonnet to protect her coiffure from the dust and wind. Then, after making a few last adjustments to her dress, Sarah drew a calming breath and stoically made her way out of the house to the waiting buggy.

The sight that greeted her as she exited the house stopped her dead in her tracks. All her men, cowboys and sheepherders alike, were scrubbed and spit-shined and dressed in what, for them, was their Sunday best. They stood in a line, practically at attention, as if they were waiting to form an honor guard for her.

Travis and Cameron stood to one side. Cameron wore a black suit and a boiled shirt with a stiff white collar that, judging from the redness of his face, appeared to be choking him. Travis was dressed more casually in brown nankeen trousers and a blue yoke-front shirt that she had never seen before and that matched his eyes.

Both men had been scowling when she walked out, as if they'd been discussing something unpleasant. They looked up, and Cameron's frown dissolved into a smile of obvious approval, but Travis's deepened.

Only when her heart sank into the pit of her stomach did Sarah realize how much she had been hoping to impress him with her new gown.

Someone gave a low whistle, and Sarah looked over to find Quinn and the other cowboys grinning broadly. The Mexicans were more circumspect, but no less appreciative, and Sarah found a little of her confidence returning.

"You look mighty fine tonight, Miz Hadley," Quinn decreed, and the other men nodded enthusiastically.

"Aye, that you do," Cameron said, hurrying up the porch steps to offer his arm.

Sarah tried not to notice that Travis hadn't moved a muscle and certainly hadn't added any words of

280

praise. Murmuring her thanks, she allowed Cameron to escort her to the buggy and help her into it.

At least, she told herself, she would have the ride into town alone with Travis during which to coax a compliment out of him. But to her surprise, Cameron climbed into the buggy beside her.

Her surprise must have been humiliatingly evident, because Cameron smiled knowingly. "Travis figured he should be on horseback in case we run into any trouble."

"Does he really think someone would try to abduct me when I'm surrounded by all these men?" she asked, loudly enough for Travis to hear.

As she might have expected, however, he pretended not to. Oblivious, he walked to where his horse was tied and mounted it. The others followed suit, and when Cameron started the buggy out of the ranch yard, they fell in behind.

"My dear mother would have told ye to be careful or ye'll trip over that lip," Cameron remarked before they'd gone too far.

"I am not pouting," Sarah informed him acidly, although she knew she had been, and not very prettily, either.

"Nor should ye be," Cameron advised. "Not when ye're got up like Cinderella on her way to the ball."

"Unfortunately, I'm not likely to meet any handsome prince who'll help me live happily ever after," Sarah remarked dryly.

"I'm thinking ye'll not be needing any prince, missus, not when ye've got something better."

Sarah eyed him uneasily. "What's better than a

prince?" she asked, with what she hoped was non-chalance.

"A real man."

"What real man are you talking about?" she asked even more uneasily, but Cameron only smiled.

Sarah had an urge to wipe that smug grin right off his broad face, and wondered what gave him the right to tease her. She only wished she could be as certain as Cameron appeared to be that she had any claim on Travis at all.

"I know ye'll have no lack for partners tonight, but don't forget ye promised me a reel," Cameron reminded her when they'd ridden a while in silence.

That reminded her she'd also promised the first dance to Garth Richardson, but Travis hadn't even mentioned the subject of dances to her. Either he was awfully certain she'd partner him as often as he wanted her to, or else he wasn't interested in dancing with her at all. If she weren't a sensible woman who considered herself above such nonsense, she might be tempted to teach him a lesson by showing him she didn't need him at all, because plenty of other men were perfectly willing to oblige her. Of course, such a silly, childish thing was beneath her dignity.

The schoolyard was already full of vehicles when they arrived, and a group of men had gathered around the whiskey barrel that had been set up nearby. The sound of fiddles drifted from the open doors of the building, and Sarah could see the figures moving inside in time to the music.

Instinctively, she reached up and smoothed the collar of the dress.

"Ye look fine, missus," Cameron assured her, and

she thanked him with a smile. Why couldn't she have fallen in love with a man like Cameron, instead of with a man whose idea of kindly reassurance was to call her a pea-brained jackass for doubting him?

Resolutely, Sarah removed her bonnet, set it on the seat, and patted her hair smooth. "Will you walk in with me, Mr. Cameron?" she asked, thinking she needed some moral support to face the crowd, many of whom might be openly hostile.

"My pleasure, but are ye sure ye wouldn't rather ask someone else?"

"I asked you, didn't I?" she replied, more sharply than she'd intended; then she consciously softened her voice. "If I'd wanted someone else, I would have asked him."

Cameron gave her one of his maddening grins and climbed out of the buggy. She took his offered hand and jumped down herself. Taking another moment to shake the wrinkles out of her skirt, she took his arm and started toward the school, acutely aware—even though she'd taken great pains not to appear to no-tice—that Travis was tying his horse nearby and couldn't help but see them.

If he objected to Cameron's escorting her, he gave no indication, and he certainly made no attempt to overtake them. Sighing with disappointment, she steeled herself to face the crowd inside, climbed the few steps, and strolled into the schoolhouse.

The three musicians, two fiddlers and a mouth or-gan player were just finishing up a rousing square dance, and the dancers clapped and stomped their appreciation for the music. In the din, hardly anyone noticed Sarah's arrival, or so she told herself.

283

She scanned the room, picking out the corner where the old ladies had gathered to gossip, another where the young wives had clustered, holding babies and trying to keep tabs on toddlers and the older children who raced in and out with little regard for their own or anyone else's safety. Elizabeth Williams sat at the edge of this group, close enough to acknowledge she should have been one of them and to keep an eye on Paul who played with the other children, but far enough away to indicate she really had no right to associate with the respectable matrons.

"Thank you, Mr. Cameron," Sarah said, releasing his arm. "I think I can make it from here all by myself."

He nodded and stepped away so she could pass into the room. She was moving toward where Elizabeth sat when she heard someone call her name.

"Garth," she said in genuine pleasure, looking up to see his tall figure weaving through the crowd.

He hurried to her side, smiling broadly. "I'd just about given you up."

"I . . . we got a late start," she said, loath to admit she'd spent more time primping than she'd intended.

"It was worth the wait," Garth exclaimed, looking her over in frank admiration. "I've never seen you look lovelier, Sarah."

"You're very kind, Garth," Sarah said, gratified to know other men found her attractive, even if one certain man didn't seem to.

"Kindness doesn't have a thing to do with it. I'm so glad to see you've decided to give up your widow's weeds, I could kiss you right here in front of God and everybody."

"Please try to restrain your enthusiasm," Sarah chided, flushing and trying not to laugh.

"Only if you'll keep your promise to grant me the first dance. That's a waltz, if I'm not mistaken."

Indeed, the opening notes were a little uncertain, but the fiddlers quickly squawked into the familiar strains of the Tennessee Waltz.

Sarah stepped into Garth's arms and followed as he swirled her into the midst of the other couples. "You look awfully handsome yourself, tonight," she observed, thinking he looked exactly like the prince about whom Cameron had teased her earlier. Tall and dark in his black broadcloth suit, he was without doubt the most imposing man present.

Certainly more imposing than a scrawny, blond gunfighter who wouldn't even tell people his real name, she thought sourly, but she didn't allow her ill temper to show on her face. Giving Garth her brightest smile, she brushed away his modest demurs and proceeded to make what she hoped was sparkling conversation.

"Son of a bitch," Travis muttered in disgust when he entered the schoolhouse and saw the man with whom Sarah was dancing. She hadn't wasted a second getting into Garth Richardson's arms, the little vixen.

"Best mind your manners in here, laddy," a familiar voice cautioned, and he looked up to find Cameron at his elbow.

"I ain't planning on actually murdering him," Travis allowed.

"Mighty glad to hear it," Cameron said cheerfully. "Ye should stop frowning, though. The look

285

on your face would curdle milk."

Travis made a conscious effort to relax his expression. "How's that?"

Cameron shook his head in mock despair. "Ye'll have to do better if ye expect to attract any partners tonight."

Travis hadn't even considered dancing with anyone. He'd planned on simply watching the crowd and keeping an eye on Sarah, but keeping an eye on Sarah while she danced with Garth Richardson held very little appeal for him, and might even prove disastrous if he couldn't disguise his feelings any better than he was doing at the moment. "I can probably attract at least one partner," Travis said, seeing her on the other side of the room. From here she looked as if she could use some company, too.

When he saw the woman Travis indicated, Cameron snorted. "No woman that pretty would dance with ye."

"She would, too," Travis informed him. "We're good friends."

"What's her name then?" Cameron challenged.

"Elizabeth Williams."

Cameron's broad face wrinkled in distaste. "The whore."

" 'Let he who is without sin among you cast the first stone,' " Travis quoted piously. "Ain't that what the Good Book says?"

"Aye, but I'm surprised ye can quote it," Cameron replied in amusement.

"A consequence of my misspent youth, before I discovered saloons." Travis frowned again as Garth Richardson swept by with Sarah. Her cheeks were

rosy and her eyes shining, and she was looking at
Richardson like she thought he'd hung the moon.
Damn it, she never looked at Travis like that. For a
moment he recalled someone who had, though, and
the vision of Elizabeth Williams's green eyes full of
admiration convinced him to follow his original impulse. He barely heard Cameron's startled exclama-
tion as he strode confidently toward where all the
young, attractive women were sitting.

They all saw him coming, and he could see the
whispered speculation. Ignoring the gasps of surprise, he stopped in front of Elizabeth. Just as he had
known she would, she smiled, her eyes as soft and
green as new spring grass.

"Good evening, Mr. Travis," she said, a little uncertainly.

"Good evening," he replied, and eyed the empty
chair beside her. "You don't look like you're having
much fun."

Her smile wavered but held. "I enjoy watching the
festivities. It's nice just to get out of the house once
in a while."

"Would you like to dance?"

Her smile vanished. "I . . . I don't usually . . ."

"Why not?" he challenged.

She considered this, her lovely face as smooth as
satin. "Why, I suppose because no one ever asks me,
and *you* really shouldn't, either."

"Why not? If you're worried about my reputation,
don't be. People usually think the worst of me no
matter what I do, so I gave up caring a long time
ago. You should, too."

"I did once, and I paid the price, Mr. Travis," she

287

reminded him solemnly. "Perhaps you should take a lesson."

"I'm too old for lessons," Travis insisted. "If you don't dance with me, I'll sit down here beside you until you do."

He could see the prospect of sitting there while every woman in the place speculated on why Travis had singled her out for attention held no appeal for her. At least if they were dancing, she wouldn't have to see them watching. "It seems you give me little choice," she allowed at last, glancing around for her son.

Paul was happily playing tag with several other boys at the end of the room, so Elizabeth rose with only a hint of reluctance and let Travis lead her to the floor.

"Maybe I should've warned you. I'm not very good at this," he said, taking her into his arms. For a second, she felt so much like Sarah that a wave of heat surged through him, but then he caught a whiff of her perfume, a heady scent as unlike Sarah as Elizabeth was herself, and the heat evaporated.

"I'll try to stay out from underneath your feet," she promised with another smile, "although I'm a little rusty myself."

She wasn't nearly so rusty as she made out. In fact, she seemed to glide as they moved around the floor, and her sweet smile went a long way toward helping Travis forget that Sarah was giving the same kind of smile to another man someplace very close by.

"I never had an opportunity to thank you, but I appreciate the way you handled Paul's questions yesterday," Elizabeth said after a moment.

"I just hope I said the right thing. I don't know much about kids."

"You're being modest, Mr. Travis. You said exactly the right thing," she assured him in her velvet voice, the one that would never hold a hint of censure or disapproval. She was, he had to admit, a real comfort to a man's dignity. Travis wondered if she did it on purpose, or if she'd simply been trained until she didn't know any better.

The dance ended abruptly, as if the musicians weren't quite sure of the final notes, and Travis released her. They applauded politely, and Travis found himself glancing around, trying to find Sarah in the crowd.

She stood with Richardson, looking up into his face and laughing at some remark he'd made. And Richardson, damn him to hell, was looking at Sarah like he wanted to take her off someplace and . . .

"Oh, dear," Elizabeth murmured, and Travis saw that she, too, had seen Sarah and Richardson.

"What's the matter?"

"What?" Elizabeth asked, obviously unaware she had voiced her concern aloud.

"You said, 'Oh, dear,' when you looked at Sarah just now."

Elizabeth forced her charming, vacant smile. "Did I? I can't imagine why."

But Travis wasn't going to let her off so easily. "Do you know something about Richardson?"

"Of course not," she tried, but she was a poor liar.

"Look, Mrs. Williams, you probably don't know this, but Sarah's in a lot of danger. Some-

289

body tried to kidnap her last week and—"

"I know."

A premonition pricked his nerve endings. "How do you know? Did Sarah tell you?"

Elizabeth looked away, obviously loath to break a confidence.

He fought to conceal his impatience. "You don't have to say, but if anybody but Sarah told you, it might be a clue. See, nobody knows about the kidnapping but us, and—"

"Mr. Richardson told me," she said softly, so softly Travis thought he must have heard her wrong.

"Richardson?" he repeated in disbelief.

"Yes, and you're wrong when you say no one knows. He said it's common knowledge. One of Sarah's men had told one of his. He said everyone in the county had heard the story."

Travis tried to make sense of this. If it were true that one of their men had gossiped, then naturally Richardson would have heard about it. But Travis had warned their men on pain of death not to breathe a word, and he was pretty sure they were all scared enough of him to keep their mouths shut.

"He came to me because he wanted someone to warn Sarah to give up her sheep before she gets into serious trouble," Elizabeth was saying. "Naturally, I don't like to meddle in her affairs, but I'm also worried about her safety."

"Don't worry anymore," Travis said. "I'll give her the message."

Elizabeth's eyes softened with gratitude, and she smiled, as if he'd just relieved her of an onerous burden. As if, he thought wryly, he'd hung the moon.

The musicians announced a reel, and the couples around them were regrouping into two long lines. "What do you say?" he asked Elizabeth, gesturing toward the ladies' line.

"I . . . I'd love to," she replied, with just the right amount of modest delight. She glided gracefully to take her place while Travis joined the men.

He'd lost sight of Sarah, but when he scanned the line of women, he found her quickly enough. She was the one giving him a look that would've drawn blood on a rawhide boot. Now what in the hell had gotten into her? he wondered, glancing over to see who her partner was.

Expecting Garth Richardson, Travis was once again surprised to see Owen Cameron opposite Sarah in the line, and the Scot was scowling at him, too. Before he could make sense of it, the music started, and the two lines sashayed forward to curtsy and bow to each other.

Now Elizabeth was frowning, too, and the next time the two lines came together, he said, "What's wrong?"

"I don't think Sarah approves of my dancing with you," Elizabeth whispered.

"What . . . ?" he began, but he had to clump back to his place before he could form a coherent question. He looked over at Sarah again and found she was still glaring murderously, almost as if she were *jealous*.

He almost laughed aloud at the thought, until he realized with a jolt that it might very well be true! Hadn't Sarah tried to test him yesterday by throwing him together with the woman she considered her rival? He'd thought he'd set her straight on the subject, but from the look in her eye just now, he could see he'd been wrong.

The lines came together, men and women clasping hands and raising them to form a bridge under which the first couple in the line passed as they danced their way to the end.

"Do you think she's jealous?" he asked Elizabeth, who was looking more distressed by the moment.

She nodded forlornly, and Travis couldn't suppress a satisfied grin as the two lines parted again. Suddenly the bitter gall he'd tasted when he'd watched Sarah with Richardson didn't seem quite so bitter anymore. Sarah might've been smiling at the rancher, but somehow Travis preferred the glare she was giving him right now.

Feeling smug, he concentrated on cheering Elizabeth up for the rest of dance. He'd actually gotten her to smile again, until Cameron and Sarah came skipping down the line. Sarah's face looked as if it had been carved from stone, and she very pointedly didn't so much as glance in Travis's direction. Cameron stomped on his foot.

Travis bit back a curse and glared at the Scot's broad back, but he couldn't really be angry. If Owen was taking revenge, Sarah must be mad enough to spit nails. When he glanced at Elizabeth, he knew she'd seen what happened. Her tentative smile was gone, and she mouthed the words, "Oh, dear."

Travis had to chuckle.

When it came their turn to travel down the line, Travis slipped his arm around Elizabeth's waist. Her gasp was audible above the squealing fiddles, but

Travis pulled her close to his side for the trip through the human tunnel. He sneaked a look at Sarah as they hurried past, and the fury in her eyes told him for certain what he hadn't really allowed himself to believe: *Sarah really loved him.*

Their lovemaking hadn't been an aberration or a mistake, and Sarah's assurances hadn't been made from a guilty conscience. As difficult as it might be to believe, Travis Taylor had won her heart. And as unworthy as he might be, Travis Taylor might actually have a chance at happiness with Sarah Hadley.

The knowledge stunned him, and the remainder of the dance went by in a blur. Before he knew it, the music had stopped, and the dancers were raucously shouting their approval.

Once again he scanned the line for Sarah, but she had already disappeared into the crowd. Instinct told him to go after her, but he couldn't just walk off and leave Elizabeth. He'd have to at least escort her back to her seat.

And Elizabeth looked as if she'd need some serious escorting. If Sarah's face had been white with rage, Elizabeth's was white with apprehension. "I knew I shouldn't have danced with you," she said, when Travis took her elbow and steered in the proper direction.

"Why not?" Travis asked, eager to hear whether Elizabeth's assessment of the situation was the same as his.

But Elizabeth just pressed her lips together and shook her head in dismay.

"Is it because Sarah got mad about us dancing together?" he prompted.

"I . . . I can't think why it should have upset her," Elizabeth hedged, and Travis realized she didn't know the extent of Travis and Sarah's relationship and was trying to protect her friend.

"Maybe because she likes me herself," he tried, taking perverse satisfaction in Elizabeth's horrified expression. "Don't worry," he assured her. "I like her right back."

Elizabeth was shocked speechless, and Travis let her drop into her chair.

"Would you like some punch?" he asked politely, thinking she looked like she needed something stronger then punch. She nodded, her mouth still open in unladylike surprise.

Travis started working his way toward the punch table, all the time watching for Sarah. Instead, he found Owen Cameron, or rather the Scot found him.

"What in God's name are ye trying to do, ye bloody fool?" he snarled.

Travis considered Owen's outrage an excellent omen. "I'm getting Mrs. Williams a glass of punch," he replied ingenuously.

"If ye go near that woman again, so help me, God, I'll break every bone in your—"

" 'Best mind your manners in here, laddy,' " Travis quoted. "And I can't very well just leave her sitting after I promised I'd—"

"Damnit, I'll get the woman some punch," Owen said, through gritted teeth. "Ye'd best take care of Sarah before she has apoplexy."

"You look a little peaked yourself, Owen," Travis noticed. "That reel must've done you both in." Grinning at Owen's outrage, Travis

294

went in search of Sarah.

Owen swore under his breath as he watched Travis weaving his way through the crowd. At least he wasn't going back to that harlot, he thought grimly, catching sight of the woman sitting alone at the far end of the room.

God almighty! He'd just told Travis he'd get the creature some punch. He glanced back in the direction Travis had gone, and sure enough, the bastard was watching over his shoulder to see whether Owen kept his promise. He muttered another curse, and wondered whether his admiration for Sarah Hadley had cost him his sanity. He supposed he should be glad most of the people in this room already despised him for being a sheepman. Nothing he did now, not even consorting with a fallen woman, could possibly lower him in their opinion. If only he could keep a good opinion of *himself*, he thought, as he fought his way to the punch table and captured two glasses of something that looked insipidly sweet.

Resolutely, he launched himself back into the crowd and struggled over to where Elizabeth Williams sat. She was too busy trying to keep track of Travis to notice him.

"Mrs. Williams?" he said.

She looked up at him in alarm, and the impact of her wide emerald gaze took his breath. She was, he realized, a strikingly beautiful woman, even more beautiful than he'd thought the first time he'd seen her across the room.

"I . . . I've brought ye some punch," he said, trying not to stammer like a schoolboy, although he suddenly felt just as awkward.

295

She tensed, and Owen had the impression she was shrinking into herself . . . or drawing away from him. "Are you speaking to me?" she asked, her voice strained, her eyes wide and frightened.

Owen cleared his throat and tried a placating smile. "We have'na met, Mrs. Williams. I'm Owen Cameron. I work for Mrs. Hadley, and—"

"Oh, yes," she said, a little relieved, but still as wary as a fawn.

"I saw Travis just now, and he . . . he had some business, so he asked me to bring ye the punch he promised." He held out one of the glasses.

She looked at it for a moment, as if deciding whether or not it was safe to take it. At last she did, being careful not to touch his fingers as she did so, just the way a respectable lady would have done. "Thank you," she said primly. "The dancing made me thirsty."

She took a dainty sip, and Owen drained his glass in one gulp. The stuff was awful, but at least it was wet.

"Mama!" a childish voice called, and a small figure barreled into her. "Can I have a drink?"

"Certainly, darling," she said, and Owen watched in amazement as her wariness vanished. Her expression grew tender as she held the glass for the child— the *bastard* child, he reminded himself—until the boy had a good grip with both hands. He took a healthy drink, and Owen had actually opened his mouth to caution him to leave some for his mother, before he remembered it was none of his concern.

The child lowered the glass and smacked his lips. His mother took the glass from him, her face fairly glowing with love, and Owen couldn't help thinking she resembled a madonna, although he chided himself for the inappropriate comparison.

The boy wiped his mouth with the back of his hand, then noticed Owen for the first time. "Who are you?" he asked suspiciously, looking Owen over from head to toe.

"Don't be rude, dear," his mother cautioned gently. "This is Mr. Cameron. He's a friend of Aunt Sarah's."

Aunt Sarah! Owen thought in outrage. How dare she use a title of such intimacy for Sarah? he wondered, then realized with a start that Sarah must have told her to.

"Pleased to meet you," the boy said, with a smile that would have melted the North Pole. He stuck out a tiny hand, and for an instant Owen couldn't think why. When he realized the child intended to shake his hand, he almost chuckled, but caught himself. No one appreciated being laughed at, and Owen figured the boy was no exception.

He took the boy's hand carefully in his own huge one and shook it solemnly. "Pleased to meet ye, too," he said.

"My son, Paul," Elizabeth explained unnecessarily, and when Owen glanced at her, he saw her wariness had returned. She'd laid a hand on the boy's shoulder, as if she were ready to pull him to her, and Owen knew instinctively she expected to have to protect him from Owen.

How could she think he would say anything to harm the boy? he asked himself, but the answer came to him instantly: she must have learned to expect cruelty from others, and so must be constantly on her guard. The outrage he'd felt moments ago over Travis's behavior welled again, this time for the injustices this innocent child must have suffered.

Paul had been studying him out of dark brown eyes that Owen knew must have been inherited from his father, since they were nothing like his mother's. "Why do you talk funny?" the boy asked.

"Paul!" his mother chided, but Owen took no offense.

"Because I'm a Scot," he explained.

Paul thought this over. "Is that why your hair's so funny, too?"

"Paul!" Elizabeth cried, jerking the boy back to her side. "You mustn't say things like that. It's rude! I'm terribly sorry, Mr. Cameron."

She looked so genuinely distressed, Owen was compelled to reassure her. " 'Tis all right, missus. I'm thinking the bairn has never seen red hair before."

"What barn?" Paul asked, confused. "And your hair's not red, it's orange. I know my colors. Mama taught me."

Elizabeth was appalled, but before she could reprimand the boy again, Owen said, "Aye, 'tis orange, all right, but they call it red, nonetheless. 'Tis one of those things ye'll not even understand when you're older."

Paul nodded sagely, as if he'd already encountered a number of such incomprehensible things, and Owen had to bite back a smile.

"Paul!" one of the other children called impatiently, and immediately the boy's attention returned to his playmates. Without so much as a backward glance, he darted away to join the latest round of rough-and-tumble.

"I'm terribly sorry," Elizabeth said the instant he was gone. "He didn't mean anything insulting, I'm sure."

Owen had an overwhelming urge to reassure her. Surely, she'd had enough real trouble in her life that she shouldn't have to be upset over something so trivial. " 'Tis nothing, missus. He's a fine boy."

"Yes, he is," she said defensively, and Owen realized he'd struck a nerve. Couldn't he say anything to her without inadvertently being offensive?

She lifted the glass to her lips and drank down the little bit of punch Paul had left for her. Then she handed the glass back to Owen. "Thank you, Mr. Cameron. I appreciate your kindness."

The words were plainly a dismissal, but suddenly Owen didn't want to be dismissed. He wanted to explain to her that he hadn't meant to be unkind about the bairn. Paul *was* a fine boy, damn it, and probably because she'd taken pains to see he was. "I . . . I'm thinking ye'd like another glass, since the boy took most of it."

"You're very kind." Her voice held no expression, so Owen could take the statement any way he wanted. If he were tired of talking with the town's scarlet woman, he could leave, and if not . . .

Owen glanced around. He didn't see a sign of Sarah or Travis. Maybe they'd gotten together somewhere, and maybe not. If not, Travis might well seek out Mrs. Williams's company again, and Sarah would be even more upset. Owen shouldn't allow that. It was his duty to protect Sarah, wasn't it?

299

He shouldered his way to the punch table, got the glasses refilled, and shouldered his way back in what might have been record time.

Elizabeth certainly seemed surprised to see him. Evidently, she hadn't expected him to return. He handed her the glass and motioned to the empty chair beside her. "May I?"

She tensed, and Owen wanted to curse the circumstances of her life that made even an innocent, friendly gesture suspect.

"I just want to talk, missus," he assured her. "Nothing more."

Still she hesitated, and he saw her gaze flicker to where the other women sat slightly removed from her. They'd be watching and even trying to listen to any conversation, and plainly Elizabeth was loath to give them any grist for the gossip mill.

Owen should probably have been surprised to find that she cared so much about what was left of her reputation, but somehow he wasn't. Whatever foolish choices she had made in the past, she clearly had no intention of making any more.

When her gaze touched him again, he found he was holding his breath while he awaited her decision. When she said, "All right," ever so softly, he released it in a relieved sigh and took the chair quickly, before she had a chance to change her mind.

Several seconds ticked by during which Owen realized he didn't have the slightest idea what to say to her, now that he was here with her. He took a swig of the lukewarm punch and racked his brain, but nothing came to mind that he could be certain wouldn't offend her. Asking about her son could be dangerous, as he'd already learned, and asking about her past was most certainly forbidden. Even talking about the present held little promise.

"How do you like Texas, Mr. Cameron?" she asked, when he had just about given up hope of finding a suitable topic.

He looked at her and found she appeared to be sincerely interested. "It's a wee bit different from Scotland," he allowed cautiously.

"I would imagine," she said, and then she smiled. Her face lit up like a candle when she smiled, and her eyes sparkled like emeralds. The sight made Owen feel strange, as if something tight were clamped around his chest, squeezing all the air out of his lungs.

"What is Scotland like?" she asked.

For a second he couldn't seem to remember, but then his brain began to function again and his mouth was even able to form the words. "It's bonny, I mean, beautiful. As green as . . ." He'd almost said as green as her eyes, but caught himself just in time. "As green as emeralds, with more trees than ye can count, and castles as big as a town, made all out of stones."

"I do miss trees," she said wistfully. "Back East we had forests and hills, even mountains. And seasons, too. I miss the leaves turning colors, scarlet and gold. Here what trees we do have just turn brown, and a week later it's winter. In Texas it's either winter or summer. Even the weather has no mercy."

Did he hear bitterness in her voice, or was he just being fanciful? Owen wasn't usually a fanciful man. "Aye, but ye must be grateful the winter here is so short and so mild. It makes the land perfect for sheep."

Her smile bloomed again. "Some would point out it makes the land perfect for cattle, too."

"Only the cattlemen would, missus," he chided.

"What brought you here in the first place?" she asked, and Owen noticed she turned ever so slightly toward him and some of the tension seemed to have eased from her shoulders. "Surely they have plenty of sheep in Scotland for you to tend."

"Aye, but the sheep belong to someone else. I was just a hireling."

"But you're a hireling here, too. The sheep belong to Sarah," she pointed out.

"She pays part of my salary in lambs, and I'm building my own flock. I'm saving my wages, too, and someday I'll have my own land. I couldna do that in Scotland."

"Why not?"

"Because the land isna for sale," he explained, warming to his subject. "Scotland is an old country and a small one. The land passes from father to son, and not even to all the sons, just to the first born so the estate stays intact. A man like me has no chance."

"How dreadful!" she exclaimed. "To have ambition but no opportunity."

"Aye, so I made my own by coming here," he said, feeling a surge of pride. He had never spoken of himself to anyone in America, not even Sarah, he realized with a start. As his employer, she'd asked him about his qualifications for the job but never about his hopes and dreams and ambitions. Elizabeth Williams had learned more about him in five minutes than Sarah had bothered to find out in almost a year.

And even if Sarah had inquired, he couldn't imagine her looking at him the way Elizabeth Williams was looking at him now, as if she admired him for wanting to better himself.

"Weren't you frightened, coming to a new place, a new *country,* where you didn't know a soul?" she asked in amazement.

"Not frightened, exactly," he said. "I couldna let myself be scared, because I had no choice if I ever wanted to be my own man."

"But apprehensive," she guessed. "Worried that things here would be too different or that you wouldn't be able to accomplish what you had planned, that you'd be disappointed here, too."

"Aye," he said, thinking even he couldn't have explained it better. How could she have known? "But I soon found out the people here respect a man who wants to better himself. Even Mrs. Hadley was willing to help."

"You mean things are different in Scotland?"

"Aye, there a man with ambition is scorned. Others think he's getting above his place."

"His place?"

"The class to which he was born. At home, a man knows his place and keeps it, if he knows what's good for him."

"Obviously, you didn't know what was good for you, Mr. Cameron, or you wouldn't be here."

She had, he decided, the most lovely smile he had ever seen, and he found himself smiling back.

"My mother always did say I was a thickheaded lout," he agreed.

"Is your mother still alive?"

Before he knew it, Owen had told her the entire history of his family, and how it had pained him to leave them, but how he hoped someday to bring them to America, too. He couldn't remember ever having such a long conversation with a woman, and certainly no woman this beautiful had ever listened to him at all.

When he had finished the tale of his family, they settled into a comfortable silence for a few moments. He studied her faint smile and the way her lashes curled up around her astonishingly green eyes and the way her raven hair contrasted with the ivory of her skin. The warmth of the room had moistened that skin and tiny wisps of hair curled damply on her nape and temples.

Owen had a sudden and very shocking urge to press his lips to those spots and taste the salty tang of her flesh. The urge jolted him, but somehow he managed to regain his composure before he actually acted on the impulse. Something must have shown on his face, though, because her smile disappeared, and he saw a hint of wariness in her eyes.

"I . . . I'm thinking that's a waltz they're playing," he said quickly, knowing he couldn't bear for her to withdraw from him again. "Would ye care to dance?"

The offer seemed to surprise her, but she recovered quickly. "I should like it very much," she said, setting her now-empty glass down on the floor and rising gracefully from her chair.

She seemed much smaller than he had noticed before, and her hand felt almost fragile when he took it in his larger one. As he placed his other hand on her back, he wondered irrelevantly if he could span her waist with his hands, and thought she seemed awfully slender for a woman who had borne a child.

She moved as supplely as a willow in his arms. Her scent came to him, a tantalizing mixture of artificial fragrance and her own muskiness. Long-suppressed desires stirred unbidden, and Owen knew a moment of annoyance at his uncharacteristic reaction. He had always prided himself on his ability to control his baser instincts, although it was only natural to respond to an attractive woman, he supposed, especially to a woman who had . . .

But he didn't allow himself to complete the unkind thought. Who was he to judge her, after all? If Sarah Hadley could forgive her, no one else had any right at all to hold a grudge. And if he hadn't known of Elizabeth's past, he would certainly never have guessed her for an adulteress. Indeed, if anything, she behaved even more circumspectly than the so-called respectable women he had known.

"And how would *ye* be liking Texas, Mrs. Williams?" he inquired, acknowledging a need to find out more about her.

She smiled wanly. "Considering I never wanted to come here in the first place and what has happened to me since, I like it well enough."

Unwilling to dwell on what had happened to her since, he said, "Ye didna want to come? Why did ye, then?"

"For my husband's health. I thought you must know. He was consumptive, and the doctors back east advised him to go west. This is as far as we were able to go before our money ran out."

305

"I'm thinking the change didna help him."

"Oh, it did at first. In fact, for a while we thought . . ." Her voice trailed off, and she sighed. "But then he got bad again and . . ."

The pain in her eyes was eloquent, and it tore at Owen's heart. "You didna go back," he said prompting her to continue past the painful memories.

"I couldn't. As I said, we'd spent all our money getting here. I'd been doing some dressmaking to support us, but I barely earned enough to live. I certainly could never have earned enough for a ticket home. Besides, with Paul dead, there was nothing to go back to."

Paul. Owen realized with a start that she had named her son for her dead husband. He wondered what Philip Hadley had thought of that, then decided he didn't care.

"When Paul died . . ." she continued, then looked away, and her expression grew grim. "Well, you must know the rest of my story. I couldn't go back."

Owen had thought he knew the rest of her story, but now he was no longer certain. Elizabeth Williams wasn't at all the wicked enchantress he had imagined. In fact, he found it hard to even picture this sweet, demure lady as the adulteress who had stolen Sarah Hadley's husband. No, he didn't know her story at all, and he found he wanted to hear it from her side. Not tonight, of course—he couldn't expect her to confide in a man she hardly knew—but sometime. Sometime when she trusted him more.

The dance ended, and Owen released her reluctantly, feeling an inexplicable sense of loss when she left his arms. They walked back to their chairs, and

306

Owen once again sat down beside her. He was trying to decide what they should talk about next when little Paul wandered over.

"I'm thirsty, Mama," he announced, although he looked far more tired than anything else.

"I'll get ye a drink, wee one," Owen offered, and Paul rewarded him with a sleepy smile.

When Owen returned with three glasses of the now-warm punch, Paul was curled in Elizabeth's lap, his head on her shoulder, his eyes drooping.

He thanked Owen politely for the punch, drank about two sips, and collapsed against his mother's shoulder again, unable to keep his eyes open another moment.

"I'm surprised he lasted this long," Elizabeth said, stroking the boy's fine hair fondly. "I suppose I'd better take him on home."

"How will ye get him there?" Owen asked, thinking the child looked like more than an armload for her.

She laughed softly in deference to the sleeper. "The same way I always do. I'll carry him."

As small as the boy was, Cameron couldn't imagine her having the strength to cart him all the way back to her house. "That's too much for ye. I'll be glad to carry him."

Elizabeth had been shifting Paul around to a more manageable position, but she stopped at Owen's offer, and looked up at him in surprise that quickly changed to alarm.

"Why, thank you, Mr. Cameron, but I couldn't allow you to do that," she said stiffly.

For a moment Owen couldn't imagine what he'd said or done to offend her again. They'd been getting along so well. Maybe she was just proud about accepting help.

"It's no trouble," he assured her. "The bairn is much too heavy for ye to—"

"Mr. Cameron," she said through stiff lips, her face white except for two fiery spots on her cheeks, "I have not invited you to my home and I do not plan to. If I have somehow given you the wrong impression, allow me to correct it right now. Perhaps you think that because of my reputation, I make a practice of allowing strange men to—"

Owen silenced her with a loud *"No!"* which fortunately was drowned out by the sudden squawking of the fiddles as they launched into a rousing reel.

Elizabeth started, and he could see she would have bolted if she hadn't been hampered by the weight of her son's limp body.

"I'm sorry, missus," Owen assured her quickly, mortified that she could have thought he planned to take advantage of her. "I ken I've made a bloody fool of myself. I didna mean . . . I had no intention . . ." He cleared his throat and tried again. "I only meant to carry the bairn home for ye. Then I will come straight back here so all can see me."

She frowned, still doubtful.

"I swear," he said, holding up one hand as if prepared to do just that. "I wouldna dishonor ye."

Something flickered in her eyes, a combination of pain and something else. "Some would say you couldn't, Mr. Cameron, because I've already dishonored myself."

Owen glared at her. "Ye have if ye've let them

308

shame you, lass. Now quit arguing and give me the bairn."

He plucked the child from her before she could protest. The boy was no bigger than a lamb, and Owen settled him easily against his large shoulder. Instinctively, the child's arms encircled his neck, and Owen felt a surge of unexpected pleasure at the boy's instinctive trust. If only he could win the mother's so easily. Owen started for the door, knowing Elizabeth would have no choice but to follow.

The cool breeze from the open door felt good after the stuffiness of the schoolhouse, but Owen paused on the steps, worried the sudden change in temperature might chill the boy. He was struggling to pull his suit coat open so he could tuck the small body inside of it with him when Elizabeth caught up with him.

"Oh, dear," she said, feeling the wind and immediately sensing Owen's problem. She'd brought a shawl that she'd retrieved from someplace, and she quickly spread it over the boy's back.

That done, they set out toward the center of town and Elizabeth's house.

"I . . . I'm sorry," she said when they were away from the din of the dance.

"For what?" he asked in surprise.

"For . . . for doubting you."

He glanced at her, but her head was down, as if she didn't want him to see her face.

"I'm thinking ye've got no reason to trust any man, especially not a stranger."

She didn't reply, and he supposed she didn't need to. They walked on into the darkness in silence until a sudden gust of wind almost whipped the shawl from the child.

Elizabeth caught it and helped Owen tuck it more snugly in place. For an instant their hands touched, but Elizabeth jerked away as if she'd been burned.

"My goodness," she said, forcing a laugh to cover the awkward moment. "Feel how cold the wind is? I think we must be getting a blue norther."

"Aye, it . . ." Owen agreed absently, until the true meaning of her words sank in. "A norther?"

"It's a storm that comes from the north. I've seen the temperature drop thirty degrees in an hour, and I've heard about even bigger drops. If it rains, too, the water freezes on everything. It's quite beautiful, like the whole world is made of glass."

Owen knew perfectly well what a norther was and what it could do. He sniffed the air and detected the unmistakable smell of a coming storm. "I'd best get ye home, then," Owen said, picking up the pace as his mind raced ahead. He had a range full of sheep ready to lamb at any moment. If those lambs were born in the midst of a blue norther, they wouldn't stand a chance.

Chapter Ten

Watching the dancers, Travis shifted his shoulders to a more comfortable position against the hard wood. He stood leaning in a vacant spot on the schoolhouse wall with his arms and legs crossed negligently, as if he weren't watching the woman he loved in the arms of another man and as if he weren't entertaining fantasies of stalking across the room and claiming her as his own right in front of everybody.

At least she hadn't danced with Richardson again, although Travis had seen the tall rancher lurking, ready to claim her at the first opportunity. The opportunity hadn't arisen, though, because Sarah seemed intent on dancing with every single man present and was encouraging them with every feminine wile she possessed.

Travis might've been furious if he hadn't been so gratified. Sarah apparently didn't know much about playing hard to get, and she kept glancing over at him to make sure he saw what she was doing. Plainly the whole show was for his benefit, and he was prepared to endure it for as long as he could. Then he would inform Sarah it was time for them to be getting home, and this time *he'd* be the one in the buggy with her for the long ride back to the ranch.

He'd just begun to imagine what might happen during that buggy ride and afterward, when Owen came striding across the room toward him, looking like a thundercloud. Travis braced himself. If Owen thought he was going to light into Travis again about dancing with Elizabeth Williams . . .

"There's a norther coming," Owen said before Travis could speak.

"A norther?" Travis echoed, momentarily confused. He hadn't been expecting a weather report.

"Aye, and the smell of rain is in the air. If those lambs start . . ."

He didn't have to say any more. "Round up the men. Sarah probably won't want to leave just yet, so I'll have the cowboys stay so they can ride back with her. I'll go with you and the herders."

Owen nodded and made for the door while Travis scanned the dancers to find Sarah. While he'd been distracted, she'd paired up with Richardson again, and the bastard was guiding her around the floor in a waltz, grinning like a cat with a mouthful of feathers. Sarah was grinning right back, probably because she knew how irritated Travis would be to see them together.

At least he hoped that was the reason.

Drawing a deep breath, he lunged into the milling bodies and fought his way to them. He caught himself squaring his shoulders as he approached, as if he could make himself taller and therefore more of a match for Richardson. Silently cursing his own vanity, he consciously let his shoulders relax and made his expression blank as he reached up and tapped Richardson on the shoulder.

The rancher turned, prepared to politely deny whoever had sought to break in on them, but when he saw Travis, his charming smile hardened into a sneer. "Sorry, old man," he began, but Travis ignored him.

"Excuse me, Mrs. Hadley," he said, with just the proper amount of respect. He was glad to note her face had lit up when she thought he was cutting in, but at his tone, her expectant smile faded. "Cameron just told me the weather's turning, and we figure we'd better get back and make sure the sheep are all right."

"The sheep?" she asked, her lovely eyes clouded.

"Yeah, we don't want 'em lambing out in the open in freezing weather," he explained.

Understanding lightened her eyes and quickly changed to apprehension. "I'll go with you."

"No need, ma'am. There's nothing you can do there, and you've been having yourself a fine time here tonight," he told her generously, holding back a smile with difficulty. "Stay as long as you like. I'll leave the cowboys behind to make sure you get home all right."

"I'll see Mrs. Hadley home safely," Richardson said sharply.

Travis looked up at him consideringly, as if he were trying to judge the rancher's qualifications for the task, then dismissed him out of hand. He turned back to Sarah. "Like I said, Quinn and the others'll make sure you get home."

Richardson made a furious noise, but Travis ignored it.

Sarah did, too. *"You're* going with Mr. Cameron?"

313

she asked, plainly unhappy about it.

"Yes, ma'am," he said deferentially, and he could see the spark of annoyance in Sarah's expressive eyes. As he'd suspected, the dance would hold little pleasure for her unless Travis were there to watch her having fun. Unfortunately for her, she couldn't say what was on her mind in front of Richardson, and Travis took a perverse pleasure in getting a little of his own back. He allowed himself a small smile. "Enjoy yourself, Mrs. Hadley."

He nodded curtly and, still ignoring Richardson, took his leave. Wondering idly how long Sarah would remain at the dance without him to torture, he went outside in search of the others. He'd have to make sure Quinn understood he was not to leave Sarah in Richardson's care, no matter what anybody said.

Sarah told herself she was leaving early because she wanted to get home before the rain started. Everyone knew how deadly a Texas ice storm could be, and when the wind turned frosty less than an hour after Travis left, most of the other revelers had started to leave, too.

If she hadn't been so worried, she might have been amused over the battle of wills taking place between Quinn and Garth Richardson.

"Travis done told me to see Miz Hadley home, and I aim to do it," Quinn was insisting.

"Suit yourself," Richardson said, "but I intend to accompany her, too. Surely you can't object to my help."

Quinn muttered something unintelligible and stomped off to fetch the buggy.

314

"My God, it's getting cold," Garth remarked, turning up the collar of his suitcoat. "I hope you have a lap robe or something."

"I'm sure I do," Sarah said absently, pulling her shawl more closely around her shoulders. She couldn't believe how quickly the temperature had dropped. A newborn lamb could chill down and freeze to death in no time at all in weather like this.

While they waited for Quinn to bring the buggy, Sarah mentally calculated the gestation period of her sheep, adding one hundred and fifty days to the day last fall when they had begun breeding. To her horror, she realized the birthing might already have begun.

"Where'd your men get off to?"

The question startled her, and she looked up into the scowling face of Abel Frank.

Her hackles rose instinctively, but she couldn't just ignore him. "They went to take care of my sheep," she said, wishing she could have thought of some lie to tell him. It was really none of his business.

"Don't tell me those critters are too puny to leave out in the rain," he scoffed.

Sarah had no intention of answering such a question, but Garth had no compunctions. "It seems the sheep are getting ready to drop their lambs, and there is some concern about them doing so in an ice storm."

The two ranchers exchanged a look of mutual contempt for such delicacy. "My cows drop their calves wherever they happen to be," Frank said. "Don't need no midwives to hold their hands and wrap 'em up in a blanket."

Garth pretended to consider this. "Do cows have hands, Abel?"

315

Frank widened his beady eyes in mock surprise. "Well, now you mention it, they don't. What do you suppose a midwife would hold? The tail, maybe? On a sheep, though, them tails is mighty stumpy . . ."

"I appreciate your concern, Mr. Frank," Sarah said sarcastically, "but you needn't worry. I'm sure my sheep will weather the storm just fine."

"And if they don't, I reckon that'll solve our sheep problems around here," Frank replied, all trace of amusement gone. "Maybe the good Lord has decided to take matters into His own hands."

Sarah's temper snapped. "What a relief it must be to you to know you won't have to kill any more of my sheep yourself."

"What the hell does that mean?" Frank demanded.

"You know perfectly well what it means," Sarah informed him.

"Well, here's your buggy, Sarah," Garth announced with forced brightness, in a transparent effort to break up her argument with Frank. "You'll excuse us, Abel. I want to get Sarah home before the storm hits."

Frank muttered something Sarah didn't catch and didn't want to. The instant Quinn stopped the buggy, Garth handed her up into the seat.

"If you don't mind, I'll tie my horse behind the buggy and ride with you," Garth offered.

Still annoyed with him for his participation in Frank's insults, Sarah was about to refuse when Quinn hoped down. "I'd feel more comfortable on horseback anyways, if somebody tries something," he said, loping away before Sarah could stop him.

With a sigh, she acquiesced to the plan. At least Garth could be trusted to make conversation. With any luck, he would help keep her mind off the weather and her sheep.

When Garth had seen her swathed in the lap robe and settled into the corner of the buggy seat, he started off at a brisk pace, apparently intending to get her home as soon as possible.

They had ridden a little way in silence when Garth said, "Did you see your man shining up to Elizabeth Williams?"

Sarah felt the words like a lash, and she stiffened defensively. "I'd hardly call it 'shining.' He only danced with her once."

"But he must have sat with her for two hours, and the way he kept bringing her punch, and he carried her . . . her *son* home for her," Garth added in disgust.

"Travis?" Sarah asked in amazement.

"No, the Scotsman. What's his name?"

"Cameron?" Sarah asked, even more amazed.

"Yes. He certainly seemed smitten. Doesn't he know who she is?"

Garth apparently thought that if Cameron did know who she was, he couldn't possibly be smitten. Sarah was too busy trying to make sense of this to worry about his opinions, though. Owen Cameron and Elizabeth Williams? They'd sat together for hours, and Sarah hadn't even noticed! Well, she supposed that was some indication of how obsessed she was with Travis. The instant he'd left Elizabeth's side, she hadn't even given her friend another thought. Hadn't even gone over to say hello, she realized with a stab of guilt. But then, she'd barely spoken two words to Amabel or any of the other women, either. She'd been too preoccupied with flirting with

317

the men and trying to make Travis jealous.

Not that she'd succeeded. He'd stood and watched in total unconcern, and when the sheep needed him, he'd left her in the arms of another man without a qualm. Her only comfort was that he didn't seem as interested in Elizabeth as Cameron apparently was. After one dance, he'd been content to leave her to another.

"I said, does he know who she is?" Garth repeated a little testily. Apparently he didn't like being ignored.

"Of course he knows who she is," Sarah snapped. "And why should it make any difference?"

"You know perfectly well what difference it makes. No man wants to raise another man's bastard." As soon as the words were out, he made a startled sound, as if he'd just realized what he'd said. "Oh, Sarah, I'm sorry. I didn't mean—"

"Don't bother, Garth," she told him wearily. "I'm not that sensitive."

He sighed. "I just can't understand how you can be friends with that woman."

"Then stop trying," she suggested, wondering if the headache gathering behind her eyes was from the dancing, or the cold, or Garth's attempts to be chivalrous.

They rode on for a few minutes in silence; then Garth said, "Are your sheep really in danger?"

"I'm afraid so," she admitted, giving up the struggle not to think about it. "You see, we breed the sheep according to a schedule, so all the lambs are born during a four-week period in the spring . . . when we're sure the weather will be warm," she added with irony.

"Do your men really have to help with the birthing?" he asked skeptically.

"I'm afraid sheep are much more difficult to raise than cattle in that respect, although in most cases the men just stand guard against the varmints that are attracted by the birthing: wolves and coyotes, even eagles and buzzards."

"Eagles?" Garth scoffed.

"Yes, they've been known to carry off a newborn lamb. And since each lamb is so valuable, we have to make sure none of them die because the mother refuses to nurse it or because the mother has no milk."

Garth grunted in disgust, and Sarah could imagine his expression even though she couldn't see it in the darkness. "Sounds to me like they're more trouble than they're worth."

"They're certainly worth a lot. Don't forget the sheep saved my ranch," she reminded him sternly. "Without them, I would've gone out of business."

"You can't blame me for wishing you had, Sarah, because then you would have been forced to marry me."

"Garth!" she scolded, glad for the darkness that hid her burning face.

"It's true," he insisted. "Believe me, the thought of riding in like a knight on a white charger and rescuing you holds a lot of appeal. And," he added, "it's a lot easier on a man's pride than trying to convince a successful lady rancher that she ought to give up her sheep and let him take care of her."

"For heaven's sake, Garth, you sound as if you were really disappointed when I refused to marry you."

"Of course I was," he said. "No man likes to be turned down."

"Your pride may have been injured, but certainly not your heart."

"My heart was broken," he claimed.

"I thought you said you don't believe in love," she reminded him.

"That doesn't mean my heart couldn't be broken."

"Garth!" But Sarah couldn't help smiling in spite of her troubles. At least Garth's nonsense had taken her mind off her sheep, just as she had hoped.

He kept up a steady banter most of the way home, but when the ranch buildings appeared as dark shadows against the night sky, the rain began.

"Oh, no," Sarah murmured, hugging the lap robe around her against the chill of the north wind. The stiff breeze whipped the icy droplets against her face. Please, she prayed silently, don't let the lambs come in this.

Garth reached over and patted her arm. "I'm sorry, Sarah. I'd hoped at least it wouldn't rain."

"So had I," she replied, blinking against the hot sting of tears.

"If there's anything I can do . . ." he offered, when they had pulled into the yard.

"Other than stopping the rain and turning the wind, I can't think of a thing," Sarah replied, not even waiting for Garth's assistance before jumping down from the buggy.

Her men were riding in behind her, and they stopped their horses nearby as if awaiting orders.

"I don't suppose there's anything we can do until

morning," Sarah told them. "Try to get some sleep, and we'll set out at first light."

"I'll take the buggy, Mr. Richardson," Quinn offered, climbing down from his saddle, his rubber slicker making him look like a monstrous creature in the darkness.

"Just let me get my horse untied," Garth said, moving toward the back of the buggy.

"Maybe you should spend the night," Sarah suggested. "I hate for you to ride home in this."

"If I go now, I'll probably get there before it freezes, but if I wait until morning, you might be stuck with me a week," Garth replied. "I'll be fine if one of your men will loan me a slicker." He was right, of course, although Sarah couldn't bear the thought of the ice lasting a week, and what it would do to her flock if it did. She sent Ace to fetch a spare slicker from the bunkhouse, and when Garth had slipped it on, he turned to Sarah and took her hand.

"Remember, if there's anything I can do, don't hesitate to call on me. Although I hate to say it, for your sake, Sarah, I'm even willing to help with those godforsaken sheep."

His kindness touched her, and she decided she was no longer angry with him for the little scene with Abel Frank back at the schoolhouse. She squeezed his hand. "Thank you, Garth. Unfortunately, I don't think there's anything you or anyone else can do."

She waved as he rode away, although she knew he couldn't see her. How simple her life would have been if she'd been free to accept Garth's proposal. She should at least be thankful she had him for a friend.

The way things were, she needed all the friends she could get.

The morning sun revealed a crystalline world where every building, every tree, every bush, every blade of grass was covered with the frozen remnants of last night's rain. Having slept little, Sarah had no trouble at all waking at first light. She dressed quickly in her longjohns and woolen petticoats beneath her riding dress, then donned her sheepskin jacket and wrapped a woolen scarf around her head.

The north wind still howled fiercely as Sarah made her way carefully across the slippery ranch yard to the cookhouse. Inside, Pepe had already begun the morning meal.

"*Buenos días, señora,*" he said when he saw her.

"Good morning, Pepe. I think we'd better pack up the chuck wagon and take it out to where the men are working. No telling how long they'll be gone if the lambs have started."

"Should not we wait to hear from them, *señora? Señor* Cameron say I should—"

"I think the fact that no one has returned to the ranch indicates they are all too busy to send anyone with a message. Anyway, I'd rather take the wagon out for no reason than to have them need it and not have it."

"*Sí, señora,*" Pepe replied doubtfully, his round face creased in a frown, but Sarah wasn't in any mood for arguing. She helped herself to the flapjacks Pepe was stacking for the men, ignoring his look of surprise, and sat down to eat. Within minutes, the cowboys

322

came in, looking as if they also had slept little.

They glanced at her in surprise, too, but were too polite to mention how strange it was to be sharing breakfast with the boss lady. When they were all seated, Sarah said, "I've told Pepe to pack up the chuck wagon. I think we should go out and see if Mr. Cameron needs our help."

She expected an argument from the men, who would, at the very least, be reluctant to set out in such inclement weather, but they all nodded solemnly. "We was thinking the same thing, Miz Hadley," Quinn informed her. "You reckon Cameron took 'em to the birthing area?"

"If he couldn't do so last night, I'm sure he'll try today. At least it's the logical place to start looking for them."

The birthing area had been especially prepared for this time. Surrounded by fields where the various flocks could graze while they waited, the area contained corrals where sheep in labor could be penned, and rows of *jaulas,* or narrow chutes, where a reluctant mother sheep could be isolated with her lamb in a space too small for her to turn around and deny her baby its milk. The birthing area also contained rough shelters for just such weather as this, although Sarah had thought when they were being built that she would never have to use them.

When everyone had eaten, they all went their separate ways to prepare for the trip. Sarah packed blankets and her medicine box and, although she didn't allow herself to think about why she was doing it, the guns from the rifle rack and enough ammunition to supply an army.

Pepe stocked the wagon with tents and enough food to feed the crew for a week, and enough dry firewood to last out the storm. The sun was well up by the time they set out, but it promised little warmth, certainly not enough to melt the ice that covered everything in sight.

The going was slow over the slippery terrain, but after what seemed a lifetime, the sound of bleating came to them across the hoary plains, and Sarah knew a measure of relief. At least they'd gotten the sheep, or most of them, to the birthing area. Soon she could see the familiar grayish blobs milling in small bunches and the men on foot moving among them.

Sarah rode ahead, scanning the confusion for sight of Travis . . . or Cameron, she told herself sternly. She was only looking for someone in authority, and either of them would certainly do.

She found Cameron first. He was inspecting a flock for ewes who were in labor, and he'd just found one when Sarah rode up and frightened the sheep. They scattered in bleating confusion, and Cameron bellowed a curse at the rider before he recognized her.

"Oh, pardon, missus," he said in exasperation. "Get down off that horse, will ye?"

She hurried to do so, and motioned for the other riders to hang back. "I'm terribly sorry. I forgot. How are things going?"

"We've been lucky so far. The herders saw the storm coming and began moving the sheep here late yesterday. We've only had a few lambs so far. Two died, but the rest seem fine. If the weather breaks . . ." He glared at the overcast sky and left the rest unsaid.

"I brought the rest of the men and the chuck wagon

324

full of supplies, and some tents, too. What do you want us to do?"

"Ye'd best check with Travis. He told me to mind the sheep and he'd take care of everything else." Cameron lumbered after an escaping ewe, and Sarah led her horse back to where the others were.

"Wait here," she told the men. "I'm going to find Travis and find out where he wants us to set up camp. Does anyone see him?"

The cowboys stood in their saddles, and Ace was the first to spot him. Sarah set out in the direction Ace indicated, threading her way through the clustered flocks until at last she saw him, too. He was working near the *jaulas*, squatting on the ground with his back to her. Her heart lurched at the sight of him, and she had to remind herself she was still quite angry with him for the way he'd behaved at the dance. Still, she quickened her pace as she approached. She couldn't see what he was up to until she was almost upon him.

"*What are you doing!*" she cried in horror, as he finished skinning a newborn lamb.

His head jerked around in surprise, and when he saw her, he scowled. "What are *you* doing?" he countered. "I thought I told you to stay at the dance."

"The dance has been over for hours," she informed him. "And I'd like to know why you're murdering my sheep!"

"I don't have to murder them," he said, heaving himself upright, the tiny fleece still clutched in one hand, the bloody knife in the other. "God's doing a pretty good job of it, all on his own. I'm just cleaning up the mess."

Without waiting for a reply, he strode off toward a

ewe who was fussing over two lambs, both of whom were trying to nurse. Apparently, she'd given birth to twins and didn't quite know what to make of them. The confused ewe kept nudging them both away, as if she couldn't make up her mind which of them should go first. She bleated in protest when Travis, after sheathing the knife, picked up one of the lambs with his free hand and carried it off.

Thinking he intended to skin this one, too, Sarah snatched up her skirts and charged after him. She caught up when he had judged he was a safe distance from the mother and set the lamb down. Sarah had opened her mouth to shout a protest, when she saw he wasn't skinning this lamb at all. In fact, he was doing just the opposite: he was putting the fleece from the dead lamb onto the live one, stuffing the resisting legs into the second skin as if he were slipping on a jacket.

Sarah watched in open-mouthed fascination. When he had the lamb securely tucked into the second skin, he picked it up again and headed back in the other direction. As he passed her, he said, "Catching flies, Mrs. Hadley?"

Sarah closed her mouth with a snap and charged after him again. By the time she caught up this time, he'd come upon a hysterical ewe who had been running in circles as if she'd lost something. Travis presented the lamb to her, tail first. She sniffed suspiciously, once, twice, then bleated happily.

Travis set the lamb down and took a step back to watch as the mother nuzzled the skin of the dead lamb and recognized it as her own offspring. Within minutes, the fostered lamb was nursing happily on his new mother.

326

Sarah was so engrossed, she almost didn't notice Travis was walking away again. "Travis!" she called peremptorily. He stopped and looked back, obviously annoyed at having to stop what he was doing.

"I've brought the cowboys and the chuck wagon. Where do you want us to set up camp, and what do you want the boys to do?"

He opened his mouth, then closed it again, sighed and wiped his forearm wearily across his face. Only then did she notice how tired he looked. His eyes were bloodshot and his skin sallow. She wondered if he'd had anything to eat, and knew an urge to take him someplace far away from this bedlam and fix him a good, hot meal.

"I'll talk to them myself," he said, looking around until he saw the chuck wagon. When he started toward it, Sarah fell in beside him, casting one last look at the lamb and its new mother, who were getting along famously.

"What you did back there with that lamb," she began, not knowing exactly how to say it. "That was wonderful."

"It's nothing sheepherders haven't been doing for hundreds of years. Sheep are too stupid to take care of more than one lamb at a time, but luckily they're stupid enough to be tricked, too. They tell their lambs by smell, and if it smells right, they don't notice that it doesn't look quite right. After a couple days, we take off the skin and the ewe doesn't know the difference."

"You seem awfully knowledgeable about all this for a cow man, Travis," she remarked suspiciously, and she noticed he looked somewhat chagrined at her observation.

327

"Uh, Owen told me about it," he hedged. "We been working here all night," he added, as if that explained how he'd become such an expert on sheep.

Sarah had a feeling Owen Cameron hadn't needed to explain anything to Travis. She remembered other times when he'd exhibited more knowledge than he should have about sheep, and the seeds of suspicion finally began to take root. She'd get to the bottom of this, although perhaps not for a day or two, she realized, remembering the current crisis.

They'd reached the cowboys, who had dismounted and now stood waiting. The men muttered a greeting to Travis, who returned it grimly. "Things couldn't be worse," he told them, "but at least the lambs haven't started in earnest yet. The Mexicans have the sheep pretty well under control, but I'd like you boys to take turns riding around, sorta keep your eyes open. You know what I mean?"

They nodded solemnly, and Sarah suddenly felt a brand-new wave of apprehension. If someone wanted to strike her when she was most vulnerable, now would most certainly be the time. Her men were distracted, and the most valuable part of her flock was all together in one place. A single night raid could wipe her out.

"Pepe, get some chow going," Travis was saying. "We only had jerky for breakfast this morning, and the men are hungry enough to eat raw mutton."

"We cannot have that, *señor*," Pepe said, with a broad grin.

When Travis had instructed him where to set up the wagon and the others had scattered to their assigned tasks, Travis glanced at Sarah.

328

"You'd better get back to the ranch. This is no place for you."

Sarah was tempted to remind him that if someone wanted to kidnap her, she'd be a sitting duck back at the ranch alone, but she decided not to give him anything else to worry about at the moment. "You're forgetting who owns these sheep. I'd like to keep an eye on them myself, if you don't mind."

His frown told her he did mind, but he said, "Suit yourself, boss lady."

The sarcasm stung her, but she realized her reminder must have stung him, too. He had already started back for the sheep, but Sarah grabbed his arm, unwilling to let him go just yet. "We . . . we brought some tents, too," she told him, her heart aching at the sight of his fatigue. "Maybe the men could take turns getting a nap."

He nodded, then glanced down to where her hand still clutched his arm. When he lifted his gaze, it held a question, and Sarah answered it by refusing to let him go. They had to get at least one thing settled, even in the midst of this crisis.

"You . . . you didn't ask me to dance last night," she tried, watching for any reaction.

Something flickered in his eyes but was gone before she could identify it. "You didn't look like you needed a partner."

"Were you watching me?"

"You know I was."

"Why?" she challenged, knowing even as she did so that she was asking for trouble.

His lips twitched into a tiny, taunting smile. "Because you were trying to make me jealous."

329

"I was not!" she cried indignantly.

"Then why did you keep looking over at me?"

"Because you were looking at me," she informed him. "And . . . and because I thought you'd . . ."

"You thought I'd what?" he asked, still smiling.

"I thought you'd want to dance with me, and I couldn't . . ." She caught herself before she could actually say she couldn't understand why he didn't.

But she didn't need to say it. "I didn't want to dance with you, Sarah," he said very softly.

Mortified, she dropped his arm, but before she could turn away, he caught her wrist and held it in an iron grip. "Or maybe I should say I didn't *just* want to dance with you," he added provocatively.

His eyes glittered with desire, and the heat of it burned away her humiliation. Instinctively, her body quickened in response. Hardly able to breathe, she said, "What did you want to do?"

"I wanted to take you in my arms and kiss you until you forgot who you were and who I was and nothing mattered but the two of us together. Then I'd carry you off someplace where nobody'd ever find us and lay you down and take off every stitch of your clothes—"

"Travis," she protested weakly, but he didn't stop.

"—and I'd kiss every inch of you, Sarah, so you'd know just how much I want you and so you'd want me just as much, and when I was inside of you, you'd call my name—"

Travis!

"—and tell me you love me—"

I love you!

"And you'd know that you're my woman."

In spite of the freezing wind, Sarah thought she

might go up in flames. She would most certainly have thrown herself into his arms if Quinn hadn't interrupted.

"Miz Hadley?" he called.

"Yes," she managed, although her voice sounded shrill and Travis's azure gaze still held her fast.

"Pepe's gonna have a fire going in a minute. He says you should go over and get yourself warmed up."

Sarah was already as warm as she ever hoped to be, but she nodded absently, still unable to break her gaze from Travis's. After what seemed a long time, he slowly released her wrist, and only when the blood began to flow back into her hand did she realize how tightly he'd been holding it.

She massaged it absently, cradling it to her chest where her heart thudded ominously. "You're a dangerous man, Travis Taylor," she heard herself say.

Instantly the glow of passion vanished from his eyes, as if it had been snuffed by an unseen hand, and his expression hardened. "I'm a danger to you, Sarah Hadley. Maybe you oughta think about that."

Then he was gone, striding away, back to the sheep, not giving Sarah a chance to say that she *had* thought about it, and she knew now it simply didn't matter.

The sheep came just as Cameron had told her they would, the ewes in each flock giving birth in the order in which they had been bred. When the lambs fell on the icy ground, the men were there to snatch them up and carry them to shelter, isolating each lamb with its mother until the baby had nursed and been accepted.

Unfortunately, not every ewe accepted her lamb, and many wandered off heedlessly, leaving their little ones to bleat piteously until they collapsed, easy prey for the cold or for some predator that had slipped by the men's vigilance.

Sarah assigned herself the task of finding these lost lambs, and while the men saw to the births, she clumped through the churning masses of sheep hour after hour, looking for lambs whose mothers had abandoned them.

When possible, she would locate the lamb's mother and have one of the men isolate the two in a *jaula*, but sometimes Sarah couldn't locate the proper mother, and she would have to carry the lamb to a place of safety until a foster mother could be found. For such small creatures, they were surprisingly heavy, or at least they seemed to grow heavier with each hour that passed.

Still she worked, hour after hour, numbed with cold, her feet leaden lumps, her arms aching with weariness. Every now and then one of the men would order her back to the chuck wagon, where she would bolt down a few spoonfuls of beans and swallow a cup of scalding coffee, but soon she would be back again, the cries of the lambs echoing in her head as she searched for the orphans.

The sun rose high in the sky, then started down again, glittering off the ice but never warming it. They built fires for warmth, but the heat dissipated into the sky and never touched them. They spread blankets for the newborns, to shield them from the ground, but the lambs would stagger up on spindly legs and wander away to fall again, and Sarah would find them frozen and dead. After a while, she couldn't even feel grief anymore. She would simply carry the stiff little body to one of the men for disposal and go out again, looking for another.

The sun slid behind the horizon and the low-hanging clouds darkened into night. The temperature dropped even lower, and now the lambs were sometimes simply born dead. Sarah had thought herself beyond anguish, but the first lamb she saw that lay limply on the cold ground and didn't at least try to lurch to its unsteady feet brought the full extent of the tragedy home to her.

Tears scalded her eyes, burning like liquid fire until they spilled over onto her cheeks, where they chilled instantly in the relentless wind. She should, she supposed, be weeping for the financial loss each death represented, but never would she have dreamed such a disaster would also involve such suffering: the lambs bleating out their death agonies, ewes calling to their dead lambs, the whole endless cacophony reverberating through the night.

When Travis found her staring at the dead lamb with the tears streaming down her face, he muttered a curse and scooped her up into his arms. She tried to protest, but the sound came out as a sob. She wondered how he had the strength to carry her when he'd been at this even longer than she, but before she could manage to ask him, he set her down beside the chuck wagon.

"Pepe!" he bellowed, and the portly cook emerged from under a pile of blankets.

"Sí, señor," he said, scrambling to his feet.

"See Mrs. Hadley gets something hot to eat and put her in one of the tents and don't let her out until morning."

Pepe nodded vigorously and hurried to

fetch Sarah some food.

Travis glared at her. She wanted to say something, but couldn't seem to work up the energy.

"I don't want to see you again until daylight," he told her. "Do you understand?"

"Travis . . ." she managed, trying to blink the tears out of her eyes so she could see him clearly. She wanted him to hold her, to tell her everything was going to be all right. And then, miraculously, his arms were around her.

He held her tightly, her face pressed against his jacket. He smelled of sheep, but she didn't care. Nothing mattered except being in his arms.

"Oh, God, don't cry, Sarah," he whispered fiercely. "I'll save them for you, I swear. Just don't cry."

She fought the tears with the last of her strength and managed at least to slow them and to hold back the sobs clogging her throat. Clinging to him, she drew on his power and felt a little of it seeping into her, reviving her.

"I'm . . . all right . . ." she said brokenly, sounding far from all right, but feeling much better than she had just seconds ago.

He released her slowly, reluctantly, and she saw the frustrated determination in his eyes. His fingers gripped her arms through the thickness of her jacket. "I won't let them die, Sarah," he promised. "Do you believe me?"

She nodded, knowing it was a rash, reckless promise, but believing it just the same.

Pepe returned, holding a plate of beans and a steaming cup of coffee, which he offered to her with a pleading smile.

"I want you to get some sleep," Travis said, firmly as if he were talking to a slow-witted child. "You won't be any good to anybody if you keel over on us."

"I will," she said, alarmed at how weak her voice sounded. If she looked half as bad as she felt, no wonder Travis was so concerned. "I'll be all right."

He squeezed her arms. "Yes, you will," he said; then he was gone.

After choking down as many of the beans as she could, Sarah crawled into one of the tents, wrapped herself in a blanket, and knew nothing more until she heard Pepe ringing the bell to summon the men to breakfast. The second day was much like the first, and once again Sarah worked alongside the men. By late afternoon, her body was past pain and fatigue, her mind numb from too many dead lambs.

She was carrying the latest of these from one of the *jaulas* when a drop of water struck her on the head, soaking right through her scarf. She muttered a curse, thinking the rain had started again, but when she looked up, another drop hit her in the face, and she realized it had fallen from the overhang of the shelter under which she stood.

"What it is, missus?" Cameron asked, taking the dead lamb from her.

"I . . . I think it's melting," she said, turning her face into the wind. The sting was gone, and when she got her bearings, she realized she was facing south.

South. The wind had shifted again, and already it was scouring the ice from the ground and the trees. Relief surged through her, and she whispered a silent prayer of thanks.

"Aye, missus, ye can feel it," Cameron confirmed.

He shouted to the other men, who all stopped what they were doing and looked up.

Sarah scanned the scene until she found Travis, and he saw her at the same time. Even from here she could see his smile, as triumphant as if he'd turned the wind himself. Sarah wanted to run to him and throw her arms around him and share this moment with him, but of course she couldn't make a spectacle of herself in front of her men. Travis was right about being discreet. He'd lose the men's respect if they found out. So she hugged herself instead, cherishing the victory and consoling herself with the knowledge that someday soon she and Travis would no longer have to keep their love a secret.

By sundown, the ice had disappeared and the men had stripped off their jackets in deference to the change in weather. And more than just the climate had changed. While the activity with the sheep was just as frantic, the sense of urgency had gone, blown away by the south wind. No longer did they need to fear a newborn lamb would freeze to death unnoticed, and the process settled into the routine tasks associated with natural lambing.

Sarah was taking a break that evening, sitting by the cooking fire and savoring a cup of coffee, when Travis found her. He hunkered down beside her where she sat on a log, and Sarah resisted with difficulty the urge to caress his beloved face. If he had looked weary the first morning she had seen him, he looked positively haggard now, and she wondered if he had slept at all. His azure eyes were shadowed, and the lines beside his mouth looked as if they had been carved there by an unkind hand.

336

"Sarah, I think you'd better go home before it gets dark. You need a good night's sleep, and we really don't need you anymore."

She tried an imperious glare, which she knew would lack some of its authority, considering her present bedraggled condition. "These are my sheep, if you will remember. I believe I am the one who should decide whether I'm needed or not."

She saw the warning glint in Travis's eyes, but before he could respond, Cameron said, "He's right, missus. I've seen dead people who look better then ye do."

Sarah hadn't noticed Cameron standing across the fire from her. She glared up at her *mayordomo,* but he only smiled benignly back. Knowing he was probably right, she resorted to the argument she'd been holding in reserve. "Are you suggesting I ride back to the ranch alone? Have you both forgotten someone tried to kidnap me only a week ago? Or maybe you *really* want me out of the way . . ."

Travis muttered something profane, but Cameron said, "Missus!" as if he were thoroughly shocked. "Ye canna think we'd send ye home alone. Travis will go with ye."

Plainly, this news was as much a surprise to Travis as it was to her.

"I can't leave," he insisted, rising to his feet to face Cameron.

"Why not? If we dunna need Mrs. Hadley, we dunna need ye, either. My men know how to birth lambs, and Quinn and the others can guard against intruders. They have at least had some sleep. Ye'll be of no more use to me until ye've had some,

337

too, and ye'll sleep better at the bunkhouse."

While Travis considered the suggestion, Sarah's mind raced. Good heavens, Cameron was sending them off to the ranch, where they'd be completely alone all night. Her outrage at being sent home melted in a heat that was half desire and half embarrassment. Why on earth would Cameron do this? Did he know about her and Travis? But if he did, surely he would be the last person to throw them together.

"I can't just leave her at the ranch," Travis was saying. "She's right about the kidnapping. If whoever did it found out she was alone—"

"Then take her into town tomorrow morning when ye've both had some rest. She can stay with the Bigelows. She'll be safe there."

"Wait a minute," Sarah protested, annoyed at being discussed as if she weren't present, as if she weren't their *employer*, for heaven's sake. "What if I don't want to go to town?"

The two men exchanged a glance, and Sarah could just imagine them plotting to bind and gag her and carry her off against her will. She had stiffened her spine, ready to light into them, when Cameron said, "Missus, I'm thinking if ye don't go to the doctor's house now, we might be taking ye in later as a patient."

Sarah recalled his earlier remark about having seen dead people looking better than she, and instinctively raised a hand to her face. If the men looked exhausted, she must look equally bad, perhaps even worse, since she wasn't used to such strenuous labor.

"We'll discuss where you're going in the morning," Travis decreed, grabbing her arm and hauling her to her feet, "after you've had a good night's sleep. Quinn," he called, "fetch us a couple of horses, will you?"

Sarah didn't allow herself to think about why she'd given in so easily, because the truth was, she hadn't really wanted to object. Every bone in her body ached, and the prospect of a hot bath and a night spent in her own bed instead of on the ground had been far more tempting than she'd wanted to admit. The prospect of spending that night with Travis, alone, was more temptation than she could resist.

The two of them hardly spoke during the ride back to the ranch. Sarah was much too tired for conversation, and she expected Travis felt the same. She entertained herself with thoughts of her bed, the bed that had of late seemed cold and empty, but which tonight she would share with Travis, she thought, as tingles of anticipation danced over her. And this would be only the first of many such nights. As soon as possible, they would marry, and she would never be alone again. Her life stretched before her now, not as an ordeal she must endure, but as an adventure of discovery, full of golden promises and the one thing she had never allowed herself to hope for: happiness.

The ranch buildings were forbidding in the darkness. She and Travis dismounted in front of the house, and Travis went in ahead of her to light the lamp. He glanced at her when she came in, but looked quickly away, making her self-conscious of her appearance. "I'll get a fire started," he said, and moved into the kitchen without waiting for her reply.

Sarah wondered at his strangeness. She'd half expected him to take her in his arms the moment they were inside the house, but, she reasoned, they were both filthy, and he hadn't shaved in days, and perhaps he was as self-conscious as she.

Light bloomed in the kitchen from the lamp he had lit there, and she followed him in. He was crouched in front of the stove, and in another instant he had a small blaze going. Without consulting her, he took the buckets stacked nearby, filled them from the kitchen pump and put them on the stove to heat.

"I'll take care of the horses," he said, and left without looking at her.

Sarah decided maybe she'd better find a mirror.

Taking the lamp from the hallway, she carried it to her bedroom, and when she finally saw her reflection in the mirror, she gasped in despair. No wonder he didn't want to look at her.

She quickly stripped out of the jacket and scarf and began to pull the pins from her matted hair. Having brushed the worst of the tangles out, she returned to the kitchen, where she ladled a basin of water from one of the buckets to use on her hands and face. After she'd washed, she went back to her bedroom and started to peel off the clothes she had worn for the past two days. When she got down to her petticoats, she shivered a little in the chill, and decided she'd better light a fire in here, too.

The small bedroom stove caught instantly, and soon the blaze was burning cheerfully. Sarah removed the last of her clothes and slipped quickly into her heavy winter robe and slippers, grateful for their warmth. She wished she had something more alluring to wear for this, of all nights, but she suspected Travis would prefer it if she wore nothing at all.

The thought raised gooseflesh all over her body, and she hugged the rough robe to her sensitized skin. If Travis didn't return soon and take her in his arms, she would be forced to go after him.

Still listening with one ear for sounds of Travis's return, she went back to the kitchen to check on the water. Finding it almost ready, she looked at the tub hanging on the wall and smiled to herself.

The tub was an old-fashioned round one, shallow with a wide brim and a seat on the edge in case one wanted only a foot bath. Sarah wondered idly if it were large enough even to consider what she was considering. They would both need a bath, though, and there was no sense in wasting a lot of time.

She heard Travis's footsteps on the porch. "Sarah?" he called from the hallway.

"I'm in the kitchen," she called back, and felt the prickle of excitement teasing the backs of her legs.

Travis appeared in the doorway, and his blue gaze found her instantly, but once again he looked quickly away. Staring pointedly at the stove, he said, "Will you be needing anything else?"

Sarah gaped at him. He talked as if he planned to leave her. Surely he didn't intend to really sleep in the bunkhouse. Or maybe he did! She could hardly credit it, after the things he'd said to her yesterday about taking her off where no one would ever find them, but here they were and there he was, looking as if he found the mere sight of her painful.

Humiliation burned her cheeks, but she'd already shamed herself twice by asking him to seduce her. She'd be damned if she'd do it again. "Yes," she said, determined to be just as cool and detached as he. "I'd

341

appreciate it if you'd carry the bathtub into my bedroom for me, and fill it," she added.

His blue gaze darted to her as if he were checking to see if she were serious, then darted away again. He moved slowly, deliberately, to where the tub hung on the wall. She watched as he carried it out, and she pulled her robe more tightly around her as she waited for him to return. Suddenly, its warmth seemed barely adequate against the chill.

When he came back, he didn't spare her a glance as he picked up the buckets from the stove and carried them out, too. Furious now, Sarah followed, fairly marching with determination to show him his indifference meant nothing to her.

She stopped in the bedroom doorway and watched while he poured the steaming water into the tub. When he had finished, he turned and stiffened when he saw her. Looking pointedly at some spot just above her head, he said, "Is that all?"

"Yes, unless you were planning to kiss me good night," she said sarcastically.

At last he looked straight at her, and his eyes narrowed dangerously. "Don't tease me, Sarah. This is hard enough as it is."

"What's hard enough?" she snapped.

"You know damn well what," he snapped right back. "Leaving you here, like this." He gestured angrily at her robe-clad figure. "Now get out of my way, and let me leave while I still can."

Sarah thought the problem might be her fatigue. That would explain her inability to make sense of all this. "Are you saying you don't want to leave?"

"Sarah," he growled in warning, and Sarah could

practically see the tension radiating through him.

She crossed her arms beneath her breasts and studied him. "Is this the same man who said he wanted to carry me off and make love to me until I called his name and—"

"*Sarah!*"

Sarah started at the vehemence of his tone, but she wasn't about to back down. "Then why are you in such a hurry to leave?"

He clenched his fists and drew an unsteady breath. "You're tired, Sarah. You need your rest."

Suddenly, everything became clear. "Are you being considerate?" she asked in amazement.

"I'm trying," he told her stiffly. "Damn that Owen Cameron. He probably knew just what he was doing, too. When I . . . What are you doing?"

Sarah closed the bedroom door behind her and smiled. "I've decided there is something else you can do for me, Travis. You can scrub my back."

Chapter Eleven

His astonishment was almost comical, but Sarah didn't laugh. Instead, she strolled over to where he stood and eyed him with what she hoped was a sultry glance.

"Better take off that jacket, Travis. It's going to get hot in here."

His astonishment turned instantly to fury. "You're damn right it is," he informed her, grabbing her hands when she would have untied her robe. "Do you know what you're doing?"

Sarah was starting to wonder if she did, but he didn't give her time to decide.

"Sarah," he said, trying for control and very nearly succeeding. He released her and dropped his hands to his sides, closing them into fists. The tension radiated from him in waves. "Are you sure . . . ?"

"Of course I'm sure," she replied tartly. "Unless, of course, *you* don't want to."

"For a smart woman, you sure say some stupid things," he replied in exasperation. "Listen, Sarah, I know the kind of woman you are, and you're not the kind to lay down with a man you're not married to."

Sarah opened her mouth to point out she'd lain down with him twice before, but he beat her to it.

"The other times were different. You were . . . upset," he said, obviously choosing his words carefully. "You're not upset now, and we're still not married, and we might never be. Have you thought about that?"

Not recently, she admitted to herself, feeling the first stirrings of the all-too-familiar humiliation. "Are you trying to tell me you're not the marrying kind, or something?" she asked stiffly.

He sighed in exasperation. "I'm trying to tell you things happen. I'm not the kind of man who can make plans for the future, and I'm sure as hell not the kind of man a woman can count on."

Sarah felt as if the ground were slipping away beneath her. "Because you might leave tomorrow," she said, forcing the words past the thickness in her throat.

"*No*," he growled. "Because it only takes one lucky shot to kill a man and—"

With a cry of protest Sarah threw herself into his arms, but he caught her and held her away, determined to finish.

"—and I might not be *able* to marry you. Do you understand?"

She thought she did, and the words burned as she uttered them. "You're afraid you'll . . . something will happen and you'll be gone and perhaps I'll be with child and . . ."

Her voice trailed off at his stricken expression. Plainly he hadn't even considered this possibility. His hands tightened painfully on her arms, and he breathed her name.

345

"Sarah?"

But she shook her head, despair a hard lump in her stomach. "I . . . you don't have to worry about that," she told him thickly. "I'm barren, Travis. Even if you do marry me, we'll never have any children. I should have told you before. Maybe you won't want me now —"

He silenced her with a shake and a curse. "Don't be a fool. Just having *you* is more than I ever dreamed of. I just don't want you to have any regrets later if I stop a bullet."

Sarah wanted to cover her ears at any mention of Travis's death. "The only reason I'll be sorry is if you didn't really love me."

He pulled her close, until their bodies almost touched, and she could feel him trembling. "I do love you, Sarah. If you don't believe anything else, believe that."

She shut her eyes and let the words wash over her, bathing away the pain and the loneliness and the very last of her doubts. Then she closed the infinitesimal space between them, slipping her hands inside his coat and offering her mouth for his kiss.

He claimed her, groaning her name as his lips covered hers, clasping her to him so their hearts thundered together. After a long time, Sarah broke the kiss, anxious to return his pledge.

"I love you, too," she whispered breathlessly against his lips.

To her surprise, he smiled. "I know."

She pulled away so she could see his expression more clearly. He looked entirely too smug. "What do you mean, you know?"

"I mean, I wasn't really sure until the other night at the dance, when you went to all that trouble to make me jealous."

"I never!" she huffed indignantly, but he kept grinning and shook his head.

"And the clincher was the way you looked when you saw me dancing with Elizabeth Williams."

Sarah didn't want to discuss Elizabeth Williams. "I told you I loved you long before that," she reminded him primly, trying to hold herself rigid in spite of the fact that Travis's hands were moving over her back, making all sorts of interesting discoveries through the single layer of clothing she wore.

"Yeah, but people say a lot of things they don't really mean when they're in bed together. I figured you *had* to think you loved me then or you wouldn't be able to face what we'd done."

"I wouldn't have done it in the first place if I didn't love you," she informed him, "and in the second place—"

He kissed her then. Apparently, he'd had enough of her arguments, and quite frankly, so had she. She melted against him, reveling in his labored breathing, his pounding heart, and the hardness she felt pressed against her belly. When they were both breathless, she pulled away again and grinned at him.

"*Now* will you take off your jacket?"

He grinned back. "It *is* getting hot in here," he admitted, as he struggled out of the heavy garment and tossed it away.

"And you smell like sheep," she replied.

"So do you," he countered.

"Then I suppose we both need a bath." She glanced

at the water that still steamed invitingly, and when she looked back at him, his grin was gone.

"Sarah?"

She wasn't in the mood for questions. Instead, she started to work on the buttons of his shirt. He went perfectly still and submitted with uncharacteristic meekness to her ministrations, although she noticed his hands had closed into fists again and his breathing had become quite erratic.

When she opened his shirt, she saw not bare flesh but another layer of cloth. Undeterred, she let the shirt fall to the floor and began unbuttoning his long-johns. At last she found what she had been seeking, the furred wall of his chest, and she lovingly slid the underwear off his shoulders. He pulled his arms free, leaving the top to fall about his waist, and he reached for her as she buried her fingers in the hair on his chest and savored the furious pounding of his heart beneath her palms.

His flesh felt molten to her touch, warm and fluid, and she let her hands slip around to caress his back as he pulled her closer for his kiss. He cupped her face with both hands until their lips met, seeking, clinging, their breaths mingling. Then he stroked downward, caressing first her throat, then pushing her robe aside to bare her shoulders. His lips followed, worshiping her, finding the throbbing pulse at the base of her throat, as he drew the robe away.

The cool air pinched her nipples erect, but he instantly warmed them against his chest, sighing raggedly when her flesh touched his. One hand slipped behind her back and tangled in the fall of her hair while he buried his face in the curve of her neck.

348

"Oh, God, Sarah, you feel so good," he breathed against her heated skin.

Desire curled in her belly, hot and compelling. Instinctively, she pressed herself closer, but the stiffness of his jeans barred her from him. "Travis," she said, her voice a hoarse whisper. As if of their own accord, her hands roved over the satin of his back, reveling in the feel of him, wanting to feel all of him. "I . . ." She couldn't bring herself to ask. Instead she said, "My . . . my bath water is getting cold."

"Mmmm," he agreed. "I'm ready to scrub your back now."

"I thought . . ." she began, but then she wasn't able to think anymore, because Travis pulled away and her robe fell completely open. Instinct demanded she snatch it closed, but Travis was too quick for her. Before she could react, he was easing the garment off her shoulders, and in the next second it lay around her ankles.

She stood completely exposed, mortified in spite of all her erotic fantasies to the contrary. To have Travis see her like this, see all her flaws . . .

But when she looked at his face, she saw no trace of disappointment, only wonder.

"My God, you're beautiful," he whispered, and for the first time in her life she really was.

All her shame evaporated in the heat of his adoration, and when he took her hand to assist her into the tub, she stepped like a queen ascending her throne.

The size of the tub demanded she draw her knees up, and she did feel a little more comfortable thus partially concealed from his avid gaze. She picked up the washrag and the bar of scented soap she'd set by the tub and dipped them both into the water.

"Aren't you a little overdressed for this job?" she asked shyly, hoping he would understand what she couldn't say outright.

Travis greeted her hint with a grin and moved over to the bootjack while she wrapped the soap in the cloth and began to work up a lather. Pulling off first one boot and then the other, he never took his eyes off her, and his gaze held hers like a magnet.

The longing inside her swirled like the heated water around her, warming her secret places and making her breath short. He returned on sock feet and knelt beside her, his eyes like blue fire, the flecks of gold glowing in the lamplight.

Without speaking, he took the soapy cloth from her nerveless fingers and touched it tentatively to her throat. Automatically, she dropped her head back in silent invitation, and his touch grew instantly more confident. The cloth slid over one shoulder and down her arm, which he lifted with his other hand; down to her wrist, then up again, gently caressing the inner curve, slowing as he came closer to her breast, but somehow not even so much as grazing it, although her nipple strained with feverish anticipation.

He repeated the process with the other arm, and this time the cloth stroked under her arm and down her side, skirting the swell of her breast to sweep across her midriff and back again, lower this time, teasing her navel and raising gooseflesh in the strangest places.

Then, as if bent on torturing her, he moved to her back, not turning her, but coming closer so his hand could reach around while his chest came within a heartbeat of her own aching nipples. With his other hand, he caught up her hair and swept it aside while the cloth slid sensuously over her spine and up again to one shoulder, and down to the curve of her hip and up again, in a maddening ritual that heated her blood to liquid flame and sent spasms of desire coursing through her.

When he had driven her near to madness, he brought the cloth around again, up and up, grazing the underside of her breasts, teasing until she arched her back, offering herself with a tiny pleading sound. At last the tantalizing heat closed over her breast, soothing and inflaming at the same time. She thrust her nipple into the comfort of his palm, and his fingers molded, kneading her fullness until she couldn't bear it another moment; then he moved to her other breast, treating it to the same delicious torture.

She heard a sigh of rapture and realized vaguely it had come from her own lips, but the sigh became a gasp as the cloth released her breast at last and slid down and down, down to her belly, where the need roiled hottest. Her knees parted, straightening to permit him access to all her secrets, but he ignored the unspoken offer, and instead the cloth slid up her thigh and over her knee and down.

He took her ankle and lifted her foot from the water. The cloth encircled it, lathering slowly, deliberately, teasing the sensitive arch before moving on, back up, stroking her calf and the delicate spot behind her knee, and up and up to where the flesh of her inner thigh tingled with need. But he stopped where the water covered her, and moved to her other leg, repeating the process until she fairly writhed with wanting

351

and her blood thrummed relentlessly and her breath came in short, desperate gasps.

"Travis," she moaned when his hand left her to dip the cloth in the swirling water. He brought it up, dripping, and sloshed it onto her shoulder. The water sluiced down in rivulets, washing away the soap, again and again, until he'd cleansed her completely and she could stand it no longer.

She reached for him and found his shoulders slick from steam and a need as great as her own. His eyes shone, as bright as glass, and when her hands moved to the buttons on his pants, he dropped the cloth and helped her. In moments he had skinned out of jeans and drawers and socks, and for one second he stood before her naked and glorious, fully aroused, until she drew him down into the tub with her.

There wasn't room for both of them, so Sarah perched on the seat on the rim, oblivious of the chill on her damp flesh. Travis lowered himself before her and drew up his knees on either side of hers. Now it was her turn to torture, and she did it with abandon, lathering her bare hands and spreading them over his sinewy shoulders and back, through the golden hair of his chest and belly, down each leg and back up, until his chest heaved and his jaw clenched and his hands clutched the rim of the tub desperately.

Then she rinsed him as he had rinsed her, letting the water flow over him until he glistened in the lamplight. When she was finished, she waited, her whole body thrumming with desire, knowing he burned with it, too, savoring this last delicious moment. Her hands tingled from his hair-roughened flesh, her belly throbbed with emptiness.

352

"You . . . you missed a spot," he said hoarsely.

She glanced down and saw the sleek shaft resting against his belly. She hadn't touched it, wanting him to know the same frustration she had felt.

She smiled. "You missed a spot, too."

He smiled back, and the hands gripping the tub rim suddenly reached for her. "Come here, then," he said.

There was one awkward moment when Sarah thought she wouldn't fit, but he showed her how, closing his thighs and parting hers so she could straddle him. The warm water caressed her like an invisible hand, and she shuddered, then shuddered again when his fingers found the place that ached for him.

She said his name on a quivering sigh as he turned desire into raging need. Bracing herself against the sleek dampness of his chest, she endured the torture until the blood roared in her ears and she felt as if she would die from wanting. This time his name was a demand.

She half expected him to carry her off to bed. Instead he said, "Put me inside you, Sarah."

Her eyes flew open, and she saw her own torment reflected in his eyes. It was a command she could not refuse. With a boldness of which she hadn't imagined herself capable, she took the burning shaft in her hand.

His hands on her waist, he lifted her until the tip met her velvet opening; then he lowered her, impaling her with ecstasy so intense it brought tears to her eyes.

"Oh, Travis, I . . ." Her voice broke on the first wave of passion, and he pulled her to him, raining kisses on her breasts and suckling each nipple in turn until the need became an agony. At his urging, she

353

rocked her hips. Gently at first, ignorant until sensation streaked through her, revealing this new mystery.

Then she was teaching him, leading him, riding him toward the goal, the shining, golden bliss only they could share. He clutched her flanks, she clutched his shoulders, raking him with her nails as she clung to him, straining and lunging, racing onward, faster and faster, until she saw it just ahead, glittering and bright, and she plunged, falling and soaring, convulsing in exquisite joy.

Afterward they clung to each other, kissing and whispering broken phrases that made no sense but which they understood nevertheless. Then gradually, the golden glow of passion faded, leaving them naked in the rapidly cooling bath water.

Reality intruded when Sarah shivered suddenly.

"You're going to catch pneumonia," Travis warned with endearing concern, and ever so gently, ever so reluctantly, lifted her from him and set her back on the seat she had so precipitously vacated a few minutes earlier. Robbed of his warmth, she shivered more violently, but Travis snatched a towel from the chair and wrapped it around her shoulders. She snuggled into its warmth and yielded to the gentle pressure of his hands as he pulled the length of her hair free of the towel and rubbed her back and shoulders.

"Oh, dear," she said with feigned distress. "I was planning to wash my hair before you *distracted* me."

He grinned unrepentantly. "You were pretty easy to distract," he observed, making her blush. "You can still wash your hair, though. I'll help."

Before she could do more than register this outlandish offer, he rose from the tub with a splash, snatched

354

up one of the towels, and began to dry himself.

Sarah sat back and savored the sight of his muscular body, so gloriously masculine even though the visible evidence of his desire had moderated somewhat.

"Keep looking at me like that, and you'll never get your hair washed," he warned, stepping out of the tub and wrapping the towel around his waist to cover the part of him she had found so interesting.

He grabbed another towel and spread it over her knees, being careful to keep it out of the water. "Sit tight. I'll be right back with some more hot water." He took one of the empty buckets with him, and when he opened the bedroom door, she could feel the blast of cold air from the unheated parlor.

"You'll freeze your . . . yourself," she quickly corrected.

"Then you'll have to warm it back up, won't you?" he countered as he ducked out of the room, considerately closing the door behind him.

Sarah clutched the towel more closely around her shoulders and wondered if she shouldn't forget the whole thing and get into bed before she really did catch pneumonia. Before she could convince her strangely lethargic body to move, Travis was back carrying a bucket of steaming water.

"Where on earth . . . ?" she asked, then realized that by now the water in the boiler must be hot.

She glanced down at the water in the tub. A film of soap scum was congealing on the top, and Sarah found herself loath to lower herself back in, even if Travis did warm it up.

As if reading her thoughts, he said, "Why don't you kneel over the side of the tub?"

The solution was logical, but Sarah glanced down at her towel-wrapped body and tried in vain to imagine preserving her dignity with her bare bottom sticking up in the air. "If I do, I'm liable to freeze *my*self," she said wryly.

Travis grinned wickedly. "Well," he allowed, with forced gallantry, "you could put your robe on, then."

He snatched it up from where it still lay on the floor nearby and brought it to her, holding it up while she removed the towel from her shoulders and slipped her arms quickly into the sleeves. As she stood up, he knelt, taking the towel that had covered her knees to dry her feet as she stepped from the tub. Then he slipped her slippers on and sat back on his heels and looked up at her as if to admire his handiwork.

Sarah quickly pulled her robe closed, wondering how she could feel self-conscious after behaving so wantonly, but feeling it, nevertheless.

He spread the towel by the edge of the tub and motioned for her to kneel beside him. Until that moment she hadn't actually believed he intended to wash her hair and, intrigued by the very idea, she knelt, shaking her hair free and gathering it with both hands to the top of her head before she leaned over the side of the tub.

She waited, fairly holding her breath and wondering what he would do. From the corner of her eye, she saw him pick up the bucket, and in the next instant the deliciously warm water cascaded over her head.

Shivering with reaction, she heard him fishing around in the bath water for the soap, which had grown soft and spongy. Rolling the bar between his hands, he shaved loose the squishy outer layer, then let

356

the bar fall back into the water and delved his soap-laden fingers into her hair.

Clutching the side of the tub, she squeezed her eyes shut and savored his touch as he found a completely new way to arouse her. The sensation of his fingers massaging her scalp and working the lather through the length of her hair sent chills racing over her. Her nipples hardened again, straining against the roughness of her robe, and renewed desire blossomed within her.

She pressed her thighs tightly together in reaction, and clutched the edge of the tub, hoping he wouldn't guess his effect on her, and yet praying he would know. After an eternity of sweet torment, he finished. His hands left her with what she thought was reluctance, and he poured the remaining water from the bucket through her hair until the last of the suds had been rinsed away.

She helped him squeeze out the excess water; then he gave her another towel, which she wrapped around her hair. When she lifted her head, her face felt hot, and she wondered if the longing showed in her eyes. Almost afraid to look at him, she lifted her gaze tentatively and saw he'd been as affected as she. His face was flushed, too, and his eyes glittered with the same desire that was pulsing anew through her veins.

But the boldness she'd felt earlier seemed to have deserted her, and she couldn't quite bring herself to glance down and see if he were *completely* aroused. Instead, she busied herself with the towel, lowering her head again and rubbing her hair briskly.

"Come over by the stove. Where's your comb?"

Oh, Lord, if he started combing her hair . . . "On

357

the washstand," she heard herself say, as she moved obediently closer to the warmth of the stove.

In a moment he returned and knelt behind her, taking the towel from her unresisting hands and continuing the process. Without her being aware of it, she had somehow settled practically into his lap. His muscular thighs were spread on either side of her hips and her bottom rested against his loins while she leaned slightly forward to allow him room to work.

Acutely aware that he wore only the skimpy towel, Sarah had to clutch her robe with both hands to keep from running them over the hair-roughened thighs pressing provocatively against her flanks. How well she remembered the way her palms would tingle at the touch of his flesh, and the memory seemed to wrap around her chest, squeezing all the air from her lungs and forcing her to concentrate on every breath.

At last he tossed the towel aside and began with the comb, drawing it through the damp, tangled locks with infinite care, as if to pull one strand might cause her unspeakable pain. The teeth teased her scalp, and more shivers danced over her. She had to bite her lip to keep from moaning with pleasure, but after a while the moan sneaked out anyway and she no longer cared.

As the tangles dissolved under his hands, the comb moved more freely, stroking slowly, sensuously, in a mesmerizing rhythm. Sarah felt the last of her inhibitions drifting away as she surrendered completely to the hypnotic spell. The grueling ordeal of the past few days finally began to tell on her, and she felt the fatigue in every muscle. Exhaustion settled over her like a cottony web, and her eyes had just begun to close when Travis realized what was happening.

"Sarah," he said, giving her a little shake.

She roused instantly. "I . . . What?" she asked groggily.

"Time for bed," he told her, amusement in his voice, but Sarah was too weary to take offense.

She tried to stand up, but found her limbs refused to cooperate, and once again Travis had to carry her. She reveled in his embrace, resting her head on his shoulder to admire his rugged profile. "I'm not usually so . . . so helpless," she said, compelled to make some explanation for her uncharacteristic behavior.

His only reply was a skeptical smirk as he laid her on the bed. When he would have straightened, she knew a moment of panic and restrained him, wrapping her arms around his neck.

"You aren't going to leave me, are you?" she asked in sudden alarm.

Something flickered in his beautiful eyes, something very like guilt. "I should," he said, but before she could protest he added, "but I won't. I've just got to put out the light and bank the fire."

Reluctantly, she released him, letting her arms slide from around his neck and savoring the feel of his heated flesh beneath her palms. He straightened reluctantly and moved away.

Sarah couldn't take her eyes from him, so when he turned she saw them, the angry red scars from where James Bigelow's knife had cut the lead from his body. She'd felt them with her hands, had even seen them, she supposed, but always before she'd been distracted by passion. This time all she could think of was what he had said about how easy it was for a man to stop a bullet.

By the time he had finished his chores and plunged the room into darkness, Sarah was wide awake again, as unwanted visions of violence flashed through her head.

Travis pulled back the covers on the other side of the bed, and it sagged as he lowered himself and slipped between the sheets. "You'd better get in here," he said. Sarah kicked off her slippers as he pulled the bedclothes from beneath her and drew them over her.

The linen felt icy, and instinctively, she moved into the warmth of his arms. The towel was gone, she realized as she ran her hand down his side, but when she allowed her fingers to steal around to his back, all other thoughts fled.

"Travis?" she said into his shoulder.

"Hmmm?" he murmured, running his hands over her, warming her through the thickness of her robe.

She touched one of the ridges that marred him. "Who shot you?"

His hands stopped, and he went perfectly still. Sarah held her breath, not certain she even wanted to hear the answer even if he were willing to tell her, and wishing she could see his face.

Seconds ticked by, and Sarah began to regret her impulsive question. "Travis, you don't —"

"Yes, I do," he contradicted her. "You've got a right to know. I just . . . I'm trying to figure out how to tell you." He sighed, his breath warm on her face.

She reached up and touched his bristly cheek. "Just tell me. If you're afraid I won't love you anymore or something —"

"No, it's not that," he said quickly. "But I lied to you."

"Lied? About what?" she asked, knowing she'd made a terrible mistake. She really didn't want to hear this. Unfortunately, she now had no choice.

"The men who shot me were trying to run me out because . . . because I was running sheep."

Sheep! she echoed incredulously "Yeah, sheep," he admitted, and she could hear his reluctance. "I was helping an old friend, Nate Kauffman. He was the one who owned the sheep, but he was having trouble, so he sent for me. He said we'd be partners if I'd help him. I didn't have much use for sheep, but I wanted . . ."

She could feel the tension radiating from him. "What did you want?" she prompted.

"I wanted to belong somewhere, Sarah. I wanted my own place, my own . . ."

"Your own home," she guessed, and knew she was right.

"But it wasn't like that," he said bitterly. "When I got there, I found out Nate didn't have his own land, just his own sheep. He was a drifter."

"Oh, no!" Sarah protested, but her protest couldn't change the facts.

"He was grazing his sheep on other people's land. He'd cut their fences. You know how it works. He only had to cut the lowest wire to get the sheep under the fence; then he'd move on before he could get caught, but the cattlemen knew what he was doing. They'd been after him, so he'd sent for me. He figured my name'd put the fear of God into them. It worked for a while, but I reckon they finally decided they'd had enough, and they attacked."

Instinctively, Sarah pulled him closer; as if her embrace could shield them both from the truth, and his own arms tightened around her, too.

"They came at night. We were sound asleep. They wanted to talk, but Nate wouldn't hear it. He started shooting before I could stop him, and . . ."

Sarah held him, hardly daring to breathe for fear of diverting him from his tale, and waited tensely for the rest of the story.

"The fight didn't last long. Nate got it in the first volley, and I didn't have any choice but to shoot back. Finally, I snuck out the window, figuring when I stopped firing, they'd think I was dead. I made it as far as the barn, but by then they'd set the house on fire, so when I rode out they saw me in the light. I caught a load of buckshot, but I got away in the dark and . . . you know the rest."

She did indeed. "No wonder you were so angry when you found out about my sheep," she said in dismay. "Why on earth did you stay?"

He sighed again. "I don't reckon I had much choice. I wasn't ready to go back and get revenge for Nate, so the next best thing was to make sure nothing happened to you. It seemed like . . . I don't know, like I got a second chance or something, and this time, by God, I was going to do it right."

Sarah pressed her mouth to his for a quick kiss. "I don't think I've ever felt quite so safe in my entire life as I do this minute."

But he didn't return her kiss, and tension still held him rigid. "You're forgetting I let you get kidnapped and —"

"You didn't *let* me do anything!" she reminded him. "That was my own stupid fault for ignoring your warnings, and you were the one who rescued me."

"But they'll try it again, Sarah. They'll do whatever they can to get rid of you, and I might not be able to stop them."

"I'm not afraid!"

"Then you should be," he told her impatiently. "Don't you know what they can do to you? Dying isn't the worst thing that can happen to a woman, Sarah, believe me."

How could she explain that she knew she'd be safe as long as he was there to protect her? Obviously, he didn't believe in his own power, and nothing she could say seemed likely to convince him. "I'm not going to take any more foolish risks," she promised. "From now on, I'll do everything you say and—"

"Give up the sheep."

"What?" she asked incredulously.

"I said, give up the sheep, Sarah. It's the only way you'll be safe."

Once again Sarah cursed the darkness that hid his face from her. She touched his cheek again and ran her fingers over his unsmiling lips. "Would *you* give them up?" she asked at last.

"That's different," he insisted, but she pressed her fingers to his lips to silence him.

"Would you?" she insisted. "Would you give in to those bastards? Would you let them win just to save your hide . . . to *maybe* save your hide?" she corrected. "Would you even do it because *I* asked you to?"

His reply was a long time in coming, and in the end he didn't answer her question at all, because he didn't

363

have to. "I had to ask you, Sarah, even though I knew you wouldn't do it. I guess if you were the kind of woman who could scare, I wouldn't love you in the first place."

When Sarah thought of all the things that did scare her, she wondered how he could say such a thing, but she chose not to argue. "And if you weren't the kind of man who'd ask, I wouldn't love you, either."

His arms tightened around her, pulling her cheek to his chest. She could hear his heart pounding, and she pressed her lips to the velvet flesh. His breath caught, and he released it in a ragged sigh.

"Better be careful, Mrs. Hadley, or you'll get more than you bargained for."

"Like what?" she taunted.

"Like this," he replied, rolling onto his back and carrying her with him so she lay atop him. He pulled her mouth to his, burying his hands in the fall of her hair, tangling his fingers in the damp strands to hold her to him. She felt the unmistakable evidence of his renewed desire against her belly, and her own desire surged to life again.

When at last he broke the kiss, she gasped, "Can we? Again, I mean?" Philip had hardly ever made love to her twice in one month, let alone twice in one night, and she wasn't even sure . . .

"My God, Sarah," he groaned, "being married to you might be worth putting up with all your backtalk."

"Backtalk!" she huffed indignantly, but he was already peeling the robe from her shoulders, and when her naked breasts spilled free she no longer felt the least bit indignant.

This time their lovemaking was completely different. Having dulled the raw edge of passion with their first coupling, they were now free to indulge themselves in an orgy of discovery, kissing and caressing, stroking and fondling, until they were both mindless with wanting.

When at long last he filled her, Sarah moaned his name and wrapped her legs around him, knowing she never wanted to be separate from him again. He tortured her with long, slow strokes that teased and tormented and drove her to the very edge of sanity, but each time she felt herself beginning to fall, he brought her back again, and again, and again, until she could bear it no more. Frantically, she clung to him, mouth to mouth and breast to chest, and when he would have slowed once more, she forced him on with urgent hands and churning hips until his control snapped at last, and together they plunged into the swirling vortex.

Travis woke at dawn out of long habit. His body craved more rest to make up for what he had missed the past few days, but he'd learned long ago how to ignore his body's cravings.

What he didn't know how to deal with was the temptation of Sarah Hadley's luscious body pressed so invitingly against his own. They lay together, spoon-fashion, her back to his chest, her sweet little bottom tucked snugly against his hardness.

Damn! Last night, he'd wondered if he'd ever recover, but apparently he had nothing to worry about on that score. Just being with Sarah was stimulus enough. She didn't even have to be conscious.

His arm lay over her, possessive even in sleep, and he pushed up on his other one very carefully so as not to disturb her, propping his head on his hand and resting on his elbow. She was, he decided looking down at her sleeping face, the most beautiful woman he had ever seen. Not merely pretty, like Elizabeth Williams, but truly beautiful in every sense of the word.

He couldn't see her glorious eyes, but her lashes lay against her cheek like black lace fans. Her lips were full and rosy . . . well kissed, he thought, with a smug smile, and her raven hair was everywhere — under his head and over his chest and trailing down her ivory shoulder, just the way he'd dreamed so many times.

What he hadn't dreamed was exactly how wonderful it could be with her. He'd thought he'd known, but last night had shown him they had only begun to discover the depths of passion they could share. Life with her would be all he was likely to know of heaven.

If he could manage to stay out of hell long enough to enjoy it.

And he'd already enjoyed it far more than he had any right to, he told himself. Sarah wasn't even his wife *yet,* and several thousand sheep still needed his protection just as soon as he could get Sarah someplace where he knew she'd be safe. He really shouldn't even be here with her in this bed, and as penance, he was going to force himself to leave it without enjoying Sarah's love one last time.

Still, there wasn't any harm in kissing her just once more, he told himself, gently brushing away the hair draped across her cheek. To his horror, he saw her delicate skin was red, chafed as if someone had scraped a grooming brush across her face and . . .

With another shock, he realized his own beard had caused the damage, and guilt wilted his burgeoning desire. Like the interloper he was, he carefully extricated himself from Sarah's body and Sarah's bed, determined that if he didn't now have the right to be here, he soon would.

Sarah awoke slowly, her weary body reluctant to return to consciousness, but her mind aware that she had important things to see to. She blinked, loath to expose her sensitive eyes to the bright morning sunlight, but at least her nose wasn't cold. That told her the norther was most definitely gone and spring had returned.

At first she didn't notice the noise, so familiar was the soft scrape of a razor on flesh and the occasional splash of water. Her groggy mind needed a minute or two to remember it had been years since she had heard the sounds of a man shaving in her bedroom.

Travis? The thought brought her bolt upright in bed, and only then did she realize she was still completely naked. Belatedly snatching the covers to her breasts, she pushed the fall of hair out of her eyes in time to see Travis glance guiltily away, as if he had no right to look at her.

Shaving lather covered half his face and the other half had been scraped clean. He was shirtless, and for a moment Sarah indulged herself with the sight of morning sunlight gilding the golden hair on his chest.

"Good morning," she offered, her voice still rough from sleep.

" 'Morning," he replied stiffly. He didn't even glance

at her.

Sarah frowned. Wasn't this the same man she'd shared a bathtub and a bed with last night? Wasn't this the same man who'd lifted her to the heights of ecstasy not once but twice? Somehow she'd expected a more enthusiastic greeting.

"Is something wrong?" she asked, thinking she might still be too groggy to figure it out for herself.

"Not a thing," he assured her, looking intently into Philip's shaving mirror.

Now she knew something was wrong. "Travis," she said in warning.

His razor stopped and his chest rose and fell in a sigh. "Yes?" he asked, turning toward her with visible reluctance.

Did she really look so terrible he couldn't stand the sight of her? she wondered, self-consciously trying to smooth the wildness of her hair. Now that she had his attention, she couldn't think what to say. She settled for "Why . . . why didn't you wake me?" The enthusiastic greeting she'd expected had involved a lot of heated tussling under the covers.

"You needed your rest," he explained logically. "I was going to let you sleep until I was dressed."

"Oh." She couldn't think of anything more profound to say, and she certainly couldn't ask him why he hadn't tried to seduce her one more time. Instead, she watched while he finished shaving and toweled the remnants of lather from his face.

She noticed he'd gotten a clean pair of pants from somewhere, probably the bunkhouse, and now he reached for the shirt he'd hung on the back of a chair. She knew a pang of regret when he slipped it on and covered himself. Sighing, she comforted herself with the knowledge that after they were married, she would be able to look at him to her heart's content.

He'd finished buttoning his shirt when she said, "Aren't you even going to give me a good morning kiss?"

His head jerked up in surprise, then he looked quickly away. "I don't think that would be a good idea."

"Why not?" she asked, stung.

He hazarded another glance at her before his gaze skittered away again. "Because . . ." He started looking around as if he'd lost something.

"Because why?" she demanded, her cheeks burning.

He sighed again and turned in her direction, although she noticed he wasn't looking directly at her. "Because we've got a lot to do this morning, and we won't get it done if I try to kiss you before you've got a lot more clothes on than you do right now."

The burning in her cheeks spread inexorably over her entire body. Well, now, so that's why he wouldn't look at her. Suddenly, she no longer felt unattractive at all. Briefly, she considered dropping the sheet to her waist just to see if he could maintain his control, but when she also considered the possibility that he might be able to resist her attempt at seduction, she decided perhaps she wouldn't test her power over him quite so boldly. "What do we have to do this morning that's more important than . . ." She let her voice trail off provocatively, but he absolutely refused to respond to her provocation.

"First of all, I've got to take you to Doc Bigelow's house."

"What?" she cried in outrage. "I'm not going to be shipped off to town where I can't . . ." This time her voice trailed off uncertainly as his steely gaze finally settled directly on her.

"Seems like I remember something you said last night about doing whatever I tell you to."

"But . . . but . . ." she sputtered.

He ignored her. "You gave me your word," he reminded her sternly.

"I don't want to go to town and just sit. You need me," she insisted.

"I don't need you to guard the sheep, and Cameron sure doesn't need you to help with the lambs. Look, Sarah," he said, trying to sound sensible and persuasive, "things have calmed down considerably now that the weather broke. There's really nothing more you can do, and if you're there, the rest of the men'll be distracted, looking out for you all the time, whether you need it or not," he added diplomatically when she would have protested. "We all worry about you, and if there's one thing we don't need, it's a distraction out there. Maybe you haven't thought of it, but if whoever's after your sheep decided to hit us right now, you'd be finished."

She had thought of it, of course, and she supposed he did have a point. She sighed in resignation. "Do you think you could hand me my robe, then? I wouldn't want to distract you from your duties by going after it in my present state of undress."

She thought his lips twitched suspiciously, but he managed not to actually smile as he walked over and

370

retrieved her robe from where he'd tossed it on the floor last night. As he handed it to her, she noticed his gaze flickered down to her bare back, then quickly away again. At least she didn't have to worry that he was no longer interested, she thought with a secret smile.

He turned away as she struggled into the robe, and once again started looking around. This time he found the object of his search, a pair of socks that lay on the same chair on which his shirt had hung. He sat down and began to pull them on.

Now wrapped securely in her robe, Sarah slid out of the bed. At first her legs threatened not to hold her up, but after a few gingerly steps, they began to function again, and she made her way cautiously over to where he sat just as he finished with his socks and rose to his feet. He came up face to face with her.

"I'm ready for my—" she began, but before she could finish, his eyes widened in shock and he dropped quickly back into the chair again. A flush rose on his neck as Sarah stared at him in surprise.

"I was going to say, I'm ready for my kiss now . . . that is, unless you still don't think I'm wearing enough clothes," she added uncertainly.

The flush deepened, and he looked around almost frantically. He muttered something that sounded like "boots," then launched himself from the chair, ducked around her and snatched up his boots from where they still lay beside the bootjack.

Her mouth had dropped open in surprise, and before she could get it shut again, he was stomping his feet into them. When they were on, he heaved what sounded suspiciously like a sigh of relief, looked up,

371

and gave her a dazzling smile. "Now, what were you saying about a kiss?"

In an instant, he'd taken her in his arms, but she was too bemused to really participate in it, pleasant though it was. Why wouldn't Travis kiss her until he'd put his boots on? The question echoed through her mind until at last he pulled away and she stared directly into those glorious blue eyes . . . which were, she suddenly realized, only a scant inch or two above her own, and she was barefooted.

Good heavens! Could Travis be *shorter* than she was? She found the idea amusing, although she couldn't imagine why it would matter, except that it obviously mattered a great deal to him. Something inside her seemed to melt as the truth dawned on her, and suddenly Travis became even more dear to her. She wouldn't dream of mentioning her discovery to him. No, he was embarrassed enough just knowing it himself, but she would love him all the more because he cared about something so silly. And because he valued her opinion of him so very, very much.

Since she couldn't tell him any of this, she simply rewarded him with another kiss, a kiss so enthusiastic that they were both panting when it finally broke.

"I . . . I guess I better hitch up the buggy," he gasped, pushing her away with what appeared to be desperation. He hurried out, leaving Sarah to gloat over her secret knowledge.

Sarah washed and dressed in record time, pausing only to examine her curiously red cheeks. Could the wild night of passion have stamped a permanent blush on her face? When she realized her skin was *chapped*, she couldn't, at least for a moment, imagine what might have caused the irritation. Then, quite suddenly, she recalled the delicious scraping of Travis's three-days' growth of beard. "Oh, my," she said to her reflection, smiling at the memory. She would have to be more careful in the future.

When she was dressed, she set about preparing breakfast for the two of them. If Sarah had imagined a leisurely, romantic meal, she was disappointed. Travis was determined to get her off the ranch posthaste, and the instant he swallowed the last bite of the hotcakes she'd made him, he was up and gone, instructing her to pack a bag with whatever she'd need for an extended visit.

The prospect of being separated not only from her home and her work, but from the man she loved, for heaven only knew how long, depressed her, but she followed his instructions, determined not to cause him any more worry than she already had.

She found they had little to say to each other on the long drive into town, because every subject seemed fraught with potential dangers. She didn't really want to know whether he expected trouble at the sheep camp, or how long he anticipated it would be until she could return home. They couldn't even plan for the future the way normal lovers did, since the future depended on so many things over which neither of them had any control. By the time they reached the Bigelow house, Sarah thought she might gladly indulge herself in a good cry as soon as she was safely ensconced in their guest room.

Hearing the buggy, Amabel had come to the door to see who might be paying her a visit and, seeing Sarah, she fairly ran to the gate to meet her.

"Sarah, what a surprise! And Mr. Travis, so good to see you again. You're looking well. Oh, Sarah, we heard you were worried about your lambs. Is everything all right?"

"It is, now that the weather broke," Sarah replied, climbing down from the buggy without waiting for Travis's help. "Unfortunately, my crew seems to think I won't be safe alone at the ranch, and they don't want me hanging around the sheep camp anymore, so they've cut me loose to find my own pasture. Are you willing to take in a stray lamb?"

Amabel blinked in confusion, but comprehension dawned a second later. "Are you asking if you can stay with us?" she asked in delight. "I can't think of anything I'd enjoy more. Oh, thank you for bringing her here, Mr. Travis. I'll be forever in your debt."

Sarah glanced over her shoulder in time to see Travis shaking his head in wonder, but he quickly busied himself with climbing down from the buggy himself and collecting her luggage from the rear.

Amabel hooked elbows with Sarah and started up the walk to the front porch. "Why on earth does Mr. Travis think you won't be safe out at the ranch alone?" Amabel asked after a few paces. "Has there been some more trouble?"

"Well, I was kidnapped on the way home from visiting you last week," Sarah said, deciding it was foolish to try to keep the secret from her friend.

"Kidnapped!" Amabel cried in horror. "Oh, dear, were you . . . ? But of course you weren't hurt, or you would have called James, but . . . Oh, dear, *kidnapped!*"

"You mean you hadn't heard about it already?" Travis asked from behind them.

"Oh, my, no, and I can't imagine why. James hears absolutely everything," Amabel exclaimed.

"We asked the men not to say anything to anyone," Sarah explained, wondering how Travis could have forgotten, since the secrecy had been his idea. "I suppose for once they managed not to gossip."

"Yeah, I suppose so," Travis said thoughtfully. Sarah thought she heard something else in his voice, something disturbing, but Amabel swept her into the house before she could decide what it was.

Travis stopped just inside the front door and set her bag down.

"Won't you join us for some tea, or coffee, if you prefer?" Amabel asked him, when he made no move to follow them to the kitchen. "James is out on a call, but he'll be back soon, and I'm sure he'd love to see you."

"Thanks, but I've got to get back to the ranch," Travis said, and Sarah's heart sank. She thought she'd have him for at least a few more minutes.

His blue gaze met hers, but in the dim interior light she couldn't quite read his expression. "I'll send you word every few days about how things are going," he said, formally as if he were speaking to his employer.

Sarah swallowed against the lump in her throat. Her arms ached to hold him, her lips ached to taste his kiss once more, but with Amabel standing there watching every move they made, she couldn't even give him her hand.

"Thank you," she said hoarsely, hoping he would understand what she could not say.

He nodded curtly, as if he, too, felt the same longing. "I'll . . . I'll see you," he said after a long moment; then he nodded to Amabel and left.

Impulsively, Sarah followed as far as the door, holding it open until he had climbed into the buggy and slapped the horse into motion. She lifted her hand to wave, knowing he couldn't see, and sighed when the small cloud of dust churned up by the wheels drifted away.

"Oh, my," Amabel breathed, as if she'd made a startling discovery, and Sarah realized she was behaving like a lovesick fool.

Gathering herself, she forced a small smile, closed the door, and turned back to Amabel. "Did you say something about tea?"

Amabel's sweet face wore a knowing grin. "So that's what's wrong with your cheeks. I thought you must've gotten chapped by the wind, but it's really whisker burn, isn't it?"

Chapter Twelve

Sarah didn't even bother to deny Amabel's theory. She was only too happy to confess her newfound love to someone sympathetic, and Amabel was as sympathetic as any lover could have wished.

Unfortunately, talking about Travis was a poor substitute for being with him, and the hours and the days dragged interminably. On the second day of her stay, Sarah talked Amabel into visiting Elizabeth and Paul. Sarah spent the morning playing toy soldiers with the boy while Elizabeth worked on a loose-fitting dress designed to conceal Amabel's pregnancy. By the time they had returned home, fed James his noon meal and cleaned up the dishes, Sarah thought she might cheerfully strangle Travis for condemning her to such boredom.

Neither woman bothered to respond when they heard someone knocking on the front door, assuming the visitor must be a patient for Dr. Bigelow. A few minutes later, James stuck his head in the kitchen door.

"Sarah? You've got a caller."

Her heart jumped clear up into her throat, so she

had to swallow before she could ask, "Travis?"

James smiled knowingly. Obviously, Amabel had shared Sarah's secret. "Sorry," he said as if he really were. "It's Garth Richardson."

"Now don't look so disappointed," Amabel scolded. "At least Garth will provide you with some distraction. Maybe you can even get him to take you for a ride."

A ride, Sarah mused as she removed her apron and made her way down the hall, was exactly what she needed.

"Sarah," Garth exclaimed, jumping to his feet the instant she entered the parlor. "I couldn't believe it when I heard you were visiting the Bigelows." He came toward her, arms outstretched as if he would take her hands in his, but she kept hers primly folded in front of her, so he settled for grasping her elbows instead. "Is something wrong at the ranch?"

"Everything is wrong at the ranch," Sarah confided, realizing she was relieved to be able to tell her troubles to someone who would understand. Moving out of Garth's quasi embrace, she went to a chair and sat, motioning for Garth to do the same.

He folded his large frame into the chair next to hers and leaned forward anxiously, a concerned frown creasing his handsome face. "You haven't had any more trouble, have you?"

"If you mean has anyone attacked the sheep, the answer is no, but we've had trouble of a different kind. I thought you'd probably heard the lambing started in that awful storm."

"Yes, but . . . Oh, I'd forgotten. You said the lambs all come at once, not like the calves."

"Yes, we breed them in the fall so we'll know within

378

a matter of days when the lambs will arrive." She smiled bitterly. "We scheduled them for late March so we'd be sure of good weather."

Garth's answering smile was sympathetic. "Northers like that aren't uncommon this time of year," he reminded her.

"They're tragic, nevertheless," she replied, shuddering to recall the terrified bleating of dying lambs.

"Did you lose many?"

"Not as many as we'd feared, but enough." She sighed. "I can't complain too much, though. If the good weather holds, we'll do just fine."

Garth smiled warmly. "I'm awfully glad to hear it. I'm afraid I've started to hope you'll make a success of your sheep business, Sarah. It's against my better judgment, of course," he added hastily, "but I suppose my admiration for you is overriding my good sense."

"Or maybe you're finally *developing* good sense," Sarah teased. "If you'd only try sheep, you'd find that—"

"Stop!" Garth cried in mock distress, holding up his hands in surrender. "If you aren't careful, folks'll set up a tent for you so you can preach the gospel of sheep throughout the land."

Sarah supposed she did sound a little fanatical on the subject. "Well, it's true," she added defensively, then struck upon an idea to convince him. "And if you'll take me out to my sheep camp, I'll prove to you how much more efficient sheep are to raise than cattle."

Garth's dark eyes widened in surprise, then narrowed speculatively. "Lady, you've got a deal," he said, after a moment's thought. "Did you bring riding clothes with you?"

"No, I'm afraid not," she said, remembering how filthy her riding habit had been after two days of birthing sheep. She'd left it lying in a heap on her bedroom floor.

"Then I'll rent a buggy from the livery," he said, rising. "I'll be back in no time."

Watching him go, Sarah smiled in satisfaction, wondering if Garth would be so eager if he knew that her real motive for going on this ride was to see Travis once again.

Quinn was the first to see their approach, and he rode out to intercept the buggy.

"Miz Hadley, that you?" he asked, peering under the buggy's roof.

"Indeed it is," Sarah replied, placing a hand over the churning in her stomach. Really, she was acting like a schoolgirl about to see her beau. A woman of her age and experience should have a little more dignity, but quite truthfully, Sarah was enjoying the novel feelings of excitement, never having had the opportunity to indulge herself when she really had been a schoolgirl. "How are things going?" she asked Quinn perfunctorily.

"Fine and dandy," Quinn reported, with an uncharacteristic grin. "Them lambs are coming so fast, we can hardly keep track anymore. An' dang if they ain't the cutest little critters, dancing around like—"

Quinn caught himself, apparently realizing how unseemly it was for a cowboy to be impressed with the antics of lambs. He affected his usual scowl. "Well,

380

anyways, ain't no more of 'em died, least not to speak of."

"I can't tell you how pleased I am to hear it," Sarah said. Even her relief was not enough to distract her from her true purpose, however, and she was unable to resist the urge to scan the horizon for the sight of one particular rider. "Is . . . Is Travis nearby?"

"I reckon he's around someplace. Want me to fetch him?"

"If you would," Sarah said, glad to hear her voice did not betray her fluttering anticipation. "We'll be waiting over by the chuck wagon."

Quinn nodded and rode off while Sarah instructed Garth where to head the buggy. She noticed he was frowning. Something warned her not to inquire as to what had disturbed him, but he didn't wait for her inquiry.

"How long are you going to keep that man around, Sarah?"

"Quinn?" she asked in surprise.

"No, that Travis fellow. You don't know a thing about him, and—"

"I know his entire history," she informed him, exaggerating only a little.

Garth looked at her in amazement. "I suppose he told you he's been teaching school for the past ten years, and he got shot up when he made the lessons too hard."

Sarah frowned at his sarcasm. "He told me exactly who he is and how he came to be wounded. It wasn't a pretty story," she added, lest Garth think she really had been taken in, "but then, he hasn't led a very pretty life. I have his loyalty, though, so I

381

needn't worry about anything else."

Garth glanced at her, his dark eyes narrowed. "Are you sure? How do you know he didn't just stage your kidnapping so he could play the hero and rescue you?"

Sarah gaped at him. "How did you know I was kidnapped?"

"Everyone knows," he snapped.

Garth was reining the buggy to a halt behind the chuck wagon, and before Sarah could question him further, Pepe came lumbering up, bleating her name.

"Señora Hadley, Señora Hadley! It is so good to see you again!" He reached up and assisted her from the buggy while Garth was still tying off the reins.

"How is everything?" she asked, anxious for a second opinion.

"Fine, *señora*. The men, they eat like hungry horses, and I cook all the time."

Sarah smiled, looking past Pepe to the approaching rider and resisting the urge to jump up and down and wave. She felt as if she hadn't seen him in weeks.

Travis couldn't believe his eyes. Had Sarah driven all the way out here alone after he'd told her . . . *No!* God damnit, she'd ridden out here with that bastard, Garth Richardson! Fury boiled up in him like a tidal wave. He had half a notion to shoot the son of a bitch on the spot.

Or maybe he should just turn Sarah over his knee.

The prospect made him smile in spite of his rage, but he wasn't going to let Sarah see him grinning like a fool. She might think he was happy to see her, which he sure as hell wasn't, not with Garth Richardson beside her.

Travis reined up and slid down from his saddle,

leaving his horse ground hitched. For the first time, he allowed himself to look directly at Sarah, and the sight of her stopped him in his tracks. Dressed in her usual black, her magnificent hair almost completely hidden by a bonnet, still she looked like a queen. Maybe that was because her face was positively radiant, her green eyes glowing with the inner fire that had warmed the hidden reaches of his soul.

Forcing himself to breathe normally, he strode over to where she waited, Richardson lurking at her elbow, Pepe beaming at her as if he'd been personally responsible for creating the world. The closer Travis got, the more he realized he was in trouble. If anybody saw her looking at him like that, they'd know for sure about the two of them. He'd have to wipe that expression off her face pronto.

"What are you doing here?" he demanded, giving her his most impressive scowl the instant he was close enough to talk to her.

To his gratification — and infinite regret — the glow vanished from her eyes and her smile disappeared. "I came to see how *my* sheep are doing," she informed him.

Good, he'd made her mad. Now they'd be all right. He allowed himself to glance at Richardson, who was frowning his disapproval.

"Is that the way your men usually address you, Sarah?" he inquired, just a shade too gently.

"No, it isn't," she replied tartly. "If you will excuse us, Garth, I have some things to say to Travis *privately.*"

Garth plainly didn't want to excuse her, but he stood fast when Sarah stalked away with Travis following obediently at her heels. As soon as they were a safe distance away, Sarah stopped and turned to face him. Her eyes were glowing green again, but this time it was from anger.

"You could at least act like you were glad to see me," she said through stiff lips.

"I *am* glad to see you," he began, and instantly her face went soft again, her eyes widened, her luscious lips parted in the beginnings of a smile. "But for God's sake, don't look at me like that. If Richardson sees you, he's going to start asking some mighty embarrassing questions."

"Like what?" she asked in annoyance.

"Like whether you let *all* your men under your skirt or not."

She made a small, startled sound, part outrage and part disbelief. "You're crude!"

"Other people'll be worse than crude if they find out about us. Not many of them'll think it's romantic that you went to bed with a no-account gunslinger who—"

"Amabel does," she informed him.

He stared at her in horror. "You *told* her?"

"Not . . . not everything," she admitted, disconcerted. He noticed the red spots on her cheeks that told him she was more embarrassed than she was letting on. "She guessed we were in love, though. You know that old saying, 'Love and smoke cannot be hidden.'"

He didn't, but he supposed it was true. "Well, you'd better hide it. I don't want anybody else guessing . . . What's so funny?"

She wasn't actually laughing, only looking like she wanted to. "Shouldn't I be the one worried about my reputation?"

He knew an almost overwhelming urge to kiss the smirk off her lovely mouth. "Since it seems you don't give a damn, I reckon it's up to me. I don't want people thinking my wife's a harlot."

Her eyes grew wide and her mouth dropped open before he realized he'd broached the unspeakable. He knew she was going to throw her arms around him, so he yelped, "Don't!" before she could move.

She jerked, as if she'd caught herself just in time, and all the color drained from her face. "Oh, Travis," she murmured. The sound of his name on her lips made him weak with longing, but he resisted the weakness with every ounce of strength left in him.

"Sarah," he growled, thinking he'd better change the subject quick. "What in the hell are you doing coming out here with Garth Richardson?"

She blinked at the sudden shift, but recovered quickly. Her eyes sparked with renewed spirit. "I have every right to inspect my own sheep—"

"But why did you have to bring Richardson?" he asked through gritted teeth, holding his temper with difficulty. For two cents, he'd shake her till her eyeballs rattled.

"Because he offered to drive me," she said smugly. "I knew you wouldn't want me coming out here alone, but Garth is—"

"How do you know Garth isn't the one who had you kidnapped?" Travis challenged.

Her astonishment was close to outrage. "Because Garth Richardson is one of my oldest and dearest friends. He's even considering trying sheep himself."

Travis glanced over to where Richardson still stood, and was surprised to find him deep in conversation

385

with Cameron, who had most likely come over to see what all the excitement was about. "He knows about your kidnapping," Travis informed her.

"I know," she replied, amazingly undisturbed. "He said everyone knows about it now. I guess someone on our crew can't keep a secret."

Travis frowned. "If the word is going around, it's funny the Bigelows hadn't heard it."

Sarah shrugged. "I'm sure Garth did his best to quell any rumors about me, so maybe that's why. I'll ask him."

Damn! Travis wanted to forbid Sarah ever to speak to Garth Richardson again, but how much of that impulse was based on genuine suspicion, and how much on petty jealousy of a man he knew to be far more attractive than he? "Yeah, you ask him," Travis said, thinking a man like Richardson would have some smooth answer ready, regardless of the truth. His kind always did.

Travis wanted to tell Sarah a few more things, but Richardson and Owen were approaching. Owen's broad face was inscrutable, but Travis had the uneasy feeling he was laughing inwardly at Travis's predicament.

" 'Afternoon, Mrs. Hadley," Cameron said, smiling broadly. "I'm pleased to report the lambing is going along well. We've lost even fewer lambs than we could normally have expected during the past two days. I'm thinking that will make up for the ones we lost in the storm."

Garth didn't give her an opportunity to reply. "And I'm thinking maybe I've been a fool to refuse even to consider sheep. Mr. Cameron, would you be so kind as to show me around the camp? Sarah warned me that sheep require more care than cattle, but from what you were just telling me, the effort may be well worth the reward."

Owen glanced at Travis, as if for approval, before replying. Travis thought his scowl was negative enough to persuade a blind man, but Owen said, "I'd be proud to, Mr. Richardson. I'll be showing Mrs. Hadley around anyway. Ye do want to inspect the sheep, don't ye?" he asked Sarah.

"Of course," she said, giving Travis what he interpreted as a rebellious look. No doubt about it, he *would* shake her eyeballs loose at the first opportunity, right after he kissed her senseless.

The oddly matched trio strolled off as Owen began to explain the set-up to Richardson, leaving Travis to follow like a puppy or remain behind. He chose to remain, not because he didn't want to keep an eye on Richardson, but because he was afraid Sarah might accidentally give him another one of her burning looks and give herself away.

Or maybe he was afraid she wouldn't.

Mounting his horse, he made a leisurely tour of the perimeter of the camp, checking the horizon as he had been doing for days now, and seeing nothing suspicious. Alternately, he watched Sarah and the others making their way around the enclosures and inspecting the newborn lambs. The sight of Richardson's tall figure rubbed him raw in places where he was most sensitive. Not only was he a fine-looking man, he was successful, too, a much fitter mate for Sarah than Travis Taylor would ever be.

Travis had to remind himself that Richardson had

never known Sarah's passion and probably never would, at least not if Travis had any say in the matter, but even this was small comfort. Travis might not even be around to know.

By the time Owen had finished his tour and led his guests back to the chuck wagon, Travis was in a foul mood. It grew even fouler when he heard what Richardson had in mind.

"I had no idea you were so vulnerable here," he was saying to Sarah when Travis approached. "Do you realize one raid could destroy your whole operation?"

"Which is why my men are guarding the camp," Sarah replied.

"Four men are hardly sufficient, especially if someone chose to attack in force," Garth pointed out. "Sarah, I'd be happy to lend you a few of my men, as many as I can spare, for the next few weeks."

If the offer had come from anyone else, Travis would have been grateful. God knew, Richardson was right about their vulnerability.

"Oh, Garth, I can't tell you how much I appreciate that," Sarah was saying, her eyes big and almost as shiny as when she'd looked at Travis a few minutes ago. "I know Travis and Mr. Cameron would be relieved to have some extra help."

Travis was damned if he'd say so, though. Fortunately, Owen wasn't as reticent. "Aye," he said into the awkward silence, "we would be. When can ye send your men?"

"I'll get them out this evening, just as soon as I get home after taking Mrs. Hadley back to town."

At last Travis felt compelled to speak. "We can take her back to town for you," he said, with just a little too much satisfaction.

Richardson read him easily. "Nonsense," he replied condescendingly. "You're short-handed enough as it is. I wouldn't dream of taking one of your men away at this crucial time."

The argument was too logical, and although Travis's instinct told him he was a fool to let Sarah go off alone with the man, the fact remained that he knew of no reason not to. No reason except his own jealousy, which didn't count.

"Well," Sarah said after a moment, "I suppose we'd better be getting back, then."

She glanced at Travis, and he thought he glimpsed his own longing in her emerald eyes. How he yearned to take her slender body in his arms and kiss her until her heart pounded against his chest and her breath came in tiny, desperate gasps and she moaned his name. Under the circumstances, he couldn't even touch her fingertips, and the constraint galled him.

Soon, he told himself. Soon Sarah would belong to him, and he would have the right to do everything he wanted and more. But for now . . .

"Yeah, I reckon you'd better be on your way," Travis agreed mildly. He looked at Richardson, who seemed to be quite pleased with the way things had gone. "You look after Mrs. Hadley real careful," he said, just as mildly, but he could see from Richardson's reaction that the other man recognized the warning beneath his words. "Anything happens to her, I don't know just exactly what I'd have to do to the man responsible."

Richardson's lips tightened like he'd bitten down on something sour. "I wouldn't want to see anything happen to Sarah, either."

"Good," Travis said, inordinately pleased to have gotten in the last word.

On the way back to town, Sarah reflected on how foolish she'd been to come at all. Seeing Travis without being able to hold him or kiss him had been terrible, and now he was angry with her, which made things even worse. Her only consolation was in seeing how jealous he'd been over Garth. The memory brought a smile to her lips.

She was still smiling when Garth said, "Sarah, do you have any idea who tried to have you kidnapped?"

She stopped smiling. "Not a clue, although it must be one of my neighbors."

"What makes you so certain?"

"Who else would want to do me harm? I got the idea from the man who abducted me that the man responsible wished to marry me to gain control over my property."

"No doubt so he could dispose of your sheep," Garth guessed, his finely molded lips quirked in amusement.

"That was my assumption," Sarah said, seeing little humor in the matter. "Which is why it has to be one of my neighbors."

"You must at least have an idea which one it is."

She eyed him speculatively. "Well, *you're* the only one who has indicated an interest in marrying me."

His appalled expression made her laugh.

"I'm only teasing, Garth. I know you'd never resort to violence to get your way."

"Don't be too sure," he said, affecting an exaggerated leer. "If you refuse the offer of my hand one more

390

time, I shall be forced to carry you off to my lair and—"

"Garth!" she scolded, giving his arm a playful slap.

He looked appropriately repentant, but he said, "Well, I will."

This time she punched him, and he howled in protest. The lighthearted mood lasted for a few minutes, until Sarah remembered a question she was supposed to ask him. "Garth, who told you about my kidnapping?"

He shrugged. "One of my men. I don't remember which one, although I can find out, if you think it's important."

"No," Sarah said, realizing she didn't really want to trace the rumor back to its source and find out which of her men had been indiscreet.

After a moment, Garth said, "I may know who was behind your kidnapping."

"You do? Why? Do you know something—?"

"Nothing substantial; it's just a feeling, but I think this thing's gone on long enough. With your permission, I'd like to make a few inquiries."

"Yes, of course!" Sarah exclaimed in relief. At last someone might be able to eliminate the worst of her problems. "And you'll let me know your progress?"

Garth smiled tolerantly. "Of course."

The next few days continued to drag by, but Sarah resolutely busied herself helping Amabel with her housework and cooking, two tasks she normally despised but that filled her time, nevertheless. If she entertained thoughts of visiting the sheep camp again, she didn't mention them to anyone. The prospect of justifying her presence there to Travis depressed her too much. Besides, she didn't have anyone to serve as a bodyguard.

On Saturday afternoon, Amabel and Sarah walked the short distance to the mercantile to fill Amabel's weekly order. As they strolled down the sun-drenched street, they saw Elizabeth running toward them.

The first thing Sarah noticed was that she wasn't wearing a bonnet. As she came closer, Sarah saw that she was practically hysterical.

"What on earth?" she murmured to Amabel, who had made the same discovery at the same instant. They both rushed forward to intercept her.

"Sarah!" Elizabeth cried when she recognized her. Panting from her exertion, she couldn't speak, but she held out a scrap of paper she'd been carrying.

Sarah took what appeared to be a page torn out of a tally book. On it someone had scrawled, "Tell Sarah Hadley we're keeping the boy until she gets rid of the sheep."

"The boy?" Sarah said, momentarily confused.

"Paul!" Elizabeth gasped.

"Paul?" Sarah couldn't make any sense of this. "Where is —?"

"He's gone!" In spite of her run, Elizabeth's face was deathly pale. "He was playing in the yard, and when I went to call him inside, he'd disappeared. I looked everywhere, and then I found this under a rock in the yard. Oh, Sarah, they've taken him!"

"Who?" Sarah demanded, grabbing Elizabeth by the arms.

"I don't know!" she cried, tears sparkling in her

eyes. "Someone who hates you, hates your sheep! You'd know better than I!"

Both women heard the rising hysteria in Elizabeth's voice. Amabel took her arm. "We'd better get you inside, out of the sun," she said urging her toward the door of the mercantile.

"I can't! I have to look for Paul!" she protested, but Sarah took her other arm, and between them, they got her into the store.

After sending the storekeeper after Sheriff Monroe and forcing Elizabeth to sit down and drink some water, they got a slightly more coherent version of the story. Sarah felt her blood running cold at the thought of poor little Paul in the hands of the same man who'd had her kidnapped.

When the sheriff arrived, Sarah explained the situation to him, holding herself rigid lest she succumb to the same panic that had overwhelmed Elizabeth. Now was not the time for indulging in female weaknesses, although she dearly wished she had Travis with her to help her bear up.

"I'll be da . . . Oh, excuse me, ladies," the sheriff said when he had heard their story and read the note for himself. "But if they wanted to get to you, Mrs. Hadley, why'd they take the Williams boy?"

"Probably because they know how fond of him I am," Sarah said in exasperation. "What does it matter? The fact remains that they've taken him. What are you going to do?"

"Organize a posse, for starters. We oughta search the town just to make sure this ain't somebody's idea of a joke, and the boy ain't hiding out someplace close by. Then we'll spread out."

"But he could be anywhere," Elizabeth wailed. "He's so small and . . ." Her voice broke on a sob, and Sarah slipped her arm around Elizabeth's shoulders.

"I think we should get Mrs. Williams home, don't you?" Sarah asked of no one in particular.

"But I want to help look for Paul!" Elizabeth insisted, struggling to her feet.

"And what if whoever took him has a change of heart and brings him home and you're not there?" Sarah asked reasonably. She could feel Elizabeth trembling violently, and knew she might well faint if they allowed her to go running around town in her current state.

"Do you think they might?" she asked, desperate to believe it.

"I think the best place for you right now is at home, where whoever finds Paul will be able to find you. Come on."

Elizabeth obediently allowed Sarah to lead her to the door. As they walked, Sarah's mind raced as she tried to think of what needed to be done. "Sheriff, can you send word to my men? Ask them to come at once to help in the search?"

"Ain't they guarding your sheep?" he asked.

Sarah was a little surprised he knew so much about her business, but then, she and her sheep had been the talk of the town for quite a while now, so what could she expect? "This is far more important than guarding the sheep. Tell them I've ordered them to help."

"I'll find a boy to ride out," he promised, hurrying off to form his search party.

"Amabel, maybe you should tell James what happened," Sarah suggested as she helped Elizabeth across the street. "Perhaps he has some medicine to calm Elizabeth."

Amabel nodded her understanding and scurried away.

Sarah tightened her grip on Elizabeth, who swayed dangerously. "We'll find him," she promised rashly.

"Yes, we will," Elizabeth responded, needing desperately to believe.

James and Amabel Bigelow arrived at Elizabeth's house a few short minutes after they did. The doctor brought a large bottle of Lydia Pinkham's Female Remedy, and he poured Elizabeth a dose after whispering to Sarah that the ingredients were primarily alcohol, which should relax Elizabeth and help make the anxiety of waiting a little more bearable. After James and Amabel left to join in the search, Sarah eyed the bottle herself, wondering what it would do to the cold knot of fear tightening in her stomach.

"All I know is the sheriff said to tell you she said it was an order," the boy explained for the third time.

Travis frowned and glanced at Owen, who seemed even more disturbed about the news than Travis was. He'd never seen the boy who was delivering the message before, but he carried a note from the sheriff explaining the situation.

"I don't like it," Travis said to Cameron.

"Aye, neither do I," the Scot agreed. "Kidnapping a bairn is the most dastardly—"

"No, I mean I don't like the idea of leaving the sheep unprotected. Whoever did this might want us to do exactly that."

Owen's round face brightened with understanding, then hardened again. "But we must look for him."

"Yeah, we must, mustn't we," Travis murmured thoughtfully as the rest of the riders arrived to see who their visitor was. Briefly, Travis explained the situation to Sarah's men and the ones Garth Richardson had sent over. The latter were, in Travis's estimation, a shifty-eyed lot. He wouldn't even consider turning his back on any of them, much less trusting them with his theories on the present situation.

When he'd answered all the questions, he turned to Richardson's men. "You fellows go straight on into town to help with the search. The rest of us'll be along directly. I want to check out a hunch I have on the way."

"Do ye think ye know where the boy might be?" Owen asked anxiously.

"Like I said, I've got a hunch. Get moving, boys." He motioned to Richardson's men.

As soon as they were gone, taking the young messenger with them, Owen turned back to Travis. "Where is he, man?"

"I don't have the slightest idea," Travis replied baldly. "And I'm not going to waste any time looking, either."

Owen started to sputter and the other men growled their disapproval, but Travis silenced them with a gesture. "Listen. Whoever took the boy expects Mrs. Hadley to send us out looking for him. That'll leave the sheep unprotected, and her, too. So we're going to let them think we went, but we aren't going anywhere."

Owen planted his hands on his hips. "Ye canna just forget about the bairn—"

"I haven't forgotten about him," Travis snapped. "But I don't think he's in any real danger. Nobody's going to be crazy enough to kill an innocent kid. Everybody in the county would be out to lynch him. I figure the boy's someplace safe, eating peppermint candy. He probably doesn't even know he's been kidnapped."

"But *we* know!" Owen insisted. "We must search—"

"They won't need *us* to search. When word gets around, every man in the county'll be out looking, and the chances of finding him are pretty slim unless we get hold of the man who had him kidnapped, which we will if he and his men attack this camp."

Owen still scowled, but Travis saw he understood. He went on to the next part of his plan. "José, you'll be in charge of the camp. The herders'll have to stay here anyways to help with the lambing, and every one of you will keep a rifle with him at all times."

"*I* am in charge of the sheep," Owen reminded him fiercely.

Travis smiled. "No, you're in charge of the women."

"The . . . the what?" Owen echoed incredulously.

"They might not be in any real danger, but somebody ought to be guarding Sarah and Mrs. Williams."

"But I canna use a gun!" Owen protested.

"Which is why I'm sending you to them," Travis explained cheerfully. "If the camp is attacked, you'll be the least use to us here. And like I said, I don't think the women are in any real danger, but they shouldn't be alone, either. I'll give you a shotgun. You don't need to aim it, just point it in the general direction.

Take my word, nobody wants to be anywhere near you when it goes off."

Owen frowned, ready to argue, but Travis cut him off. "Look, Owen, I need somebody I trust with Sarah, somebody who won't lose his head if something happens. The least you could do if there was trouble is go for help." Then he added what he suspected would be his most convincing argument. "Besides, Mrs. Williams is gonna need a shoulder to lean on through all this. You got the biggest set around here."

The other men were grinning, but Owen didn't notice. He was too busy trying to think of something to say back to Travis. Travis waited patiently, ready for anything.

Owen said, "Where's the shotgun?"

It was near suppertime when Sarah heard footsteps outside and ran to the door, thinking someone might be coming to tell them something.

"Mr. Cameron!" she cried, almost as happy to see him as she would have been to see Paul himself. "Do you have any word?"

"No, I'm sorry to say," he told her with a wan smile. "Travis sent me to keep watch over ye ladies and do whatever needs doing here."

"We don't need a thing," Sarah insisted, stepping aside to allow him to enter Elizabeth's front room. He glanced around, obviously looking for Elizabeth. "She's resting. The doctor gave her something and—"

"Sarah?" Elizabeth called weakly, then appeared in the doorway to the bedroom. Seeing Owen, she brightened instantly. "Have you heard any—"

But he dashed her hopes with a wag of his head. "I'm sorry," he repeated, looking even sorrier than he had before. "I'm to be your companion."

Elizabeth looked confused, and Sarah quickly moved to help her to the sofa. When Elizabeth was seated, she explained, "Travis sent Mr. Cameron to guard us."

Elizabeth's eyes widened in alarm. "Does he think we're in danger, too?"

"Oh, no," Owen assured her, managing a self-deprecating grin. "Which is why he chose to send me, since I canna hit the side of a barn with any sort of firearm. He just didna think ye ladies should be alone at a time like this."

Elizabeth's eyes filled. "I'm . . . I'm very grateful, Mr. Cameron," she said brokenly. "Everyone's been so kind . . ."

"There now, don't cry," Sarah soothed, casting Owen a black look for upsetting Elizabeth all over again. They'd had her practically asleep after multiple doses of Lydia Pinkham, but now she was overwrought again.

"Have ye ladies eaten yet? It must be suppertime by now," Owen suggested, and, grateful for the distraction, Sarah suddenly felt less inclined to murder him.

"No, we haven't, Mr. Cameron," she said with forced cheerfulness. "You must be hungry, too. Elizabeth, why don't you help me fix something for Mr. Cameron to eat. We should show our appreciation after he rode all the way out here to be with us."

"Yes, of course," Elizabeth said vaguely. She was drunk, or at least decidedly tipsy. Sarah took her arm and led her toward the kitchen.

"I'll check around outside," Owen called after them, and Sarah waved her acknowledgment.

She sat Elizabeth down at the kitchen table and began to cast about for something she could quickly fix.

"Paul must be hungry, too, by now," Elizabeth said, her voice watery with tears. "Do you suppose they'll feed him?"

"Of course they will," Sarah said, more sharply than she'd intended, because she, too, couldn't bear the thought of the boy going hungry.

"This is all my fault," Elizabeth said suddenly, while Sarah rummaged around in the pantry.

"How can you say such a thing?" Sarah scolded. "If anything, it's my fault for—"

"No," Elizabeth insisted. "God is punishing me because I didn't want Paul. Before he was born, I wanted him to die."

Sarah went cold at the naked pain in her voice. She hurried to the table and sat down in the chair next to Elizabeth's, taking one of her icy hands in both of hers.

"Of course you didn't want him to die," she insisted. "Naturally, you were afraid, but—"

"No, I wanted him to die," Elizabeth insisted, her green eyes glittering from tears and the alcohol as she stared off blindly into space. "I was afraid he'd be simpleminded. Children of rape are simpleminded. Didn't you ever hear that?"

"Rape?" Sarah echoed, not quite comprehending. "But Philip didn't . . ." Her voice trailed off as the first glimmer of truth flickered before her. "Are you saying . . . ?"

"He forced me," she said angrily, turning to Sarah.

400

"I tried to stop him, but . . ." She caught herself, as if she'd suddenly realized to whom she was speaking. "Oh, no!" she cried, covering her mouth with her free hand.

"Philip raped you?" Sarah repeated in outrage. "How could this have happened? I thought you were . . ." She gestured vaguely.

"Lovers?" Elizabeth asked bitterly. "That's what everyone thought, but it wasn't true, at least not for me. Oh, Sarah, you've got to believe me; I never set out to steal your husband."

Elizabeth's fingers tightened painfully on Sarah's, but Sarah hardly felt it. "I . . . I don't think I ever really believed you did," Sarah admitted, finally saying aloud what she had secretly thought from the beginning. "I guess I assumed you just fell in love by accident and . . ."

Elizabeth was shaking her head in vehement denial. "I thought he was my friend," she said, dashing tears from her cheeks. "After Paul died, I was so terribly lonely, and I really didn't know anyone here very well. Some of the men tried to call on me, of course, but they . . . they wanted a wife, and I couldn't even imagine being married to anyone but Paul . . ."

Belatedly, Sarah remembered the handkerchief in her pocket and produced it, waiting anxiously while Elizabeth wiped her face and blew her nose, terrified she would suddenly realize what she was saying and stop.

When Elizabeth was finished with the handkerchief, Sarah ventured, "Then Philip came to visit you."

Elizabeth nodded. "He was picking up something you'd ordered; I don't remember what." Sarah felt a twinge when she recalled Travis's accusations, but she let it pass. "He was charming," Elizabeth continued. "He made me laugh, and I hadn't laughed in a long time."

Sarah nodded, remembering how pleasant Philip could be when he wanted something.

"I knew he was married, so naturally, I thought he was just being nice to me. I never dreamed he was interested in . . ."

"No, of course not," Sarah said quickly, thinking Elizabeth had been the victim of her own naïveté. In her place, Sarah might have made the same mistake.

"It was nice having someone to talk to, someone who didn't make any demands on me, so when he came back a few more times, even when he didn't have any business here, I welcomed him," Elizabeth continued, her voice raw with anguish. "Then, one day he . . . he . . ."

"I know," Sarah soothed, when Elizabeth couldn't say the words. "I know. Why didn't you tell someone, though? The sheriff or someone? Why didn't you at least tell *me?*"

"Who would have believed me? He even said he'd tell everyone I was a whore, that I'd lured him into my house so I could seduce him. It was his word against mine, and I was a nobody, while he was a landowner, a pillar of the community. After he died, I wanted to tell you, but you wouldn't have believed me then. With him gone and unable to defend himself, you would have thought I was making up a story just to make myself look good in your eyes."

And she would have been right, Sarah thought furiously. No one would have believed her, least of all

402

Sarah. They probably would have tarred and feathered her for being a loose woman. "But why did you continue to see him after what he did?" Sarah asked.

"I didn't, at least not at first. I told him never to come back, and he didn't. But then . . . then I found out about the baby. It had been too long since Paul's death. I knew I'd never be able to pretend Paul was the father, and in a few months everyone would know . . . Oh, Sarah, what else could I do?"

Indeed, Sarah thought in despair. A woman alone, bearing an illegitimate child. No decent women would patronize her dressmaking business. She and the baby would starve without a protector. "You sent him word," Sarah guessed, imagining how Philip would have loved the idea of having Elizabeth completely at his mercy after she had scorned his advances. With Sarah at home nagging him about his many failures, here was a woman who would have no choice but to feed his masculine pride and cater to his needs.

"He came the same day," Elizabeth said, as if the fact still astonished her. "He was *happy*."

"Oh, yes, of course he was," Sarah said. "You could no longer turn him away."

Understanding flickered in Elizabeth's eyes. "No, I suppose I couldn't," she murmured thoughtfully.

"You could never afford to offend him or even disagree with him. For Philip, you were the perfect companion."

"I hated myself," Elizabeth said with surprising vehemence. "I hated him, too, and I prayed the baby would be born dead, so I could go someplace where no one knew who I was and . . ."

Her voice broke on a sob, and Sarah took her in her

403

arms, crooning soothing sounds. "You didn't know Paul then, you didn't love him, but God knows you don't want him to die any longer, and He'll protect him, I know He will."

Elizabeth cried softly for a few minutes, and Sarah continued to hold her, wondering if she should offer Elizabeth another dose of medicine to help her drown all these unpleasant memories. Glancing over to where the bottle sat on the dry sink, Sarah caught sight of the back door, which stood open to the spring breeze. A shadow lay across the porch, the broad shadow of a man. "Is that you, Mr. Cameron?"

The shadow jumped, and Owen Cameron instantly appeared in the doorway. "Aye," he said, smiling, although Sarah saw that his cheerfulness was rather forced and his face was even ruddier than usual. "I was just coming to see if ye've got supper ready yet."

He'd been listening, Sarah knew, and she was glad. Elizabeth would never have shared such intimacies with a man, but somehow Sarah knew Owen Cameron wouldn't betray her confidence. In fact, she thought, noticing the tender concern in his eyes when he glanced at Elizabeth, giving him this information, even inadvertently, might prove to be a turning point in Elizabeth's life.

Elizabeth was busy wiping the last of the tears from her face in an effort to make herself more presentable, and she even managed a small smile for Cameron's benefit. "I'm afraid we haven't made any progress at all on supper, Mr. Cameron, and it's all my fault. I've been crying on Sarah's shoulder, and she's been letting me."

"No one has more right," Cameron said stoutly,

looking as if he wouldn't hesitate to offer his own shoulder for such a purpose.

Inspired by the thought, Sarah said, "Elizabeth, why don't you take Mr. Cameron into the parlor. I think I could work much faster if you were both out of my way."

"Oh, dear," Elizabeth said, instantly repentant. "I'm sorry, I didn't think—"

"Don't be sorry," Cameron advised. "Come, lass." He took her arm with one hand, still carrying his shotgun in the other, and led her from the room. She went meekly, smiling a little shyly in gratitude.

"You're so kind," Sarah heard her say as they walked away, and Sarah nodded in approval. Some good might come of this whole ordeal yet.

If they were able to find Paul, safe and sound.

Chapter Thirteen

"Where do you think they've got the boy hid?" Quinn asked. The cowboys had concealed themselves at various places around the camp. Quinn was at the other end of the shelter where Travis hunkered.

"I wish to hell I knew. I'd've sent Cameron straight there to fetch him. I can't imagine they've got more than one man guarding him. Even Cameron could handle that."

Quinn chuckled. "I reckon he could, 'specially since it's Miz Williams's boy. I figure he's kinda sweet on her."

Travis figured the same thing, and Cameron's willingness to leave his beloved sheep and go to town to guard her pretty much proved it. "Quinn, who you figure we're waiting for?" Travis asked to fill the silence.

"You ask me, it's Abel Frank. He's the one been after Miz Hadley most about getting rid of her sheep. He was even saying something to her about it at the dance the other night. Goddamn sneaking—"

"Did you hear what he said?"

"No, but from the look on Miz Hadley's face, it

406

wasn't very friendly. He's just the kind to send gunny-sackers out to set poor ignorant sheep afire, too."

Travis had come to a similar conclusion, although one thing still didn't quite fit. "But is he the kind of man who'd kidnap a woman and a boy?" Travis prod-ded.

Quinn considered the question for several minutes. "Might could be," he allowed at last, and Travis knew Quinn shared his foreman's doubts on the matter.

After another long silence, Quinn said, "If Pepe don't bring us some supper pretty soon, I'm gonna start gnawing on this post."

"I told him to wait until dark in case somebody's watching to camp."

"You figure somebody is?"

"If I was planning this thing, I'd have somebody watching to make sure there weren't any riders patrol-ling. By now Richardson's men have got word out that we're gone."

"Who do you reckon they told?"

"Even if they only told Richardson—and you can bet your last dollar they stopped by to see him on their way to town—everybody'll know by now."

"How long you figure we've got to wait for them to attack?"

"Full dark, at least, maybe close to midnight," Travis said, being optimistic. He hoped Frank—or whoever it was—would figure they shouldn't wait too long, since they couldn't be sure somebody wouldn't just happen across the boy, take him to his mother, and end the crisis, thus sending all the searchers back home.

Of course, if the planner was really smart, he was

holding the boy in a place where no one was likely to find him, like the planner's own home. He'd have men out looking, too, just like everyone else, so no one would think of searching his property. If that were true and their enemy felt completely secure, it might be days before the attack came.

Travis didn't know if Sarah and Elizabeth could stand to wait for days. He knew for damn sure he couldn't.

Several hours later, Pepe delivered their supper, cursing and swearing as he stumbled in the darkness, and reported no unusual signs of movement. From his hiding place, surrounded by milling sheep, Travis wondered if he himself would even be able to hear a full-fledged attack.

But of course he did.

It came near midnight, before the moon rose. Travis had been dozing, slumped in a corner of the shelter, when some sixth sense woke him. Perhaps the sheep had warned him, shifting restlessly in the darkness, or perhaps years spent planning and executing such attacks himself, or trying to second guess those who did, had created an instinct for such things.

Whatever, he was instantly awake, scanning the horizon where the black sky met the even blacker earth. He saw them at once, even before they lit their torches, and he gave the call, the howl of a coyote.

To his right, he heard the rustling as Quinn awoke and took his position. Around the camp, the rest of the men would be doing the same, taking the places Travis had assigned them, waiting, sweating, and listening, straining for some sign of what had alerted Travis.

Before another minute had passed, the first torch flared. Travis wondered idly whether they intended to set the flock on fire again, or whether they were simply going to go after the lambs, smashing in the tiny heads and thus destroying any hope Sarah had of a future.

Usually at moments like this he felt nothing except the feverish anticipation of battle, but now an unfamiliar rage welled up in him, rage and outrage that anyone would dare to harm the woman he loved. At least they would pay for the privilege, he told himself resolutely, and if Travis had anything to say about it, they would pay dearly.

He settled the solid stock of the rifle against his shoulder and pointed the barrel at the illuminated riders. His finger tightened on the trigger, ready but not quite yet. He waited until the last of the torches had been lit and the raiders let loose the blood-curdling yell announcing their attack. The sheep rose up in a body, bleating in terror, as the riders raced toward them across the rolling prairie, and still Travis waited, knowing his men were poor shots, knowing they grew more determined with each passing second, knowing they chafed with blood lust to avenge all the unspeakable horrors these men had already perpetrated.

Then, at last, when the riders were no more than fifty feet from where the sheep were running frantically before them, Travis took careful aim at the lead man and squeezed the trigger. The rifle jolted in his hands, smoke and flame belched from the barrel, and the rider careened from the saddle, his torch arcing against the night sky.

Travis's shot had been the signal, and now the night

exploded into a roar as rifles all around the camp spit flame. Like one huge, undulating body, the sheep recoiled from the sound, then surged forward again, driven by the riders behind them. The raiders came on, juggling torches and reins while they pawed for pistols, but Travis and his men granted no quarter.

Firing as rapidly as they could jack shells into the chamber, they peppered the raiders. Driven by their own momentum, unable to stop, the riders charged into their destruction, shouting their panic, their horses screaming in terror above the frantic bleating of the sheep.

The melee seemed to last forever, although it could only have been minutes until, one by one, the raiders dropped from their saddles or managed to charge away into the night's impenetrable darkness. At last Travis's men began to realize the fight was over, and the firing slackened, then ceased altogether.

Most of the sheep had escaped, and an eerie quiet descended on the camp as the last gun ceased its roaring. A few torches flickered feebly on the ground, illuminating the grisly scene of bodies strewn across the now-deserted sheep bed. Travis rose cautiously from his hiding place, lowering his rifle only when satisfied the fight was won.

"José! Get your men after the sheep! Quinn! Ace! Shorty! Let's take a look at what we've got, but keep your guns handy!"

The three men shouted their replies and slowly emerged from hiding. Keeping his rifle in his left hand, Travis drew his pistol with his right and proceeded across the open ground, dodging the occasional stray sheep that lumbered by in terrified

410

confusion, and crouching so as to present a smaller target in case one of the fallen was only playing 'possum.

Five men lay bleeding. Some moaned, others were deathly still. The first man Travis encountered posed no further danger to anyone, so he continued on, squinting in the feeble light from the dying torches, until he reached the man he'd shot first, the leader.

The fellow clutched a gaping chest wound with both hands, but when he saw Travis looming over him, he made a grab for his holster. Travis planted a boot on the man's wrist, holstered his own pistol and jerked the man's gun free.

"Who is it?" Quinn asked, loping over from the dead man he'd been examining.

"Nobody friendly," Travis replied mildly. "The son of a bitch tried to pull a gun on me."

Quinn stooped down and pulled the gunnysack from the man's head. His face was vaguely familiar, but before Travis could place him, Quinn muttered a curse. "It's Pink Yates, Garth Richardson's foreman!"

The rage welled again, bitter and overwhelming, and Travis roared a curse of his own.

"Travis, these is Richardson's men," Shorty yelled, having unveiled several others.

"Richardson," Travis growled, spitting out the word because it left a vile taste in his mouth. "Where's the boy?" he demanded of Pink Yates.

The man's homely face set stubbornly. "I don't know."

Travis shook his head in mock regret. "That's too bad. See, if you did know, I'd be inclined to get a doctor to patch that hole in your chest. Might even put a

411

bandage on it myself, to keep you from bleeding to death while you waited. Now it looks like you're gonna die lying in a pile of sheep shit. Quinn, let's see if any of these other fellows is interested in saving his own hide."

Travis had already gone three steps before Yates's hoarse grunt stopped him. "Damn you to hell, I'm prob'ly gonna die anyways!"

"You won't have any chance at all unless you tell," Travis remarked, sparing him only a glance before starting away again.

"He's . . . he's at the ranch," Yates groaned.

Travis turned abruptly and strode back to where Yates writhed on the ground. "Whose ranch?"

"Richardson's." Yates grimaced in pain. "I'm bleeding pretty bad."

"Who's there with him?"

"Just a couple, three men." Yates didn't even sound reluctant anymore. "He sent the rest into town to help search."

"Pepe!" Travis yelled, and the fat cook emerged from under his wagon and came loping across the empty field. "Get what's left of these fellows patched up as best you can. When the other boys finish gathering up the sheep, send one of them to town for the doctor. We'll probably get there first with the boy, but just in case we're delayed . . ."

"Sí, señor," Pepe said, nodding vigorously and lumbering away again.

"You wouldn't keep a man waiting for some damn sheep, would you?" Yates complained.

"A man, no," Travis agreed readily. " 'Course somebody who'd kidnap a woman and a boy and slaughter

412

another rancher's property ain't my idea of a man. You'll have to wait your turn, Yates. We got important things to do before we tend to you."

Quickly, Travis and the other men gathered up the wounded. Only three of the raiders remained alive, and Travis doubted any of them would last until James Bigelow arrived, but that wasn't his worry. His worry was a four-year-old boy who must be getting pretty scared by now.

As soon as the wounded men had been tended, Travis and the three cowboys mounted up and rode off.

"You think the ones who got away'll warn Richardson?" Quinn asked.

"If they have any sense, they'll forget they ever knew Richardson, and head straight for Indian Territory. We'll know when we get there, I reckon."

They made the rest of the ride in grim silence and found the Richardson ranch quiet. Lights burned in the house, but the other buildings were dark.

"Could be a trap," Quinn suggested.

"And it could be they're gone, or at least that they've taken the boy away. If Richardson was warned . . ." Travis stopped. No use speculating. They wouldn't know until they rode down and found out.

Travis sent Quinn and Shorty to cover the back of the house. Travis and Ace would take the front. They left their horses and approached on foot, silent in the darkness, half running across the shadowed yard up to the front porch steps.

There they crouched, waiting and listening, prepared for resistance but hearing none. Hearing, in fact, not one damn thing. Light spilled from the front window, but they could see no one inside. Were they too late? Had Yates lied to save his skin? Was . . . ?

Then something moved inside: a man, walking across the room between the window and the lamp. Either he was a damn fool or he feared nothing, Travis thought, recognizing the tall figure of Garth Richardson. That meant he wasn't expecting trouble, so he probably hadn't been warned.

Travis nodded to Ace and motioned toward the door. When Travis moved, Ace followed him, darting up the steps and across the porch. They flattened themselves on either side of the door for a few seconds, pistols poised, ready, but no sound from inside betrayed alarm.

After several seconds, Travis raised one foot and kicked, sending the door flying open with a splintering crash. Inside someone shouted, and booted feet ran. Travis threw himself into the doorway and dropped instinctively to a crouch as a gun exploded in the room, filling it with smoke.

The bullet slammed into the wall above Travis's head, as he scanned the room, taking a quick inventory of its occupants. Two men, he noted: Richardson, who was lifting a rifle, and the other, who fired again, aiming for Ace, who now crouched beside Travis.

Just as the gun spit flame, Travis fired. Someone screamed — not Ace, Travis noted vaguely — then he turned his gun on Richardson, firing again instinctively, not even bothering to aim.

Richardson's rifle roared, and the wall behind Travis burst open, sending stinging splinters flying everywhere. Travis dodged, then fired once more, aiming through the smoke at where Richardson had been.

The rifle roared again, and this time Travis fired almost simultaneously at the spot just above the red flame. The rifle clattered to the floor, and Richardson screamed a curse. Travis spared one glance at the other man, who still lay just where he had fallen. No problem there, he judged. From the rear of the house, he heard more gunshots and men shouting. Quinn and Shorty had found the rest of the guards. Travis lunged into the smoke after Garth Richardson.

He found him clutching his left shoulder while he tried to inch his way over to where the Winchester had fallen. Travis scooped it up and pressed the barrel to Richardson's throat.

"Where's the boy?"

"Just what the hell do you think you're doing, breaking into my house and shooting the place up?" Richardson demanded with just the proper degree of outraged fury. "I'll see you strung up for this, you son of a . . ."

"It's too late, Richardson," Travis informed him calmly. "We know you've got the boy. The men you sent to attack the sheep camp told us all about it . . . just before they died."

Richardson's shock was genuine, but before he could reply, Quinn hollered, "Travis?"

"We got 'em. In the front room."

Quinn and Shorty appeared in the doorway that apparently led to the rear of the house. "There was a fellow in the kitchen, but we took care of him," Quinn reported, eying the man slumped motionless by the wall, a bullet hole between his eyes.

"You boys keep Richardson company," Travis said. "Quinn, let's see if we can find the boy."

Travis took one of the lamps sitting on the mantel

and started off toward the rear of the house, pistol still poised as he made his way cautiously along the darkened corridor. Several doors opened off the hallway; all were closed. As they approached each one, both men stood back while Quinn threw it open and Travis quickly shone the light inside.

The first two were empty bedrooms, but the third wasn't quite empty. On the bed lay a small figure. It didn't move when the men burst in.

"Jesus," Travis murmured in alarm, racing for the bed. The boy was bound hand and foot, his head covered by a gunnysack, a sack in which no eyeholes had been cut. When Travis jerked it away and shone the light full in the boy's face, the small eyelids twitched, and he moaned in protest.

"I don't wanna get up yet, Mama," he whined.

Travis went weak with relief. "You all right, partner?" he asked, not a bit surprised to hear the roughness in his own voice.

"Wha . . . ?" Paul blinked a few times, then focused on the two men standing over him. "I know you," he announced. "You're Aunt Sarah's friend." He frowned. "Are you gonna shoot me?"

Travis instantly holstered his gun. "No," he said, unable to keep from smiling. "We came to take you home. You ready to see your mama?"

The boy came instantly awake, struggling against his bonds as he tried to sit up. Quickly Quinn and Travis freed him. He yowled in pain when they massaged the feeling back into his tiny arms and legs. When the worst of it was over, he looked up at Travis through tear-spiked lashes. "I knew you'd come. I told him you would."

416

"You did?" Travis asked in amusement, picking the boy up and settling him on his hip.

"He said nobody'd care if I was gone," Paul explained, "but I knew my mama would. Is she gonna be mad? I missed supper."

"She won't be mad," Travis assured him. "I fact, she'll be so happy to see you, I reckon you'll be able to get away with just about anything for quite a while."

"You think so?" Paul asked in delight, as Travis carried him into the front room.

Richardson was sitting in a chair, still clutching his wounded shoulder and muttering imprecations. Paul took in the scene at a glance.

"That's the man who took me for a ride," he said, pointing to the dead man in the corner. "He said he'd bring me right back, but he didn't. Why won't he move, and what happened to his head?"

"He bumped it," Travis explained.

"No one will believe you," Richardson warned. "I'd found the boy myself and was just bringing him back when you waylaid me—"

"Uh-uh," Paul contradicted solemnly. "You wouldn't let me go home, not even when I said please." He looked at Travis. "They put a sack over my head so I couldn't see, but I knowed it was him because he talks so mean. He came to my house one day and talked mean to my mama. I remember."

"Good for you, Paul. I'm sure the sheriff will want to hear all about it," Travis said. "Shorty and Ace, go round up the horses and see if you can't find one for Mr. Richardson, too. Quinn, make sure our friend doesn't have any hideout guns on him, then help him up, will you?"

"Aren't you going to bandage my shoulder?" Richardson said, when Quinn had him up and heading for the door.

Quinn and Travis exchanged a look. "We ain't doctors," Travis protested mildly. "We figure we'll get you to town quick as we can, where you can get expert help."

Richardson cursed them roundly as they forced him into the yard and up onto a horse.

"He won't go to heaven for talking like that," Paul informed Travis, when he had seated the boy in front of him on his own horse.

"You're probably right," Travis agreed. "Now you just sit tight, partner. We'll have you home in no time at all."

"You sure my mama won't be mad?" Paul asked again, twisting around in an attempt to see Travis's face. "She don't allow me out of the yard, but when that man offered to take me for a ride, I went."

Travis gave the boy's small shoulder a reassuring squeeze. "She'll forgive you. Just make sure you don't ever do it again."

"I won't," Paul promised, snuggling down into a more comfortable position against Travis as the horse began to move. In a few minutes the boy's head drooped, and Travis realized he'd dropped off to sleep again. Of all Richardson's victims, Paul would most likely be the least affected. Travis only hoped the rest of them would be able to recover so quickly.

As he cradled the boy's body and tried to cushion it from as much jostling as possible, Travis thought ahead to the coming confrontation. Not even Travis had truly believed Richardson was behind the attacks on Sarah and her sheep. He'd blamed his intuition on jealousy and ignored all the signs, which just showed how a woman could distract a man.

Being married to Sarah might just ruin him completely, which would be just fine, he realized with a start. Trying to imagine a life in which he didn't have to check every building he entered for a possible escape route, or suspect every man's intentions toward him, strained his capacities, but he was certain he could get used to it in next to no time.

Unfortunately, he still had some unfinished business to take care of before he could start.

The town was amazingly quiet when they rode up, and Travis figured most of the citizens were either asleep or still out looking for the boy. Lights shone in Elizabeth Williams's windows, though, in spite of the late hour. With a pang, Travis thought of the worry Elizabeth and Sarah had endured, but at least he could put an end to it now.

"Help our friend down, will you?" Travis asked the other men, while he tried to lower himself from the saddle without waking his sleeping companion. "And bring him inside. He's got some explaining to do."

"Wha . . . ?" Paul murmured when Travis hoisted him into his arms. "Are we home?"

"Yes, sir," Travis said, clumping up the porch steps so as to give the occupants ample warning of their approach. "Sarah? Mrs. Williams?" he called.

Just when Travis had realized he didn't have a spare hand with which to knock, the door flew open. Sarah stood there, looking startled and only half-awake, her lovely hair mussed, her eyes unfocused.

"Travis? What on ear . . ." Then she saw the

boy in his arms and fairly shrieked. "Elizabeth! Mr. Cameron! They've found him!"

Before Travis could open his mouth, Sarah had snatched the boy from him and carried him into the house, leaving Travis to follow. Another shriek split the night stillness as Elizabeth emerged from the bedroom and saw her son. The women were laughing and crying and carrying on, hugging Paul between them while he squirmed to be free and Owen Cameron looked on with a benevolent smile.

Behind him, Garth Richardson was mounting the porch steps with unsteady tread, and Travis stepped aside to let him pass just as Sarah turned toward them.

"How did you find . . . ?" she began, then saw Richardson's bloody figure. "Garth! You're hurt!"

She rushed to him with an alacrity that set Travis's teeth on edge, but her solicitude would end soon enough, he told himself, as she led Richardson to the settee and sat him down. "Get some water," she commanded, but no one moved.

Elizabeth stood stock-still, clutching her son and staring in horror at Richardson's crimson shirt. Cameron was looking at Travis, a silent question on his broad face, and Sarah glared accusingly.

Travis was ready to tell her straight out to wipe that disgruntled frown off her pretty face, but Paul beat him to it. "He paid the man who took me for a ride, Mama," he piped ingenuously. "They took me to his house, and Aunt Sarah's friends came and got me, and I'm awful sorry, and I'll never do it again, I promise!"

"Of course you are, darling," Elizabeth murmured

420

absently, her eyes wide as she stared at Richardson.

Sarah stared at him, too, but impatiently. "This can't be true," she insisted.

"It isn't," Richardson assured her, his usual charming smile a little strained, but effective nevertheless. "I had just found the boy and was keeping him at my house until morning when your hired gunnies came storming in and murdered two of my men and . . ." He gestured weakly at his wounded shoulder.

"Good heavens!" Sarah exclaimed, horrified but, Travis was gratified to notice, not quite able to believe what she was hearing. "Travis, what happened?"

About time she asked him, too, Travis thought. "I figured the kidnapping was planned to get us away from the sheep, and so we stayed put and—"

"You didn't go out looking for Paul?" she demanded, outraged until Travis cocked his thumb at the boy to remind her *he'd* been the one to find him. She had the grace to look embarrassed, and at least she closed her mouth and let him finish.

"We stayed put, and sure enough some riders attacked the camp along about midnight. We'd laid an ambush, and we got them before they could do any damage except stampeding the sheep. When we pulled the gunnysacks off their heads, we saw they was Richardson's men."

"I can't help what my men do when I'm not with them," Richardson insisted. "Everyone knows how much cowboys hate sheep. They knew your men were going off to look for the boy, so they must have—"

"Then how come your foreman knew the boy was at your place?" Travis challenged.

"He knew I'd found him and . . ." Richardson grim-

421

aced in pain and clutched at his shoulder.

"Oh, dear," Sarah said, her hands fluttering helplessly. "Shouldn't we send for the doctor?"

"Good idea," Travis said, turning to the cowboys peering in the open door. "Why don't you boys take care of the horses. On your way, stop by Doc Bigelow's place and see if he's back yet."

"Back?" Sarah echoed. "Back from where?"

"Back from seeing to Richardson's men. Some of them were only wounded."

"But you said—" Richardson began, then caught himself. Travis could practically read the thoughts going through the man's head. He'd intended to bluff his way through this when he thought all his men were dead, but now . . . "I'd like to see the sheriff, too," Richardson continued. "I want to report the way these men broke into my house and murdered my men."

"Yeah, see if you can find the sheriff. He'll want to hear everything," Travis added, closing the door behind the departing men.

Elizabeth had sunk down into a chair and gathered the boy into her lap. He'd wrapped both arms around her neck, but they both continued to watch Richardson as if afraid he might pounce.

"I don't understand," Sarah was saying. "If Garth was only keeping Paul until morning, why did you—"

"If he was only keeping him until he could bring him home, why did he have the boy tied hand and foot?" Travis finished for her.

"Tied?" Sarah scoffed, looking at Paul in disbelief.

"They put a sack over my head, too, Aunt Sarah," Paul reported, "so I couldn't see who they was, but I knowed his voice because he talked mean, just like he

422

did when he come to our house that time, Mama."

A tremor shook Elizabeth, either a chill or a shudder, and Travis noticed that Owen moved closer to her and put a comforting hand on her shoulder. She hardly noticed, though. Her stricken gaze was riveted on Richardson, who ignored her to concentrate on his one potential ally.

"Sarah, you mustn't believe any of this. I warned you about this man, but you wouldn't listen, and now you see what's happened. He's murdered half my men, shot me, and accused me of . . . of . . ." He closed his eyes and lolled his head back against the cushion, as if he couldn't bear to think of the crimes of which he'd been unjustly accused.

Sarah studied the man, a frown marring her lovely features, and Travis found himself holding his breath as he waited for her decision.

"Garth, I hope you'll have some better explanations for the sheriff when he comes. Meanwhile, I think we can see our way clear to bandage you up even if James isn't back yet." She turned to Elizabeth. "Do you have any clean rags we can—"

Richardson moved so quickly, no one had time to react. Before Travis could even think about reaching for his gun, Richardson had Sarah around the throat with one arm, and the other held the barrel of a shotgun to her head. Where on earth . . . ?

Travis's gaze darted instinctively to Owen, who stared in abject horror. He'd left his weapon leaning in the corner within easy reach of the sofa, since he hadn't realized Richardson was anything more than another innocent victim. Even Travis had felt no need to cover the wounded Richardson.

423

Apparently, he wasn't hurt as badly as he'd let on. Richardson was hauling himself and Sarah up off the sofa. Sarah's face had gone white, but her eyes darted around as if she were looking for a means of escape. Travis felt the sharp edge of terror pressing against his heart. If Richardson so much as bumped the trigger, he would blow Sarah's head off.

"You'll never get away with it," Travis tried, speaking as calmly as he could under the circumstances.

"No, but I can at least get away, and I can take Sarah with me, just like I planned. I always figured once I got rid of Philip, I could have *both* his women, and his water, too. He loved to lord it over me about how he had two women while I had none, and then he started talking about putting up a fence so people would have to pay him to use his water. Taking care of two women was expensive, you see," he explained with unnatural calm.

Travis's hand flexed instinctively, and he could almost feel the smooth handle of his pistol just inches away from his palm.

"Don't even think about it," Richardson warned, with a feral grin. "She'd be dead before you even cleared leather. Now get out of my way."

It took every ounce of self-control he possessed for Travis to move away from the door. His mind was racing, looking for the slightest opportunity, but Richardson was watching him too closely and the room was too small. Even if Richardson didn't get Sarah, he might hit Elizabeth or the boy.

Behind him, Travis heard Owen whispering to Elizabeth, telling her to get the boy out.

"Don't move," Richardson commanded when Elizabeth started to rise. "Everybody stay right where you are. I've been waiting a long time for this. You were good enough to whore with Philip, but you thought you were too good for me, didn't you, Lizzie? Well, folks'll be grateful for one less whore and one less bastard on this earth."

Elizabeth cried out, hugging the boy to her, and Travis instinctively stepped in front of them both, while Sarah clawed frantically at the arm holding her throat.

Richardson's grin broadened. "Perfect," he said to the tableau before him. "I can get all three of you at once." Sarah uttered a strangled sound and increased her struggles, but he tightened the hold on her neck, cutting off her air.

Sarah gasped desperately, her eyes fairly bulging. *Sarah!* his mind cried, and he took a step forward. Instantly, the barrel of the shotgun swung toward him, and he knew he'd take the full blast himself, but at least he'd save everyone else. He lunged.

The shotgun roared. Travis's body hit Richardson's and Sarah's, and they all went over in a heap. Travis felt no pain, and feared he might already be dead, but to his relief his body still responded to his commands. He drove his elbow into Richardson's throat and grabbed for his own pistol before he remembered Richardson still held the shotgun. But when he tried to reach for it, someone else was already wrenching it away.

Owen! The burly Scot jerked the weapon free and brought it crashing down again, smack against Richardson's skull. Blood spurted everywhere, and Travis reared back instinctively, dragging a shirtsleeve across his eyes, but even before his vision cleared again, he knew. Garth Richardson was dead.

And Travis soon would be.

Sarah leaned wearily against the side of the buggy roof as it jounced along the road, her eyes closed against the pounding in her head and the glare of the morning sun. If only she could sleep, perhaps she might be able to forget all the terrible events of the past several weeks that had culminated in the horror of a shotgun blast. Unfortunately, sleep eluded her, as it had all night. After the scene in Elizabeth's parlor, Sarah feared she might never sleep again.

"I still can't understand how it happened."

Braving the searing sunlight, Sarah opened her eyes a slit and studied the man driving the buggy. Haggard and unshaven, he looked as bad as she felt, perhaps worse. Or maybe that was just because of the bloodstains on his clothes. Sarah had her share, of course, but they didn't show much on her black dress.

"I should be dead," Travis insisted, not for the first time.

"I wish you'd quit saying that. You almost sound sorry you aren't," Sarah complained wearily.

He favored her with a disgusted glance. "I just don't—"

"—understand how it happened," she finished for him. "We told you, while Garth was watching you, Owen managed to move around beside him. When you lunged for him, Owen hit the barrel of the shotgun and—"

"—and it blew a hole in Mrs. Williams's ceiling instead," Travis said, repeating the story as she and Owen had explained it to him early this morning after the body had been taken away and Elizabeth and Paul put to bed under medication.

Remembering that gaping hole, Sarah shuddered, thinking what the blast would have done to Travis's body. Instinctively, she slipped her arm through his and laid her head on his shoulder, needing the reassurance of physical contact. Last night, for one horrible nightmarish moment, she had thought she'd lost him forever, and she didn't want him ever to be farther away from her than he was at this minute.

"Do you think he killed Philip?"

Travis shrugged under her cheek. "We'll never know for sure, but it seems likely, from what he said. He certainly had good reason, or at least what he thought was good reason."

Sarah sighed. "I just can't believe it. He was always so kind to me."

"Yeah," Travis agreed sarcastically, "like when he drove you out to the sheep camp so he could get a good look at the place and figure out the best way to attack it."

Since they'd already berated themselves for this, Sarah decided not to pursue the subject. Instead she said, "I remember how strangely Elizabeth acted when I told her he'd proposed to me. Can you imagine? I thought she was jealous because she wanted Garth for herself."

"She should have told you right then how he'd come to her right after Philip died and tried to make her his mistress."

"How could she?" Sarah asked straightening. "I

would have thought . . ."

Sarah didn't know exactly how to put it into words, but Travis had no such problem. "You would have thought she was just trying to convince you *every* man who wanted to marry you really wanted her instead."

"If I'd believed her, I would have been terribly hurt, and if I hadn't, it would have ruined our friendship. Poor Elizabeth found herself between a rock and a hard place."

"She still should have—"

"But she didn't have to," Sarah defended her, "because I told her right then I had no intention of marrying him. You heard what she said this morning. If she'd thought for one minute I was considering it, she would have told me."

"That woman is so nice, she's dangerous. She should have a keeper," Travis grumbled.

"I think she will," Sarah told him with a smile, her first in several days. "If Owen takes as good care of her as he does of my sheep, she'll never have another worry in the world. Which reminds me," she added, trying for coyness, "how soon can you and I be married?"

She'd expected at least a grudging grin in response. Instead Travis stiffened in resistance. Before Sarah could even think to be alarmed, he said, "Not until I get back."

"Get back? From where?"

He didn't answer right away, as if he were carefully selecting his next words, and foreboding lifted the hairs on the back of her neck. "Travis . . ." she said in warning, but he ignored her.

"I told you about my friend Nate. They killed

428

him, Sarah, and they tried to kill me. I can't just pretend it never happened."

"Why not?" Sarah demanded. "You barely escaped with your life the first time. Only a fool would—"

"Sarah, I can't walk away, not if I want to keep my pride. How could I look at myself in the mirror? How could I live with you if I—"

"How can you live with me if you're *dead!*" she retorted. "You almost got yourself killed again last night. How many times does it have to happen before your luck runs out? I thought you loved me!"

"I do!"

"Then you won't go running off to settle some stupid score that doesn't need settling at all—"

"I think it needs settling," he informed her. She heard the edge of steel in his voice, but she was too angry to care.

"Oh, you do, do you?" she challenged. "And what would you do if some no-account drifters started running their sheep on *our* range, stealing *our* grass and *our* water?"

He refused to meet her eye. "That's different."

"No, it isn't, and you know it. Maybe your friend was a good man who didn't deserve to die, but what the two of you were doing was wrong. You know it was; you were ashamed to even tell me about it, and if somebody did to us what you and your friend did to those men, you'd run off that somebody just like they tried to run you off, and if they wouldn't run, you'd . . . you'd do whatever you had to do."

She was right, she knew she was, and he knew it, too. He didn't seem too happy about it, though. In fact, he looked downright furious, but at least he'd stopped arguing. He saw reason; he just hated to admit it. She'd make it easy for him. They would simply never discuss the subject again.

The ranch buildings were in sight, and they finished the trip in silence. Sarah sighed to think of a night spent in her own bed with no more worries to keep her awake. And soon Travis would be sharing that bed with her, holding her close, loving her. She shivered at the thought and laid her head on his shoulder again. He still held himself rigid, silently resisting her, but Sarah knew he wouldn't resist for long. He wasn't stupid.

Travis stopped the buggy in front of the house, climbed down and reached up to help her out. His hands felt wonderful at her waist, strong and sure, and she would have melted into his arms, but he held her away. When she looked into the icy blue of his eyes, her heart turned to stone.

"I can't say how long I'll be gone, Sarah," he said, as if she'd never informed him of all the reasons why he shouldn't go.

She opened her mouth, but no sound came out. Outrage had strangled her, and for an instant she thought she might choke on it. "You . . . you . . . you can't leave me!"

"I'm not *leaving* you," he explained impatiently. "Some things a man has to do whether they make sense or not. You'll just have to understand—"

"I most certainly do not have to understand!" Sarah cried, the sting of tears blinding her. She wanted to scream and stamp her foot and cling to him and beg him not to go, but she knew none of those things would work. Instead, she pulled herself up to her full

430

height and looked him straight in the eye, praying she was as imposing as she needed to be. "But *you* need to understand something, Travis 'Colt' Taylor. If you leave this ranch to go off on some fool's errand of revenge, you needn't bother to come back."

He flinched as if she'd struck him. There, she thought, knowing she'd finally found the one threat guaranteed to keep him by her side. She knew how much she meant to him, how much he longed for a home and the love she could give him. No man in his right mind would risk losing what he'd spent his life trying to find. She lifted her chin and waited while the reaction reverberated through him. She saw rage and pain give way to acceptance and resignation. After what seemed an eon, he smiled sadly. "I should've figured you'd say that," was all he said before he turned, climbed back into the buggy and drove it off to the barn.

Sarah watched, realizing her victory felt a little hollow, but knowing she'd done the right thing, the *only* thing she could have under the circumstances. What good was pride to a dead man? she asked herself as she climbed the porch steps. Travis would have come to the same conclusion himself, sooner or later. She'd get cleaned up and give Travis a little time alone before she summoned him back to the house. By then he might have cooled off enough to admit she was right, but even if he didn't, she knew just how to make him forget all about it.

A little later, Sarah heard the rest of her cowboys returning to the ranch. When she glanced out the window, she saw that Owen Cameron was with them and smiled to herself. Who would ever have imagined he would be so attracted to Elizabeth Williams? Sarah felt foolish for never having introduced them before, but she would certainly do everything in her power to make sure they had ample opportunity to see more of each other in the future.

When Sarah had removed her bloodstained dress, bathed away the residue of the past few days, and dressed in the gray gown Elizabeth had made her, she heard footsteps on the porch. Thinking Travis had come on his own to tell her she'd been right, she hurried out and threw open the door, to find Owen Cameron.

He blinked in surprise at her enthusiastic welcome but quickly recovered. "You're looking much better, missus."

"I'm feeling much better, too. How was Mrs. Williams when you left her?"

"Very happy with her son," he said with a fond smile. "Mrs. Bigelow was going to stay with her for a while."

Sarah nodded, looking past his shoulder to see if Travis happened to be in the yard.

"Could I have a word with Travis?" Owen said.

"I'm sure you could if you wanted to," Sarah said, "and when you're finished, would you send him here to me?"

Owen frowned in confusion. "I thought he was here with ye."

Sarah frowned back. "No, he . . . he must be in the bunkhouse."

"I looked in the bunkhouse. He isn't there, and . . ." His voice trailed off uncertainly.

"And?" Sarah prompted, feeling the first prickles of

alarm.

"Well," he continued reluctantly, "I saw the way things are between ye two, so when I saw his clothes were gone, I thought — "

"Gone? What do you mean, gone?"

Owen backed up a step in the face of her vehemence. "I mean gone. His clothes, his bedroll, everything."

Sarah felt the blood rushing from her head. The world tilted dangerously, and Owen grabbed her just before she fell.

Travis didn't get far before his body reminded him he'd had precious little sleep for several days. He figured it was around suppertime when he made camp, but he didn't feel a bit hungry, so he settled down under a lone cottonwood and spread his bedroll without even building a fire.

Every bone in his body ached from weariness, but the pain in his heart was the worst of all. Of course he should have known there were no happy endings for men like him. This was what he got for getting above himself.

Or maybe it was what he got for falling in love with a stubborn, bossy woman who was too used to having her own way. Just who in the hell did Sarah Hadley think she was, anyway? What gave her the right to decide what he should and shouldn't do? No man worthy of the name would put up with that, and sure as hell, no man would let a woman tell him he couldn't do what was right.

Which was the real problem, because right and

433

wrong had somehow gotten twisted around in this particular case. What Nate had done was wrong, no question, but Travis had helped him because he owed him, which was right. The men who'd attacked them had been within their rights, although Travis couldn't quite bring himself to admit they'd been right to kill Nate and to try to kill him. But nobody would argue that when somebody killed your best friend, it was right to avenge him. This was the code by which Travis had lived his life.

The problem was, until Sarah had challenged it, Travis had never bothered to decide whether it made sense or not. Certainly, a lot of things *Sarah* did didn't make sense. Raising sheep in cattle country was a damn fool thing to do, and only an idiot would have failed to recognize what a traitorous skunk Garth Richardson was.

An idiot or a lovesick fool, Travis amended, remembering his own failure.

And only a coward would be worried about risking his own hide to do what was right. Travis had never worried about such things before. When his time was up, it was up, and no great loss.

But that was before he'd met Sarah and realized what he was missing and the kind of life he might have had, and here he was, ready to throw it all away for some futile act of revenge.

She'd told him not to come back if he insisted on doing what he thought he had to do, but if he gave in to her, she'd think she'd won and he'd be no more a man than Philip Hadley. Living with Sarah after that would almost be worse than not living with her at all.

Almost, but not quite, he admitted wryly, and if he

434

could only figure out how to go back without actually giving in, maybe it wouldn't be bad at all.

Sarah had been right when she'd prophesied she might never sleep again. Yet another night had passed during which she had barely closed her eyes.

When she and Owen had determined that Travis was indeed gone, Owen and the other men had wanted to go after him the way they had before. Sarah recalled how violently Travis had fought against being taken that time and he hadn't even really been leaving. She shuddered to think what might happen to her innocent men if they tried to bring him back against his will.

No, if Travis valued his pride, Sarah valued hers even more. She had to accept the fact that once again she'd driven a man away with her dominecring ways. What a fool she'd been to threaten him, knowing he was just as stiff-necked as she. Her ultimatum had left him with no choice but to leave her forever. Why couldn't she have remembered for once that she was a woman and tried *charming* him into staying?

Sarah almost laughed aloud at the vision of her trying to seduce Travis into changing his mind. What a disaster that would have been — not only a failure, but a humiliating one at that. Sarah supposed she was simply one of those women doomed never to find love and happiness. Her character drove away men weaker than she, and made it impossible for her to get along with a man as strong as she. Travis had said he wasn't afraid of her, but that hadn't meant he could live with her, either.

And in her stupid stubbornness, she'd destroyed any possibility that he could even come back.

She would have wept if she hadn't already wept herself dry hours before. Her swollen eyes burned, but no tears formed as she stared into the cold hearth in her parlor. She couldn't remember the last time she'd moved from the wing chair in which she sat. Morning had come, but Sarah had made no move toward breakfast, since the mere thought sent her stomach into spasms of revolt.

She heard footsteps on the porch. She intended to ignore the knock, but whoever it was came in without knocking. Mercifully, she sat with her back to the door, so whoever it was—probably Cameron—wouldn't be able to see her tear-ravaged face.

The footsteps stopped in the parlor doorway, and Sarah said, "Do whatever you feel is necessary, Mr. Cameron, and kindly leave me alone in my misery."

"Sorry, I can't do that."

The firmness of the refusal, spoken in the voice she'd never expected to hear again, sparked every nerve in her body. Sarah sprang from her chair and whirled to find Travis standing in the doorway, hat in hand. For an instant, he looked uncertain of his welcome, but the sight of her face made him frown.

"Have you been crying?"

"Certainly not!" she lied, hastily scrubbing her palms across her cheeks to destroy any lingering evidence to the contrary.

He seemed unconvinced, and took several steps toward her. "Why were you crying? Did somebody do something to you?"

Sarah's shock gave way to fury. "Of course somebody did something to me!" she exclaimed. "The man I love walked out on me without even bothering to say good-bye!"

"You told me to go and not come back!" he reminded her.

"I most certainly did not! I didn't *want* you to go, which is why I—"

"Sarah!" he said sharply, stopping her in mid-sentence. "Were you crying because you thought I left?"

"You *did* leave," she reminded him.

"I didn't get very far."

She waited, but when he offered no explanation, she asked, "Why did you come back?"

"Maybe the question you should ask me is why I left in the first place," he said, but he didn't give her a chance to ask it. "I left because I wanted you to know I could have. I could have ridden away and done whatever I wanted for the rest of my life, however long or short that might have been. I wanted you to know the choice was mine, and I had to know you weren't going to send your men after me to drag me back."

"I thought about it," Sarah admitted morosely.

His lips twitched as if he might smile, but he didn't. Instead he said, "So if I stay, we both know it's because I want to stay, not because of anything you did or didn't do."

"What do you mean, *if* you stay?"

Suddenly he looked uncertain again, but only for an instant. "I mean, if you still want me to stay. You said if I left—"

"I didn't mean it!" she cried in dismay. "I only thought . . ." Now she was embarrassed to meet his eye.

437

"What did you think?" he asked, but she could tell he already knew. "Did you think I'd be too scared to leave if you threatened me?"

Sarah wanted to cover her face. "That was stupid, I know. When I found out you were gone, I realized I'd pushed you too far, left you with no choice at all. If you'd stayed after that, you'd be just like Philip."

"Well, maybe not just like him," he said, and to her relief she saw a smile twinkling in his eyes, like the first break in the ice at spring thaw.

"You would have felt like a lapdog," she tried, as the hope inside her blossomed into something bigger and far sweeter. "I don't want a lapdog, Travis. I don't want to control you or order you around or —"

"Yes, you do, Sarah," he said, and the smile in his eyes spread to his mouth, softening the accusation. "You want to spend the rest of your life ordering me around. You just don't want me to take it. You want me to argue with you and tell you when you're wrong and give in grudgingly when you're right . . . like I did today."

She shook her head in confusion. "Today?"

He looked a little sheepish. "Yeah, you were right about me going back. It would be stupid to invite those men to kill me when I would've done exactly what they did, especially when I've got so much to live for now."

"Oh, Travis!" she cried, and would have thrown herself into his arms, but he caught her shoulders and held her away.

"Not so fast," he warned. "We've got to get a few more things settled first."

His eyes looked like blue steel, cold and hard and

438

uncompromising. Sarah told herself she wasn't intimidated, but she loved him, so she was willing to humor him.

"All right," she said, as meekly as she could.

His eyes narrowed as if he didn't quite trust the meekness, but he said, "First of all, which one of us is going to run this place?"

Sarah blinked. She hadn't really considered the possibility of giving up her control over the ranch. "I . . . I think I do a very good job keeping the books and ordering supplies and finding markets for the wool and . . ." She let her voice trail off.

"But you'll let me run the rest of it, giving the men their orders and making sure the stock is taken care of, all that?"

He wasn't going to try to turn her into a housewife! She nodded quickly, only too happy to agree to such an arrangement.

"And if I decide to get rid of the sheep?" he challenged.

Outrage swelled in her, but she bit it back, telling herself she'd be a fool to surrender to anger at this moment. "Then I will do my best to convince you you're wrong," she replied with only a slight tremor in her voice. "If you are half the man I think you are, you'll be willing to listen to reason."

"And when I'm right, and you're wrong?"

Sarah had so seldom felt she was wrong, she hardly knew how to answer. "*If* that ever happens," she qualified, "then I'll try to be as gracious in defeat as you are."

The last of the frost melted from his eyes, and his mouth spread into a joyous grin in the instant before

439

it closed over hers. He pulled her to him with a strength born of desperation, and she wrapped her arms around him with the same desperation. This time she would never let him go.

As if from far away, she heard someone calling her name, but only when Travis broke the kiss did she realize the person was a lot closer than she'd guessed. A second after they pulled apart, Owen Cameron burst into the room. He stopped short at the sight of them, his broad face red with exertion.

"Travis," he gasped breathlessly, his gaze darting between the two as if he knew perfectly well they'd been kissing, and couldn't figure out why they were standing so far apart.

"Owen," Travis replied, his face as calm as if they'd just been discussing the weather. "Will you hitch up the buggy for Mrs. Hadley. She's going to town."

"I am?" Sarah asked, prickling instinctively at this cavalier treatment.

"Yes, you are," Travis replied, silently daring her to argue.

Sarah had no intention of going to town, not when she had Travis all to herself and everything between them was settled at last and . . .

"And Owen, you'll want to come along, too," Travis was saying.

Owen's gaze darted back to Sarah, not so much asking her permission as trying to judge her reaction. She refused to give him any satisfaction at all.

"By all means, Owen," she said, having decided to wait until he was gone before letting Travis know her new spirit of cooperation did not extend to allowing him to boss her around.

She thought Owen smirked just a bit before he turned away and lumbered out of the house. The instant the front door closed behind him, she turned on Travis.

"And just why are we going to town?" she challenged, crossing her arms belligerently.

"Because," Travis replied smugly, crossing his own arms, "I'm going to sleep here with you tonight, and every other night from now on for as long as we both shall live. I don't care much about the proprieties, but I thought you might want to be married to me before I move in."

Sarah's jaw dropped open, and for once she couldn't think of a single thing to say. Not that Travis gave her much chance. Seeing her mouth otherwise unengaged, he took up where he'd left off when Owen had interrupted them.

Epilogue

Sarah sat at her dressing table, pulling the brush through her hair with rhythmic strokes and listening for the sounds of her husband's return. Looking at her reflection, she was amazed to see the change love had wrought in her. With her hair loose, her arms and throat bare above her nightdress, and the glow of happiness lighting her face, she was actually pretty. At least Travis thought so, which was all that really mattered.

At last she heard his footsteps, and the bedroom door opened. He found her instantly in the light from the lamp, and his satisfied smile sent a shiver of anticipation racing over her.

"Let me do that," he said, coming toward her with a hand outstretched to take the brush.

She surrendered it eagerly and settled back in her chair for the sensual assault that was becoming a ritual with them.

"Is he asleep?" she asked dreamily, as Travis pulled the brush through the length of her hair with tantalizing slowness.

"Yeah, finally," Travis said, his fingers grazing the

442

back of her neck lovingly as he lifted the fall of hair and let it trickle through his fingers. "I can't figure why he wanted me to put him to bed instead of you."

Sarah had closed her eyes. "I got the feeling he had some questions he wanted to ask a man."

"He had some questions all right." She could hear the amusement in his voice. "He wanted to know if Owen was really going to bring his mother back, or if they intended to leave him here with us forever."

"Oh, dear!" Sarah cried, thinking she'd been negligent in not explaining everything to Paul, but she'd thought he understood he was just visiting.

Travis's hands stroked her soothingly. "Don't worry, I explained the purpose of a honeymoon to him, and he—"

"You did *what!*" Sarah squeaked, her eyes wide with alarm.

"Not the *entire* purpose," Travis assured her with a grin. "Just the part about two people needing some time alone to get to know each other."

Sarah sighed her relief and settled back down to Travis's ministrations. "It was a beautiful wedding, wasn't it?"

"A lot different from ours," he recalled, and Sarah murmured her agreement as she remembered the hasty ceremony performed with the Bigelows and Owen and Elizabeth standing by looking dumbfounded.

"Somehow, though," Travis continued, "I got the idea that when Reverend Gilbert said, 'You may kiss the bride,' that was the first time Owen had ever laid a hand on Elizabeth."

Sarah smiled knowingly. "It was. Poor Elizabeth,

443

she didn't know what to make of it, until Owen finally explained to her that he wanted everything between them to be perfectly proper. He assured her, however, that once they were married, he would no longer show any restraint whatsoever."

"Smart fellow," Travis said, his fingers trailing through her hair and raising gooseflesh all over her body.

Desire swirled in her, but she resisted it, knowing she had one more thing to discuss with Travis before surrendering to their passion. "You're awfully good with Paul," she remarked.

"He's a good kid."

"Do you like children?"

He considered. "Never thought about it. Never had much to do with them before."

"Do you think you'd mind having one of your own?"

His hands stopped, and his gaze sought hers in the mirror. His blue eyes held an unspoken question.

She smiled beatifically.

Travis frowned in confusion. "You said you couldn't . . ."

"I was wrong," she explained blithely. "You see, there were a lot of things I didn't know about marriage from living with Philip."

"Like what?" he asked warily.

"Like how often a man and woman can make love. You see, Philip hardly ever applied himself to the task, while you apply yourself almost constantly—"

"Sarah," he said sharply, his fingers closing over her shoulders. "Are you . . . ?"

"Going to have a baby?" she offered, trying for non-chalance but falling somewhat short. Suddenly, she

444

was no longer confident of his reaction. "Yes, I am, or perhaps I should say *we* are."

For one agonizing moment his gaze held hers in the mirror, and she was so terribly afraid . . . But then he hauled her up out of the chair and into his arms in a bone-crushing embrace that he released at once.

"Oh, God, did I hurt you?" he exclaimed in remorse.

"Of course not, silly. I won't break. You can even kiss me if you want to."

He did, long and hard, while his hands moved over her, cherishing her. When at last he lifted his mouth from hers, his expression was troubled. "I don't know anything at all about being a father."

"You didn't know anything about being a husband, either, and you've performed remarkably well," she reminded him.

"Well, I had a little pre-marital instruction," he recalled, grabbing her hand when she would have smacked his bottom in retaliation.

"You can practice your fathering on Paul until Owen and Elizabeth get back from their honeymoon," Sarah said. "You should be an expert by then."

"Right now, I think I'd rather practice my husbanding, if you don't mind," he replied, scooping her up into his arms.

Sarah didn't mind a bit.

Author's Note

I hope you enjoyed *Sweet Texas Surrender*. The conflict between sheepherders and cattlemen has become one of the enduring legends of American history. In fact, sheep were among the earliest settlers in Texas, and grazed alongside cattle in many parts of the state for decades, before trouble arose late in the nineteenth century. Most of the battles were fought with cuss words and threats and very little violence, although quite a few sheep met unpleasant ends at the hands of the infamous gunnysackers.

Charles Schreiner, an early sheepman, established the first wool warehouse in Texas in Kerrville. He became a successful businessman, and he believed in sheep so much that he made a rule that whenever someone borrowed money from his bank, they had to invest at least half the loan in sheep. The practice helped spread sheep husbandry throughout the state.

Please let me know how you enjoyed this book. If

you would like to receive a newsletter and a book-mark, please include a long self-addressed, stamped envelope. Write to me at:

Victoria Thompson
c/o Zebra Books
475 Park Avenue South
New York City, NY 10016